Anniversary Edition

~

Mobster's Girl

Awakening Mobster Series:

the Mobster

Mobster's Vendetta

Bonus Epilogue

Copyright © 2013 *http://www.amyrachiele.com*

To: Joh,
I hope you enjoy
the series! No comments
to Tim about how I
know — ☺
Best Wishes,
Amy
10/30/13

BOOK 1

Mobster's Girl

Chapter 1

Medigan (meh-di-ghan): a seriously non-Italian person.

Megan:

"Megan!" I hear my mother calling me with her slight Irish lilt. My mother and father wanted to fit in when we came to New Jersey after Gram died. I'm not really sure why we had to move to America, but leaving my beautiful Irish cottage behind was hard. Erin was two and I was five when we moved here. Erin and I have authentic semi-Jersey accents. That would have made us fit in to this all Italian neighborhood except for our flaming red hair and milk pale skin. We stick out like firecrackers exploding on a hot July night.

"Megan! I'm not calling you again!" my mother screams.

"Coming!"

I jump down the stairs in the hall and scamper past my sister sitting on the couch watching T.V. in the living room.

"Mom wants you," Erin says, never taking her eyes off the screen.

"Yeah thanks, I heard," I quip sarcastically. As I cross the room, I brush my hand across the strings of my harp that sits patiently waiting for me every day. The only time I feel complete and content is when I am seated securely behind it.

In the kitchen, my mother is standing by the sink peeling potatoes. I know-cliché.

"I need you to go to the store for more potatoes and eggs. The O'Connells are coming for dinner now, and I don't have enough for all of us."

"Okay."

The O'Connells are another Irish family that we spend time with. My mother met Mrs. O'Connell at a church meeting. They don't live in our neighborhood. They live a town over. They have two sons. Connor is Erin's age, fourteen. Troy is a year older than me, eighteen. He graduated last year. Me? One more year, thank God. Knowing it's almost over is enough to keep me going. Notre Dame here I come. I received an early acceptance.

I grab Erin's old red wagon. I always take it to the store when I go for my Mom. I know it's stupid but I really don't want to carry the groceries four blocks. I have been trying to convince my dad to get a second car, but he keeps saying no. My mother doesn't drive, and I'll be headed to college. He says it's not necessary. They did let me get my license though.

I pull the old wagon out of the tiny garage onto the city sidewalk. There is no grassy buffer between our house and the sidewalk. It is house, sidewalk, busy street. That's how close it is. There's no breathing room. Not like Ireland. When I was young, my mother and I used to have to walk half a mile to reach a road. I remember being small and holding her hand as we strolled through lush green groves. Then we came here to cement, exhaust fumes, and a culture we'll never fit into.

Block one down. I pass the pastry shops making Tiramisu and Cannolis. Then the bakeries making breads, pizza, and rolls. It's a hot August day. All this stuff would smell great, if it wasn't for the smog and bus exhaust. The wheels of the wagon rumble along the lines of cracked cement.

The thumping of drums echoes thickly through the air as a shiny black Cadillac with darkly tinted windows bowls up the street. The car slows down and paces me. My heart races nervously, and I keep walking-faster.

The tinted window slides down to reveal a guy I recognize from school. He has a dark complexion like most people around here. He's handsome in a mischievous way. I can't remember his name, Quedo, Zito, Lito….

"Hey, Red? Looking mighty fine pulling your little red wagon. How about I let you pull on something else? I got what you need right in this car."

There must be more people in the car because I can hear them snickering. I ignore him and keep walking.

"What's the matter, baby?" voice suggestive. "Come on, I'll give you a ride." His words are laced with double meanings.

"Leave her alone Vito!" a female voice calls from the backseat. "Andiamo!"

Vito (Oh yeah, that's his name) laughs wickedly and hits the gas. They spin away, and I make it to block three. Sweat is gathering on my forehead from the August heat and the run in with the senior hoodlums.

The grocery store is packed as usual. A lot of Italians in the neighborhood like to get their groceries fresh, almost every day.

Concetta the cashier, totals my food. "That'll be $9.50 Megan." I hand her ten dollars. "You getting ready for school to start?" she asks bagging my food. She always has a pleasant smile.

"Yes, thanks," I hook my hands in the bags and head outside. Waiting patiently is the little red wagon. I am always surprised that it is still there when I come out of the store. I am sure one of these days someone is going to pilfer the rusty thing or throw it in the dumpster because they think it's trash.

I sip on the ice cold cola I bought at the register. It feels good on my dry throat. I flip the handle of the wagon in to my hand and start back up the street. Block four down.

Block three coming up. I always play this little game with myself. It makes the uncomfortable, lonely walk tolerable. Bakeries at block two. They're in my sight, a few more buildings. Lost in my thoughts, I don't notice until I am steps from him. Oh no! I feel my chest tighten. No, no, no…shit, shit, shit. Antonio Delisi, Jr. Shit!

If you are going to avoid anyone in this town, avoid Antonio Delisi, Jr., the Mob boss's son. I've managed to basically stay clear of him and his friends over the many years we've lived here. These moments don't happen often but when they do they're frightening. My mom says, 'He's got the devil living in him.' She may be right because seeing him right now; he looks nothing like an angel.

I'm just going to keep walking. Maybe he'll ignore me. My hand tightens on the wagon handle, slipping with sweat. I drop my soda bottle to my side, my steps planted with determination.

Antonio confidently pushes off from the cherry red Camaro he's leaning against and flicks the butt of the cigarette he was smoking into the street. He steps right in front of me glaring down at me. He's blocking my path. Shit!

I look down to the ground, face heating. He makes my heart race because he is the most beautiful "devil" I've ever seen. I try to step around him. He blocks me. I timidly glance up into his face that's a foot higher than mine. Our eyes lock, and there is an unidentifiable emotion on his face that passes quickly. His dark brown hair hangs slightly into his dark brown eyes. His mouth is pulled up in a half grin that says either 'Don't fuck with me' or 'I'm hot and I know it.' Goosebumps surface on my skin, despite the scorching heat. His low riding jeans and white sleeveless t-shirt hug his swarthy muscled body.

He probably learned at the age of three how to kill someone with his pinky finger. A couple weeks after we came to Jersey, my mom had taken me to the playground near the elementary school. She wanted me to play with the kids in the neighborhood. You know, get to know them.

I was in the sand box letting the rough sand filter through my fingers. A little boy came over and sat in it too. It was Antonio. His skin was darkly tanned and smooth. Antonio made up a game in the sand called bakery. We made sand pies with buckets and pretended to make different kinds. Antonio was a cute kid. He even pretended like he was eating some of them. He kept saying, 'mangia, mangia.' I remember laughing at the funny word.

My mom had Erin on her lap and was sitting on a bench talking to a pretty lady who had on lots of makeup. It was weird…one minute my mom was talking, the next she was at the sand box grabbing my arm. She was trying to lift me out. I started crying that I didn't want to leave. She dragged me down the street with Erin on her hip towards home. I never even said good-bye to Antonio.

Five-year-old Antonio was cute; eighteen-year-old Antonio is chilling- beautifully scary, dazzlingly intimidating, heart-throbbingly gorgeous, and standing in my way.

A sharp voice pulls me from my trance like the vortex of Antonio's striking eyes. "Tonio!" An old grandmotherly woman leans out the window of the house next to us. I've seen this woman before. We talk sometimes when she's sitting alone on her steps. She starts gesturing with her arms and yelling in a Sicilian accent. "Tonio! Leave ta medigan alone! Come, mangia!"

A wolfish grin crosses his face, and he climbs the steps two at a time. He looks back at me before heading into the house. I let out the breath I didn't even realize I was holding and pull the red wagon home.

Chapter 2

Mangia (mahn-ja): to eat, and eat, and eat more (even if you're not hungry)

Antonio:

I walk into Nonna's apartment still thinking about her-Megan. I'll admit I saw her coming. So I dragged out my cigarette a little longer than necessary. How could I not see her coming with that shock of beautiful red hair on her head? Ever since her family moved in, I was always silently checking my surroundings for her at school, the movies, even the streets.

Meatballs, tomatoes, and basil mix into an aroma that wafts through from the kitchen. Even when Nonna isn't cooking you can still smell the ghost of Italian food in the air and on the plastic covered furniture.

"Tonio!" she yells again, "You leave ta girl alone, gabish!" Nonna scolds with a ladle, waving it at my face.

"What, Nonna? I wasn't doing anything." Nonna's orthopedic shoes shift on the linoleum floor.

She harrumphs, "I knew boys like you. I was young too, ya know! I saw yous lookin' at her like she was strawberry gelato! You're your father's son!"

"Nonna, please." I shake my head.

"You gotta prove your worth!" You could always count on one thing with Nonna, yelling. It's how she talks. When she's quiet-you're in trouble. "Now set the table!"

Nonna loads me up with dishes of food to take home to my ma. I place it all on the floor of the backseat of my car for the two-mile drive home. I kiss her good-bye like the good grandson.

My phone beeps with a text message from Vito:

Vito : Where r u?

Tonio: Jus leavin' Nonna's

Vito: Meet me @ the dock

Tonio: Can't. gotta meet Pop

Vito: K

Mom's beamer is there when I get home. I carry the food into the house.

"Ma! Nonna's got food for you." I call out heading over to the fridge to put the dishes in. While my head is still in the fridge, Mom comes around the corner.

"Hey, Sweetie," she leans into kiss me.

"Hi, Ma," I flip the door closed and pop a can of soda. Caramel-colored soda sprays all over the front of my white shirt. "Ugh, fanabola!"

"Hey! Don't swear," My mom yells and clips me with her hand on the back of my head. Her slap echoes in my skull.

"Sorry," I mumble as I strip my shirt off. "I gotta change before I go see Dad."

I climb the stairs to my room. My room hasn't changed much over the years. I've added some posters and pictures of friends but that's it. I rummage through my drawer to find a clean t-shirt. Wow, I really need to do laundry. I fish to the bottom of the drawer and feel a piece of paper. A picture, an elementary school class picture from 5th grade. This must have been stuck at the back of my drawer for years. It makes me laugh. I scan up and down the rows of pictures. Vito, Ronnie, Alessandra, Louie and there in the third row, Megan O'Neill. Her freckled face and wild red hair made my heart slam even all those years ago. I had drawn a heart around her little tiny picture. What a stunad I was!

I throw an old black t-shirt on and hurry down the stairs. Pop will be mad if I'm late for a meeting. Turning eighteen means that I have to attend; it's not optional anymore.

I jump into my Camaro, an eighteenth birthday gift from my dad, and race to the restaurant. All the meetings take place at Gino's Restaurant. It's a co-owned place that I sometimes work at as a waiter when I'm needed. The heads of the town's families all own it. My father started it and named it after his father, my grandfather, Gino Delisi.

I walk in, and the first person I see is, Mr. Maranzano, my friend Alessandra's father.

"Ah, Antonio!" he beams, "What a boy?" He grabs my face in his hands and kisses me on both cheeks. "You're eighteen now, you call me Vinny! Eh!" Then he smacks me gently. My mother calls them 'love taps.' I call them annoying and sometimes painful.

"Thank you, Vinny," I say appreciatively to Mr. Maranzano. People are already starting to treat me differently.

I spin around to see Luigi Prazzo. I watch him size me up. He looks me up and down. Instead of a greeting, all I get is a nod in my direction. I never liked him. I don't trust him either. His son Dino is an asshole.

"Is that my lady-killer nephew!?" Uncle Tutti comes strolling in from the kitchen. "Come 'ere goombah!" I walk into my Uncle's arms. He slaps me on the back in greeting.

"Hey, Uncle Tutti." His name is Mario but everyone calls him Tutti. I don't know why, they just do.

The restaurant is closed on Mondays, so that is when the group usually meets. But tonight, they closed the restaurant on a Saturday night for me and my initiation. My father claps his hands together and everyone turns their attention to him.

"Let's sit." He walks to me and hugs me. "Antonio, my boy," he says as he pats my face. "Sit next to me, son."

I walk to the large table that is set up just for these meetings. There are eight of us tonight. My friends, Ronnie Contini's son and Louis Ferretti's son, don't show. They won't be eighteen for another year, so their attendance is optional. Dino Prazzo is away at college. He's a chooch. I can't stand him or his father.

A waitress comes from the kitchen to pour wine into everyone's glasses. My father starts to speak. "My family, today we welcome a new man, my son, Tonio. He has been an exceptional student, and learned many valuable lessons over the years. He joins us with a full heart, and we welcome him with open arms. He, like all our sons, is the future of Palmetto, New Jersey. So let us raise our glasses to Antonio Rinaldo Delisi, Jr." My father raises his glass. "Vino, Antonio, Salud!"

A chorus of 'Salud' echoes off the restaurant walls. I pick up my glass and drink with them.

Chapter 3

Salud, Salute (Sa lood): to your good health, a toast (hopefully you're not wearing cement shoes when you're toasted.)

Megan:

The O'Connells arrive just before six. I have vacuumed and scrubbed the pans my mom used to make dinner. Erin has set the table and lit the candles. Everything is perfect like my mom always wants.

My mother acknowledges her friends, as Patrice and Aidan wobble through the door carrying a platter of assorted desserts. Behind them come their two sons, Troy and Connor. Connor immediately heads for the living room to look for Erin.

Connor has had a crush on her for years. He used to be shy around her until last year. Our parents had a joint birthday party when Connor and Erin turned fourteen. Connor must have matured or something because now he is perfectly normal around Erin. Well, as normal as a fourteen-year-old male can act.

Troy on the other hand has never grown up. He's sneaky, silly, and my best friend. Troy can always make me laugh. It doesn't hurt that he's a striking Irishman with blue eyes and thick dirty blond hair. Two years ago, he shot up, and now he towers over my 5'4" frame.

"Ahh!" I squeal as Troy picks me up and spins me around like I'm a little kid. I throw my head back laughing.

"Okay you two," my mother scolds. "Go put this in the kitchen, Meg." My mother hands me the dessert. Troy and I head into the kitchen following orders.

"So. Spill!" I yell at Troy as he takes some cheese and crackers off a plate on the table.

"Spill what?" he asks, cocking his head to the side.

"You start college in a week! You excited?"

"Umm, yeah," he says sort of quietly.

"That wasn't too convincing," I retort, popping a cheese cube in my mouth.

"Come on…" I say grabbing Troy's arm and leading him to my room. "Let's go talk." Obviously, something is bothering him. He's never not excited about something. He makes pumping gas for a car an adventure.

"So why didn't you text me that you're not happy about going to college?" I ask, opening my bedroom door. Troy flops down on the bed his blond hair trailing into his eyes.

"I just think I'm not ready," Troy responds, scrunching my pillow under his chin. "I really wanted to try traveling. You know see the world. And you're not going to be there at school for another year," he pouts. Troy's voice sounds worried and a bit lonely.

"We've never gone to school together. You'll be fine. It will go by like that," I snap my fingers. "Then it will be the next year, and I will be there." I push his shoulder to get him to look at me. "Come on, you'll be fine," I reassure him. I can't wait to get out of Palmetto.

I hear a thump come from the other side of the room. Thump. Giggle.

I gingerly open my closet door to find Erin and Connor sitting on the floor looking very guilty.

"What are you doing?" I ask exasperated.

"Nothing," Connor says while my sister sits there red faced.

"Well, I'm glad to know nothing considering my sister's face matches her hair!" I toss my hands up and turn to Troy, "Do you believe this?"

Troy stares at the two on them on the floor from his position on the bed. "Yeah. I'm just mad I never thought of it before."

"Why you!" I lunge at the bed and grab my pillow out from under him. I start hitting him with it. He grabs my waist and throws me down on the bed tickling me. "Stop!" I yell. "Stop!... I can't breathe."

"Sucks to be you," he says and tickles me harder. I kick and thrash on the bed trying to free myself, only I'm laughing too hard.

"Megan!" my mother screams. We both still to listen. "What's going on up there!?"

Troy still poised over me looking down on me with a wicked gleam in his eye answers softly and sarcastically only to me. "Well, Connor is ravishing one daughter in the closet. As for me, I am straddling the other on her bed." Laughter bubbles up in me again.

"Unfortunately, this is all true," I say as Troy lets me up, and I am out of breath. I walk back to the closet because the door has been shut again. This time I fling it open. All I can see is the back of Connor's head. "Get out now!" I say. Troy and I watch as Erin and Connor scramble away.

Chapter 4

Chooch (choo-ch): Jackass!

Antonio:

Glad that the meeting didn't run late, I head down to the dock. Vito, Louie, and Ronnie are still there. The tires of my car on the wooden boards thrum and bump as I stop in front of the guys. I kill the engine and get out. Vito tosses me a beer. I catch it and smoothly pop the top. I take a long pull off it.

"So, how did it go?" Vito asks me.

"Good," I say as I sit on the hood of my car. "They're watching Sommersville though. Pop says Sommersville is getting fuckin' greedy." Louie lets out a loud burp while Ronnie cranks up the stereo on his car.

"Shit, Louie!" I curse at him. "I can smell your Ma's cooking ova here!"

"Sorry, Dude. Got some serious agita…" he says banging his fist on his chest. I light a cigarette.

"Hey, Tonio? Why'd you get a red Camaro? I thought black was more your thing, man," Louie asks between belches.

"Ooo, speaking of Red. The Irish Princess looked fuckin' hot today. Didn't she?" Ronnie yells over the music.

"Shit yeah!" Louie says, "I'd like a piece of her!"

I felt my back stiffen at the mention of Megan. My friends and I talk shit about girls all the time, but this is different.

My father told us years ago we all had to stay away from her. Pop meant 'don't fuck her' or 'fuck with her.' He never said why, but I keep my distance like everyone else.

Megan is beautiful, sweet, and smart. It's no wonder everyone is into her. Just listening to them talk about her makes me want to punch something. I don't get a chance to remind them to stay away from her because a black sedan is coming towards us. I take another puff of my cig and watched Donny, the Knife, pull up in his Lincoln. The dark window rolls down as I stroll over to Donny.

"Hey, Tonio," Donny says. "Give this to your Pop." He hands me a bulky manila envelope. "Tell him Johnny is all set, but there is no juice."

I hang my cig out of my mouth to take the package and shake hands with Donny through the window.

"No problem, Donny."

"Ah, you're a good boy." He taps me on the cheek with his hand. "Stay out of trouble, eh?"

I know better than to open the envelope. Juice means Donny collected some money, but there was no interest on top of what was owed. Donny's the Enforcer. He works for my pop. He collects on debts or he fucks you up. It's that simple. There's a Cleaner, too. No one knows who it is. The Cleaner ices people who don't pay or who rat out to the cops. The secret identity of the Cleaner keeps everyone loyal.

I open my car and shove the package under the seat. The guys are still hanging out and drinking. No one even flinches at the sight of Donny the Knife. I lay back down on the hood of my car after I've had about five beers. The conversation about Megan is over. I'm buzzed. The music is rocking, and I'm feeling very relaxed. Vito comes over to sit on the hood.

"School starts Monday. It fuckin' sucks. Why can't summer be six months instead of three?" Vito crushes his beer can and throws it into the river.

"At least we're seniors," I say. "It'll all be over by May. I jus' wanna get it over with."

Louie taps my car to get our attention. He points towards the end of the road that leads to the dock. "Company," he says.

I reach into my car window to the glove compartment and grab my glock. I shove it in to the back of my pants. Ronnie grabs a blade.

The music is still playing, and we are all focused on the car stopped at the end of the alleyway. I hear a rush of movement and an oaf from Ronnie.

From the water side of the dock, six ski-masked guys jump us. We're outnumbered, but we hold our own. I get pushed to the ground, and my assailant gets in a good punch to my face. I thrust up with my legs and push him off. He flies backwards and lands smashing his head on the boards. Only seconds have gone by, but it feels like an hour. I scan and see Ronnie, Vito, and Louie all fending off attackers.

I reach behind me into my waistband and grab my gun. I fire a shot into the air. It startles everyone. All eyes stare at me. I lower my piece and point it directly at the fucker who jumped me.

My eye is trained looking down the barrel of the gun at the asshole. "You have less than three seconds to get the fuck out of here. One...." my voice is menacingly deep. They all jump up and start running. The four of us watch as the chooches run their asses off. I learned how to intimidate people at a young age. I also learned from the best-my pop.

"What the fuck?" Vito yells, brushing himself off. "Do they think this is a Jackie Chan movie? Those dickheads were all dressed in black like fuckin' ninjas!"

Some of the tension slowly leaves my body. I lightly touch my eye that got socked. "Wow, Tonio, your eye is gonna be really black and blue for church tomorrow," Ronnie comments.

"Yeah, thanks," I say deadpan.

Chapter 5

Stunad (Stew nad): You're just stupid!

Antonio:

In the morning, while I'm putting on my suit, Pop walks in. "Thanks, Tonio. I got the package you left." He looks at me. "Eh, what happened to you?" He grabs my face to examine my eye. I yank away from him.

I continue getting dressed, staring into the mirror tying my tie. "Got jumped."

"What? Who? Tonio!"

"I don't know... some fuckers dressed in black. I pulled my glock on them and they ran." I grab my keys and wallet and shove them in my pocket shrugging my shoulders.

"You think it's Sommersville?" he asks me.

I shake my head, "I don't know, Pop."

"I'll send Donny to look in to this. Stay away from them docks for a while." I don't look at him. "Eh!" he smacks me. "You got me?"

"Yes, Pop."

*****

Megan:

My family goes to St. Mary's Church. We could leave and go to an Irish Catholic church like St. Patrick's in another town where the O'Connells go, but St. Mary's is close to our home. So as my father says, convenient.

I have on a summer silk cherry-red sundress and put my hair up in a messy bun. The temperatures on this last day of August are supposed to reach 90 degrees, and there is no air conditioning in the church. I am thankful that we are going to an early morning mass. Going to a later one just means it will be hotter in the church.

My father drops off my mom, Erin, and me at the entrance. St. Mary's is a huge Cathedral-like structure; all stone and stained glass. A twenty-foot cross with Jesus on it hangs behind the altar. It's a lovely church. On special occasions the Priest says Mass in Latin.

I typically don't run into kids from school too often here. There are five different times Mass is run on a weekend and usually we go to the less crowded one late on Sunday. Today, I'm not so lucky.

"Ugh, it's hot already," My mother complains as we climb the massive stone steps into the church. Behind me are a couple of senior boys from my class. One of them was in a bunch of classes with me last year, Louie Ferretti.

We walk down the aisle and my mother selects the emptiest row she can find. The three of us kneel and make the sign of the cross as we slide down the hard wooden bench. Louie's family and his friends slide in the row behind us.

I pick up the Missal in the bench pocket in front of me. I need something to do. I can hear whispering behind me. I know it sounds paranoid, but I always worry. I can't hear what they're saying. I hope it isn't about me as I pretend to read.

A cell phone drops down directly next to me on the bench, onto the skirt of my dress that is draped around me. It startles me for a second. No one notices but me. My mother is on the kneeler praying, and Erin is texting someone (probably Connor) while waiting for Mass to start.

I turn my head to look behind me. Not two inches from my face is black Cadillac guy, Vito. He whispers seductively in my ear.

"Why don't you put your number in that phone so I can call you sometime?" I can feel his breath on my neck blowing some loose curls that have fallen out of my bun. My breath hitches from his closeness. What I really want to do is drop his cell phone in the Holy Water fountain at the front of the church. Why doesn't he just leave me alone?

I notice movement out of the corner of my eye-behind Vito. Standing and waiting for his family is Antonio Delisi. Vito's face becomes distorted and out of focus in my vision as I stare at Antonio in a striking black suit. What a breathtaking sight! He always carries himself in a suave and regal manner like the royalty he is around here.

He and his mother are waiting patiently while his father speaks to one of the priests.

Antonio spots me watching him while Vito is still leaning into me. He speaks to his mother, takes her hand and leads her towards us. I quickly turn around.

I hear Vito stand and hug Mrs. Delisi and pat Antonio. Others behind me say their hellos as well. I strain to hear what is going on. I steal a glance at Erin and she is still texting away. I suck in a strong breath, cross my legs and rest my folded hands in my lap like a young lady who has got herself together.

Then something happens. Something I never would have expected. Antonio Delisi sits down next to me. I quickly look his way unbelieving. His eyes are smoldering, and he has a knowing look on his face. "Good morning," he says to me.

"Good morning," I return, and then repeat it to his mother.

The cell phone still lies next to me resting on the silk of my dress that spills around me. Antonio reaches down, grabs it, and holds it behind his head without turning around.

In a deep guttural voice, he says, "Vito."

Vito's hand comes around and snatches the phone from Antonio. He knew. Antonio knew what Vito was doing. I blush. A couple of seconds later the organ begins to play and Mr. Delisi slips into our pew next to his wife.

At some point my father sat down next to my mother at the other end because I could see his burly hands resting on his thighs. I am hyper aware of Antonio next to me. I find myself noticing every twitch or movement of his body.

When it is time to stand and sing, Antonio opens the hymnal to the correct page and holds it for me to share with him. I notice his hands, a dark tan color and his fingers are long and slender. It must be awkward for him to share with me because of our height difference. It is sweet. I am singing with the Mob boss's son in church. It is terrifying and seems right all at the same time.

Over the loudspeaker, the priest announces, "It is now time to pass the peace of Christ." Everyone stands. I don't know what to do first. I turn to Erin. I lean over and give her a sisterly half hug. I kiss my mom and dad. Murmurs of 'Peace be with you' are heard throughout the church. I shake hands with Louie and his family. I am glad Vito is absorbed in Mr. and Mrs. Delisi.

I turn all the way around, and Antonio is there facing me…inches from me. I look him straight in the eye, and he is smiling devilishly at me. I notice his eye. It's black and blue. I have this uncontrollable urge to reach out and touch it. I want to clutch a cold pack to it and whisper to him that the pain will go away soon. My thoughts of touching him run away from me. I am in a surreal bubble.

He takes my hand in his, gently, then leans down and kisses my cheek. A bolt of excited shock pierces through to my stomach. He whispers, "Peace be with you," in my ear. He stays there a fraction of a second longer than necessary. My heart speeds up even more, I feel tingles from where his lips touch my cheek, and it radiates all the way down to my toes.

I am frozen stuck in one place. Everyone is starting to sit down, and I am still standing there like an idiot. Erin reaches up and yanks me down. My butt connecting with the hard wood bench jogs me back to reality.

*****

Antonio:

How much of a stunad can you be, Delisi? Stupid, stupid, stupid…

We all slowly file out of the church. I can sense Megan behind me. It takes every ounce of strength I have not to reach behind me and put my arm around her waist to guide her out of the church like she is mine.

"Oh, Antonio," Father Gio says. "A senior now, school starts tomorrow." Father Giovanni always tries to remember something about everyone in his church. He shakes my hand then he turns his attention to behind me. "My beautiful Megan! You're a senior too… Oh, that reminds me. Do you think you would be willing to play your harp one Sunday? What a treat that would be."

I hear the hesitation in her voice as I move forward with the crowd. "I would love to Father."

"Great, great. How about next Sunday, this same Mass?"

"Okay.

"Bless you, child."

I linger so I can be around her a little longer. The harp? She plays the harp? My thoughts are interrupted when Vito comes up to me and lightly punches my arm.

"Slick, Delisi. -That was very slick," he says smirking.

I shrug and walk through the Sunday crowd following my parents to the car. I hear her before I see her. No one can mistake the whiney twang that accompanies Maria Silvati's voice.

"Tony! Wait up!" Maria yells repeatedly. "Wait up!" Her hand comes down on my arm, and I spin around to face her. "Didn't you hear me calling you?" she asks. I plaster on my best smile.

"Sorry."

"Hey, I was wondering, you busy this afternoon? Nonna Silvati is cooking today. You want to come for dinner?"

"I can't," I say looking away from her. I catch myself scanning the crowd for Megan. After all these years, it's like an obsession.

My mother hears Maria and my response. She hits me on the arm. "Tonio! Don't be so rude." My mother scolds me. "You can go with Maria's family. You were just with your Nonna the other night. Go with your friend."

If my mother only knew! Maria is the senior class whore. When guys want a lay, they seek her out, and she delivers. Me, I never want anything to do with the skank. I don't want someone else's leftovers or to know my goods have been the same place as my friends. Ugh, fuckin' gross!

"Tonio, I am talking to you." My mother continues to berate me, and I hang my head in defeat.

"Yes, Maria. Thank you. What time should I be there?" I reply tonelessly.

Maria squeals, "Yay! 2 p.m. See you then." She gives me a ridiculous wave and walks away. I scrub my hand down my face in annoyance. Great, the last day of summer, and I've got to spend it with her. Fuckin' great.

"Eh, what's tha matta wit you?" My mother slaps the back of my head. Her words are clipped off, she's pissed. "I raised you betta than that!"

I sigh and say nothing.

"What's wrong wit you? You neva have a girlfriend. You don't want to go anywhere except with your friends or Alessandra. You got somethin' goin' on with her?" I'm surprised by this outburst from my mother. We never talk about this shit.

"What are you crazy? She's like a sister to me," I half yell back.

Speaking of Alessandra, my phone beeps with a text:

Alessandra: What's goin on today? You hangin out?

Tonio: No I have to have fuckin dinner at Maria's!

Alessandra: LOL See ya later

My mother and I stand there waiting for my dad to finish talking with Donny. Most of the church goers have gone. Actually, new people are starting to arrive for the next Mass. I squint, the sun in my eyes. I see Johnny Nero slowly coming up the steps giving my family a wide berth.

He's limping slightly. He has his arm in a sling. I catch a glimpse of his face, and he has long red scratches down his cheeks and above his eyes. I know he knows I'm watching him. I know by the way his eyes stay focused on the stone of the steps and the change in his gruff breathing.

Some serious large must have been in the envelope last night and Johnny Nero must be in some deep shit.

Chapter 6

Nonna (naw-na): Grandmother. (Watch out! She'll smack you just as hard as your mother.)

At 1:59 p. m., I stop my car in front of Maria's house. Her cousins are outside. They all go to high school with us. She's probably slept with some of her cousins, too. I shudder at the thought as I walk up and say hello to everyone. Dino Prazzo, Luigi's son, comes strolling out of the house eyeing me warily. He's always been fuckin' scared of me, so I'm not sure what this look is about, but I give it right back. He's Maria's cousin. I wonder what he's doing home. I thought he left early for college. He wasn't at the meeting Saturday night.

"Tony!" Maria screeches and runs over to me, enveloping me in a hug. I graciously and lightly hug her back and step away. She slips her hand under my arm and leads me into the house.

During dinner all I can think about is Megan, being next to her, her silk dress, and the way I wanted to shove Vito's cell phone down his throat. I know he'd never do anything. He's too afraid of my dad. It's just when it comes to Megan my thoughts get oobatz.

Three hours and five courses of food later, I am ready to leave. I can't take another minute of Maria hanging on me, and I'm ready to smack the smug look off Dino's face.

I stand to give my regards to Mrs. Silvati and her mother. "First day of school tomorrow, I've got to be getting home."

"Oh no, Tonio, stay," Maria's grandmother pleads. "Maria was so looking forward to you coming today."

"I can't. My Dad needs me," I say. If I ever have to get out of something, the only thing I have to say is 'My Dad needs me' or 'My Dad's waiting for me.' No one argues with that.

"Okay, Tonio." Nonna Silvati says, "I hope we see you again soon." Not if I can help it.

Maria grabs my arm to walk me to my car. I say my good-byes and let her lead me.

"Thank you for dinner, Maria." I say politely while pulling my hand away from hers.

Maria doesn't take the hint though. She tugs me into the empty living room. Everyone is still in the dining room at the table. I feel the need to get away again, but I don't want to hurt her. She's got a tough hold on my hand. Maria spins around and reaches up practically jumping to smash her mouth with mine.

I am momentarily stunned, but I recover quickly. I grab her upper arms to delicately push her away.

"What's wrong with you Tony?" she says. That is the second time someone has asked me that today.

"Nothing," I say. "Then why don't you want me? You're the first guy to ignore me-to say no to me." I don't want to tell her that the reason is that I have absolutely no interest in her or girls like her. I really don't want to tell her that my skin crawls when she's around. So, I do what I do best, lie.

"Maria, I have a lot of responsibility. I don't have time to have a relationship. You deserve more than I can give you." I don't like lying like that on Sunday. It feels more wrong than it does during the rest of the week.

Her brown eyes start to glisten like she's going to cry. Oh, no. I hate it when girls cry. Then she surprises me by hugging me quickly and saying, "That is so sweet, Tony." She sniffles once and lets me go. Whew! Close one.

*****

Megan:

When people say they're walking on cloud nine, I totally know what they mean now. After church, I am totally beaming. A butterfly flutters its wings in my belly every time I think of Antonio leaning down to kiss my cheek. In fact, this morning is the first day of my last year of high school, and it isn't even giving me same depressing feeling I get at the start of every year. I'm invigorated. I catch myself smiling in the mirror as I brush my long hair. I know that Antonio was probably just playing with me because of Vito but who cares. Just looking at Antonio makes my blood race. My phone chirps with a text from Troy:

Good luck on ur 1st day!

Antonio and I are never in the same classes. I only know him by chance meetings, the neighborhood, and by reputation. No one messes with him. He walks on water at Palmetto High. Every girl wants to date him. I'm not sure if it's his good looks or the fact that his father is Antonio Delisi, Sr., ruler of all Palmetto.

I walk to school because like I said before my dad refuses to buy another car. I am halfway to school and a little blue hatchback rolls to a stop next to me.

"Hey girl! Get in." It's Raven Ramirez, the only other medigan at school. She's Hispanic and just about the only person I talk to or hang out with there. We have most of the same classes together. We're a lot alike. Neither one of us fits in.

"Congratulations!" I tell her. Up until last year, both of us didn't have cars.

"Thanks! My mom and dad gave it to me over the weekend. They have been talking about it for a while. Now they finally bought it. Yeah ME!" she screeches. "And to top it off, I am going to take you home too, Homegirl." Raven beams with pride.

"Now it's 'yeah me!'" I say. Raven starts looking at me closely.

"You look different," she pauses. "You have sex or something?"

"What?!" I squeal.

"Whoa, take it easy, I'm just messing with you." Raven laughs.

Raven drops the subject as we head to school. The subject changes to classes, teachers, and summer gossip.

"How many blow-off classes did you take?" Raven asks.

"Home Ec, Music appreciation, and Auto Mechanics." I reply

"Auto Mechanics! Why would you take that? You don't even own a car," Raven says laughing.

"I think it's important to know the basics about cars. How to change the oil, fix a loose hose... the basics."

"I guess," she says, as she turns her car in to a tiny spot near the picnic tables. I unbuckle my belt and reach for my bag. I get out of the car still defending my class selection of Auto Mechanics to Raven. I hear laughing and glance towards the picnic tables. Sitting on top of the one in front of us, looking like he doesn't have a care in the world is Antonio. Sitting next to him is Alessandra, and that kid Vito.

Alessandra's thick chestnut hair is styled into perfect soft waves. She has on designer ripped jeans and three inch high heels. Alessandra is an Italian goddess. And she's sitting with Antonio. I always suspected they might be secretly dating or something. It's a rumor I've heard, and I have seen them together a lot over the years. Just seeing them together confirms my suspicions that Antonio is just playing with me. What would he want with me? A stab of jealousy punctures my stomach where butterflies for Antonio hide.

A guy, whose name I don't know, calls out, "Hey, Red?!"

I try to ignore them while I sling my bag over my shoulder. I steal a glance, and Vito is elbowing Antonio. Raven is on the other side of the car, waiting for me.

"Hey Red?" the guy calls again.

Alessandra shushes him and says, "Ashbet, Ronnie!"

I feel my face flaming. I keep walking. Raven falls into step with me and we speak quietly to each other until I hear footsteps behind us.

"Megan, wait up."

Alessandra is catching up to us. Raven and I stop.

"Hi," she says.

"Hi," Raven and I say simultaneously.

"I just wanted to apologize for them." She points back to the picnic table. "They can be obnoxious." My eyes shift to where Alessandra is pointing, and my eyes lock with Antonio's. Heat crawls up my neck and face. It's not just embarrassment, but intense desire.

"Yeah, well." I didn't know what to say. They are obnoxious.

"I'm having a party at my house Saturday night. You know a back-to-school party. I thought you might like to come."

"Ummm..." again speechless. I have never ever been invited to Alessandra's house.

"Both of you." She pulls out her cell phone. "Here, give me your number, and I'll text you my address."

"Ummm..."

"Come on. It'll be fun," she says encouraging me.

I give Alessandra my number. Raven and I walk away in stunned silence.

True to her word, Alessandra texts me her address about a half an hour later. I send back a T.Y. for thank you. Electives don't start until next week, so I have three long hours of study hall.

During hour number two, when I will be having my auto mechanics class, Antonio comes strolling in late. He scans the room. I hastily look down at the notebook I am scribbling on because I finished all my homework during hour one. I pretend that I am immersed in doing something important when I hear books thunk down on the table next to me.

Shit! I glance over my shoulder as Antonio sits down next to me.

"Hi," he whispers.

"Hi," I say back. Panic is building in my stomach, and my thoughts stray back to the kiss yesterday. Startling me, my phone buzzes with a text message from Troy:

How's ur day goin? Can I come over 2nite?

I'm holding my phone in my lap so it doesn't get taken away by the study hall teacher. Antonio is watching me. I text back

Okay. Weird actually. Yeah, definitely come over.

Troy: C U @ 6

"Friend?" Antonio asks quizzically, part of his mouth turned up in a half smile.

"Yeah," I respond shyly.

*****

Antonio:

I feel my breath getting shallower just looking at Megan. She is stunning. I want to talk to her more but I don't really know what to say. This is new for me. I am never feeling out of my element.

Talking to girls has always been easy for me. But no girl has ever been Megan. There is something so wholesome and good about her, and it draws me.

Seeing her four times in a three day time span is not good for me. The sad part is yes, I'm counting. Maybe I'm being punished. My punishment is seeing her every day, but not being able to do anything about it. I had to keep saying the Hail Mary to myself for my unclean thoughts about her during church. That dress was my undoing. Kissing her cheek and whispering in her ear was definitely a bold move, especially in front of my father. But I loved every second of it.

"So you're taking Auto mechanics too?" I ask.

"Yeah," she says, not looking at me.

"That's cool. Everyone should know a little bit about cars." As I talk to her quietly in study hall, I just want to reach out and touch her long hair.

She glances up at me, a small smile on her face, "That's what I said. Raven thinks I'm crazy." How could anyone think this girl is crazy? I'm the one who's oobatz!

Chapter 7

Oobatz (oo-bot-z): Crazy

On the drive home from school, I think back that this is the first time in my entire life that I didn't hate study hall. Megan and I didn't say a whole lot. I just loved looking at her.

I know where she lives. Hell, I know where everybody lives, what they do for a living, who they're related too. I have to know. Pop has maintained his position so long by knowing everyone else's shit. I typically avoid her street. It has always helped me over the years not to think about her. At first, I thought it was because Pop said she's off limits. I know deep down that's not the reason. I'm drawn to her, always have been.

I pull up to my house. Donny's car is parked out front. I can hear Pop and Donny talking on the side of the house. They wave me over.

"Hey, Pop. Donny." I say.

"Tonio, you need to take a ride with Donny to take care of some things for me."

"Okay. Let me throw my books in the house."

Donny and I ride in his Lincoln to the docks.

"Your Pop says you had some trouble the other night."

"Yeah, me and the guys got jumped by six dudes with ski masks. They tried to beautify my face, but I pulled a glock on them."

"Yous remember anything about them?"

"Nah, it happened fast, and they took off running."

"Well, if you or the guys remember anything you tell me, eh?"

"Yeah, Donny, I will."

Donny slowed the car down to a crawl scanning in between the crates and stuff that litter the docks this time of year.

"Who we looking for?" I ask.

"Johnny Nero."

"Johnny Nero? Didn't you fuck him up already?"

"Yeah, but he still hasn't finished payin'."

"Fanabola! He's walking with a limp. I saw him at church yesterday."

"Well, he betta start prayin' because here's your first beatin' as an enforcer. This is how it goes Tonio. Collect whatever money you can. Give a couple of hits, and I want you to break two of his fingers. I left the fingers for you 'cause I knew your Pop was going to send you in when Johnny didn't have all the money last night."

"Now repeat to me. What do ya do?" Donny asks arching his ear to me like I'm repeating a grocery list he gave me.

"Collect the money. Hit him a couple of times. Break two fingers. Got it," I say matter-of-factly.

"Good boy. This is an easy one. He ain't gonna run on ya. Make it quick 'cause it's easier on everyone."

Thinking back to the drive home from school, the last thing I thought I was going to have to do tonight besides homework is kick the shit out of someone.

"Look, here he comes. He just got off work. Take him behind the building. GO!" Donny yells.

I jump out of the car. I saunter over to Johnny. He's talking to some guy I don't know. He breaks his conversation immediately and we walk out of ear shot of the people milling around after work.

"Give me the money, Johnny," I say.

He reaches in his pocket and pulls out a wad of rolled up hundreds. "I can get the rest. Tell your Pop I'll have it this weekend," he pleads. I shove the money in my pocket. I don't count it or even look at it.

"Shit, Johnny!" I say as I let my fist fly. It connects with his jaw with a sickening crack. I don't dwell on the noise because an adrenaline rush hits me and my arm is cocked back again, ready to strike before Johnny can recover. SLAM! I fucking hit him again. He's staggering, and I have to move forward so I can get his hand. I plant my foot, grab the pinky and ring finger of his left hand, and twist hard. It sounds like two twigs snapping. Johnny screams. He's on the ground writhing in pain.

I stand over him, and say in a low voice, "Get the rest of the fuckin' money, Johnny. I'll be back on Saturday." I turn to walk back to the Lincoln. Standing behind a crate watching me is Donny. He nods to me, and I nod back.

As soon as I get home, I get ice out of the freezer for my hand. I wrap the plastic bag full of ice around my knuckles. They're throbbing and red. My pop comes in the kitchen.

"Good job, Tonio, good job. Donny was very pleased. You did exactly like he told ya to."

"Thanks, Pop."

When I have to do something like that, I don't think about it. I just do it. It's the way of life here. You don't pay, you get hit. You don't pay again, you get hit and something broken. You don't pay a third time you get something really important broken. There are rules.

Pop counts out five hundred dollars from the money I just gave him and hands it to me.

"Here get yourself something for your new car or take a pretty girl out." He throws the bills on the table in front of me.

There is only one girl I want to take out and I don't think Pop would be too pleased.

*****

Megan:

Troy came over after dinner. I change into cutoff jeans and a tank top and we head outside for a walk.

"Well, I have to say one thing about starting college. I'm glad it's starting soon. I'm so bored at home. Connor's at school, Mom and Dad are working... It's boriiiing," Troy drags out the word.

"Soon you'll be knee deep in work and wish you were alone again." I tell him.

"You're probably right," he says taking my hand. We continue down the street holding hands. It is always so comfortable with Troy. I can be myself. We laugh, joke, and have a great time together. The weather is hot and sticky.

"How about ice cream?" I offer.

"Sounds great!"

I lean in conspiratorially, "So this is how it's gonna go." I talk to him like it is a top secret mission. "The ice cream shop is two blocks down. Last one there buys." I quickly release his hand and take off running.

"No fair!" he calls.

We race down the sidewalk avoiding obstacles like trash cans, bicycles, and people. I am still ahead and Troy with his long legs is gaining on me.

I'm laughing when I see Troy start leaping over trash cans instead of going around them. Then he sneaks into the lead.

"Hey! No fair!" I yell. I speed up. We both make it to the outdoor ice cream counter at the same time. But he scoops me up by the waist and plops me down behind him so he's first.

"Hey," I stomp my foot like a baby. "That's cheating!" I yell.

"I believe Madam is mistaken. I am the winner," Troy says dramatically pointing to himself. He turns to the window to order his butter pecan ice cream. I am still fuming and not paying attention. A ton of people are enjoying ice cream on a hot night. I hear someone call my name.

"Megan!" It's Alessandra.

"Oh, hi," I say surprised. She's with a couple of girls from school. Troy comes over without any warning and rubs his ice cream cone on my nose. "I'm gonna kill you," I hiss as I wipe my nose off with the back of my hand.

"Being a sore loser just doesn't look good on you," Troy says.

Alessandra clears her throat and brings Troy and I out of our little world. "Oh, ummm... Troy, this is Alessandra. She's goes to my school."

Troy immediately sticks his non-ice cream carrying hand out to Alessandra. "Hi. Nice to meet you." He turns back to me. "I believe, young lady, that you have some unfinished business with that gentleman behind the counter," Troy points melodramatically.

"You are such a goof," I say giggling. "I'm going." I put my hands up in defeat. I go to pay for the ice cream. I ordered my favorite, mint chip.

We sit with Alessandra and her friends for a few minutes while we finish. Troy pulls my hair, tells Alessandra outrageous stories about us and is his usual dynamic self. Alessandra is acting odd. I have never spent more than five minutes with her, so I guess this could be her normal.

"Well, we should be getting back," I say standing and Troy follows suit.

But Alessandra pipes up, "Did you tell Troy about my party Saturday night?"

Whoa! Where did that come from? "Ummm, no."

She speaks to Troy. "I'm having a party this weekend. I would love for you to come-with Megan, of course," she adds.

"As I would love to spend more time with my Besty," Troy says with fake conviction, putting his arm around me. "I am heading to Notre Dame this weekend to join the world of collegiate academia."

"So you're college bound, huh?" Alessandra says smiling.

"As hard as it is to believe, yes," he says, bowing like the weirdo he is.

"Well, maybe I'll see you around when you're home on break," she states.

"I don't think so." He swivels his head, scanning the surrounding area. "I don't believe I even live around here."

It is truly a good thing that Troy is handsome, because with the way he acts, people tend to think he's a nut-job.

"Megan!" He pats the top of my head and says in a fake panic. "Megan! He's feeling my head all over like a dweeb. "Is that you?" He looks down at me, "Oh, sorry. I was temporarily blinded by your hair." I elbow him hard in the ribs.

"Shut up." I look at Alessandra. She's smiling at me. "Bye."

"Bye."

The ice cream was delicious and just what I needed. We hit block two, and the kids have opened up the fire hydrant. A heavy stream of water is spraying all over the road. Barefoot kids are running, jumping, and kicking the cold water. We stop to watch.

Troy looks down at me, and an evil grin spreads across his face. It takes one second for me to register what he's thinking, and I start running. I don't even get a step away, and he tosses me over his shoulder heading straight for the hydrant.

I yell and fight. I even smack him in the butt, but he smacks me back. I try pleading with him. But to no avail. He plops me directly in front of the heavy, cold, stream of water. I let out an earth shattering screech. My clothes and hair are immediately soaked. He holds me so I can't move. Troy's getting wet too, but not like I am. I try to dodge out his reach, and he thrusts me back.

I lunge to get out of the stream, but he's too fast. He grabs me and forces me back to the spot directly in front of the water. We're struggling and laughing. I'm squirming and feeling like I'm in a wet t-shirt contest. The kids are egging Troy on. They think we're hysterical. The commotion is enough to wake the dead.

Troy notices something over my shoulder, and I feel him stiffen. He doesn't let me go, though. I am still held under the rushing water. I look over my shoulder when I hear two car doors slam. The doors belong to a black Cadillac. Uh oh!

Chapter 8

Marrone! (mar-own): Dammit!

Antonio:

I was on the fence about going out with Vito tonight to throw a few beers back. I wanted to unwind after the ass-kicking but I'm tired too.

I get out of the car, after sitting with Vito watching Megan play dirty dancing in the water with some tool I've never seen before. I realize I am being punished or tested, or something.

She looks like a super model in a naughty photo shoot. Her pale skin glistening against her slick wet hair. All of her curves showing through the thin material of her clothes. I think I licked my lips like a fuckin' stalker.

I couldn't take it anymore. I had to get out of the car. To do what? I don't know. Stop it? Talk to her; find out who this chooch is she's with? Kidnap her and take her back to my house? Shit! I am a fuckin' stalker.

There's a creeping thought in my brain that this guy might possibly be her boyfriend. And that makes me want to hurl and punch him at the same time.

I lean against Vito's car and light up. "What are we doing, Dude?" he asks me. "You're acting oobatz! What the fuck is wrong?"

I shrug my shoulders and take a long drag off my cigarette just watching.

"Do we need to fuck this guy up or something?" I don't answer him.

Vito goes quiet resting his hand against the door of his car. Without warning, Vito starts laughing uncontrollably. "I know what this is!" he says between fits of laughter. He slaps his hand on the roof of his car. "I got it! You fuckin' like her! You don't just want to screw Red! You... You like her like a girlfriend. Holy shit! I never thought I'd see this day." He's getting louder and really pissing me off.

"Keep your fuckin' voice down." I flick my cigarette butt and glare at him.

"So what do you want to do? Mess up this chooch?" he asks, getting serious.

I look over at Megan and her 'whatever' and they're staring at us. Probably wondering what we're doing. At least they stopped fooling around.

"Nah, I can't do that. She's already petrified of me," I say disgusted. Yeah, I want to mess him up, but I can't. It would hurt her. I reach for the door handle to Vito's car and get in. I guess I achieved what I wanted. They stopped, and I realize the only person I want her doing that shit with is me.

Vito pulls away from the scene that contained any guy's fucking nightmare involving a girl he likes. "Ugh!" I punch the dashboard. "I'm in fuckin' trouble, dude!"

All Vito says while laughing is, "Yeah, you are."

Vito drops me off at home, and I sit on my bed replaying beautiful Megan in the water. She was so carefree and breathtaking. I'm still hard from watching her. Who was that fuckin' guy? He had his hands all over her. Jealousy sweeps through me, and I know that I'm losing the battle to stay away from Megan.

Buzzing sounds from my dresser. I pick it up. Text from Alessandra:

You home?

Antonio: Yup

Alessandra: I'm coming over.

Ten minutes later, I'm still lost in my boiling jealousy when my bedroom door opens, and Alessandra walks in.

"Hey, San," I say too depressed to even get up off the bed.

"Hey," she says, plopping down in my desk chair.

I sit up. "What were you talking to Megan about this morning?" My interest is totally piqued.

"Oh… I was doing you a favor," she says, walking to the bed were I'm lying and starts poking me in the chest.

"Me?"

"Yeah you. I'm sick of you looking like a stunad whenever she's around."

"What?" I quickly sit up.

"How stupid do you think I am?" she asks sarcastically. "I have known you way too long for something like a crush on the Irish

Princess to slip by me. It's just gotten to the point that you're getting pathetic."

"Huh?!"

"Oh, puh-lease, Tonio!"

I hang my head. She knows. Everybody knows. Even my grandmother knows.

"So," she says excitedly, "I invited her to my house on Saturday night." What?! "And I got her phone number! I think you should call her."

"My father will shove my feet into cement and throw me in the river!"

"What? Why?" San asks incredulously.

"Because my father gave me and everyone else the 'don't date her; don't fuck her' speech about five years ago."

"Ohhh... that explains a lot." she says thoughtfully, "She really is nice. No wonder you guys treat her like a leper. Well, anyway. She's got this really cute friend. He's tall and blond..."

"Whoa! Stop right there." My heart halts in my chest. "What are you talking about?"

I was at DeMarra's Ice Cream and Megan shows up with some guy. Well, they show up running, actually. They were racing or something..." she trails off. "Anyway, I went up to Megan to say hi, and we all started talking. Troy is very funny. He made me laugh so hard... He starts college next week....He can't come to the party... I hope I see him again... I want to..." San was talking a mile a minute.

"Stop! You know the guy's name? Is it her boyfriend?" I practically yell.

"You know, I was gonna ask her, but I got different vibes. I got the brother/sister vibe and the boyfriend vibe. I was planning on texting her to ask."

"What? You besties with her now?" I ask feeling slighted. "Besides I get the boyfriend vibe."

"What do you mean?" San looked disappointed.

"They were putting on a fuckin' wet'n'wild show an hour ago at the fire hydrant near her house. It was fuckin' disgusting."

"How disgusting?"

"Wet, clingy clothes and hands all over. Laughing too. There was lots of damn laughing."

"Hmmm." she says, grabbing her phone. "I'm gonna text her." San types on her phone and shows it to me:

Boyfriend or crazy friend? LOL

I look at the text. "Why LOL?"

"He was really crazy," she says beaming.

Alessandra sends the text, and we sit in silence waiting. I feel sick to my stomach. My heart is pumping way too hard. The anxiety is killing me. Friend I can deal with. I think. Boyfriend? I think I will fuckin' kill someone-starting with Troy. Troy? What kind of an asshole name is that? Wasn't that a country like a thousand years ago? What if she doesn't see the text? I don't think I can stand the wait. I am just about to suggest that San call her when I hear my father call me.

"Tonio! Come down here!"

"I'll be right back," I say to Alessandra.

I jump down the stairs and see my dad standing with Donny in the living room.

"Yeah Pop?"

"I know school just started but I need you to go with Donny tomorrow. You need to help get a few things done for me."

"Sure Pop, no problem." My thoughts dip even lower because now I know I definitely won't see her tomorrow. I open my bedroom door and San is right there holding her phone in my face. The screen says:

Friend

My heart spikes! I am relieved and know I don't ever want to feel that way again. It's time to do something about my feelings for Megan. I just hope my father doesn't pound my fuckin' face in.

I don't just miss one day of school. It's going on day three. Donny and I have collected over twenty thousand dollars and fucked up two people. Donny says the farther he has to travel and the more time he wastes tracking them the more he fucks them up. We take turns. Each time Donny tells me exactly what to do. 'Hit him two times in the face, Tonio.' Or 'Pull the arm back till you hear a pop. That means the shoulder has been dislocated.' Donny could have been a doctor in an emergency room. He really knows a lot about anatomy. I even got to count and organize the money. Donny shows me the way to count large sums of cash. He has taken money bands with him.

When I'm done, Donny checks it. Then he hands me ten one-hundred-dollar bills. "Here, your pop said to give you this. You're doing a great job, Tonio."

We're still here in northern New Jersey because we got a runner.

We trapped him yesterday but he evaded us again. We're in a hotel resting up to go after him in the morning. Donny gives me some ointment for my knuckles. They're really sore. The ointment shit stinks, but feels good.

Alessandra had given me Megan's number. I'm so tempted to text or call her. I have no fuckin' clue what I would say, though-'Hey, how's it going? I think you're beautiful. I wish I could see you tomorrow, but I have to beat the shit out of people. Bye.'

She doesn't even know I have her number, besides the fact that she's scared shitless of me. The haunting images of her with that chooch Troy invade my mind. I try and concentrate on last Sunday at church and the red dress.

I need to get out of the hotel room. I have a grand burning a hole in my pocket and pent up energy from the adrenaline rushes I've had over the past three days from beating the shit out of people. Donny's lying on his bed watching the news.

"Don, I'm gonna go shopping."

"Shopping? What the fuck for?"

"I don't know. I gotta get outta here."

"Okay, Tonio. Don't be gone long."

I take Donny's keys off the bedside table and head out the door. I drive down the main drag until I come to a huge indoor mall. I park at Nordstrom's. I decide that I'm going to pick up some of my mother's favorite perfume.

I am immediately accosted by sales clerks, some holding bottles of spray cologne. A pretty petite girl with blonde streaked brown hair and perfect make-up comes up to me.

"May I help you?"

"Uh, yeah. I need a bottle of Chanel."

"For men or women?" she asks.

"Women," I say and follow her to a sales counter covered in jewelry, perfume bottles, and scarves for sale.

"I have the 5 oz or the 8 oz spray bottle."

"I'll take the biggest one," I tell her. She slides the counter door shut and places the shiny box on the glass top.

"That'll be eighty-five dollars, please."

I grab a hundred out of my pants pocket and clerk is smiling a little differently at me, playfully. She takes the hundred from me and asks,

"Is this for your girlfriend?" I see the look in her eye. I know that look. I get it a lot.

"No, my mom," I say then instantly feel despair. I would take every dime I have and spend it on Megan. I wouldn't even flinch. In fact, I wish I could. It would make me happy. "What is the most popular perfume for a girl?"

"How old of a girl?"

"Your age, eighteen or so," I say.

"Oh, that would be Juicy Couture or Coach Poppy."

"Can I see those?" I ask, getting excited.

She sprays some stuff on a little piece of white paper and hands it to me. I bring it to my nose. It smells good, feminine. She hands me the next one. It smells even better. But I ask her, "Which one do you like?"

"Oh, I'm a Juicy girl," she says, smiling provocatively.

"I'll take that one then."

"That will be another eighty-five dollars please." She's still smiling, and her mouth is getting wider and wider. I toss another hundred on the counter, and she hands me my change. The clerk starts to wrap the perfumes and puts them in the same bag.

"Can I have those in separate bags please?"

She laughs lightly and says, "Sure." I'm not positive, but I think this girl believes I am buying her perfume. She puts them in pretty bags and ties each one with a ribbon that has the name Nordstrom running along it. "Will that be all?"

"Yes. Thank you." And I snatch the bags off the counter. Her face falls, and I book it to the entrance of the mall.

I wander around for awhile and pass all sorts of stores selling clothing, make-up, and shoes. I pass Ralph Lauren. I pick up some pants for myself. Then I walk by a jewelry store. The display in the window has all sorts of silver necklaces. I decide to go in. I slowly peruse the necklaces and bracelets.

"Can I help you?" a tall woman in a business suit asks. She has a bracelet of keys dangling from her wrist.

"I'm just looking," I say still peering down into the glass.

"Is it for someone special?" she asks.

What am I doing exactly? Why would I come into a jewelry store? I don't want anything for myself.

"Do you have anything Irish or Celtic?" I ask.

"Come right over here." She points to a tall cabinet made of glass. Inside are intricately made pieces. Some have green stones in them-emeralds I'm guessing.

"This one is a Claddaugh..." she starts explaining what it means. "The heart means love, the hands mean friendship, and the crown means loyalty. It is white gold and encrusted with diamonds around the circle. All Celtic jewelry has some type of meaning."

She hands the delicate necklace and pendant to me. It's beautiful. It's small, but I don't think Megan is showy like my mom. I can just picture it resting on her neck against her buttery skin.

I look up at the clerk, "How much?"

"That one is five hundred and fifty dollars, Sir."

"I'll take it," I say without hesitation. She smiles at me and goes to wrap it in a nice box with a bow.

When I get back to the room, Donny appears to be sleeping, but when he hears me come in, he jolts and grabs for his gun.

"It's just me, Donny."

"Eh, Tonio, what did ya get?"

"Some new clothes... perfume for Mom." I leave out I got stuff for someone I wish was my girlfriend.

"You're a good boy," he says.

The next morning we get up early. The early bird catches the worm or the chooch who stiffed my father out of five G's.

There is a text on my phone from Alessandra:

Where have u been?

Antonio: Running errands for Dad

Alessandra: Will u be at the party?

Antonio: YES!

Donny did some searching on this dude who ran. He has a sister on the other side of town. We arrive at her house at seven in the morning and park on the street a little ways down. One thing I've learned is that doing this kind of stuff can involve a lot of waiting. I text Vito and Ronnie and ask about school. I search the XBOX website for new games coming out. I play a game of Angry Birds and wait and wait.

Donny breaks the silence.

"Tonio, tomorrow night don't forget you gotta collect from Johnny again?"

"Yeah, I know."

"I'm gonna send you alone. Do you think you can handle it?"

"Sure, no problem."

"If he gives you anything less than three G's, you gotta break his leg." I look up from web surfing. He continues. "You count the moola, then break his leg if it ain't all there."

I hesitate, but I say, "Got it."

Donny's head turns, and he sees the guy who ran. Simultaneously, we get out of the black Lincoln. My adrenaline starts humming through my veins. We pace each other then fan out. The asshole sees us. He starts to bolt, but I take off like a shot. I catch up with him instantly and swing out my leg. My leg rips his out from under him, and he goes down-hard. His head smashes on the cement sidewalk. I hold him down with my foot pressed against his throat. That's what twelve years of martial arts training will do for you.

Donny gets to us. He riffles through the guys pockets. He finds fifteen hundred. Not even close.

The guy pleads, "Donny, I need more time."

"You're a runner! I don't like to fuckin' chase people!"

"Donny, please, I just need another week."

"Thirty-five hundred next week." Donny says to me, "Take care of this Tonio." And I do.

I grab the guy by his shirt and pull him to a standing position in one fluid motion. I cock my fist back like I've been doing all week and plant it in the guy's face. His nose makes a crack sound, and I know I have broken it. I've heard that sound before. I wind my hand up again and punch. The guy wails and staggers. While he's staggering backwards, I grab his hand and snap two fingers. He howls long and loud.

I walk away. Donny already has the Lincoln running and waiting. I don't look at the guy crumpled up on the ground as we screech by.

Chapter 9

Cappatosta (ca bah dos): thick headed, stubborn

Megan:

All week Raven has been talking about going to Alessandra's party. On the way to school, what she's going to wear. On the way home, she's changed her mind and picked a new outfit. She has gone over and over whom she thinks is going to be there.

It's Friday, and she is driving me home.

"Okay," she says, "I'm going to pick you up at seven. Be ready. Do you think that guy Louie will be there?"

I roll my eyes at this question. She has asked this same question no less than ten times this week. I have offered to text Alessandra and ask, but Raven yells, "No! She might tell him I was asking."

"Yes, I do think he will be there. He is friends with Alessandra," I reassure her again.

I don't mean to be short with her, but I've got my own issues going on. All week I have been waiting to see Antonio. The anticipation is killing me, and every day I am let down. He doesn't show up for study hall.

I have been dwelling on the way Antonio looked at me when I was with Troy. His face was murderous. I'm not sure why but it seemed like Vito was laughing at him. What were they doing anyway? Besides just standing there glowering at us. I had an ugly fear deep down inside. It wasn't for me. It was for Troy. Then they just left. Just like that.

Troy and I walked home, and the atmosphere between us was not as jovial as before. Troy was uncommonly quiet. He called me a few times this week, but there was something unspoken between us. He promised to call me tonight because he leaves for Notre Dame in the morning.

Later that evening he calls.

"Hello."

"Hi Megan."

"You all set to go?" I ask getting excited for him.

"Yeah."

"Come on, Troy. It will be great. I want you to call and tell me all about it. I want to know everything from where the cafeteria is to how annoying your roommate is."

Troy's voice gets quiet. "I wanted to ask you about that party tomorrow night."

"What about it?"

"Is that guy with a hard-on for you gonna be there?" he asks softly.

"What?!" His harsh words shock and confuse me. "Ummm, what are you talking about?"

"Don't act stupid Megan." He is practically yelling at me. In all the years I have been friends with Troy, he has never talked to me this way.

"What is wrong with you?" I ask heatedly frustrated.

"The guy, Megan! The guy leaning against the car smoking! The one that looked like he wanted to rip my throat out then have his way with you." Hurt filled his words.

"Troy, I have to go practice," I force out. "I'm playing the harp in church on Sunday. I'm sure you've got stuff to do for tomorrow. Give me a call when you get settled in."

"Yeah, whatever. Bye, Megan." And he hangs up. The dead air on the other end of the line makes me feel yucky. I'm not sure why I don't want to talk about Antonio to Troy. I'm not sure about anything.

"Megan!" my mother calls from downstairs. "Your father wants to talk to you!"

I find my father in the living room with his feet up on the coffee table watching soccer.

"Dad?" I say, "Mom said you wanted to see me." He turns off the T.V.

"Your mother tells me that you're going to a party in the neighborhood."

"Yes, my friend Raven from school is picking me up."

"I'm not sure how I feel about you going."

"What's that supposed to mean?" I ask warily.

"You know what it means. We live here but we don't belong here. I don't know if I can trust those kids," he says.

"Alessandra has been very nice to me."

"Megan, those kids are trouble makers."

"Dad, I'm going to be eighteen. This is my last year of school then I am off to join Troy at college. I don't think hanging out with Alessandra and a few other kids from school is going to make a difference now since I have never done it in all the years we've lived here."

Dad seemed to consider this. "Make sure you make good decisions. If Antonio Delisi is there, or any of his friends stay away from them. Okay?"

"Okay," I say and head back to my room for bed. It has been an exhausting week. Different images of Antonio keep popping into my head, some delicious and some scary. I fall asleep to the delicious ones.

It's Saturday and Raven has called me every hour on the half-hour to make sure I'm still going and to find out what I'm wearing.

I fix my hair so that my red curls lay in waves down my back. I put on a crimson-colored halter top and dark skinny jeans. I take a cue from the shoes Alessandra always wears and select a pair of matching high heeled sandals. If Alessandra can walk everywhere in high heels, so can I. I shove money and my lipstick in my pocket. I sit on my front steps waiting for Raven.

In front of Alessandra's house, a bunch of people are hanging out. Everyone seems to have a plastic cup in their hand. I reach for the door handle to Raven's car when she asks,

"Ready?"

"Ready," I say. Startling me, my door opens it up on its own. A tall guy with light brown hair and green eyes stands holding open the car door.

"Oh, uh, thank you." I stammer.

"Hi." He smiles brightly revealing beautifully white teeth. "I'm Dino." He holds out his hand to help me out of the car. I blush and take it.

"Hi." Raven comes around the car to where we're standing.

"Hi," Dino says to her.

"I'm Megan, and this is Raven," I say, waving to my friend.

"Yeah, I know who you are," he says. "I've seen you around."

I don't have a chance to respond when Vito, Antonio's friend, pops out of nowhere. Shockingly, this is more attention than I've had since I moved here.

"Hey, Red, you want a drink?" he asks.

"Uh, sure." After the cell phone scene at the church, I'm a little leery of Vito. Louie is now standing behind him drinking a beer.

"Hi Megan," he says. I notice Raven go ridged next to me. I can see why she likes Louie. He is cute. I never paid attention before. He's not as tall as Dino or Antonio or even Vito. But he definitely takes care of himself. He's also smart. I've read some of his papers in English class.

"This is Raven." Louie salutes her with his beer and Vito nods.

"What don't you come in the house and pick what you want?" Vito says. It seems like he was trying not to make it sound like an order. My father told me to stay away from Antonio and his friends. It's kind of hard when they're greeting me at the car.

Alessandra hugs me when I walk in her house. I know I haven't really been friends with her all these years but I always liked her.

"Ooo, love the shoes!" she says. Dino, Vito, and Louie are right behind.

"Thanks."

Raven meets up with some kids from our classes. I scan the crowd quickly. No sign of Antonio. My heart plummets, a little disappointed. I follow Alessandra to the kitchen. She fills cups lined up on trays with a pink liquid.

Dino leans against the counter. He seems to be assessing me. There is a gleam in his eye that is anything but just friendly.

"Megan? Can you help me with these?" Alessandra asks.

"Sure," I say glad to do anything. I feel uncomfortable here. I've never spent much time with these people. There is also a ton of people here I've never met before-Dino being one of them.

I wrap my hands around the handle of the tray. I turn to go to the living room.

"Can I help you?" Dino asks, moving to take the tray from me. I catch Vito out of the corner of my eye. His face is threatening. He is staring at Dino like a panther ready to pounce on its prey.

"No thanks, I've got it." I smile and retreat in to the thrashing bodies dancing in the living room.

Antonio:

Johnny Nero didn't have the all the money again. I need to break his leg now so I can get home, shower, and get to Alessandra's party.

Johnny's face is still swollen from last week and he is still walking with a limp. I wonder if I should break the limping leg or the good one. Should I make the one that's hurt worse or make the good one bad? I don't need this right now. I've counted the money and the time has come. He's only five hundred dollars short. Should I really break his leg for five hundred of juice? Thinking is bad. My pop would say 'don't think-just do.'

So I make it fast. I push Johnny to the ground and snap his leg.

I get home and dressed in record time. I'm just getting my shirt on when my dad walks in.

"He didn't have it all, huh?" Pop asks.

"No."

"You break his leg?"

"Yup, all set." I tell him. My voice sounds as casual as if I just told my Dad I went to buy milk.

"Here, some money for tonight." He sticks another $500 in my hand. I fold my fingers around it. My dad pats me on the cheek.

"You're a good boy," he says smiling. "Your ma loved the perfume."

"Thanks, Pop."

I come through the door at Alessandra's house, and the party is already rockin'. People are smashed together dancing to a deep beat coming out of the stereo system. A few couples are making out in the corners of the living room. Everyone I pass says hi to me or claps me on the back. Others, when they see me coming, move out of my way.

Most people only want to be my friend because they don't want to be my enemy. I don't give a crap. There are very few people that I care about or trust among these individuals. My limbs are still humming with the beating I just gave Johnny, mixed with my anticipation to see Megan. Calm and collected just is not working for me right now.

The kitchen is filled with people drinking beer, wine and some pink shit San made. At the table Louie, Ronnie, and Vito are playing poker with some other kids from school. Maria is standing over Vito's shoulder watching with her cousin Dino. What the fuck is he doing here?

Maria squeals, "Tony!" and rushes over to hug me. Over her shoulder I see Alessandra by the refrigerator mixing drinks. Standing next to her helping is a sight that makes my knees weak, long waves of red hair spilling over her shoulders. She turns with a tray of drinks in her hands and my heart stops. Megan looks fuckin' gorgeous!

Maria still has her arms around me, and I am immobilized to the spot I'm standing in. I don't even notice that Maria is talking to me.

"Tony, dance with me?" she whines. She's clutching the front of my shirt now. I barely register what she's saying because I am too busy watching Megan walk away with Dino following her.

I pull Maria's hands off me and say, "Can't," without even glancing down at her. The only person I can look at is Megan and the beauty of her form and grace. Maria storms away.

Vito shakes me. I notice he's standing next to me now. "Where the fuck have you been? San and I are trying to keep Dino off her. San asked Red to help out just so we could keep an eye on her. Go make a move, Paesan. I'm exhausted and about three seconds away from wailing on Dino."

I nod and enter the living room to see Megan passing out drinks while Dino tries to talk to her. She seems to be polite but trying to ignore him. That's how I feel she acts with me. I am silently praying I don't get shot down.

Megan is done passing out drinks and is headed right toward me because I'm in the pathway of the kitchen.

"Hi," I say, stepping in front of her.

"Hi," she says and moves to step around me.

I reach out and gently touch her arm to stop her. My heart's racing at the touch of her skin. She looks down where I've touched her and gets a panicked expression. Is it fear? Just as I'm about to say something else, Dickie Saco comes up to me.

"Hey, Tonio, how about those Red Sox?" I swing my head at him and my anger goes from zero to sixty. I'm so pissed that this little fuckin' weasel is bothering me when I am trying to talk to Megan. Every time I see this guy, he wants be my friend. He's the biggest fucking empty suit! Get a life!

"I don't fuckin' know! Who the fuck cares?" My voice booms as I glare at him. A couple of people turn around to stare at me. Dickie shrinks back and Megan scurries away. Fanabola! I roughly scrub my hands down my face trying to get a hold of myself. I notice that there is a wide open area around me. The dancers have shifted away.

Dino is leaning against the wall in the kitchen watching Megan. Louie calls out to me, "Hey, Tonio, how about a game?"

"Nah, I don't feel like it right now," I say. Alessandra is talking to Megan. They are deep in conversation by the refrigerator again. What the fuck are they talking about?

I step closer. "So he likes college?" San asks.

"Yeah. He's hasn't said too much. It's probably a really big adjustment," Megan replies.

They're talking about the chooch, Troy. Marrone! That really doesn't help my attempt to calm the fuck down.

This night is not turning out the way I was hoping. I wanted to show her she doesn't have to be scared of me. I want her so bad. All of the bottled up, repressed feelings over the years coupled with the adrenaline of today's beating consume me. I shake my head in frustration and disgust. I slip outside for a cigarette. Maria must have seen me leave because she snaps up right in front of me.

"What's the matter, Tony?" she asks.

"Nothing," I tell her.

She sidles up to me and wraps her arms around my waist.

"You wanna have some fun?" she asks suggestively.

"Maria… I just want to be alone right now." I push her away. I don't know what else to say. This girl just doesn't take a hint. My phone buzzes with a text message, it's San.

Where did u go?

Tonio: Outside 2 smoke. Send someone out for Maria. NOW!

"Who's that?" she asks gesturing to my phone.

"Alessandra," I say as Vito comes outside.

"Maria, come on. Let's go have a drink." He takes her hand and she follows him inside.

My phone buzzes from Alessandra again.

I'm gonna bring Megan out there. Don't fuckin' scare her away!

I laugh at the stupidity of this night. It's like friggin' middle school all over again. I hear the door open. Alessandra is talking. "My parents put this deck on the house last year."

The screen door opens. Alessandra and Megan are standing in front of me. Megan gasps a little. That can't be good.

"Megan, why don't you keep Tonio company? I have to get back in the house." San immediately leaves. Megan stiffens. I need to come up with something to say, fast.

"How was the first week of school?" I ask. Whew! That came out easy and normal sounding.

"Okay…" she says timidly. A long pause fills the awkward air around us. "How come you weren't there?" She noticed I wasn't in school, that's a good sign.

"I had some stuff to do for my dad," I tell her.

"What kind of stuff?" she asks. I am taken back by her question. No one ever asks me that. Once I say I had to do something for my Dad-the conversation is over. No one pushes for more information.

"Work stuff." The front of her blouse dips down just enough for me to see the swell of her breasts. I subconsciously lick my lips again. My stalker is back. Red is such a killer color on her. Her hair is different tonight, the waves are like zig-zags. I want to reach out and touch her hair, but I'm afraid she'll run away like an abandoned kitten.

"I saw you the other day." Why am I bringing that up?

"I saw you too," she says.

"You looked beautiful…" I take a step closer, she takes a step back. "But there was something I didn't like about it." I move a little closer. Are you stupid Antonio? You're going to frighten her away again!

She doesn't step back again as I move closer. I notice her breathing getting heavier. Her lips are glossy. Warning bells are going off in my head that I'm pushing too much. But I can't stop myself, I feel drawn to her. I lean down and whisper in her ear. Her breathe hitches and her eyes close. "I didn't like that it wasn't me playing in the water with you."

"Do you even know how gorgeous you are?" I move my hand to cup her face. I brush my hand down. It is so soft. Softer than I ever would have imagined. I want to kiss her. And I do just like I did in church. I brush my lips against her velvety cheek.

The door opening jolts us. Dino comes out and his eyes narrow at me when he sees us. What the fuck dude? Go away! Go to college already!

"Megan, do you want something to eat? Alessandra just put out some pasta." The douche talks directly to her.

"No, thank you," she says in a low voice. She clears her throat. "I'm all set." I don't move away from her. Her breathing is raspy. Hopefully, asshole gets the hint to leave us alone. I don't give a shit that Dino's still standing here.

He finally shakes his head and goes back into the house. I whisper in her ear again. "I've wanted to be this close to you for a long time." I continue to brush my lips across her cheek and down her scrumptious neck. I hear a faint moan in the back of her throat. My fuckin' heart is pumping like the engine of a train. I better quit smoking or she's going to give me a heart attack. I search her eyes.

"Do you want to get out of here?" I feel her freeze beneath my gaze. "I promise it'll be okay." My voice is still low. She doesn't answer right away.

"I came here with Raven." She pauses, thinking. "I need to tell her."

"Let's go find her." I lightly take her hand and lead her back into the house. She is uncertain at first.

The poker game has broken up but the music is still on. The house seems to have cooled down. People are mellowing out now. When we get to the living room, a few people are dancing; everyone else is coupled off into their own world. I find Vito making out with Maria on the floor. I kick his outstretched leg.

"Hey, Vito, have you seen Raven?" He breaks away from Maria, and she looks at me. Maria is staring at my hand holding Megan's. Jealous sparks ignite in her eyes.

"Yeah," he says, pointing to a dark corner. "Over there."

Megan and I walk over. She is making out with Louie. I look at Megan her and face is flushed. So I do the honors. I tap Louie. He pulls away from a very glowing Raven.

"Raven, I'm going to take Megan home."

She just nods her head. I take that as she understands. I get my keys out of my pocket and lead Megan to my car.

Chapter 10

Paesan (pie-zan): friend

Megan:

Antonio is holding my hand as we walk to his Camaro. I'm still reeling from his whispers. I have circling butterflies in my stomach. I am not sure if they're because I'm excited or terrified. My feet stop and I hesitate. I think about what my father said. Antonio notices my apprehension.

"Hey, don't worry." He leans towards me again with his smoldering brown eyes. "It'll be okay. Trust me." And for some incomprehensible reason I do, even after everyone has told me not too.

He opens the car door for me, and I slide in. The car still smells new. The black leather seats are shiny. It's an awesome car. Well, every car is awesome to me because I don't have one. Antonio slips in and starts the engine. He's grinning from ear to ear and he asks me, "You alright?"

"Yes, thank you," I say shyly. He looks unbelievable. I've never seen him smile so wholly before.

"I want to show you something."

"Okay."

Antonio drives out of town. I am thankful in case someone sees us. We are silent for a long time. I stare out the window because he keeps glancing at me while he's driving and it's making me uncomfortable and exposed.

"You want to listen to some music?" Antonio flips on the radio to a Top 40 station. His hand moves to my lap. He takes my hand into his and places our intertwined hands on the armrest. My nervousness spikes. He looks at me as if to say, 'Is this Okay?' It is, and I don't move my hand an inch. Antonio's hand is huge and dark. He must have observed the same thing because he says,

"Wow, your hand is tiny." I blush. I am so nervous. I feel like I'm being naughty. I am going against my father's wishes, and that part of me feels disobedient. But my rebellion is warranted. Antonio makes me feel like I never have before. He's beautiful, amazing, strong, and powerful. He can command a room just by being in it.

I bet it is rare that someone sees him this way, caring and controlled.

He pulls into a park-like area I have never been before. It overlooks the river. The lights from a nearby bridge reflect off the water. He parks the car and we get out. Antonio takes my hand as we walk towards the river. The rippling noise of the water is serene.

We go and stand in front of the wrought iron railing. It's a stunning sight. Antonio arms corral me in front of him with his hands on the railing, "Megan," he whispers into my neck. He rubs his nose into my hair. Antonio feels so good. Standing here with him is strange. "I want to… take you somewhere." Really! My eyes snap open. I wasn't expecting that. He doesn't let me answer. "I know you're afraid of me… but I want to show you that you don't have to be." He spins me around to face him. "I'll take you anywhere you want to go." He sounds unsure and hesitant when he says, "I'd like to spend some time with you."

Antonio Delisi, Jr. wants to spend time with me! I am so embarrassed at his words. But joy spears me. His brown eyes search mine. He seems uncertain, yet wanting all in the same gaze. My heart sinks when I remember my father's warning. He'd be livid if he knew I was here alone with him. My phone buzzes with a text, I shift away a little from Antonio, but he still holds on to my waist. His fingertips send shivers up my spine. It's Raven:

U OK

Megan: Yes

Raven: U still with him?

Megan: Yes

"Is that your friend?" Antonio asks tightly.

"It's Raven, checking on me." I'm still looking at my phone screen, when Antonio says in a low, seductive voice, "Tell her I'm gonna kiss you."

I don't even have a chance to react, as he crushes his lips to mine, and passion explodes between us. My phone clatters to the ground. My arms wrap around him. His muscled back is heaven under my fingers. He grips me tighter lifting me up closer to him. The ache that fills me creates a fog over my brain. Rockets of want pierce me. Antonio's kisses radiate a kind of cherished that is foreign to me. I'm not sure how long we stand there in each other's arms, acting on an emotion that has been bottled up for a decade.

On Sunday morning it feels like I dreamt everything that happened the night before. Antonio was mystifying. I had always been so scared of him that it felt weird. Those emotions melted away when I saw him on the deck alone in the moonlight. His desire was palpable. And when he leaned down to whisper in my ear like he had at church a week ago, it was my undoing.

I was always attracted to him, just like the rest of the females at my school. People move out of the way for him as if he is a ruler of a kingdom. He can be with any girl he wants, yet I've never seen him with anyone other than Alessandra. And it appears that, after last night, he wants me.

When I left him last night, I felt bereft; I wanted to stay with him. I decided to have Raven pick me up and take me home. I didn't want my parents to see or hear Antonio's Camaro outside the house. I offered to give him my number, but he said he already had it. About five minutes after I got into bed, my phone buzzed with a text from him asking if I got home safely. Warmth spread through my body just thinking about my time with Antonio.

Chapter 11

Andiamo (on-dee-ahmo): Let's go

"Megan!" my mom yells. "It's time to get ready for church."

Oh yeah. I have to play the harp in front of the entire congregation. Why did I agree to this? My hands start sweating immediately. I shower and dress in long black palazzo pants, the ones that look like a dress but are really pants, and a pink chiffon shirt. I hear my dad moving the harp out the door as I come into the kitchen. Mom is holding the door for him. It's a good thing my dad is really strong. The harp is heavy.

"It is a real honor that Father Giovanni asked you to play," my mother says to me like I don't know this.

"Yes, it is."

"You need to do your best for him and the Lord."

"Yes, Mom."

"I think you should wear your hair up, it looks more respectful than hanging down. You look almost wild. Can't you do something about that?"

"Yes, Mom." I pass Erin on the stairs.

"Where're you going? I thought we were leaving," Erin asks.

"Yeah, well, I have to fix my hair," I say aggravated. I twist it up in a clip and rush back to the kitchen.

"Ahhh, much better," my mother says. "Softer. Very nice."

Wow! Praise from my mother.

In front of the church, people are on the steps mingling. My father opens the back of our mini-van to get out the Harp. I am just opening my door when I see two people stroll over towards us. The morning sun blinds me.

"Can we help you with that, Sir?" One of them asks. I step out on to the curb and it's Antonio and Vito. Holy Crap!

"That would be great boys, thank you," my dad says very civilly. Antonio smiles at me in his charcoal gray suit that looks lip-smacking on him. My face heats when I think of him kissing me last night. The deliciously tight clenches my stomach made with him so close. Ugh, it was sooo good. My father starts to give them instructions on how to move and carry the harp. My hands shake as I follow Antonio, Vito, and my father up the big steps to the church entrance.

*****

Antonio:

So this is her harp. It's awesome. Vito and I very carefully carry it to the altar. Mr. O'Neill helps us to stand it up just right. Megan and her family sit in one of the first rows. I smile at her as I pass by to go sit farther back with my friends. She looks stunning in pink. My parents are sitting with the Ferretti's on the other side of the church.

Vito and I make the sign of the cross and slip in the pew to sit with Louie and Ronnie.

"So how was last night?" I ask Louie. He looks at me funny. As if to say, 'what the hell are you talking about?' "Uh, Raven." I say.

"Oh, yeah. She's cool." He starts to say more, but Dino Prazzo slides into the pew right behind us with Maria and some of her other cousins. I hear Dino talking to Glenn Prazzo, a junior at our school.

"Hi Tony," Maria says in my ear as she leans in to me from behind.

"Hi, Maria," I don't turn around when I say it. I look at Vito out of the corner of my eye, and he's rolling his.

Maria doesn't get a chance to say anything more because we all rise as the organ begins to play. Dino and Glenn are still whispering. I want to turn around and tell them to shut the hell up when Father Giovanni calls Megan to the altar.

"We have a very special treat during today's Mass. Miss Megan O'Neill is going to play Ave Maria on the harp for us."

Megan gracefully walks to the altar, makes the sign of the cross, and gently slides behind the harp. Dino comments viciously saying,

"Wow, I'd like to be that harp, sitting between her legs... I'd rather put my face between her..." I am moving before I even distinguish my fist colliding with Dino's face. There is an audible GASP! from the church-goers and I hear my mother yell,

"Antonio!"

Vito grabs my arm to stop me from winding my arm back again to smash Dino's face a second time. Ronnie is blocking me from jumping over the bench. I am lethal. Dino's cousins are shocked. Maria is yelling something to me. Dino's lying on the bench. Ronnie and Vito push me out of the pew. I hear Louie trailing behind stopping Maria from following. There's loud talking and commotion in the recesses of my hearing. Dad is standing at the end of the aisle looking really pissed. Vito and Ronnie haul me outside.

I take a deep breath. The air feels good. The sun is bright and making me narrow my eyes to slits.

"What the hell is wrong with you?" my father booms from behind us.

The guys let me go and we stand way off to the side of the church.

"I'm talking to you!" my father yells.

"Dino's a fucking prick!" I say back not looking at him. He whacks me on the head.

"Watch your mouth, we're at church!" My father yells at me. "So..."

"I didn't like what he said," I murmur.

"You just punched someone in church! Your mother's going to be saying the Hail, Mary for a week! Why did you punch him?..." I say nothing. "Answer me!" My father's face is red from yelling.

I glance at Vito. Ronnie and Louie are standing back like they're either body guards or they're ready to stop me from pummeling others that are here to pray. We hear the organ playing again and some commotion at the door. Dino's cousins are walking him out. My anger flares. I jolt ready to pound him again. Louie and Ronnie make a wall to stop me.

"Whoa!" Ronnie says. I halt, but watch Dino go to the car. Maria looks over, shakes her head, and follows her cousins. My adrenaline is still spiking.

"Take him over there." My father points to a granite bench. The guys walk me over, and I sit down. They are all hovering. My dad sits down beside me. He's calmer.

"Tonio, I need you to tell me what's wrong. I can't fix something if I don't know what it is."

"There's nothing to fix, Pop." I stare straight ahead.

"Then what is it?"

"You aren't going to like what I say."

"Tell me," he says. The guys move away, far away. At first I think it's to give us some privacy. Then I think it's what I am going to tell him.

"Dino said something... disrespectful about Megan." I still stare straight ahead.

"Megan. Megan O'Neill?" he asks. I nod still not looking at him. He pauses. Then he realizes what I am saying.

"Fanabola! Tonio. You can have any girl you want!" He scrubs his face with his hands. "Shit!"

"Pop, we're at church." I say sarcastically chastising his language.

My mother comes out of the church stomping towards us in her high heels. "Antonio Rinaldo Delisi, Jr.! What has gotten in to you!? You embarrassed me. How dare you? In God's house!" She makes the sign of the cross and looks heavenward. "You are going to go in there and apologize to Father Giovanni!"

"Ma, ummm." I don't know what to say. I know it was wrong, but I just reacted. I didn't think. I don't regret it, but I could have waited till church was over to pound his face in. I'm ashamed of where it happened, but not of what.

"He's interested in Megan," my father says slowly.

"What? What are you talking about Antonio?" she asks my father. She's still pissed. I am ready for the blow to the back of my head that I know is coming from my Mom.

"You wanted him to be interested in a girl. He is… with Megan." She blinks a couple of times. My mother's reaction startles me. She's not mad like my dad. She's happy. She's really happy, in fact, she's beaming at me.

"Oh! Tonio!" She claps her hands and bends down to hug me-her Coach© bag trailing on the ground. "Thank God!" She makes the sign of the cross again. "Finally!" With her hands waving, she is talking a mile a minute. "She's smart too. She got in early to Notre Dame. And talented, you should've heard her play that harp…."

"Yeah, I should've." I say feeling my shame at the spectacle I made in church. My phone buzzes with a text from Megan…

U OK

My mother's eyes go immediately to my phone. "Is that her?" she squeals. My mother is giddy like a school girl. "How cute! She wants to know if you're okay." I turn to my father. He hangs his head.

"How long has this been going on?" he asks.

"It hasn't. We saw each other at Alessandra's last night. I've liked her for a while, Pop. I just didn't say anything."

"Alright…" he pauses for a long time then says, "I'll talk to her father."

My mother uncharacteristically jumps up and down in her heels. I hope she doesn't twist her ankle. I stand, and she hugs me tightly, the fact that I have knocked someone out in church forgotten.

*****

Megan:

I was lucky to get through Ave Maria without throwing up. I couldn't get the image of Antonio hitting Dino in church. It came out of nowhere. I had just settled behind the harp when the room exploded.

Through the entire Mass, I saw a replay in my mind of Antonio spinning around and punching and Dino's head snapping back. I wouldn't be surprised if Dino had whiplash. From the backseat of the mini-van, I could hear my mother talking to my father.

"That kid is no good. He's got the devil in him!" she says still fuming. "If he was my boy, I would take him over my knee, then smack a for sale sign on his fancy car." She went on and on. I thought I was going to start crying now that the shock was starting to wear off. "You see now why your Father told you to stay away from him?" Pointedly, she's looking at me as she swivels in her seat to face me. When my mother gets going on something, there's no telling when she'll stop. My father says nothing.

My phone buzzes with a text from Antonio:

I'm sorry! Can I C U later?

I quickly text back:

Not sure yet

Sweet elation pumps through my veins at just the idea of seeing Antonio. He was gorgeous in his Sunday suit this morning. The searing kisses from last night mingle with the visions of his fist flying. I know I should be afraid, but I'm not. I want him. I don't think in my entire life I have wanted anyone. One day I'm running from him; the next day all I want to do is run to him.

My father's cell phone rings while my mother is still going on and on about the horror show at church today. My father's words are short and one word at a time.

"Yes." Pause. "No," he sighs. "No, I didn't know." A long pause. "Okay, this afternoon."

My father hangs up but not before doing something to his phone. Silence hangs in the air.

"So, what was that about?" my mother asks.

"Antonio Delisi and his son are coming over this afternoon," my father says with absolutely no emotion.

"What? What does he want?" my mother asks in a panicked voice.

My father does not respond, and my mother knows better than to press further. Erin glances at me, a smile creeping on her face.

My mother is a wreck. She races through the house, cleaning in one room, then running into the next not finishing what she started in the first. She is barking orders at Erin and me.

"Erin, put this is your room. Megan, vacuum the stairs." We all work like crazy in a knowing silence. No one talks or asks why the Delisi's are coming.

The doorbell rings and all of us stop in our tracks. My mother flattens her skirt while my father answers the door.

"Hello, Patrick," I hear Mr. Delisi say from the doorway.

"Hello," my dad says and invites Antonio and his father in.

They come in the door and Mr. Delisi immediately acknowledges my mother. "Hello," she says lightly.

Antonio steps forward handing my mother a foil covered dish. "Hello Mrs. O'Neill. This is from my mother. It's Tiramisu."

"Thank you," she says tightly.

Antonio smiles at me and winks. I am standing just behind my mother. Embarrassed and not sure what to do, I take the plate from my mother and head to the kitchen. As I am just shutting the door to the refrigerator my mother and Erin walk in.

"The gentlemen would like to speak privately." my mother says through pursed lips. Excitement dances through me. Antonio in my living room talking to my dad, I never thought I would see the day.

Erin stands in the door way to the kitchen off to the side. I see her.

"What are you doing?" I ask.

"Shhhh… I'm listening."

"Erin," my mother scolds quietly.

But Erin's eyes go wide at what she is hearing. Her hand flies up to cover her mouth. "They're talking about you," she whispers. "Holy Crap. Antonio wants to date you." Her face is incredulous. I approach to listen too. My mother is standing rooted to the kitchen floor with a scowl.

I lean and take the same position as Erin.

"We had an agreement," my father says. I'm surprised at the tone my father is taking with Mr. Delisi.

"Well, things change, Patrick," he says. "My son is asking respectfully if he can spend time with Megan. I did what you asked. Tonio knew very well to stay away from her."

"I understand your concerns, Mr. O'Neill," Antonio says.

"No, I don't think you do, Antonio," my father says with an angry tone, "I didn't want her involved."

Involved in what? My cell phone rings on the kitchen table startling Erin, my mother, and me. I dive for it. It's Troy.

"Hello," I say softly.

"Hi Megan," Troy says quietly. "I just wanted to…"

I cut him off. "Troy, I gotta call you back." I hit end and stand with Erin again. My mother must have turned on the coffee pot because I can smell it brewing. Erin whispers what I missed. "Antonio's father said that he will be very polite and treat you cordially while you're out. And he personally vouches for his son."

"I need to talk to my daughter," my father says, breaking Erin and I out of our quiet conversation.

My father enters the kitchen. He looks to my mother. "Will you and Erin please see to our guests? I need to speak with Megan."

My mother passes us with a 'Hmmmph,' carrying coffee and Tiramisu. As soon as Erin and my mother are gone, my father stands in front of me. I have no clue what he is going to say.

"When were you going to tell me?" my father asks.

"What?"

"That you have a thing with Antonio Delisi," he says aggravated and pointing to the living room.

"Dad, I just spent time with him last night."

"I told you not to Megan!" My father's almost yelling. He never yells. He notices his tone and takes it down to a lower level.

"It was unavoidable," I say looking at the floor.

My father paces a little. "I knew he was interested in you."

"Huh?"

"I knew Megan. Anytime we ran into him or saw him he always watched you."

"How do you know that?"

"I'm a father, Megan. It's my job to know." I felt that my father was leaving something out of that statement.

"What about Troy?" my father asks.

"He's a friend, Dad."

"Well, I hoped he was something more."

"He's not," I respond.

"Do you like Antonio?"

"Yes," I say, staring at the floor again. Very much!

I'm guessing those aren't the answers my Dad is looking for.

"Well. I am going to give you permission to see each other. Hopefully, it will be over before it starts. You're both off to college next September. Please, Megan, be careful. I don't want you to get hurt." It seems as though hurt has a double meaning in his tone.

My father and I join everyone in the living room. Antonio beams at me as I walk in the room. We sit down and take the plates my mother offers to us. It is uncomfortably quiet. My mother makes small talk with everyone. Erin clears the plates and goes with my mother into the kitchen.

"So." Mr. Delisi says.

"I am going to give my permission to Antonio." Antonio's smile brightens, and I think how eighteenth century this seems and formal. "Please keep her away from… trouble," my father says.

Mr. Delisi stands and Antonio follows. "I have some business to tend to. Patrick, don't forget to take care of that matter."

"Yes." We all stand, and I wonder what Mr. Delisi is talking about.

"I'll see you at school tomorrow," Antonio says, "Thank you." he says to my Dad.

"Bye." They walk out to Antonio's car. I watch from the front window. I see them talking in the car as Tonio lights up a cigarette, then pulls away. The excitement of having Antonio here in my home is paralyzing. I'm in a daze. No one has ever made me feel this way.

"Patrick!" my mother yells. "What is going on?"

Erin runs up to me. "Meg, I can't believe it. He is so gorgeous!"

I turn to my sister. "When did you become so boy crazy?"

My parents are talking loudly in the kitchen. "I heard Antonio tell Dad why he punched Dino." She is practically jumping up and down.

"Why?" Now this was something I wanted to hear.

"He said that Dino made a rude remark about you! So that's why Antonio decked him!"

"Wow…" I said stunned.

"Megan, can I see you please?" my mother calls.

I find my mother at the kitchen table with her hands folded.

"Sit please," she says.

I reach for the back of the chair and pull it out to sit.

"Your father tells me that he has agreed to let Antonio come around, to call on you, if you will." This is the eighteenth century!

"You realize that Troy would be better for you." My mother draws out his name and gives me a knowing look. "He has the same background as you."

"Troy is my friend."

"Let me make myself clear. I don't trust Antonio Delisi. His family is corrupt and dangerous. We have worked at keeping you and Erin at a distance from them over the years. You need to be wary and careful. Do you understand me?" My mother's tone is harsh and angry. With her hands folded, she's trying to stay in control.

"I understand. I need to call Troy back."

"Fine."

I swipe my cell phone off the table, and I go to my room in bewilderment. My fingers itch to call Antonio. I wanted to head out the door with him this afternoon. The bittersweet taste of having him in my house but yet at an arm's length, it was so formal and awkward.

Troy answers on the first ring.

"Hello."

"Hey, college guy. How's it going?"

"He was there wasn't he?" I am shocked at his question.

"What? Who?"

"That guy."

"Troy what is going on with you?" Now talking to Troy felt awkward. We have always been so close. Where is this coming from?

"Just answer me, Megan. That fuckin' guy was there." I suck in a breath through my teeth.

"Yeah…" I am angry. I try to switch subjects back, "How is the dorm? Are you close to the cafeteria?"

"What's his name?" Troy's tone gets louder.

"Uh… Antonio."

"Holy shit! Megan! That was Delisi wasn't it? The guy watching us."

"How do you know the Delisis?" I ask.

"I'm not stupid Megan. I may not live in the same town as you, but I live in the same state. Don't you think our parents talk too? I'm not living under a rock."

I'm not sure where this conversation is going. I am still trying to process the past eight hours, and then I get this crap from Troy, my friend.

"Are you going to tell me about school or are you going to keep this up?" I'm getting mad.

"I gotta go," he says softly. This whole thing is so unlike him. "I'm going out with a bunch of guys from the dorm. See ya."

He hangs up. Again!

Chapter 12

Stai zitto (sta te zeet): SHUT YOUR MOUTH!

Antonio:

I've always hated school. I have to put up with the phony kids who try to be my friend, the made-up bleach blondes that hang on me and the teachers who can barely look me in the eye. Don't get me wrong; years ago I took some Barbies up on their offers and used my position to influence some grades. I didn't do it for long. It just didn't feel right. I stay pretty low key at school. Most people stay away from me anyway.

I park next to Vito's Caddy. I scan the parking lot and benches looking for Megan. Raven's little blue car is a few cars down.

I slam my door and in front of me is Vito.

"What happened yesterday?" he asks, smirking. "You talk to her dad?"

"Yup."

"What did he say?"

"He said yes."

"You are shitting me! Even after you kicked Dino's ass in church?"

"Yup."

"Dude, that's awesome!"

My mind is racing about what I'm going to say to Megan today. Today is the first day of auto mechanics and Megan is in my class. We're assigned lockers our freshman year and keep them until we graduate. I always try to make it a point to walk by Megan's locker in the morning. Now I'm headed there with a purpose. I have this insane urge to let everyone know that she's mine. My stalker is back because we have barely been together.

Megan is just slamming her locker as she hikes her bag over her shoulder. She smiles when she sees me coming. I take that as a good sign.

"Hi," she says blushing. Her hair is hanging straight down her back.

"Hi." There is an awkward pause. "What class do you have first?"

"Home Ec." I don't even give myself a chance to think. I take her hand in mine, and lead her down the hall to her classroom. The hallway is still full. Some people rush out of the way when they see me coming. Others stare from the outskirts near their lockers. Their eyes travel to my hand wrapped around Megan's. The hallway is unnaturally quiet as we get to her classroom. It's a short walk. "What class do you have?" Megan asks.

"English," I say.

"You're going to be late. That is the other side of the school... Thanks for the dessert yesterday."

"Don't thank me; thank my mom." I don't have any patience so I ask her. "Can you go out Saturday?"

"Ummm, yeah, I guess. I don't have any plans." She watches me. "That was pretty brave coming over and talking to my dad. It was awkward as a matter of fact."

I stop short in front Home Ec. "What are you saying?" Does she not want to go out?! Shit!

"Nothing. Just that it was weird. Nowadays, guys don't usually ask a girl's parents to take her on a date."

"My father wasn't for it at first. He said he wanted to talk to your dad." I was starting to get an eerie feeling. "Do you not want to go out Saturday?"

"No, it's not that… I would love to go."

I try not smirk at her admission. I let her hand go and brush my fingers across her cheek. She visibly shudders.

"Good," I say. "See you next class." And I head to English. Whew! I have her all to myself Saturday.

Vito and I slip into two desks all the way at the back of the classroom. Mr. Treat, what a fucked up name, comes into the classroom carrying English Anthologies.

"So…" Vito says.

"So what?"

"When you takin' her out?" Vito asks.

"Saturday."

"What's your 'big plan' with Red?" He air quotes his words.

I plan to blow her fuckin' mind with the plans I have. I don't want to tell Vito because:

    1. He has a big mouth.

2. He's going to know I have it bad.

"I'll tell you about it on Sunday."

"What!?" Vito's voice raises and Mr. Treat sends us a warning glance. We could talk all class if we wanted. He just wants us to be quiet. I'm feeling generous today because I have a date and a class with Megan; I don't send the warning glance back to him.

I show up outside her door at Home Ec to walk with her to auto Mechanics. Vito is with me. She looks stunned when she walks out of the classroom.

"Uh, hi," she says.

"Hey Red," Vito pipes up. I shoot him a look. Why the hell is he using a nickname for my girl? Whatever! He has been referring to her as Red since forever.

"Hi," she says again.

"Come on." I grab her hand and the three of us walk down the hall. Vito makes playful jabs at Dickie, the empty suit. Dickie loves every minute of it. He wants to hang with me and my friends so bad. He is such a freakin' poser. He probably would have pissed his pants the other night when we got jumped. He doesn't have the heart for it.

"Hey, you hear about Johnny Nero?" Dickie asks Vito. My adrenaline spikes at Johnny's name. I spin myself towards him pulling Megan with me. He sends a leery gaze to Megan like he doesn't want to say it in front of her. I get the message. I continue to lead her to class. Vito will fill me in later.

We enter the classroom. I lead us to the back black top tables.

"Is this okay?" I ask her.

"Sure." She puts her stuff down and sits on the gray stool. The classroom smells of oil and metal. She seems nervous.

"I'm gonna pick you up early Saturday."

"Where are we going?" she asks eagerly.

"It's a surprise." As soon as the words are out of my mouth, Maria comes bouncing in the room headed for the teacher's desk. I groan inwardly. I watch her give the teacher an add slip. Fanabola! Maria turns and starts waving to me frantically. I catch Megan out of the corner of my eye, appraising me.

"Friend?" she asks.

"Not really," I answer, as she appears aggravated now.

Vito sits on a stool next to our table. He gives me a knowing look. Maria bounces down the aisle towards Vito. My elation of having a class with Megan is squashed as Maria and her stiletto heels clunk down onto the stool beside him.

"You are going to be broken up into groups of four," the teacher, Mr. DeRobbio, announces. "This will be your group for projects. This is a hands-on class."

Vito chuckles and waggles his eyebrows at Maria. Mr. DeRobbio casts him a warning look and continues. "Today we are going to break down into our groups and do an activity."

"I can think of a few activities," Vito smirks.

Maria slaps him on the arm, giggling.

"Stop it."

Other kids in the class chuckle too. The teacher definitely heard Vito this time, but won't say anything.

"Break up into groups of four. Choose wisely." As Mr. DeRobbio says this, he gives a pointed glance at Megan. Vito immediately stands up and drags his stool towards Megan and me. Maria watches. Vinny Maranzano's kid, Joey, comes over.

"Hey Tonio. Can I be in your group?"

"Sure man," I say.

"Me too," Maria says, moving towards me.

"Uh, Maria. This group is full." Is she stupid? We have four. Megan's face goes pink. Maria eyes her up and down.

"What about me?" Maria whines. "Who am I going to go with?" Her face scrunches up and she folds her arms across her chest in a pout. Like I need this fuckin' drama. What am I, the freakin' organizer? I know she is not going to stop so I call over Alessandra's friend, Sophia.

"Maria needs a group." It's all I have to say.

"Come on Maria," Sophia says. Then she walks Maria over to her group. She already has four. Sophia shoves out some kid I don't know. The kid gets up and walks to another group. I can tell Maria is seething as she stares at me from across the room.

I didn't get to talk much to Megan. Well, I did but not the conversation I wanted to be having with her like learning every little thing about her. The groups had to label a diagram of a car. We only had five minutes then Mr. DeRobbio lectured the rest of the class.

Sitting next to Megan is distracting. I have no fucking clue what the teacher has been talking about. I want to reach out and stroke her hair then rub the pad of my thumb across her pink lips.

DING DING! Thank God, the bell rings. I wait for Megan to pack up her stuff.

"What do you have now?" I ask her.

"English." she says.

"Hey, is Louie in your class?"

"Yeah, history too. He seems to be in my classes every year," Megan says as I take her hand. I see a slight flush rise to her cheeks. I feel a stab of jealousy.

The hallway is loud and bustling. More gawks follow us as we walk. I peer down at Megan. Her face is smooth with a smattering of pinkish freckles. I have to control myself from shoving her into an empty classroom and kissing every freckle on her face. The more I spend time with her the more breathtaking I find her. I'm in deep shit!

I haven't stopped thinking about the other night. I am walking hand in hand with Megan and my hard-on inducing thoughts when a young girl comes up to us. It's Megan's sister. The flaming red hair is a dead giveaway.

"Hi!" She is bouncing on her toes.

I see Megan roll her eyes.

"How's the start of freshman year going?" Megan asks her.

"Great! So far my classes are a breeze." Megan's sister is stealing glances at me and grinning.

"Hi," I say to her because she's just staring at me.

"Hi," she says giggling.

Out of what seems like nowhere, Vito pops up.

"Hey Dude," I turn to him. He doesn't say anything; he just flanks my right side. My attention goes back to Megan and her sister.

"Okay… see you later Erin," Megan says as we watch her sister walk away with lively steps. "Sorry. My sister is a little excited."

"About what?" I ask.

"About you."

"Me? Why?"

Megan flips her hand against her forehead in an exaggerated motion. "Antonio Delisi asked you out! Oh my God!" Obviously, she is making fun of her little sister. Vito snorts and walks away.

Megan's animated expression makes me laugh. She is so sweet and smart. This is the most relaxed I have seen her, except when she was with that chooch. My hand clenches into a fist at my side remembering her care free smiles.

Alessandra calls out to me, "Tonio! Wait up." Both Megan and I turn as San bounds over to us.

"Hi, Megan," she says smiling. Then she whispers to me.

"Did you hear about Johnny Nero?" I don't know what is going on, but from the way people are mentioning his name this morning, I doubt it is anything good considering he still owes my dad five-hundred in juice money. I give her a look and shake my head slightly giving her the message, not now.

Alessandra is one of my smarter friends, and she catches on right away. Just like she caught on about how I feel about Megan.

San eyes us curiously. Her appraising stance makes it as though she can flush out all our secrets.

"Megan, some of my friends and I are going to the mall Saturday. Do you want to come?"

Megan's face is shocked at the offer, but she says, "Antonio and I are going out that day."

"Wow, great! Well, I have to get to History. Bye."

The rest of the day flies by. I am standing by my car smoking, when I see Megan and Erin walking down the sidewalk. Raven is sitting in her car probably waiting for them. Megan sees me and smiles, and her sister whispers something to her.

"Can I give you a lift?" I ask as they approach.

"Um, well." Megan says.

"Oh please, Meg?" Erin begs. "I've never been in such a nice car, please?"

"Let me go talk to Raven," she says looking torn.

She is back in a minute, and Raven's car leaves the parking lot. Erin is jumping up and down giggling. I'm not used to giggling little red headed girls.

I open the passenger door for Megan, and Erin is giddy. I shut her door for her and she is squirming in the backseat. Ugh, kids!

When I get in the car, Megan is scolding Erin to sit still.

"How fast does this go, Tonio?" Erin asks.

"Buckle up." I tell her and rev the engine. We pass Vito and his Caddy. I wave. He doesn't wave back but is staring into the backseat of my car. When we reach the main road, I gun it. Erin squeals in delight. Megan is clutching the door handle and arm rest.

"This is so cool!" Erin shrieks.

The drive to their house is shortened by my exceeding of the speed limit.

"Thanks for the ride, Tonio. That was awesome!" Erin says as she clamors out of the car.

"You okay?" I ask Megan.

"Oh yeah, much better now that you aren't risking my little sister's life," she says sarcastically.

"It wasn't that bad." I tell her.

"Uh huh."

I reach out, peel her hand off the armrest, and bring to my lips to kiss it. Her face is surprised and inviting. I lean in to kiss her sweet lips. I breathe in a scent of cherries. I wonder if it's her lip gloss or something. Megan leans in closer to me to deepen the kiss. It takes an effort but I restrain myself. I want to flip the switch to recline the seat and cover her with my body. Reluctantly, she pulls away.

"My mother may be watching. I should go. Thanks for the ride." She is flushed pink. I jump out of the car wanting to be a gentleman and open her door. We stand facing each other, and she lightly kisses my cheek.

"Bye."

"Bye."

I only have a couple of hours before the meeting tonight. Thoughts of Megan swirl around in my head. I can't wait to take her out Saturday. It's been a long time since I felt this kind stirring anticipation. I swing my car into the driveway and my dad and Donny are talking by the side door. My father motions me over.

"Eh, Tonio, good day today?"

"Yeah Pop."

"Donny and I wanted to tell you... don't worry about Johnny anymore." He clasps my shoulder. "We're all set."

"Why?"

"You don't need to think about it. Johnny's been clipped."

"You take care of him, Donny?" I ask. I knew all the talk of Johnny today had to be that he was dead, but the initial words from my dad send a nasty jolt through me.

"Nah, I don't do that. Yous know that. Now, about those other chooches from last week. We gotta collect. We're leaving after the meeting."

I turn to Pop, Johnny's death pushed to the back of my mind. "What about school?" I really don't give a fuck about school. I am more pissed about not seeing Megan in class.

My Pop pats my cheek, "You're a smart boy, you'll be fine."

*****

I arrive at the meeting at Gino's. Everyone is gathered around the table. I sit down next to my Dad.

I spot Dino down at the other end of the table. The skin around his eye is swollen with a blackish tint. He is staring at me. I glare back at him. My blood boils just thinking about what an asshole he is. Pop starts speaking.

"Sommersville is not playing by the rules. Their crews have been spotted around town. My Tonio and some of your own sons were jumped last week."

"Eh, what the fuck is their problem?" Mr. Maranzano asks. The room is quiet while everyone waits for an explanation.

"We're not sure. Donny is looking into it." Pop motions for Donny to speak as he reaches for his wine glass.

"Sommersville is getting too close," Donny starts. "They are showing up all over. Shit was stolen out of the chemical warehouse by the docks."

Shit! Sommersville is getting ballsy. My friends and I getting jumped and a break-in. Fuck!

Zing-thwack! Donny clasps his side and hits the table sending papers soaring and wine flinging like droplets of blood. Pinging sounds ring out. Without thought, my body leaves my seat and connects with my dad's hurling him to the hard floor. Chaos erupts. I feel his gun against my side under his suit jacket. I reach for it. In a split second, I quickly crawl on the floor holding the piece in my hand, adrenaline surging.

I move to Donny on my way to the window where the shots are coming from.

"I'm okay, Tonio," Donny rasps. "Get those fuckers…" he winces out. I don't think, I move.

At the window I crouch, Mr. Maranzano and Mr. Ferretti are huddled on the carpet, already popping up in succession to exchange shots with the intruders. Others at the meeting are lying low. Red fills up my field of vision; it's not blood I see but rage.

"I'm going outside," I murmur to them. I check the clip and scurry across the floor to the back door. I find Dino lying flat on the floor of the kitchen as I make my way through. Fuckin' pansy!

From low down, I push the back door slowly making sure no one is there. I knew these assholes wouldn't get out of their car. Never lifting myself higher than a door knob, I sneak around the building constantly searching and scanning for attack. I see the black Escalade that has bullets exiting. Its windows lowered only to slits. They must have brought a special vehicle-bullet proof glass.

The shots coming from the restaurant are doing nothing but making plinking noises and webbed cracks. The only way to puncture through is with a long succession of shots in one spot.

I get up close enough to the edge of the rear bumper. I peer in the darkened glass. They are so fuckin' stupid. No one is watching behind them. Four people are smashed up to the windows facing the restaurant. I only have a few more seconds before these fuckers drive away.

As low as I can get, I point my gun close to the glass and fire six shots firm and fast in the same spot. I don't dwell on the fact that one of the bullets could ricochet and hit me. The fifth bullet penetrates and the sixth one flies. The car jerks forward as the driver stamps on the accelerator. Instead of gunshots, the noise of screeching tires fills the air and the smell of burnt rubber assails me.

Chapter 13

Fanabola (fa na bowl a): Shit!

Megan:

My instincts were right. My mother was watching me from the window of our living room. When I walk in, surprisingly she goes easy on me. She only asks about my day.

While I'm getting ready for bed my phone buzzes on my nightstand. I flutter a moment, hoping it's Antonio. It's only been since after school that I've seen and talked to him but I sort of miss him. Is that possible? I mean, it has only been a few days since we started seeing each other. Can someone really grow on you that much? I look at the screen, and my heart falls a little. It's not Antonio; it's Troy.

"Hey Troy!" I push some extra exuberance into my voice. After our last few conversations, our relationship has become very strained.

"Hey Meggie!" Troy laughs. "Meggie, Meggie."

This doesn't sound like Troy at all. I'm immediately on alert.

"Troy, you okay?" Concern fills my voice.

"I am great. Fab-u-lous-es." Fabulous is completely slurred. This is so not like Troy.

"Have you been drinking? Are you okay?" I panic a little. "Troy?"

He doesn't speak. "Troy?" I try again.

"Hmmm?"

"What is going on?"

"I'm missing my girl." His voice drops. He sounds depressed.

"What girl?"

"Have you always been this stupid, or is it just 'cause you're hanging with Delisi?" He sounds mad.

"What?!"

"Are you still my best friend?" he asks, sounding sobered.

"Of course."

"Will you still be my best friend after I tell you this?" Troy asks quietly.

"Tell me what?"

"Answer me."

"Do you have fun with me?"

"That's a question Troy, and you know the answer. Come on what's wrong?"

"I thought... I thought...." I was losing him again to the alcohol. "I thought... I was gonna marry you," drives out of his mouth.

My body stiffens from his declaration, and I'm forced into surprised silence.

"Ummm."

I don't know what to say. Troy and I always had a gentle understanding. We are friends, best friends. His words shock me. Upsetting him while he's drunk is the last thing I want to do. The silence between us lengthens. I can hear people laughing in the background over his cell phone. A girl screams and snickers in the din.

"Troy?" He didn't answer right away.

"I gotta go… there are people here," he slurs, and the phone clicks off. Sitting on my bed, I stare at the wall. How did my life change so quickly? Troy's words replay in my mind, 'I thought I was going to marry you.'

I'm not sure how long I stare at the wall because, when I opened my eyes, the first thing I see is my ceiling. I must have fallen asleep. My phone buzzes with a text. A lump forms in my throat. But it isn't from Troy, it is from Antonio:

Have to do some stuff for a few days so won't be at school. Can't wait for Saturday! I will miss u.

His words about missing me stir feelings I never felt before. I miss him too. I am giddy and sad at the same time. I am happy he will miss me, but depressed I won't see him for a couple of days. Those four little words mean more to me than Troy's professing of marriage and a part of me despise myself for it. I am falling too hard and too fast. The butterfly is back in my stomach flying in happy circles. I text him back:

Okay. I'll miss u 2

*****

Raven picks me up for school, and Erin catches a ride with us. For this ride, Erin isn't bouncing in her seat like she was in Antonio's car. Thinking his name causes a pang in my chest.

Walking down the hallways is odd. I have done it for the past three years. This is different though. The last few days with Antonio walking with me and being in auto mechanics class with me changed something. I actually enjoy the anticipation of seeing him and just being with him. He has been a perfect gentleman. Even Vito is starting to grow on me. Louie talks to me in all my classes now. He is really a nice guy.

People I don't even know say hello as they pass me in the hall. Maria obviously is not happy about me spending time with Antonio. She is constantly trying to get his attention. She stands in front of me to talk to Antonio. Maria interrupts conversations to put in her two cents. It's annoying! Antonio always dismisses her forward advances. I can't help but wonder if they have had something going on before.

"Hey, Red!" Vito says as he sits down next to me in auto-mechanics class where Antonio usually sits.

"Hi," I say back. I see Maria coming down the aisle between the black-topped desks. A frown mars her features. If my mother saw that face, she would say that she better watch out or her face might freeze that way. There is something about Maria, I just don't like her.

Vito stiffens next to me.

"Who am I gonna sit with?" Maria complains as she runs her fingers through her long black hair.

Vito regards her like he wants to say something, and I am guessing it wouldn't be nice. Maria sat at the vacant table on her stool with a huff. I roll my eyes at her grumbling.

"How's Tony, Vito? I heard last night was brutal."

Vito glances at Maria across the aisle, giving her a severe warning. Maria doesn't take the hint and I don't want her to. What happened last night? Worry and wonder creep into my chest followed by sharp panic.

"Is it true that the gunfire shot up the entire restaurant?" My panic shot up to alarm.

Vito's eyes shine feral anger. A low tone rumbles out of him, "Shut the fuck up, Maria." Obviously, Vito was told not to mention whatever happened.

Finally finding my voice I ask, "What happened?"

Vito's expression softens, "Everything is fine."

Maria hmmphed, "That's not what I heard."

I grab my phone and hold it under the table. I quickly text Antonio:

R U OK? I heard there was shooting last night!!!
Antonio: Who told U?

Antonio didn't answer the question. He didn't have to.

Megan: Maria
Antonio: Don't worry. And don't listen to Maria. I still miss U.
Megan: Me 2

My scalp prickles as I read his words, Don't worry. Everyone always worries when someone says that. I just don't know how worried I need to be.

*****

Antonio:

I am rip shit mad. Maria is going to fuck this up with Megan. This guy I'm waiting for is going to find his day much more unlucky than he thought. Red clouds my vision as I sit in my car waiting. I am still pissed about last night. Donny getting shot. The whole freakin' frittata at the restaurant irks me. Who knows how long I'll have to fill in for Donny. My mind is off. I just want to spend time with Megan. And this loser asshole is keeping me from her.

My phone buzzes. It's Pop.

"Yeah," I say into the phone.

"Tonio, forgetta abou' this guy. The cleaner's comin'. I changed my mind. His three large ain't worth the jerk off he's been givin' me. Get out of there."

"Kay, Pop," I say. Part of me wishes I was the cleaner because I really feel like killing someone right now. I crush the gas pedal to the floor of my car and speed away.

I head home glad I don't have to spend another night in a hotel. Randy's Liquors is right down the street from my house. I grab a six pack. Randy never cards me and never refuses to sell to me. One of the perks of being me.

I punch the tab on my beer can and lay down on the couch in our living room trying to calm the fuck down.

"Eh," my mother says, standing behind the couch, "what are you doing here?"

"Dad called the cleaner in, so I'm done for the day."

"Johnny Nero's funeral is tomorrow. You goin'?"

"Yeah, then I have some stuff to do for Dad."

Mom doesn't say anything else, she just walks away. If I sit and really think about things, it's fucked up. I am going to a funeral of a guy who I beat up then my father had killed. I need do what my dad always says, 'don't think, just do.'

Megan gets out of school in a half an hour. I find myself off the couch and sitting in front of the school waiting for her. Finally, I am calming down. I spot her walking out the door with Raven and Erin. Louie is next to Raven talking to her. Erin sees me first because she points to my car and shakes Megan's arm. A smile forms and Megan's entire face lights up when she sees me. My chest stirs with contentment.

She is walking towards me as I lean against my car. It's like my vision is a tunnel. All the shapes around her are blurred; her face is the only thing I see clearly. As soon as she is within arms distance, I reach out and pull her to me. I wrap my arms around her then lean down and kiss her. She eagerly wraps her hands around me too. My anger fades as I hold her. She is so calming. All I need in life is this girl.

"What are you doing here?" she says, when I loosen my hold but don't let go.

"I finished early. I thought I could take you home."

Megan turns to her sister. "You coming with us?"

"No, I'm going to Connor's tonight." Megan's face has a hard-to-read expression, a little sad maybe. I don't know what to think. I can take her sister too. Raven and Louie are in their own world. They say their goodbyes and walk towards Louie's car.

A mini-van rolls to stop in front of my car. A kid gets out.

"Connor!" Erin squeals and walks right up to him.

The window of the van opens and a woman, definitely not Italian, calls Megan over. Possessiveness overtakes me, and I walk to the van with her never letting go of her hand. The lady in the van just looks me up and down like she was sizing me up.

"Hi Mrs. O'Connell," Megan says.

"Hi Megan," the lady says with a curt tone. "Tell your Mom that I'll be dropping Erin back at your house about seven."

"Okay," Megan replies a little too brightly.

"Aren't you going to introduce me to your friend?" Mrs. O'Connell drags the question out like it was hurting her to say it. My eyes automatically narrow.

I gently reach my hand through the open window and say with a polite smile, "Hi, I'm Antonio... her boyfriend."

Mrs. O'Connell sucks her teeth and plasters on a fake sharp smile, "Nice to meet you." Only an idiot would believe she means it. Medigans all look at me the same way, with disgust.

I see Vito out of the corner of my eye taking in the whole scene. Megan and I back away from the van as Erin and the kid get in. Vito is still staring, but he isn't looking at me or Megan. He is watching the van door close.

Megan and I decide to go to the dock and hang out. Well, I convinced her that's what we should do since we don't have to take her sister home, and it's a gorgeous day. We haven't been there since the night of Alessandra's party. The sunlight on Megan's hair makes it glow different shades of red. I brush my hands on the back of her neck having the best of both worlds feeling her soft curls and tender skin. I wanted to stand there kissing her for the rest of the day and night.

There is something about her. Something that I can't explain. Being with her is like a blanket of sweetness and warmth.

Megan breaks away from our kiss. "I have to ask you something but I don't think you'll tell me."

"What?" I ask concerned.

"What happened last night? Why weren't you in school?..." She pauses. "Where did you go?"

I sigh long and hard. This girl makes me want to spill my soul and loyalty onto the ground. I don't want to keep anything from her.

"Ugh... Megan there's just stuff that happens that I can't tell you. And you probably really don't want to know anyway." I pause collecting myself. "What I can tell you is that, last night the restaurant I was at was shot up." Her face morphs into fear and I caress her cheeks in my hands, "Look at me, I'm fine... And, when I'm not in school, I'm doing stuff for my Dad."

I see her breathe to say something so I jump in with, "No, I can't tell you what." I smile at her then give her a peck on the lips.

My brain registers that it's back, fear. She's afraid of me again. Fucking Maria! Megan wouldn't even have known about last night if it wasn't for her.

"Maria..." Megan starts.

"Stop right there. Don't listen to Maria. She's a slut who can't keep her mouth shut." My voice came out harsh and mean. Megan takes a step away from me. I see her eyes fill with tears, and I immediately feel sick to my stomach.

"Whoa, come 'ere," I say softly, reaching for her. "I'm sorry. I didn't mean to get upset."

Reluctantly, she comes back to me, and I hug her. I take a deep breath relishing her scent and closeness. It's like a dream. After all these years, I am holding her in my arms.

Chapter 14

Agita (ah gi ta): upset stomach

Megan:

I knew Antonio was intense, but I didn't imagine I would be on this quiet rollercoaster. I am getting my shoes on the sunny Saturday morning of my surprise. Antonio said he'd be here early. I hear my mother on the phone.

"I know, I know... He's got the devil in him that one." (pause) "Yeah, unbelievable." (pause) "Well, I just hope he can keep our Megan safe while this lasts." I creep closer to where she is. I'm hanging on every word. "It's not going to last. Her father and I are counting on that. Give it a couple of weeks, and he'll move on to the next girl." (pause) "If that happens, then we'll just send her to visit Troy. She needs a little perspective."

I don't have time to seethe with the anger growing in me from listening to my mother talk about Antonio dumping me, because there is a knock on the door.

My whole family turns up by the front door in a matter of seconds. Erin is grinning from ear to ear. I swing open the door to see a smiling Antonio in all his dark and smoldering beauty. He is just gorgeous. Light musky cologne wafts my way, and I close my eyes a second.

I open them when I hear Erin ooooing and ahhhing. I follow her gaze to the street, and there is a limousine. A long black stretch limousine with a driver waiting patiently with his hands folded.

"You ready?" Antonio asks me.

My parent's expressions are of disapproval. "Where are you off to?" my father asks Antonio.

"New York for the day. We'll be back this evening."

Erin did her trade mark squeal, "New York!" I am beaming. New York in a limo-Holy Shit! I snatch my pocketbook off the couch. My mother stops my steps towards the door.

"Do you have your cell phone?"

"Yes," I tell her.

"Have a nice day," my mom says, but after her conversation with whomever she was gossiping with, I don't believe her. I kiss my father good-bye, and he looks down at me warily.

I slip into the limo first as the driver holds the door open for us. I am giddy as Antonio buckles in beside me.

"I can't believe you did this."

"So, you're surprised?"

"I'll say."

"There is another surprise. I've had it for a while. I was waiting for the right time to give it to you, but I can't wait anymore."

Antonio retrieves a small box from a compartment in his door. He hands it to me. My hands are shaking.

I tug the bow off and stick it on his head, and he laughs as he pulls it off.

"I hope you like it," he says.

With my hands shaking, I open the box to find a striking Claddaugh necklace. I am in awe.

"It's white gold and the clerk said it means love, friendship, and loyalty."

I shake my head agreeing with him, "Yeah, I know." I say as I stare at it. "It's beautiful. Thank you so much." I lean in and kiss him. Then I lift my hair and swivel so that he can put the necklace on me. I immediately feel his breath on my neck, and then his lips are moving over my skin. I shudder because it is amazing. He moves away and says huskily, "It's on. Lemme see."

When I face him again, his eyes are lustful and searching mine. He looks at the necklace and smiles. "Now it's beautiful," he says, and I can't resist kissing him again.

We stop and get breakfast at a little diner off the highway. Everyone in the restaurant stares at us as we come in. I'm guessing they saw us get out of the limo. I giggle.

"What's so funny?" Antonio asks me as we stand at the front holding hands waiting to be seated.

"Nothing," I say.

He gives me a look that says, yeah right.

"I was just thinking that all these people probably thought someone famous was coming to eat here because of the limo. And I just want to yell out to them. I pretend to yell and cup my hand over my mouth, "Nothing to see here, just the mob boss's son from New Jersey out for breakfast."

"Wow," he deadpans. "No one has ever called me that to my face."

I laugh again, "What are you going to do Mr. Delisi, tie me up and throw me in the river?"

"I wouldn't throw you in the river, but tying you up has been on my mind before." His face is serious, and he squeezes my hand to jerk me closer. The waitress interrupts us and yanks us out of our reverie.

We order eggs, bacon, and toast. I am still reeling by what Antonio said. A blush creeps up my face by just replaying what he said in my mind. He has an unbelievable ability to make me want and fear him at the same time. I am so out of my league. I've never had a steady boyfriend. In fact, these feelings of passion and lust are new to me. But regardless of how confused and new this is, I wouldn't want to be here with anyone else.

We arrive in New York City and Antonio takes me to the Empire State Building. We have lunch at the Ritz. Everywhere we went Antonio paid with one hundred dollar bills. It made me uncomfortable. I was starting to question where he got all this money-the limo, the necklace, and our two hundred dollar lunch. Did his parents just give it to him? I was trying not to let my thoughts sour this awesome day.

My phone buzzes with a text message:

Enjoying your day in NY? Did he get in ur pants yet?

It's from Troy. I don't respond. I'm too mad. So this is how it's going to be between us. I shove my phone back in my pocket. I refuse to let Troy ruin this perfect day.

Antonio takes my hand and tells the driver to meet us at Central Park. We walk slowly, taking in the sights and sounds of the city. We pass shop after shop, window after window of everything from clothes to tools. The streets aren't too busy because it's a Saturday.

Every couple of blocks, Antonio tugs on my hand and we stand close to the buildings away from the foot traffic. And every time, he scrunches his hand in my hair and kisses me. The first few times, they are sweet and slow kisses. The closer to Central Park we get the more heated and wanting they become. The more heated the kisses become the more dazed and drugged I feel.

At the entrance to Central Park, a man with a weathered cardboard sign sits huddled on the ground. His clothes are tattered and dirty with what seemed like years of filth.

Antonio's pace slows as we get closer to the gates of the park. He releases my hand. We stand a few feet from the man who appears homeless. Antonio reaches into his left front pocket and takes out a crumpled hundred dollar bill. Less than two weeks ago, I was afraid of Antonio. Now I think he's the sweetest guy I know. He hands it to the guy, picks up my hand again, and leads me into the park.

*****

Antonio:

I know that the text she got is from her 'friend' Troy, the chooch that Alessandra thinks is so wonderful. But I'm not going to let it bother me because she's here with me all bouncing red curls, luscious lips, and smiles.

The park is crowded. People on roller blades, bicycles, and wearing fancy jogging suits litter one of the slices of green grass and trees in New York City.

We walk for a little while. The sun makes shadows on the sidewalk through the tree limbs.

"So," I ask her, "are you looking forward to college next year?"

"Yeah, I'm glad I got into my first choice. What are you planning to do next year?" She asks squeezing my hand.

"Don't know yet. I've been busy," I say, not wanting to meet her gaze.

"You must want to go somewhere?" I get a sickening feeling when I think of her going off to college without me. My question had been meant to be light and conversational, but now I'm sorry I brought up her going away.

We approach a large group of people standing huddled together in a circle. Loud music begins to ring out. A bunch of guys start dancing. Megan obviously wants to watch because she leads me over to the crowd.

"Wow, they're good," she says. I position her in front of me and rest my hands across her middle while we watched the show. It is awesome just to hold her.

The driver picks us up at the entrance, and we drive down the congested streets.

It's getting late. I need to bring back something for my mom. I spot a Godiva Chocolates store on 40th street. The driver steers the limo to the curb.

"I'm gonna grab something for my mom. You want anything?"

"No, I'm all set," she smiles at me and I notice her playing with the necklace I gave her.

"Wait here. I'll be right back." And I smile at her too.

The smell of melted chocolate drifts over me like a warm blanket. I walk around looking for Mom's favorite. I pick a large box of them. I should get something for Megan's mom too. Then I second guess myself and get another large box of assorted chocolates for her sister. Then I grab one for Megan too.

I stand at the register as the clerk rings it up when my phone buzzes with a text from Vito,

Ronnie's been jumped, your pop is calling a meeting tonight, what time will u be back?

Shit! Figures.

"That'll be 195 dollars please." The cashier jars me from my thoughts of having to rush back home. I snatch a couple of hundreds from my pocket and hand them over while texting Vito:

7:30 if no traffic

I take the huge bag off the counter and get back in the limo.

"Did you buy out the whole store?" she says giggling at me. Megan holds the bag under her nose. "Wow, it smells awesome! Did you mug Willy Wonka or something?" My anxiety melts away at her teasing. I lean over and kiss her. She laughs again. "YOU even smell like chocolate." She rubs her nose over my neck and hair like a cat. I hit the button for the privacy screen between us and the driver while I pin her beneath me.

The magic that is Megan ensnares me. For the next two hours we kiss, talk, and laugh. She is the most amazing person. I can't imagine how I lived so long having her at an arm's reach. I don't know how I am going to let her go when it is time to drop her off at home. I want to tell the driver to head for Canada. My stalker is back! And I tell her that.

With my face nuzzling her neck and my hand cupping her hip I say, "I don't want to let you go. I want you all to myself."

"What are you gonna do, kidnap me?" she says joking.

She stiffens under me when I say, "I have resources you know."

"I bet you do." The joking tone was gone.

I look up at her, "Don't be afraid of me... I can see it in your eyes sometimes."

Megan straightens forcing me to sit up. "Well, I am afraid." She won't look at me.

I tip her chin forcing her back to me. Tears well up in her eyes again. "No, honey, don't cry." I feel sick to my stomach. "I know I get angry at times, but I won't hurt you." My own words stun me. I can't recall ever calling someone 'honey' in my life.

Her eyes still glistening, tears threatening to fall she says, "That's not why I'm scared."

"What is it then?"

She is really killing me with those tears. When girls I don't even like cry, it bothers me. This is torture watching her try to stop her tears from falling.

"Ugh, I don't even think I could explain it all."

"All!" I choke. "All's not good."

She waits then says, "You're gonna hurt me when you get tired of me." It seems like it took a lot for her to say that.

"Tired of you!" My voice goes up. "I just told you I didn't want to let you go."

"Yeah, well, guys like you can be very charming."

"I just threatened to kidnap you! That's charming!" That makes her laugh. "I'm afraid too, Megan." And I am.

"Huh? What can the great Antonio Delisi be afraid of?" I could feel the bite of her sarcasm.

"If this is confession time, here it is. I am so see through about my feelings for you that even my grandmother knew. Alessandra told me to stop moping around and do something about it. I never even told San how I felt about you. She said she had always known from when we were kids. San really likes you."

"I like her too."

"And Vito… the asshole laughed so hard when he figured it out, I wasn't sure he could pull himself together enough to drive."

"Why was he laughing?"

"Because he's an ass and he knew how bad I wanted you. But I had to convince my father to allow it."

"Hmmm, my father warned me away from you," she said quietly.

"If I had a daughter, I wouldn't want her hanging with me either." She smiles again, but I know that isn't everything. "That's not it though is it?"

"No," Megan sucks in a breath. "I'm also scared something will happen to you… You won't tell me what you do all day…. And what happened the other night, you're keeping things from me."

She is right I am. But it isn't because I don't want to tell her. I want to protect her.

"I can't tell you." I kiss her. "And I don't want you in that part of my life. That scares me." I kiss her again. I reach my arm around her slim waist and slip my hand under the hem of her shirt. I graze my fingers over the soft, warm skin of her belly.

A barely audible groan sounds in the back of her throat. Her need and want excite me. I brush my hands higher up her sides. Megan's kisses become hungrier and I'm finding it hard to stop myself. I want her.

The stopping of the limo pulls us from our passion filled daze. We are right in front of her house. I don't want this to end. I don't think she does either.

"This is your stop," I say. Megan's hair is wilder looking than usual. It probably didn't help that I kept running my fingers through it.

"Yeah, I guess it is," she sounds disappointed. "When will I see you again?"

"I need to check out the schedule for the week," I say. "I'll text you." I kiss her again and walk her to the door.

After I drop Megan off, I have the limo driver take me right to the docks at the warehouse where the meeting is being held. There are so many of us when Pop calls a meeting like this that we won't all fit at the restaurant. Regardless of the fact that right now it is boarded up.

Dino's outside with some of his younger cousins. They all watch me get out and pay the driver. The limo pulls away, and I light a cigarette. I didn't need one all day with Megan, until now.

Dino calls out to me, "What's the matter? You have to fuckin' wine and dine her with limos to get any from her?" I was calm all day then Dino has to go and fuck with it.

I don't even hesitate. I take two strides and blast him in the face with my fist. He is ready for it this time-unlike in church. He tries to hit me back, but I duck and smash him again. A cut forms over his eye and his jaw lumps up. Like a stupid fuck, he tries to hit me again, but I dance back and swing my leg out. He goes crashing to the ground. No one, not one of his cousins or any bystanders, interfered.

Uncle Tutti must have heard the commotion. He comes outside and sees Dino lying on the ground.

"Aww, Tonio," he says sounding disappointed. "Will you stop beatin' that kid up?"

I light a new cigarette, since I tossed the other one on my way to pummel Dino. I take two drags and flick it at him.

"Stay the fuck away from me and Megan."

I mumble, as I blow smoke out of my lungs, "Sorry Uncle." I pass him to go into the meeting.

I step into my father's arms as he pats me on the back. "How was your day?" he asks.

"Good, real good," I say. Donny's already seated with his crutches leaning against the table. He looks decent for being shot the other day. I give him a tap on the back.

The place is packed; even sons as young as 14 are here. This brewing fight with Sommersville has all the families of Palmetto coming together.

My father stands at the front table and everyone sits down in a folding-chair. The tables are plastic party tables set up in a huge square on the cement floor. Dino sits all the way on the other side of the room with his Dad. He is sitting there seething. He baited me on purpose because he thought he could take me. He's a fuckin' stunad!

Vito sits at my right with Louie and Ronnie who is sporting a black eye on my left. Normally they're not here. They sit with me to show their loyalty.

"Sommersville has gotten on my last nerve. I'm done with this shit." Some nod in agreement. He points to me. "My Tonio will lead the hit." His hands gesture as he speaks. "Tonio has proven his worth." I am shocked and honored that my father trusts and believes in me enough for this responsibility.

All faces turn to me. Admiration is on the young faces, and pride is on the old. I stand to acknowledge my pop with a respectful nod, letting him know I accept.

Vito nudges me. I can tell he is psyched. I catch Dino staring at me. I just look away; he is not worth my time. Louie picks up on it and whispers to me,

"I know why he isn't at college. He gotten fuckin' kicked out for selling drugs."

"Fuckin' stunad," I mutter.

Pop brings up the attack at the restaurant. "Tonio, selflessly snuck up on the bastards and pumped iron in the back window till it broke, frightening those fuckers away." I am embarrassed by Pop's accolades. I just reacted. I don't think it was selfless. 'Don't think, just do!' replays in my head.

A week of doing Donny's dirty work goes by. On the days I am close to home, I pick up Megan from school. Vito offers to take Erin home so Megan and I could be alone for a while, but Megan always says no. I don't think Megan trusted Vito with her sister. It's okay because just seeing her for a short time makes everything I do worthwhile.

Pop never discloses at the meeting when the attack is going to take place. He knows there's a snitch somewhere. So he says he'll let me know when the time is right.

Vito, Ronnie, and Louie are pumped up. They plan on coming. They don't have to, but they want to. Vito says that he has my back always.

It's Friday, and I really want to pick Megan up, but I have a runner. The guy took off. I chase him, and I know where he's going. He has a sister who lives about thirty miles away from Palmetto. I'm going to stake out her house.

Chapter 15

Capisce? (ga-bish): Do you get it?

Megan:

I'm sitting in history class thinking about Antonio of course. I have a habit now of touching the necklace he gave me. It's the nicest gift I have ever received. We made plans to go to the movies this weekend. I really want to go to the mall to get some new clothes with the cooler weather starting. It would be nice to have a new outfit for our date.

"Megan," my history teacher calls me.

"Yes, Mrs. Touti?"

"You're needed at the main office." I pack up my books and walk down the hall.

As I turn the corner into the office doorway, I am taken aback. My father standing there.

"Hi, Meg," my father says quietly.

"Uh, hi Dad. What are you doing here?" In all the years I have been in school, I can't remember my father ever coming to school. I had a music recital in which I played the harp in middle school, and he didn't even come.

"I signed you out." I pause while he continues. "I have somewhere I want to take you."

"Uh, okay." The secretary waves to me from her desk and I say goodbye. Dad and I walk to the mini-van and get in in silence.

Weird. That is the only word to describe this moment. We drive for about ten minutes, still in complete silence.

"Where are we going?" I ask.

"You'll see."

"Is it a surprise?"

"You'll see when we get there," Dad says stoically.

I want to ask more questions, but my father's demeanor is actually starting to frighten me.

"Did Antonio give you that necklace?" He asks never taking his eyes off the road.

"Yes." I immediately touch it and smile.

"Are you going out again?" his voice never changing.

"Yes, we're going to the movies. Why?"

My dad doesn't respond; he just kept driving.

After a while we drive into a neighborhood with small houses and tiny front lawns. It's the middle of the afternoon so there isn't anyone around, most likely because kids are at school and parents are at work. My dad parks in front of someone's house. No clue whose house or even where we are.

"Where are we?" I ask.

"Megan..." my father says, not looking at me but at the steering wheel. "This is for your own good. Get out."

My heart is racing with worry and a lot of fear. What is this all about? I slowly open my door. My father comes around the van to stand next to me. He grabs my wrist and starts pulling me down the sidewalk. He's not rough, but not gentle either.

"What are we doing Dad?"

"Quiet," he warns.

I can faintly hear yelling as we walk farther. Still clutching my wrist, my dad walks us over to a tree. The yelling is getting louder. My dad moves us slowly to the edge of some house. I still have no clue what we're doing or whose house this is. Are we trespassing? One of the voices is familiar, and the tones are sharp and mean.

"I told you to never fuckin' run from me!" I hear as my father pushes me a little to see around the corner of the house. He is right behind me. Two men are standing and struggling in the backyard. The smaller man is in a headlock. He is reaching behind him to try and grab his assailant. I put my hand on the house to steady myself, and bits of peeling paint crumble in my hand.

"Where's the money? I'm not asking again." Those words help me to understand the horror I'm witnessing. It's Antonio! Within seconds, Antonio gives two kicks to the man's kidneys. The guy yells and falls to the ground. Antonio reaches for the man's leg and, with a quick twist, snaps his left leg. My body jolts and cringes with the break and snap. The man screams and so do I, but my scream is muffled by my father's hand over my mouth. Hot tears burn my eyes as I watch Antonio's face. It's full of rage and hatred. It is an expression that I can't even imagine on the most infamous criminal, heartless and cold. Tears continue to flood my eyes and roll down my face and slide down my father's hand.

As the man is writhing on the ground, Antonio punches him twice in the face and says, "Shut the fuck up!" He rifles through the man's pockets and finds a wad of cash.

I feel the scratch of vomit welling up in the back of my throat. My body convulses with panic.

Antonio kicks the guy hard in the leg he broke, shoves the money in his pocket and says, "Next time, if you run, I won't be so fuckin' nice."

That's it. I lose it. I wriggle to get away from my father and push off from the house. I vomit into the bushes. My father grabs my hand and starts jerking on me to run. But I can't see through the tears, and I collapse with more dry heaves wracking my body. My father reaches down and picks me up slinging my arm over his shoulder, but he doesn't stop moving. I am so afraid, and my body just doesn't work. He handles me like a rag doll.

My father gruffly says, "Keep moving Megan." Keep moving where? There is nowhere to go that can save me from this. The man I love dishes out merciless and unfeeling beatings. Oh God! The man I love. And I vomit all over the street.

I've heard of people blacking out when they witness something horrific. So that is the only explanation that I can figure out when I wake up on my bed with a cold facecloth on my head. My throat stings from vomit and screaming. My face is achy, and my legs are numb. My mother is sitting on a chair in my room watching me.

"You knew, didn't you?" I ask in a raspy voice.

She nods yes. Her face is blank except for her pursed lips. I take her expression to be righteous, and I lose it again.

"Get out of my room!" I scream. "I hate you!" I throw the facecloth at her. She stands; she is acting all high and mighty. Shouldn't a mother be sympathetic when her daughter learns her boyfriend is psychotic? "Get out!" I say again.

"We were just doing what is best for you," she humphs as she leaves the room. The river of tears I cried comes back in shuddering waves. I can't stop them. The pain is so intense it's like someone stabbed a knife through my sternum and into my heart.

I don't know how long I have been crying, but a soft knock sounds on my door and a whisper says, "It's Erin."

The door opens quietly. I hear her through my sobs gently pad in the room. She sits on the bed and rubs my back. I look over at her. There are tears in her eyes too. Exhaustion overtakes me, and I fall asleep.

*****

Antonio:

I don't make it to pick up Megan. That pisses me off. So I call her. I can't reach her. I call and text her all afternoon. She doesn't respond. That's not like her.

My phone buzzes and I pray that it's Megan. It's Vito.

"Hey what's up?"

"We're headed for the docks. You in?"

"Yeah, I guess so," I say. "I don't have plans with Megan or anything."

"Is Red okay? She left school early today."

"What? I've been trying to call her."

"Yeah, Paesan, she left early. Her father picked her up."

"Thanks. I'll catch up with you later." I hang up and drive to her house.

I knock on the door, but no one comes. Their van is in the yard. Someone has to be home. Maybe she's sick. Did she go to the hospital? I knock again and slowly the door opens. Mr. O'Neill is standing soundlessly and looking his usual somber self.

"Hello." He doesn't say anything. "Is Megan okay? I tried calling her but she didn't answer. Vito told me she left school early today." Mr. O'Neill just lets me ramble on and on. He doesn't take his eyes off me. "Can I come in? Is she here?" The expression on Mr. O'Neill's face makes me feel anxious.

"I don't think she wants to see you," Mr. O'Neill says indifferently. He starts to close the door. I wedge my foot in between the threshold and door.

"Wait!" I say. "Is she okay?"

"She's not your concern." he says ominously. He crushes my foot with the door. No way!

I push the door open and Mr. O'Neill stumbles back. "What's going on?" Megan's mother appears. She glares at me.

"She doesn't want you anymore," Mrs. O'Neill says sternly with her hands folded across her chest. I am dumbfounded. I can only hope that I heard her wrong.

"What?"

"You heard me, she doesn't want you anymore. She knows what you're like now."

I walk into the room, astonished. "What do you mean?"

Mrs. O'Neill gestures to her husband. "Megan went on a little field trip today." I want to knock the smirk off her face. "She's seen you in action now."

"What?!" I yell. "What do you mean?" Fear and anger surge through me like a missile.

Mr. O'Neill shoots his wife a warning glance. "Antonio, I don't think it's going to work out between the two of you," he says

I clench my fists. "What do you mean she's seen me in action?"

"I think you better leave," Mr. O'Neill says.

"No! I want to know." I stamp my foot, the tips of my fingers digging into my palms. Icy cold realization slithers down my back. "You!" I point at Megan's father. "You!" It's getting harder for me to breathe. My chest is closing up at the comprehension that Megan must have seen me today. She must have seen me break Scott's leg; beat the shit out of him.

"I want you to stay away from her," he says, "This is as far as the relationship is going."

"No," I rush out, the words stinging. "I just got her... Don't do this." I see Erin sitting at the top of the stairs holding her legs and rocking back and forth. She's silently crying.

My brain wants me to yell, Where's Megan? I want to take her away from here. Just run. Go somewhere together. Leave. I feel sick.

The air is too thin in this small room. The hurt is so intense, more than any fight I have ever been in. My eyes tingle with an unfamiliar sensation.

A knock sounds on the front door. The person just walks in. It's my father. Mrs. O'Neill must have called him when she left the room. I am stuck, frozen.

I look at Pop, and he is sympathetic. I rub my eyes unsure of what to do. I need to see Megan, but I don't think anyone is going to let me. Part of me feels that this is a conspiracy, that this was planned all along. It was too easy to convince my pop and Megan's father to allow us a relationship, even one that barely got started.

I've been betrayed. Set up. Megan seeing me taking care of business for my dad would do her in, make her hate me and be afraid. They knew it. I should have told her when she asked. I should have confided in her to make this less of a blow. Maybe I could have made her understand, help her to deal with that side of myself that I don't even like to think about. I would never hurt her. EVER! I'm a monster, bred, raised, and trained right here in Palmetto by the best, my father.

"Tonio," Pop says quietly. "I think we better go."

"I want to see her," I choke out. "I want her to tell me that she doesn't want me anymore." I plead, "Let me just talk to her."

Megan's mother leaves the room and her father just shakes his head 'no' as he opens the door for Pop and I, motioning for us to leave. I shoot a glance at Erin, who is still sitting at the top of the stairs hugging herself. I drag my feet to move towards the door.

At the sidewalk, Pop clasps me on the back. "I'm sorry. It really is for the best." I throw my shoulder back and push my father's hand away. "Come on, we gotta get ready for the hit," he says quietly. I don't say anything. I don't want to do anything that I'll regret later. I jump in my car, rev the engine, and shoot off down the street.

Vito, Ronnie, and Louie are at the docks drinking. Beer just isn't going to cut it for me tonight, so I stop and grab a bottle of vodka.

"Whoa, Antonio, what's with the hard shit?" Ronnie asks as I swig the clear alcohol from the bottle.

"Is it Red?" Vito asks.

I snap. I spin around and hurl the bottle against the brick warehouse in front of me. It shatters and rains tiny bits of glass over the dirty pavement.

I don't answer the question, but I say, "Mannegia!" The rage doesn't subside. I squeeze my eyes tight. "The hit's tomorrow night. Meet me here at eight. I gotta fuckin' go." I can't even look at my friends. I just pop in my car and squeal away.

I get home around 1 a.m. I had sat down at the river side, where I kissed Megan for the first time wondering why I didn't see this whole frittata coming. My mother startles me when I walk into the kitchen. She's sitting at the table with her hand wrapped around a coffee cup.

"Hi," she says.

I immediately wonder if she knew this whole fuck-up-things-with–Megan-plan. She stands and pours me a cup of coffee.

"Thanks," I say as I take it from her.

"How are you doing?" That question answers mine. She knew. Does she really need an answer? I glare at her.

She starts again, "Tonio, I disagree with this whole mess. Are you okay?"

"Do I fuckin' look like I'm okay?"

My mother gives me a stern expression but doesn't chastise me for swearing.

"Your father is going along with the O'Neill's, okay? He really doesn't care if you see her. She's a nice girl, Antonio. We like her."

"Then what is the problem, fanabola?!" I half yell.

"You have to understand that her father wants to keep her safe."

"You've been married to Pop for over twenty years, and nothin's happened to you!" I say frustrated.

"There are things you just don't know, Tonio. Let it go." My Mom pleads while resting her hand on my arm.

My throat is closing up, it feels odd. "I don't think I can," I choke out. "Ma, I think I love her."

She reaches out and hugs me tight. When she pulls away, I see tears glistening in her eyes. "Try to get some sleep."

The next morning brings big changes. I have a tutor now. I'm not going back to school. My father has signed me out and made me an independent student. He says he needs me too much. The only hope I had to see Megan was at school, and they took that away too.

Chapter 16

Cavone (gahv-own): ignorant Italian

I am sitting cleaning my gun getting ready for the hit tonight trying to psych myself up, but instead feeling this hole left gaping open in my chest when my dad comes in to go over the plan. He never mentions what happened yesterday. He doesn't even apologize. Pop is all business.

"Now, don't forget to go pick up Uncle Tutti's old Chevy. And make sure Louie has a car ready."

I nod as he talks.

"It's all you, Antonio. You're leading this."

I nod again. He continues to go step-by-step through the hit. I half-listen without looking away from my piece. I've tried Megan's cell phone at least ten times. It goes directly to voicemail. The compulsion to talk to her is eating me alive. It's crippling to think she hates me.

Everybody is pumped. The adrenaline flowing through everyone's veins is creating an unquenchable need in me to search out and destroy. We are in groups. I have taken on the responsibility of the most important parts of tonight-hitting the hive. It is a Laundromat on South Street in Sommersville. It isn't too hard to figure out it's their place of business because the people going in and out rarely have laundry or look the type to even do their own laundry.

Mr. Maranzano and Mr. Ferretti are leading two other groups. They will come in the back way.

My voice doesn't feel like my own. It is crisp and sharp. and I feel outside of myself. Dino is with Mr. Ferretti so I don't have to look at his fuckin' face. I'm desperately trying to shove Megan to the back of my mind. I have to suppress my hurt and anger or it will rule me tonight.

Vito loads the back of Louie's car with vodka bottles stuffed with rags, handmade, good old fashioned grenades.

Vito, Uncle Tutti, and Ronnie all pile in the old Chevy. The drive to Sommersville is about 25 minutes. The car is an old clunker. The engine grinds and whines every time I speed up or press the brake. No one speaks but Uncle Tutti, giving advice and words of assurance.

We park the car on the side road near the alley in front of the Laundromat. A warehouse is to the other side of us, perfect for cover. I had scouted this out last week on one of my many long days of running Pop's errands.

A car bomb is a good way to flush Sommersville out. Vito puts the bomb on the seat of the old Chevy. Pop is great at making bombs. Sommersville will definitely know it's us.

We skulk out of the diversion car. My pistol is raised, ready to shoot. Uncle Tutti and I jut out towards the back of the warehouse waiting for Vito and Ronnie. We cover the entrance to the Laundromat. Two shots ring out, and Ronnie takes one in the shoulder. He trips, but regains his footing as he runs towards us. What the fuck? Where did those come from? It's dark as I scan the surrounding area. Wasting time is not an option. It's a few minutes early, but I tell Vito to blow it.

"Now!" I say to him as Ronnie pants on the ground behind me. With one tap on the detonator the old rusted Chevy blows up and metal debris showers the road.

"Cover us, Tonio!" Uncle Tutti shouts over the sounds of the blast. He leans down to tend to Ronnie's shot up arm.

Where the fuck did those shots come from? Red clouds my vision as I hear Ronnie's grunts of pain. "Don't think, just do!"

Using the building as cover, Vito and I scan the area, guns moving in succession like we were taught as kids, ready to rain lead in the air if anything moves.

The car blazes in front of us. Even from as far away as we are, I can feel its searing heat. Uncle Tutti jerks Ronnie to a standing position.

"Move," I say. We need to get out of here. Someone has tipped off Sommersville. Pop suspected a mole but now its official, fanabola!

I nod to Vito; he dodges around the trash bins. We move and prowl like we're in a cop show. Rage is boiling from the tips of my fingers to the top of my head. I can see Vito's face in the low light of the street lamps, it's twisted brutality like mine. He knows there's a fuckin' mole too. Loyalty is something you don't mess with.

The road ahead of the alley is quiet, too quiet. Slowly we continue to advance. I have the Laundromat in my site. Ronnie has regained himself from the shot, surviving on pure adrenaline. Malice coats his features too. The street ahead suddenly gets darker. The street lights have gone out. I know the other two teams are still surrounding the building.

The ping of gun shots flying through the darkness ricochets around us. We drop to the ground and start firing. Using only instinct in the darkness, I listen to where the bang of the bullets come from and fire. A strangled screech echoes in the distance. The firing abruptly stops.

"Move!" I say. We all bolt forward still staying behind the cover of brick walls. Gun fire starts again, but it is muffled like it is coming from inside the Laundromat. We're pinned down and in the dark.

I see shadows up ahead; two people are dragging a body. Down the street is the car and Louie. "Go!" I yell to Uncle Tutti. "Take Ronnie. Get your asses out of here." I squat and position my gun right at the dark figures to cover them. If they even raise a finger, I'm firing. Uncle Tutti doesn't argue with me. He knows I'm fucking running the show.

I give a quick look behind me to see if they made it to the car. Vito is right there. He didn't go with them.

"Dude, I'm not leaving you," he says low. I nod. Vito may be a lot of things, but one thing I would never do is question his loyalty.

"1..2..3..Go" I say. Vito and I continue our sweep-and-scan moves until we get in our final position to make our hit. The air is so noiseless that the only thing I can hear is the swish of Vito's leather jacket.

The Laundromat is dark like the street. It is hard to see inside. I cross over the doorway so one of us is on each side of it. I am getting ready to kick the door when I see a flash of movement through the window.

I motion to Vito to get ready. I swing myself up to see a person by the window. It's a Sommersville chooch. I fire three shots through the window. The guy yells out in pain. With my gun held high, I check for damage. I got him in the thigh.

Vito immediately kicks the door in, stays low, and crosses the threshold. I follow him. I check the area and quickly kick the gun away from the kid who is clutching his thigh and writhing on the floor. Vito picks it up and stuffs it in his waistband.

"That's for Ronnie you fucker." I stare down at him with disgust.

We leave the kid moaning and move through the darkness. Pounding and slashing sounds are coming from behind a closed door. Slowly we advance and flank. I nod and Vito kicks in this door too. A knife fight is in full force.

It's Dino and some ass I don't know. Dino is holding his own. His shirt is torn in three places, but no blood. The other guy, on the other hand, has blood dripping from his arms, legs, face, and hands.

"Move!" I say, and Dino hurries behind Vito and me. I'm a little surprised he listened to me. "Where's your piece?" I say never taking my eyes off the kid who is barricading himself behind some old dryers.

"Lost it," Dino says through heaving breaths.

A door on the other end of the room opens. About ten Sommersville guys rush in.

"Move!" I command again. Vito heads back out the way we came while I protect his back and Dino's. Within seconds, we are back where I shot the kid. He is losing a lot of blood. Then back on the street, we work together, exchanging positions until we see Louie's car.

"Go!" I yell, and we fly to the doors and jump in. Vito takes two Molotov cocktails and lights them. He hurtles them out the window to stop our pursuers. The smashing sound of the glass bottles is the first thing we hear, then the front of the Laundromat lights up like fireworks. Louie hits the gas, and we sail down the road.

*****

Megan:

I'm not sure what has happened now; it's all a blur. I haven't seen Antonio in over a week. He never came back to school. I never talked to him after that horrible day. I'm a zombie-I eat, go to school, and play the harp. I'm a Zombie harpist. I play the harp until the tips of my fingers are raw. I will the music to transport me somewhere away from the pain.

The only person in my house that talks to me, and that I'll talk to, is Erin. Most nights she carries my dinner to my room for me. At school, Vito won't tell me anything. None of Antonio's friends even look my way. I think they're afraid I'll ask them something they can't answer. Alessandra came up to me right after it happened and hugged me, then walked away.

Troy calls every day to check on me. He has to call on the house phone because I no longer have a cell phone. My father took it away and didn't give me a new one. I feel bad that it's a one-sided conversation when he calls. It's usually Troy doing the talking, trying to cheer me up and telling me about college. He never ever mentions

Antonio or the uncomfortable time he told me he thought he and I would get married someday.

"Guess who is coming to Notre Dame? Guess, guess! You'll never guess." Troy is his bright and cheery self.

My voice never raises or elevates. It's too much of an effort. My chest is heavy, and the lump in my throat that never goes away keeps me from being able to speak properly. "I don't know," I say not the least bit curious.

"Miss/Megan/O'Neill!" He says my name like I'm someone famous.

"Huh?"

"You, my friend, have won a fabulous trip for one to the beautiful campus of Notre Dame! Five nights and six days of college life…airfare and meals included." Troy declares like I've just won a prize on the The Price is Right©.

"What?"

"You're coming for a visit. It's all arranged. Your parents already booked your flight. You leave on Friday. Isn't it awesome? I can't wait to see you, Meg."

Gripping my chest is the only way to hold myself together, or what's left of me will fall out. The past week has enlightened me on one thing. I don't care. The shock of the event has worn down, but not the hurt and betrayal. The fear of Antonio I always had had been warranted. Deep down I always knew he had a dark side. I knew he wasn't rescuing kittens from trees when he said he had things to do for his father. But does that take away the love I have for him? No. Our parents keeping us away from each other for the past ten years, knowing him only as someone in town, doesn't change the fact that I love him.

I can't pinpoint when I fell in love with him. Was it when he was leaning against his car with a mischievous smile, heated eyes scorching into me, or was it when he was playing in the sand box? It doesn't matter.

But I can pinpoint when I realized that I don't care where he comes from or what he has to do to survive in his mafia family. My life and what's important to me has changed in a very small amount of time.

Troy's voice yanks me from my revelations. He must have noticed I wasn't listening to his rant about all the great things we were going to do at Notre Dame.

"Troy? I gotta go. There's something I have to do. Bye."

Alessandra. I need to find Alessandra. I shove my feet into sneakers and walk out the front door. I start walking to Alessandra's house. It's a long way by foot, but I barely notice. When I get closer, I start running. I know what I have to do.

Luckily, Alessandra answers the door when I knock. I'm breathing heavy from running. She has a very concerned look on her face.

"Megan? Are you okay?"

Grasping the doorframe, I say, "Yeah, yeah. Just out of breath."

"What's the matter?"

"I need to find Antonio."

She gives me a sympathetic look. "No, seriously, I need to find him. I need to talk to him."

Alessandra takes my hand and tugs me through her house to her bedroom. I take being dragged through her house as a sign we're going to talk, but what I find in her bedroom astonishes me.

Sitting on the floor against the wall, jean clad, knees bent, head in his hands is Antonio. His whole demeanor is of someone in despair and lost.

Finally, he glances up. His face registers different emotions; elation, happiness then wariness. He jumps to his feet still as shocked as I am. He is just as gorgeous as always. Intensity stares at me through his eyes. Alessandra is still holding my hand. She lets go and walks out of the room shutting the door behind her.

Antonio steps towards me, reaches out, and crushes me to him in one fluid motion, "Megan..." he says into my hair. "I'm sorry. Don't hate me." My arms wrap around his toned waist. He is the most delicious guy I have ever known. His words sound like they have been on the tip of his tongue for a while, but have never had a chance to spill out, until now. "Tell me you still want me." This is so unlike Antonio. His words sound insecure and unsure.

I hold him tighter and say into his chest, "I never stopped wanting you." We hold each other, squeezing, and my chest compresses. He loosens his hold. We stand a long time not saying anything, just clinging to each other. Gently he strokes my hair as he holds me. Deep down we both knew, no matter what, we belong together.

Desperation and loneliness has consumed me all week. Grasping the betrayal of my family and the images of Antonio thrashing that man haunted me day and night. Standing in his arms right now is amazing, and I'm not sure how I have survived so many years without it.

"I'm sorry." he says again. "I should have told you."

"It's okay," I tell him, and I mean it.

I leave Alessandra's feeling liberated. Antonio and I are going to see each other tomorrow night. We're going to talk. Figure things out. Alessandra holds me tight when she says good-bye.

Chapter 17

Cazzo (kaatso): Balls!

My lips are still tingling from Antonio's rough kisses. I catch myself smiling all the way home. Antonio offered to drive me. He had his father's car. He said he hasn't been driving his much because it reminds him too much of taking me back and forth to school. I still didn't want to risk my parents catching us together. We are going to have to sneak around and lie if we are going to keep seeing each other. Just knowing that I am going to see him is enough to sustain me.

The way my mother's been treating me, I could care less. She looked triumphant and smug the day Dad took me to see Antonio. I won't let someone like that ruin my happiness, even if it is my mother.

The darkness of evening sneaks up on me. The days are getting shorter as autumn wanes. By the time I climb the stairs to go into the house, it is totally dark out. The house seems exceptionally quiet. Well, it's been real quiet since last week.

Feeling better than I have in the past week with the lump in my throat finally gone, I head straight to the kitchen. I reach for the light switch, and a hand grabs my wrist and painfully forces my arm behind my back. My eyes adjust to the shadowy room. I see my mom and Erin bound against our kitchen chairs. Panic surges through me.

My assailant shoves me into a chair and presses on my shoulder to hold me down. I struggle and clutch at them, but they're too strong. I hear a ripping sound from behind me. Quickly, they bind my hands in what feels like duct tape. Harshly, my hair is tugged so that my face it thrust up, and my attacker says,

"Don't fuckin' move."

I definitely don't know this person. I can see better now. He is tall with blue eyes. His face is scruffy, like he hasn't shaved in a few days. I glance at my mother and sister. Tears are streaming down my sister's face with no sobbing cries. My mother is staring straight at me like I have all the answers in the world for what's going on. But I don't.

"We're just gonna sit here and wait for the Cleaner," he says sitting down in the fourth chair. He crosses his arms and legs in a gesture that says he's got all the time in the world. He is holding a pistol in his right hand, up against his chest. It has a long cylinder-like piece on the end. From watching way too many cop shows, I'm guessing it's a silencer.

Wait! What?... Cleaner? Is he expecting Merry Maids to show up?

I look over at my mom again. Questions are filling my brain, but no panic. But my mother is not the haughty person she before, her eyes are like saucers. She appears panicked now. But I'm not. Why? I shuffle my hands around slightly behind the back of the chair. The tape is loose.

Our attacker speaks again in his unruffled demeanor. "The cleaner is gonna get what's comin' to him. He killed my family, I kill his," he chuckles. "An eye for an eye."

My heart is pumping wildly. It's not fear though, its vehemence and confusion. Who is this person?

"When Patrick gets here, you're going to wish you never stepped foot in this house," my mother says.

"He ain't gonna get by Butch, lady." He says with complete surety.

What?!... Dad's at work. Who the hell is Butch?

A loud thump comes from outside on the back steps. The guy jumps up and grabs Erin by the back of the neck.

"Don't fuckin' open your mouths." He holds the silencer up to his lips like it's his finger, shushing us.

With one of his hands buried in Erin's hair, he points the gun at her temple. I scream, and it startles him. I force my hands apart, ripping the loose tape, and spring. I ram the guy in his stomach with my shoulder. The shock of my actions takes him off guard, but not enough to knock him down. We scuffle a bit, but he gets me.

His arm is suffocating me where he's trapped me against him. He points the gun at my temple now. My breathing is shallow. It hurts. I reach down into myself for courage. This son of a bitch is trying to take away all that I've gained and struggled for! Not happening!

Erin screeches, and I ram the back of my fist into his groin. He lets out an oaf and steps back from me. Involuntarily, he doubles over, and his hands immediately go to his crotch.

I take a chance and grab for the gun. With all my might, I twist it out of his hand. He reaches for me, but I scrabble back. The cold metal in my hand. The back door flies open, and my father rushes into the room. Dad tackles the guy still reeling from my hit. Dad subdues him in seconds, crushing the intruder's face into the tile floor.

My father yells at me, "Get something to tie him!"

I reach for the roll of duct tape that was conveniently left by the stupid ass that broke into our house. I pass it to him with my free hand.

With swift agile movements, he confines our attacker in silver duct tape like a mummy. My father, never leaving the guy, grabs the gun from me and smashes the guy on the head with it, knocking him out. Dad stands.

Erin's shrieks and cries break through the scene. I rush to her and get the tape off. I look up at my mother who has said nothing, but has eyes that are puffy and red. I notice my shoulder hurts. I absently rub it, and my hand involuntarily clutches my necklace. Then I walk over and free my mother. Erin is in Dad's arms whimpering uncontrollably. Remarkably, I don't feel much of anything.

Erin is still clutching Dad when he hands me the gun. I take it. He sits Erin back down in the chair. Dad picks up the man like a sack of potatoes. "Follow me," he says in his typical monotone voice. So I do.

The man is limp in his arms as we walk out the back. The spotlight on our house illuminates another man who is lying on the steps. He looks odd. His body is twisted awkwardly. I step closer, his eyes are open. This man is not just unconscious, he is dead.

Dad's arm is bleeding. There is a gash about 5 inches long down his forearm. Blood is trailing behind him as he slumps the intruder in the back of our van. I gingerly skirt around the dead man on our steps. I stand next to my dad at the back of the van. The scene before me is surreal in a horrifically ordinary way.

"I need you to wash down the kitchen and back steps with vinegar and water. Wash everything. Call the O'Connell's and have them come pick you up. Stay with them until I come to get you. Pack a bag because you may be staying the night." He rattles off instructions stoically. He takes the other man from the steps and puts him in the back of the van too, then shuts it.

He looks directly at me for the first time. "Take care of your mother and sister. Make sure you all stay at the O'Connell's. Go."

Chapter 18

Mannegia (mah-neg-ah): Damn it!

In the kitchen, I find Erin and Mom. Erin is sitting in Mom's lap. The heavy object in my hand registers and I notice I am still carrying the gun. I put it on the counter and take a bucket out from under the sink. I run hot water into it. The cabinet with the vinegar is right there too. I pour the white vinegar and mix it with the scalding water. The steam and vinegar burn my eyes.

I take a dishtowel and wipe down the gun. Then I wrap it up and place it in the center of the kitchen table. The bucket sloshes as I move it from the sink to the floor. I wash the counter, table and the chairs, the refrigerator, even the light switch. I take more dish rags and start cleaning the floor on my hands and knees. Soon the kitchen smells like an Italian sandwich, tangy and sour.

I don't look at Mom and Erin. I just do the job my dad asked me to. I don't think about why, or how at this moment I could have been dead or cleaning up my sister's blood right now-I don't think, I just do.

My mother and Erin get up. "Pack a bag," I say, still washing. "Then call the O'Connell's to come get us." My voice carries a familiar tone, low and resigned.

*****

Antonio:

I am so fucking relieved. I didn't lose her. She came to find me; my beautiful Megan came to find me. I can hardly believe it. I could have held her all day. I knew she was strong.

Once, I was walking home from school in the sixth grade. I was alone, which didn't happen very often. Even in elementary school, people gravitated towards me.

I heard a girl yelling. It wasn't a crying or sobbing yelling. It was an angry yelling. The high pitched shouting was filled with vehemence. I turned the corner to find Megan backed up against a wall with two kids from our class advancing on her. They were two assholes that moved out of town years ago. They were closing in on her. To this day, I don't know what was going on, if they were teasing her or just being the asses they always were, but Megan wasn't taking it. She was giving it right back. She swatted her backpack at them and told them to go to hell. Her fiery red hair was blowing loosely around, her sweet, but fuming, face.

In an instant, the shouting and yelling stopped. Megan's eyes locked with mine. The two chooches turned to see what had caught her attention. One look. One look was all it took. They ran like the devil was chasing them. I moved towards Megan slowly. She looked scared. I only wanted to see if she was all right. I thought maybe I could even walk her home. But she mouthed the word 'thanks' and sprinted away from me.

Down at the docks, Vito and Louie are drinking some beers. Ronnie isn't here. His shoulder is really bad. He has to keep it immobile. The doctor's afraid that the wound will heal wrong because of all the tissue the bullet shredded.

"Hey, Tonio!" Vito says, handing me a beer. "When is the next hit? I am pumped to rip the shit out of Sommersville again."

"We'll see." I didn't want to tell anyone that Pop has a meeting with the boss of Sommersville. The two bosses are going to try to call a truce, even though Sommersville fucking started it.

"How's things with Red?" he asks non-chalantly. I don't want to talk about her either. I don't want to screw things up. These guys could slip to someone that we're planning to sneak around. I can't wait for tomorrow night. I want her with me always. I have to know she's mine. Megan calms and soothes me. I have a sense of completeness when she is around. I want all of her.

"I gotta take a piss. Be right back." I use nature to get away and avoid these questions.

I slip between some crates and large green recycle bins. I lower my zipper. A thwack and a heavy shuffle noise come from the other side of the building towards the water. I zip back up without pissing. I crouch. Sommersville comes to mind, Are they really going try again?

A couple of slashing sounds resonate. I move forward. The light is weak, so it is hard to see. A dark liquid is running across the boards of the dock and into the water, thick like blood. My gaze shifts to the cause.

Spread out on a plastic sheet is a body. It's missing an arm; definitely a man. My vision scans the gory scene in front of me. The other arm of the body is being sawed off. And the person that is doing the sawing is Megan's father, Patrick O'Neill. Holy Shit! The fuckin' cleaner!

He moves in quick jabs with efficiency. His face is impassive. The way he is gutting this guy proves his experience and strength. The performance is actually masterful. I watch both sickened and in awe as he reaches for a bottle. A sizzling sound trickles from the extricated arm's fingers. He's burning off finger prints. Mr. O'Neill continues to dismember the body methodically. Then he walks the pieces wrapped in plastic down to the river out of my line of sight.

My mind is reeling, processing. Does Megan know? She can't possibly know. What do I do? Part of me is still rip shit at this guy. . He betrayed me and lied to me. The part of me that is still mad as hell at this guy wants to walk right up and call him a hypocrite. This is going to hurt Megan. Haven't I done that already? Now this. Would she even believe me if I told her?

Mr. O'Neill comes back to pick up more carefully and professionally wrapped body parts. Red blotches and spots have dried on his face and clothes. The wicked part of me wants to strike a deal with this man. A callous and evil deal in which I keep my mouth shut in return for Megan. Would he do it? OR would he try to slice me up and stuff me at the bottom of the river? Shit!

He takes another body that was hidden and lays it out on another plastic sheet. "I know you're there." Mr. O'Neill's voice is commanding and low. Is he talking to me? He begins working again.

Mr. O'Neill takes a syringe and plunges it into this man's leg. Then he starts again.

"I know you're there, Antonio. I haven't been doing this for twenty-five years and not know when someone is watching me." I take two tentative steps towards him. "All I wanted to do was keep them safe." It doesn't sound like he's talking to me, but I know he is. "My girls being with anyone in the mob puts them in even more danger. I've been so careful." His voice is reflective. "This happened before."

What happened before? I want to ask, but yet I don't want to interrupt his thoughts. I come out of the shadows and stand across from him, the corpse sprawled between us.

"I was away at a job in Dublin. There was a runner." He pauses. "He just irritated the Boss so much I got called in to finish the guy." He puts his hand on the neck of the man on the ground, seemingly checking for a pulse and keeps talking. "It happened in the middle of the night. Two guys broke in to my cottage. We lived miles from the nearest neighbor. The way my wife tells it, she was sleeping. The girls were in our bed too. They always slept there while I was away." He smiles to himself. "The two guys rushed the bedroom. Megan was only five years old. She slipped down onto the floor and went into my nightstand. She took out the pistol I kept there. I didn't even know she knew about it.

"My wife said all she heard was three shots in the darkness and two bodies hit the hardwood floor. She grabbed the girls and ran. She drove them all the way to Dublin and stayed in a hotel. I found them in the city.

"My girls never even went back to their home. I disposed of the bodies and grabbed what I could of our stuff. We got on a plane to America. I contacted your dad and he gave me this job, which we have been able to conceal for the past twelve years."

"What about Megan? Does she remember?" I ask.

"No," he says. "She doesn't remember anything. The child psychologist we spoke to said she repressed it, but it could surface at some point in her life. Another thing I'm afraid your lifestyle could contribute to. Erin was so young; there is not much chance she would ever remember." He is quiet and still.

"You have to do something for me Antonio." He puts his fingers to the guy's throat again, then lifts the body. He starts wrapping it loosely.

"What?" I ask.

"I need you to take Megan away from here… I don't want her to go alone. I know you are very capable. You can protect her in ways others can't. There are not many people I trust."

I pause trying to process what he is asking. Maybe Megan and I have been soul mates all along. Maybe it wasn't her beauty or intelligence that drew me to her. The first monster she's ever loved is standing right in front of me. I'm a monster too. And she's used to loving monsters.

"You just told me to fuckin' stay away from her. You tried to sabotage our relationship. You put her through hell! You're telling me you trust me. What about you? I can't fuckin' trust you!" My anger escalated.

157

"That was all before what happened tonight. I realize now that I can't protect my girls from this. I put her in the danger that I swore would be you, but it wasn't. It was me."

"What are you going to tell her?" I hiss sarcastically. "Oh, I was wrong, Antonio's a great guy. Go away together, have fun!"

"I already booked her on a flight to Notre Dame for Friday. But now you'll leave in the morning. After tonight, she'll understand. She needs to get out of here while I sort this out. I'm going to send Erin to some friends of mine out of state. I want them going in opposite directions."

"What happened tonight?" I ask, anxiety settling in. Mr. O'Neill looks down at the man on the ground.

"They came after my family."

Fuck!

I walk back to the guys.

"What happened? You shit too?" Vito asks laughing.

"Ha," I deadpan. "Funny asshole!" I quip back. "I'm out of here. Ciao."

Her father thinks some fucked up crap. I'm dangerous and bad news, but he's not?! What kind of dream world is he living in? I guess I'd be like that too if I have been doing what he has all these years.

I just jetted out of there. Talk about the shit hitting the fan, mannegia! Talk about fucked up! My movements are on automatic as I weave through the streets towards home. Patrick, the Cleaner, O'Neill wants me to go from boyfriend to freakin' bodyguard. Shit, I'll take it. A fresh burst of red flashes across my vision when I think of Megan in danger tonight.

Thank God, Patrick is going to talk to my father. I don't want to see his face when he finds out I'm leaving with Megan for Notre Dame in the morning. With Donny getting better, it shouldn't be such a problem, but I'd prefer not to piss him off.

Chapter 19

Ciao (chow): Goodbye

The next morning, I roll up to a nice house outside Palmetto on a small country road. The house is light blue with a picket fence. The grass is pristine, like someone cuts and trims it painstakingly with scissors. Even through this mess of shit, I am stoked to see Megan to kiss her and hold her. Go away with her! Even if I have to see that chooch Troy, it's worth it. Last night Megan's dad wrote this address down of where to pick her up. I ring the bell. I only wait a second before the door flings open. It's Erin and she's sobbing. Oh shit! Crying girl!

Erin lunges at me still sobbing. She wraps her arms around me and attaches herself like a tick. I feel the wetness of her tears staining my shirt. I lift my hand to her back to console her.

For a split second, I have an amazing big brother twitch. Comforting her is my concern. I have never seen this girl anything other than happy. Then my mind races with, Why is she crying? Whoever made her cry is going to be beaten and bloodied. Was it the guys from last night breaking in her house and she's still upset? Is Megan okay? Is someone hurt?

Megan appears in the doorway. Her eyes are red-rimmed and teary. Erin pulls away from me. She wipes her eyes and looks at her sister. Megan steps forward and takes her into a hug. Then she shuffles forward with her sister in her arms and encapsulates me in the hug too. I feel like I'm in a fuckin' Hallmark© commercial. I don't know why everyone is crying and it hurts to see it.

"What's going on?" I ask softly into Megan's ear. She shakes her head, not wanting to talk about it. I rub my fingers down her cheek, feeling sick at seeing her this way. We all disengage from the hug and quietly walk into the house.

I see luggage waiting by the door. I can hear voices speaking low from the kitchen area. In the corner huddled in a chair, looking very guilty, is that kid from the other day. The one whose mom picked up Erin.

Megan's mom comes out from the kitchen. She doesn't speak to me.

"You have everything?" she asks Megan.

"Yes," Megan replies.

"Hello, Mrs. O'Neill," I say. I want her to know I got her number. I know she hates me.

"Hello Antonio," she haughtily replies. "Could you put those in the car?" Then she narrows her eyes at me.

Great, fuckin' bodyguard and valet! I would have done it anyway.

I pick up the luggage and head out to pop the stuff in my trunk. I put the bags next to my own duffle and shift the school work that my new tutor gave me aside. As I snap the trunk shut, I see Patrick with Erin on the side of the house. She's still crying and waving her arms. Patrick looks weary and tired. He holds up a finger to her to tell her to wait a minute. He strides over to me.

"Antonio. Thanks for doing this," he says with effort.

"I'm not doing it for you. I'm doing it for Megan." I say. I would do anything for her. Being with her is all I want.

"What did your father say to you?" I light a cigarette before I answer and take a long drag. All this crying girls and shit does me in.

"Pop was put out…I guess. But he's got plenty of others to do the jobs. He feels more comfortable when it's Donny or me, especially with all the shit going on with Sommersville." I pause. "My mother was the one that said I should go."

"I need your help with something else," he says.

"Wow," I say sarcastically. "For someone who wants me to stay the fuck away from their daughter, you're asking for a lot of help." I crush out the butt of my cigarette and drag the ashes across the driveway with my foot.

"With what's gone on last night and what's gone on here this morning, I need Erin to go with you too. I'm afraid she's close to snapping."

"That's fine." I say. I like the girl. Megan would feel better having her. I know it.

"Who were you going to send with her?"

"I hadn't figured that out yet. I was planning on asking you. I have to keep my girls safe." His voice sounded almost desperate.

"You're relying a lot on me," I say. "Vito would be your best bet. Missing school isn't going to be detrimental to his already horrible grades."

"I don't trust him," he says.

"You didn't trust me either." We just stare at each other.

"If he puts one finger on my daughter, I'm holding you responsible."

"Are you serious? She's a kid," I say disgusted. So that's where he's going with the trust issue.

"Well she's my kid," Patrick's voice is filled with menace, "and she's been hurt."

"He's got a reputation, but he's not a child molester. Mannegia!" I don't know what has happened over the past twenty-four hours. But whatever it is, you're scared. I get it." I wait, but he doesn't respond so I add, "You asked my opinion and I gave it. It's your call."

A frown mars his face. "Okay. Call him…You guys better hurry up or you'll miss the flight." Geez, he's the one holding us up. I can't fuckin' win.

I go back into the house to get Megan and Erin. A new bag is by the door. Erin is bellowing at the kid slumped in the chair. Megan, with a carry-on bag on her shoulder, takes Erin's hand trying to pull her away.

"I hate you!" Erin screams at the kid.

"Connor!" a woman calls out. "Come into the kitchen." He gets up head hanging. Erin kicks him in the leg and storms out of the house. I shake my head and take her bag. I reach for Megan's hand and squeeze it.

"What's all that about?" I ask.

Megan leans in and whispers, "He's cheating on her." SHIT!

Red forms in front of my eyes, and I snarl. I spin around to go after him. Megan grabs my forearm.

"Please don't!" she cries. "Let's just get out of here." I allow her to lead me out.

Patrick is settling Erin into the back seat of my car talking softly to her. Her arms are crossed, and her face is horribly tear-streaked. I have a lump in my throat watching her cry. I set the bag in the backseat next to her. If being next to Megan hadn't calmed me down, I would have torn that kid's face off. Patrick kisses her, then tugs Megan in for a hug.

Mrs. O'Neill is standing in the window watching this exchange. She doesn't come out of the house. I'm guessing she doesn't approve of this little arrangement, me taking her two daughters away.

I get in and so does Megan. She leans her head against the glass of her window. She looks totally spent. Patrick leans down into my open window, giving me last minute instructions.

"You know the drill. Be cautious of everyone. Don't let them out of your sight." He hands me a piece of paper. "Here's the address at Notre Dame. I got you two guest suites on the campus. I will contact you when things are safe enough to come back."

"Got it."

"Where is Vito meeting you?"

"He'll be waiting at the gate."

"Good."

Sniffling is still heard from the backseat. I throw the car in reverse and start driving towards the airport.

Megan doesn't lift her head, but reaches for my hand and squeezes it. I notice her face is still moist with silent tears.

"Jesus Christ, Megan, what happened?" I stroke her hand with my fingers wishing I could hold her until the tears stop. But I have a job to do. I need to get Megan and her sister out of here and on a plane.

*****

Megan:

I can't stop them. They just keep coming. Tears flood down my cheeks as the car rumbles down the road.

Where should I begin to even remotely answer his question? Should I tell him the part that makes me numb or the part that makes me cry?

The tears are for my sister. The beautiful, loving, happy sister I almost lost to a bullet. Then I lost her to an asshole. Erin has never been this way. I fear for her state of mind. Her hurt and uncharacteristic behavior frightens me. I felt the crushing of my sister's heart when she found Connor with that girl. I wanted to kill him for it. She needed him. After the fear of last night, she needed comfort. But only found pain. I'm worried about how much she can take.

I'm trying really hard not to succumb to the horror of last night or the repulsion of the hidden life my father leads. When my father finally made it to the O'Connells, he told me. I can't rid myself of the ickiness that is crawling up my throat. His words of confession rattle

165

around in my mind. Disgust and anguish sicken my stomach where butterflies used to be.

The betrayal of my parents singes my soul. I'm a victim, a victim of my environment, just as much as Antonio. My father is the devil, and I am his spawn. Antonio and I are more alike than I could ever even imagine. This upsurge of emotions crackles and burns underneath my skin. They are a moan and mumble of discomfort and shame. The only solace I have is that Antonio and my sister are here with me. Right now, they are the only two people I trust.

Where the fuck do we go from here?

End of Part One

BOOK 2

Awakening the Mobster

Mafia is a process, not a thing. Mafia is a form of clan-cooperation to which its individual members pledge lifelong loyalty. Friendship, connections, family ties, trust, loyalty, obedience—this was the glue that held us together.

Joseph Bonnano, Mob Boss

Chapter 1

Scumbati (scoom-bah-dee): Messed Up!

Megan:

The airport is crowded. Travelers rush to and fro with a solid purpose, to get somewhere. The wheels of their bags make whirling sounds across the floor. A monotonous female voice echoes through the terminal giving instructions for lost bags and gate changes.

Antonio is beside me holding our carry-on bags. I can feel his free hand caressing the small of my back as he guides me and my sister, Erin, towards security. I look up into his dark brown eyes to reassure myself that this is all real. That we are running away. He glances down at me, and it is powerful. His eyes shine with strength and confidence.

With my sister's hand clutching mine, I take my place in line...a line that will take us away from Palmetto, New Jersey. I face forward to stare at the backs of heads. There are so many different types. Long flowing hair, short crew cuts, even bald spots. Each person has their own destination. Each person has their own hopes and dreams.

My hopes and dreams were simple up until a couple of weeks ago. Finish my senior year at Palmetto High and start college at Notre Dame. Simple. Normal.

169

Antonio's strong hand rubs my back with small circles.

"You okay?" he asks.

"Yeah." Trying to sound normal or unaffected is hard. Antonio's question sparks me to turn to look at my sister. Her typical pale complexion is almost gray. It's like her soul has been sucked out of her. Her once consistently bright blue eyes are outlined in red and bloodshot.

I release her hand and put my arm around her shoulders holding her to me. This close up, I gaze down at her again to see our fiery red hair mingle together. Despair coats her face.

In less than twenty-four hours, our world has fallen apart. My family was held hostage in our kitchen. A man died on our back steps at the hand of our father. The man would have killed us all.

My father's hidden life—assassin, murderer, and, what the mob calls him, the cleaner—surfaced and rattled our lives. For my entire existence, I never suspected anything. My father went to work every day. We never owned anything flamboyant or ritzy. No expensive vacations or a big fancy house. We only have one car, for God's sake, and it's a mini-van.

The mini-van fit my harp. I really need my harp right now. If I could step out of this insanely slow moving line and sit on a bench and strum my fingers across the strings, I'd feel at home.

Just the thought of home...it's a strange place to me. More foreign now than ever. An all Italian city with a subculture that I never fit into until I started spending time with Antonio Delisi, Jr.—the Palmetto mob boss's son.

The breathtakingly beautiful man is standing right next to me—holding me, reassuring me, protecting me. Antonio is my savior. Having him with me makes the ickiness that is stuck in my stomach tolerable. He's smart and strong. I know because I have witnessed it first-hand on more than one unpleasant occasion. My father arranged this escape, or whatever you want to call it. He is sending us away hoping to protect us.

I was supposed to be visiting Notre Dame at the end of the week anyway. I am going to college there next fall. My father had wanted me far away from Antonio, but recent events sped up the trip...and I have three additional passengers with me—Antonio, Erin, and Vito, Antonio's friend. I bet my father never saw this coming.

Dad sees Antonio as dangerous because of his lifestyle and who he is. I lay comatose on my bed for a week suffering with the images of Antonio's brutal attack on someone who owed his father money.

Antonio didn't put that in my head, my father did. He wanted me to see Antonio for what he really is. My father is the one who gave me a front row seat to the ugliness. I did witness it. A cold and cruel beating, but I don't see what my father thought I would see. I see Antonio as a man raised to be what he is. He is what he was taught and trained to be.

"We're next," Antonio says softly to Erin and me, as if we are fragile and much too breakable.

I remove my shoes and place them in the blue bin, gliding it over the rollers. Erin follows. A security officer waves a wand up and down my body, checking to see if I'm dangerous.

Leaning against a cement pillar and watching us navigate through security is Vito. His dark hair brushes the top of his collar, and a leather shoulder bag is hanging on his side. His face is impassive. It has only been a couple of hours since Antonio called him and asked him to join us. By the sound of the conversation, Vito didn't even hesitate to agree. He is a large, intimidating guy.

Erin's eyes are glued to the floor as she walks with effort towards the gate entrances. I caress her shoulder again as Antonio and Vito say their hellos.

"Hey man," Antonio says, slapping Vito on the back. "Thanks for doing this."

I observe Vito. The hard slab of muscle underneath his shirt shifts when he moves towards us. I think he is looking at me, but he's not. His focus is solely on my sister.

"Hi," I choke out around the dryness and misery lodged in my throat. Vito nods at me.

Erin moves with automatic motions, not acknowledging anyone. She hasn't spoken since we left the O'Connell's house and her cheating ex-boyfriend, Connor. I clutch her hand. I'm worried.

We make our way through the long passageway to the gates. I study the large blue numbers jutting out above our heads, searching for gate twenty-nine.

Antonio is attached to my other side while Vito trails behind.

"Over here, honey," Antonio says, the endearment surprising me. I allow him to lead us over to a seating area.

A sea of fake black leather chairs faces the large glass windows. Airplanes line up outside. Sprinklings of people take up space in some of the chairs. Erin releases my hand and lies down across an empty row of three.

I hear Vito whisper to Antonio as I sit across from her.

"What the fuck is wrong with her?"

"A lot of shit," Antonio says in a low voice. Then he sits down next to me and takes my hand. We both stare at Erin who seems lifeless while lying down, her face covered with her arms.

"I'm going to get a coffee," Vito says. "You guys want anything?"

"Yeah, I'll have a coffee," I say. "Cream and sugar."

"Me too," Antonio responds. "Black."

"What about her?" Vito asks.

"Her name is Erin," I say crossly.

"I know her name, Red," Vito states. "Does she want anything?" Antonio stiffens at Vito's words. He always calls me Red, and apparently Antonio doesn't like it.

"An orange juice would be great." It is the only thing I can think of. When we're sick, my mom always gives us orange juice. It's the electrolytes, I guess.

I take my bag from Antonio and rifle through it looking for a hair tie. I find one. I lean over my sister and gather up the hair that has spilled all around her threatening to knot up. I gently pull her hair through the elastic. Erin doesn't budge.

Sighing, I sit back down with Antonio. We both stare at her, probably thinking the same thing. What's wrong with her?

Antonio leans in and kisses my temple. Electricity jolts through my body. "She'll be better when we're away from here."

"I hope so," I say, trying to believe it.

Seemingly from nowhere, Vito hands me a cup.

"Thanks," I say, taking it. The warmth of the coffee through the paper cup feels heavenly. A gloomy coldness has been fighting to consume me since yesterday.

He hands a coffee to Antonio, too.

Unexpectedly, Vito takes two short strides over to Erin. He squats down with his back to us.

He is talking to her. Erin leans up on her elbows. Her face is splotchy and red. Lines have formed across her cheeks where she was leaning on her arms.

Vito pops the top off some high-priced organic juice and hands it to her. Erin sips it slowly and hands it back to him. He takes it and brushes some loose strands of hair I missed from her face.

"Flight four-thirty-two to Indiana is now ready for boarding."

"That's us," Antonio says. We gather up our stuff. Vito helps Erin to stand.

My legs are like lead. I'm so tired and numb. It's as if a four-hundred-pound boulder is resting on my shoulders. I ignore my discomfort, and head towards Erin. I pull her to me, my arm around her shoulder, as we make our way to the gate.

A crowd quickly forms in the small area in front of the catwalk entrance. Kids, bags, and people huddle around us. It's hard to breath with everyone so nearby. A tickle of anxiety crawls its way into my chest.

Antonio and Vito are close, right behind us. They're talking softly to each other. They are examining our plane tickets when Erin is pushed from behind. The blow affects me as well since I am holding her. We stumble forward a few steps. Antonio steadies us.

Vito's arm immediately flies out and shoves a tall guy with glasses. I assume he is the culprit. He is just as startled by Vito's reaction as I am. The guy, obviously intimidated, mumbles an apology.

It was clearly an accident. I shift my sister and myself over a bit towards Antonio. His arm snakes around my waist. Antonio shoots Vito a knowing look.

Maybe asking Vito wasn't such a good idea. I gaze down at my sister who is still unresponsive. Vito acts as a wall and moves directly in front of the pusher, blocking him from our view.

Thankfully, the line starts to dissipate as passengers start loading the plane. Antonio hands four tickets to the flight attendant.

"4a, 4b, and 5a, 5b," she says with false cheerfulness. Shit, we're not together!

Erin and I sit down in the seats in front of Antonio and Vito. The third seat by the aisle is vacant. More and more people file onto the plane, seats filling up. The sound of belts clicking and bags sliding across the plastic overhead bins fill the cabin of the plane. Erin's head is resting on my shoulder as I watch all of the hustle and bustle before take-off.

No one sits down next to us. There are only a few more people loading. The jet engines roar to life.

"Find another seat," Antonio mutters from the seat behind me. I turn my head and peak to see the tall guy with glasses scurrying down the aisle towards the back of the plane.

Did that guy have 4c? I'm too tired to care.

"Fuckin' chooch," Vito murmurs.

*****

Rushing air hurts my ears, I'm falling. My arms and legs flail as I plunge downward. I can't stop myself. I panic as I watch blue sky and clouds surround me. I'm helpless to stop myself. The air ends, and cold dark water envelopes me. I open my eyes, but I can't see—everything is murky and dark. I try to push up, but I don't know which way that is.

I can't breathe. The water is crushing my chest. I have an uncontrollable urge to take a deep breath, but if I do I'll inhale the ocean.

Hands encircle my ankles. I scream into the water. It's a muffled nothing of huge bubbles. I try to kick the hands away, but they hold on. The hands move up my ankles to my calves, then to my thighs. They grab me by the waist and propel me up. I break through the surface of the suffocating water, choking and sputtering. I focus and Antonio is there bobbing in the water smiling at me with rays of the sun shining behind him.

I jar awake. Sweat makes my shirt stick to me, and my limbs are heavy. Arms are around me.

"It's okay," Antonio whispers. "You were having a bad dream."

"Ugh." I rub my head. It's throbbing like little men are hammering on my skull. I squint to look at him. He is positioned against the window with me in his lap.

"Where's Erin?" I ask in a panic. Antonio points behind him.

Chapter 2

Scootch (sk-oo-ch): a pain in the ass!

Antonio:

Vito and I moved the girls when they were both fidgeting in their sleep. I carried Erin and placed her in my seat, and then settled in next to Megan, molding her body to rest over mine. My beautiful Megan lies crushed tightly to my chest. The soft white skin of her neck calls to me while I watch her sleep. I restrain myself from trailing kisses across it. I finally wake her when she started kicking.

Erin lies sprawled across two seats behind Megan and me with her legs in Vito's lap.

"Does your head hurt?" I ask her.

"Ugh, yes...bad," she says, and I push the button above us for the attendant. "How long 'til we land?"

"Not long."

An attendant comes down the aisle and stops at our row.

"Can I help you?" she asks.

"Do you have any aspirin?"

"Of course." The attendant leaves.

I massage the back of her neck with my hand, and she moans. I reflect about all that Megan has had to endure over the past two weeks. I want to rip someone's fucking head off just thinking about it.

Her fucking father did this to her. Megan didn't grow up knowing this shit—beatings, money, hits. Patrick-the-fuckin'-cleaner-O'Neill. I didn't see that coming. The son of a bitch tried to make me out to be the bad guy. And all along he was chopping up Pop's clients who didn't pay.

This makes me in awe of her though. I haven't met many girls that could take it. I'm thankful that Megan isn't bowed over in a catatonic ball like her sister. Her father has put her and Erin through hell, and it truly pisses me off.

"Here you go." A cheery attendant returns with a small white packet and a miniature glass of water. She hands them to Megan.

Megan gracefully gulps down the pills and then returns to resting against me.

"I had an awful nightmare," she says into my chest. "I was falling, then I landed in the ocean."

"It was just a dream," I soothe, brushing her hair with my hand.

"It was so real," she shudders in my arms. "But you pulled me up to the surface of the water."

"I'd swim the Atlantic for you. In fact, I'd do anything for you." I say straight into her eyes.

I tip her head up by her chin and gently press a kiss to her lips. Megan shifts and snakes her arms around my neck. She kisses me back, greedily, like she was looking for something and found it.

I caress her back with my hands and part her lips to make the kiss deeper. Oh, how I love this sweet girl! My heart is slamming in my chest. I raise my hands to her thick mane of wavy red hair, and I am lost. No hum of plane engines, no attackers, no hurting people.

Thump, thump.

My chair snaps forward twice. I swivel my head and give Vito a brutal stare. Megan shifts away from me dazed. He's lucky he's my best friend because, if it were anyone else, I would rip their fuckin' head off.

Vito points to Erin, who is now awake and watching us make out through the space between the seats. Her face is discolored and vacant.

I get the message loud and clear from Vito and nod to Megan.

"Your sister's up," I say.

Megan twists around and taps Erin's knee.

"You okay?" she asks.

No response. But Erin unclasps her seatbelt and stands. Megan snaps up too. What is she doing? Erin leaves her seat and walks to the back of the plane. Megan follows her.

"What the fuck, dude?" Vito asks me. "Keep that shit to a minimum. People were rubberneckin' to watch you."

"I don't give a shit!" I huff. "She's mine."

"Well, her sister's already zoning the fuck out, she doesn't need to watch that shit too."

"Fine," I concede.

"Hey, does that chooch Troy even know we're coming? He's going to be pretty surprised when Megan shows up with us."

"I hope Patrick told him," I say, my blood starting to boil. "That pansy better keep his hands to himself when it comes to Megan.

Memories of them together at the fire hydrant have been seared in to my brain."

Vito laughs, "That was one...hot...fuckin' show."

"Thanks ass-wipe," I mumble, and he laughs harder.

Turbulence makes the plane dip and shake. I do the opposite of the little red sign that reads, "Please fasten seatbelt." Megan and Erin haven't come back yet. The plane isn't that big, but, when I check up and down the aisle, I don't see them.

I motion to Vito and point towards the front. I knew they had headed to the back of the plane originally, but I wasn't taking any chances, weird shit happens on planes all the time.

Even with the warnings over the speaker system to sit down, Vito and I walk the aisle in opposite directions.

At the galley area I find them, Erin is in a jump seat by the bathroom throwing up in a federally-regulated barf bag. Out of the corner of my eye, I see Megan in another seat in the corner by the huge aircraft door. The sound of the engines is much louder back here.

The big brother twitch finds me again. I lean over a panting, green-faced Erin, and kiss the top of her head. I can feel Megan's eyes on me and glance her way. She is smiling broadly at me. She is so fuckin' pretty!

One of the flight attendants takes Erin's bag and hands her a new one. Vito stands in the aisle at the last seat watching the scene. His face has an unfamiliar expression. I can't pin point it. He motions me over.

"Shouldn't they give her something?" he asks. "She's gonna dehydrate."

I shrug my shoulders. The crackle of the loudspeaker sounds again. "We will be landing in South Bend in approximately ten minutes. Please take your seats. Make sure your seatbelt is securely fastened. And as always thank you for flying with us!"

Megan gets up and helps her sister to stand. We walk single file back to our seats. The girls sit together again as we land in Indiana.

Down the passageway and out into the terminal, it's like we landed on foreign soil. I am totally out of my element. This is not New Jersey, and it makes me uneasy. Even the faces of people in the airport seem to have a different shape and context to them. I have a burning need to get my hands on a weapon. It would comfort me.

Vito is on high alert, too. It is crowded and, for all intents and purposes, we are on alien ground. My Mafia education kicks in, and I will have to rely on only that until I can get my hands on a piece. That will be my first order of business once we settle in.

We rent a car. Vito wants to rent two sports cars to tool around in. I nix that idea and rent a black Porsche Cayenne SUV. Definitely more practical, and with the money Pop gave me, we can afford to be extravagant and comfortable.

I pull the vehicle to the curb. I pop the rear door, and Vito loads the luggage in. I jump out to help.

"Wow, this is 'mob-ish.'" Megan deadpans.

"How does the saying go, 'If the shoe fits...?'?" I trail off, smiling at her.

Erin's complexion isn't blotchy and red anymore. It is a perpetual grayish-green. She sits in the backseat, and Megan sits next to her.

I drive while Vito rides shotgun. Vito uses his phone to put in the address of the campus.

"Pull in here," he says.

I navigate into the parking lot of a convenience store. Vito gets out and goes in. I turn in my seat to check on the girls.

Erin is staring into space, and Megan is looking at me. She shoots her eyes to Erin, deliberately, letting me know without words that she is worried.

The passenger door opens, and Vito slides back in. He has a box of saltines and a large bottle of Gatorade. He opens the saltines and tosses one in his mouth. Then he reaches diagonally behind him and waves the box at Erin.

With effort, she reaches into the sleeve of crackers, taking a few. Slowly, she puts one in her mouth and chews. We sit there waiting and watching Erin. She never looks anywhere but out her window.

Vito then twists the top off on the Gatorade and hands it to Erin. Either she doesn't notice or doesn't want it. Megan takes it from Vito's hand and holds it under her sister's nose. She won't take it.

"Come on, Erin, have a small drink," Megan pleads quietly. Erin remains unresponsive.

Vito unclicks his belt and gets out of the car again. What is he fucking doing now?

He opens Megan's door. "Why don't you ride next to Tonio?"

Megan gets out and sits next to me while Vito buckles in next to Erin. He whispers to her. Then Vito reaches forward and motions for

Megan to give him the Gatorade. Erin drinks it. It is only a couple of sips, but at least it is something.

I pull out of the parking space and get back on the road to Notre Dame.

"So, this is cool. You get to visit the college before you come here next year," I say to Megan to fill some of the silence in the car.

"Yeah," she responds quietly.

I take her hand in mine, and Megan leans her head back and closes her eyes.

*****

The campus is huge. I thought it felt foreign here in Indiana, but nothing could have prepared me for the Gothic European buildings.

Vito gives me directions from the backseat to O'Neill Hall, where Troy is living. The irony of the name is not lost on me.

Large stone structures, with church-like pillars adorn all of the fancy structures. It's another country right here in America. Students carrying heavy backpacks flood the sidewalks and step right out into the street without looking.

O'Neill Hall is on the other side of the campus to where we enter. It is slow going amongst the pedestrian crowds. Megan sits up and watches. There is a small smile on her face. I can see it in her profile. Is she happy that she's at the campus, or happy to see Troy? Fanabola!

"Tonio, turn right here," Vito directs me.

Chapter 3

Bombaleed (bom-ba-lead): messed up! or poor quality.

Megan:

The Cayenne rolls to a stop at a four story pale brick building. A large sign on the door reads, O'Neill Family Hall. Some distant relatives must have donated some serious money for this place. My heart is pounding, and I'm not sure why. Seeing Troy is important to me. The thought didn't hit me until I saw his dorm.

Troy has been my best friend for a long time. I tell him everything. He's like the big brother I never had. I need him. We have had some great times over the years. He has been such a big part of my life. He has kept me grounded to my Irish heritage.

I turn to Erin from my seat. Antonio has already stepped out of the car. She looks like she's going to cry again. Vito holds out his hand to help Erin out. She takes it.

Room three-twenty-three is of course on the third floor. We ride in the pristine elevator in silence. When I picture college dormitories, I imagine something dirty or messy. Not this immaculate and modern building.

Antonio's face is hard. I've seen that expression before. I give him a reassuring squeeze of his hand. I cringe at the thought of how many times his hands have punched or hit someone, or snapped a limb. The same hands that offer me reassurances and kindness.

The four of us are a sight. We look like we've been traveling for days not just the morning.

I step up to Troy's door. I raise my hand to knock, and the door flies open. It's a girl...a tall girl with long blonde hair. She's rumpled and is adjusting her shirt.

"Hi," she says and then walks past us. "Bye," she says and throws a cute little wave over her shoulder. Which I immediately think is directed at Antonio.

I gaze into the room. It's small and neat. Troy is lying on the bed, shirtless; his arm is thrown over his eyes. In a matter of seconds, he sees me and jumps up. Troy's face is hard, just like Antonio's. I am still processing the girl leaving when Troy walks to me in the doorway.

"Hi, Meg," he says, and pulls me in for a gentle hug. Antonio's hand shoots out to stop him. Troy allows the interference. Then he takes his T-shirt and yanks it on forcefully with his back to us.

"So what do I owe the pleasure of seeing you today?" he sighs, rethinking his sarcasm. "Meg, you weren't supposed to be here until Friday."

We are all still standing in the doorway/hallway. I'm not even sure if Troy saw anyone but Antonio and me.

I step into the room with Antonio, and Troy faces us with a changed expression. He is trying to be pleasant. "What's with the bodyguard?" Troy chuckles.

"It's boyfriend, asshole!" Antonio retorts sinisterly.

"Oh well, pardon me," Troy hisses sardonically.

There is a charge of male electricity in the room, raw and feral.

"Didn't my father call you?" I ask him, trying to defuse the glowering males in the small room.

"No."

"Oh," I say, surprised. "I'm going to be visiting longer than expected. Erin is here too."

I swivel around to the doorway, but she's not there. I step back into the hall, a little flustered. Leaning against the wall is Erin, and she is staring at the floor. Vito is standing next to her. He shakes his head at me and I understand. She doesn't want to go into Troy's room. I can sympathize with her not wanting to see Troy; he does look a lot like Connor.

Troy tries to follow me, but Antonio stops him with a hand on his chest. "I don't think she wants to see you dude." Wow, Antonio is very intuitive.

"Last I heard, the O'Neill's put an end to your little fairytale," Troy says vehemently to Antonio. Antonio's posturing at the comment sizzles the atmosphere, and his upbringing rears its head.

"Meg...?" Troy asks frustrated. "Can you tell me what's going on?" Troy scrubs his hand down his face. I snap back into the room not wanting a fight.

"There's been some trouble, Troy. We need to stay here for awhile. My father sent us here," I tell him trying to calm the situation.

"I don't think we'll all fit," Troy spits acerbically and gestures to his small room. Antonio steps forward, and I cringe.

"We're staying at the guest suites on campus," Antonio says, pushing forward invading Troy's space. His voice matter-of-fact, "I am going to take the girls there to get some rest."

Antonio sees Troy's phone on the nightstand and picks it up. "Here's my number. Call us when you get your shit together."

Antonio reaches for my hand and pulls me from the room. He is moving quickly. The four of us get back in the elevator. Erin is still speechless. Vito and Antonio are ticked off.

That just wasn't what I envisioned would happen seeing Troy. I left the dorm feeling betrayed, for what I'm not sure. Watching that girl leaving his room startled me, but I wouldn't say it bothered me. I know he has a life, but one minute he's saying he wants to marry me, and the next he's sleeping around?

Maybe betrayed isn't the right word. I think I feel gipped. I didn't find the normal solace I usually find with Troy, and that makes me sad. It's like I lost something with him. But I just have to turn and look at Antonio, and everything I feel I lost with Troy, I have gained ten-fold with Antonio.

*****

We arrive at the guest suites. They are beautiful and richly furnished. The campus really went all out for visitors. They even have small kitchens. There are two bedrooms in each suite. The units are adjoined by a door in the living room.

I flop on the couch in the suite I am sharing with Erin, exhausted. Antonio and Vito move the bags into the respective rooms. Then I catch them doing something weird. They are looking out every window, moving every curtain, checking the locks on doors. They are moving succinctly like they're cops staking out a building.

Erin slips into her room after it's checked and shuts the door.

"Don't lock it," Vito orders at the closed door.

Antonio sits down next to me and leans in to give me a sweet kiss.

"I have some stuff I need to do," he says. "Why don't you go lie down too?" His request is syrupy, but with a hint of command behind it.

Vito hovers by the door that connects the rooms. Antonio gets up, checks the bolt on our main door and leaves with Vito. They don't shut the adjoining door, but I still can't hear them.

I go to my room and grab a blanket off the bed. I lie down on the couch and close my eyes.

A phone buzzing on the coffee table wakes me. Antonio is reaching for it.

"Hello," he says, "Yeah." (pause) "Everything is fine." The other person is speaking. Then Antonio continues, "How's everything there?" (pause) "Good. I wish I could tell you but I can't." (pause) "I don't know how long. No, I know. (pause) I'll talk to you later, bye."

I yawn and stretch.

"Alessandra says hi," Antonio says.

"How does she know?"

"I'm gone, you're gone. Alessandra is pretty bright."

Antonio's phone buzzes again. I get up feeling the call of nature when I spot the table in the kitchen area. It is loaded with stuff — guns, ammunition, phones, crackers, chips, and a jar of peanut butter. Holy Crap!

"Hey," his demeanor is totally different. "Everything is good here." (pause) "Yeah, I sent Vito." (pause) "He should be back any minute. I will. Bye." Antonio hangs up.

He comes over to me and kisses me. My stomach flip-flops, and I reach up and wrap my arms around his neck. He kisses me deeper. He tastes like spearmint gum. His arms come around my waist, and he tugs me closer. Antonio pushes me back a little, and I fall onto the couch cushions. He hovers above me — kissing me, worshipping me with his passion. I've never felt so wanted in all of my life.

"Dude! Come on," Vito says walking into the room annoyed. He's carrying a map. He lays it across the coffee table in front of us.

I glance at it. It is all marked up with a highlighter.

"What are you guys doing?" I ask.

"We're learning our surroundings," Antonio says. "We have to know where everything is."

I point to the kitchen table covered with stuff. "And that?"

"Shit we need," he replies.

"But where did you get it?" I ask intrigued.

"We have resources," he says flatly, and Vito laughs still reading the map.

There is a very faint click behind me. Slowly Erin's door opens; she walks out with a very bad case of bedhead. Her red curls jut out in all directions framing her face. Vito stands.

"Feeling better?" I ask. Erin just shrugs her shoulders.

Vito has made it to the refrigerator and grabs an orange juice. Wow they've been busy while we've been asleep. He hands it to Erin.

She seems to sip it gratefully. Antonio's phone buzzes again. Angry lines form on his forehead.

"Yeah," his tone is intimidating. "No, you can talk to me, asshole." I immediately know it is Troy. "They're fine." (pause) "Tomorrow would be better," he says. "Fine." Antonio hangs up.

"What was that about?" I ask.

"Troy wants to get together. We have stuff to do and talk about. He'll have to wait."

Antonio is a very take-charge person. It is comforting and scary all at the same time. Erin sits in an overstuffed chair, sipping her orange juice. Her eyes go wide at the accoutrements strewn about our kitchen table. She gets up and moves next to me on the couch. Vito watches her every movement carefully.

Antonio takes the two phones off the table.

"These are for the two of you. I want them charged and on you at all times. They shouldn't be traceable." He hands them to each of us. Erin and I take them from him. Then Antonio points to the map on the coffee table. "This is a map of South Bend and the surrounding areas."He points to a highlighted area. "If anything happens or we get separated, this is where we meet. The address is programmed in your phones. You are not for any reason to leave these rooms or go off by yourselves. You have to be with Vito or myself."

I am in the middle of a military briefing hosted by Antonio Delisi, mob-child.

"If you suspect anything weird going on or hear any weird noises... Do. Not. Think. Twice. Get one of us. Do you understand?"

"Yes," I say. Erin nods.

"Just like we have resources everywhere we go or can find them, so do the people your father is worried about," Antonio hovers over us. "Any questions?"

Erin and I shake our heads no. Part of me felt like we just got a lecture or a scolding. I know Antonio is trying to keep us safe, but I immediately felt safer the minute we took off and away from Palmetto. We are so far away and in a totally different environment. Who'd find us here? I wonder if my father has called.

"Did our father call or anything?" I ask.

"He texted me," Antonio replies. "I said everything was fine."

Chapter 4

Schifioso (skeevotz): Yuck! Gross!

Megan:

Vito and Antonio take us to a pizza place off campus for dinner. We sit at a booth in the corner. Antonio has a clear view of the door. Antonio's face screws up like he tasted something sour when he bites into his pizza.

"This is schifioso! It tastes like shit!" Vito exclaims. "My five-year-old cousin makes better pizza sauce than this." He throws his piece down on to his plate.

Antonio taps his plate with the crust, white against his dark Italian skin. "This might be bullet proof," he says.

It is tasteless, but I didn't care. It is food. Erin plays with her pizza, not talking. We let her be. I'm not sure when she'll come around, but everyone handles things differently.

Vito gets up, and speaks to a waitress, and comes back. He stands out in the room, darkly confident and menacing looking, like Antonio.

A few minutes later, soup is placed in front of Erin. It appears to be chicken. Vito leans over and whispers in her ear. Erin reluctantly picks up the spoon and starts eating.

Antonio's hand brushes my thigh under the table, and I jolt in surprise. He gives me a knowing smile, and I relax. It feels so good to have his strong hands on my leg. His hand creeps higher and I stiffen, heart racing.

*****

By the time we make it back to the campus and made our way to the rooms, I am beyond tired. It is as if my legs can't function. I stumble on the carpet in the hallway. Antonio secures me back to a standing position and opens the door. He leads me to the couch.

Erin is next to me. Her eye lids droop and her head starts to hang. Antonio and Vito scan each room checking every inch. Antonio lifts Erin up off the couch and carries her to her room.

*****

Antonio:

It's a good thing that I never had a sister because these feelings overwhelm me, and I'm not use to it. I have been raised to be loyal and in control. Protecting Pop's interests, family, and friends has been ingrained in me since I was small.

Seeing Megan's sister, Erin, so messed up bothers me. I really need a cigarette. I gently lay Erin down on the covers in her room. I pull the comforter out from under her and tuck her in like she's two.

Different emotions sparkle and crack in me swallowing up the dark ones. The monster that rages in me softens. I never had to deal with these before...they're new and overwhelming. It could get us killed if I don't stay focused. Vito has subtly hinted at it. He knows.

I come back out into the living room, and Vito is cleaning and loading the guns. All the parts are spread out. He has a rag in his hand.

"Where's Megan?" I ask.

"In the bathroom," he replies, never looking up from his work.

The bathroom door opens, and Megan steps out in a skimpy tank top and sweatpants. Immediately, my mouth starts to water like I am a wolf stalking its prey. The smooth skin of her arms calls to me as her long hair falls in waves around her shoulders. I catch Vito ogling too. I give him my death-stare, then walk over to Megan.

I rub my hands down her arms. Oh, shit! Like silk!

"I'm going to go to bed too," she says.

My jeans start to feel tight as I stare at her. I give her a quick peck on the lips. Anything more would be bad, very bad.

"Okay," I reply. "Good night."

"Good night." Megan goes to her room and shuts the door.

After a minute of silence, Vito says, "Keep your head in the game, Tonio."

"I am." Even as I say it, I don't believe it either.

Vito is diligently cleaning and organizing the weapons. I stand across from him.

"I'm not going to get any sleep tonight," I say matter-of-factly.

He looks down at my crotch, then up into my face, "No, you're not."

I finally manage to calm my passion-filled body down after two trips outside for cigarettes and watching Simpsons© re-runs in bed. Vito and I are taking turns sleeping on the couch in the girls' living room. Vito suggested he go first. Probably a smart decision.

I think about the events that led us here. The emotions of getting Megan and then losing her, floods through me. I never want to feel that helpless or lost again. Nothing in my screwed up Mafia life compares to that.

The last time I looked at the clock, it is twelve forty-five a.m. My eyes drift open and closed a few times. A shriek jars me out of my semi-sleep.

I jump up and race to the adjoining door and dash through it. Vito's not on the couch. Another shriek, louder this time, comes from Erin's room. I dive to the doorway. The door is open and Vito, bare-chested, is hovering over a thrashing Erin. Her legs are kicking the covers; her head is flinging from side to side, eyes closed. Vito grabs her shoulders trying to wake her up.

"Erin!" he yells. "Come on, babe, wake up!"

Megan flies into the room and stops short at Vito's attempts to wake her sister.

Erin is kicking and screaming. "No! No! Don't let them hurt us, Daddy! No! I can't run that fast! Don't leave me! Meg! Shoot him! Shoot him, now!"

"Come on, babe, wake up!" Vito continues in a soothing yell.

"Hurry, Meg! Don't let him get away! Shoot!" Erin screeches.

Megan's hand covers her mouth, tears stream down her face, as she watches and listens to her sister's haunted ranting.

Vito tries a different tactic; he leans down and sits her up. She gets a good hit to his cheek, but he doesn't even flinch as he desperately tries to get her into his lap. Her flailing slows as he gently rubs her back, but she still doesn't wake up. Erin is slumped, eyes closed, in Vito's lap. This is some scary shit!

"Shhh, it's okay," he says into her ear. She calms down, and I help Vito lie her back down.

"Maybe, I should stay in here with her?" Megan comments.

"No way!" I answer a little too loudly. "You could get hurt. These are night terrors or something."I pull the covers back over Erin and straighten them.

The three of us stand there watching Erin as she returns to a calm sleep.

"I'll stay up and watch her," Vito says.

"What? We all need the sleep. You and I will take turns." I order.

"No, she is my sister. I'll stay with her," Megan says determined.

"Vito, come 'ere," I sigh. He reluctantly follows me to the couch. "Help me move this."

We pick up the couch and move it near the door to Erin's room. Facing the bed, so that whoever lies there has a clear view of Erin.

Erin's feet start thrashing again. Vito immediately goes over and strokes her arm to try and calm her. Erin stills.

That decides it. I go to Megan's room and grab blankets. I come back and lay them on the couch.

"You and I," I point to Megan, "are going to sleep here on the couch. Vito is going to sleep right next to your sister. I don't give a fuck if she beats the shit out of him. This way you can see that she's okay and keep Vito an honest man."

Megan gives me a triumphant smile, "Thank you."

"Problem solving, it's what I do," I reply.

Vito gets in bed with Erin, while Megan and I get comfortable on the couch. She stretches out in front of me, her soft hair smothering my face. I smooth it down so I can breathe, then wrap my arm around her tiny waist. Megan's entire body relaxes and her breathing slows. I silently pray that I can sleep too.

Chapter 5

Fangul (fon-gool): FUCK!

Antonio:

A morning hard-on wakes me up. Megan is curled up against my body, and I have to maintain restraint. The sun is beaming in through the windows in Erin's room. I glance at the bed. Vito and Erin are sound asleep. Her head is on his shoulder as he snores lightly on his back. Thank God, no more nightmares!

Megan stirs, and I feel light kisses on my neck. No, no, no. Bad! Very Bad!

I don't have the will-power to push her away. She trails kisses down my chest. The blood in my veins sings. My eyes feel like they are going to roll into the back of my head. I rub my hands up her thighs and cup her leg to bring it over mine, trying to get her body even closer.

A soft hoarse voice calls out, "Meg!"

Startled, both of us shoot our attention to the bed. Erin's eyes are closed, and she is calling for Megan.

Megan goes and sits on the side of the bed next to Erin. Gently, she rubs the hair from her eyes. Vito is still sleeping and has turned over towards the windows.

"I'm here," Megan says quietly.

"What's going on?" Erin's voice is groggy and thick with sleep. She looks small and vulnerable hunched up in a ball on her side.

"You had a bad dream last night," Megan coos.

"Meg, you had a gun. I keep seeing you with a gun when I close my eyes."

"Shhh, it was just a dream. You've been through a lot the past few days, and that plays tricks on your mind. Remember, I took the gun from that guy the other night. That's why. Try to go back to sleep."

"Is Daddy a bad person, Meg?" Erin asks innocently.

That's it. I had to get up. This kid is tearing at my heart. Is Daddy a bad person? This poor kid is so fucking traumatized.

I make coffee and clear off the kitchen table. Megan helps her sister to the bathroom and closes the door. She comes over to help me, avoiding the guns and bullets. I move those.

"Do you think she's going to be okay?" Megan asks me.

"I have no clue. I never had to deal with this shit before." I say, putting things away a little forcefully.

"What's the matter? Are you mad?" Megan asks.

"Hell yeah! I think your father screwed up!"

"What do you mean?" Megan asks horrified.

"He shouldn't have kept this from you! He should've raised you with it!" I gesture with my hands. "Helped you to understand the lifestyle."

"Hey!" she gets angry. "I'm doing okay. At least, I think I am."

I walk over and hug her.

"Yes. You are. But I think it's you. Everybody is different. I think it's in your blood to handle it. Erin? Not so much."

She squeezes me tighter. "Then what is wrong with her?"

Vito comes strolling out of the bedroom, scratching his balls. Nice! In front of my girlfriend...ASS!

"I bet she has PTSD," he says, grabbing a mug and pouring coffee.

"What?!" Megan asks.

"I saw it on the military channel. It's post-traumatic stress disorder. I googled the symptoms on my phone. Erin's got a shit load of them." Vito rubs his head and sits down sipping his coffee. "Tired, depressed, nightmares, lack of energy, loss of appetite."

Megan and I both stare at him.

"Wow, dude, you did look it up. You almost sounded like a friggin' doctor for a second."

Vito smirks at me, and Megan sits down next to him.

"How long does it last?" Megan asks intrigued.

"It's different for everybody. Weeks...years. But the first step to recovery is being removed from the situation. So coming here, I suppose, was a good thing," Vito says.

"I think she needs to fully come to terms with what your father does for a living," I say, then turn to Vito. "Oh yeah, that reminds me. What did you say yesterday to make her drink and eat?"

"Yeah, what did you say?" Megan is curious too.

Vito sips his coffee, "I just told her I would break a different body part on that kid who cheated on her every time I needed her to drink.

What's his name? Connor? I hope she's better today because I'm running out of shit to hypothetically break."

Megan shook her head, laughing, and I slap Vito on the back. "Good thinkin'."

All at once, my phone rings and Erin calls Megan from the bathroom. Megan scurries to her sister, and I answer the phone. It's my mom.

"Hello."

"Hi, Sweetie. How is everything?"

"Everything is fine...except Megan's sister isn't taking things too well."

"What's she doing?"

"Nightmares, not eating, quiet."

"Sounds like she's in shock, honey. That's understandable," my mom says comfortingly. "How's Megan?"

"She's taking things really well so far," I say.

"Aw, that's cause she's got you, Baby. Is Vito staying out of trouble?" she asks joking.

"Yeah, he's been good."

"Your dad is going to be calling for you to do a couple of things for him," she says. HERE! What the fuck!

"Okay."

"Take care of those girls, sweetheart. I love you," she says.

"Love you too, bye." And I hang up.

A knock sounds on the door. Vito and I both move. I grab a gun. We position ourselves on each side of the door. Vito cautiously looks through the peephole. He visibly relaxes. "It's the chooch."

I look over at Megan and her sister. They are staring at us wide-eyed. They must have been moving from the bathroom to the bedroom. Erin is wrapped in a towel. The two of them are frozen in one spot.

"It's Troy," I mouth to Megan.

The girls continue to the bedroom. Vito flings open the door. He looks down the hallway in both directions then yanks Troy inside. Troy trips in, and I slam the door.

"How did you know where we were?" I ask not so nicely.

"I went to the downstairs desk," he says, surprised and aggravated.

"What do you want?" I ask, threatening.

"I want to talk to Megan," he says. "I didn't bother trying the phone again," he adds sarcastically.

Megan comes out of Erin's bedroom. She is in her pajamas like the rest of us. I place the gun on the table.

Troy walks over to her in a movement that says, I am going to hug you.

"Not so fast, asshole! She's not dressed!"

"Hmmm," Troy says mockingly, not turning around. "Funny, I have hugged Megan before in her PJ's." He is advancing on her. She just looks between the two of us. "In fact, she has slept over my house, repeatedly, over the years."

I fucking lose it. I grab Troy by the collar and shove him to the floor. Vito knows better then to intervene. He just stands there posturing, while I push my forearm into Troy's neck. His blond hair is tangled and not as perfect as when he walked in. "Not anymore!" I spit at him.

Troy doesn't fight me. He just grins and says, "Jealous much?"

I let him up. Megan is gone. The door to her bedroom is closed.

"Why are all of you here?" Troy asks, standing up and brushing himself off.

I shrug my shoulders, "I'm spending some time with my girlfriend."

He clearly doesn't believe me. He smirks. "So you just decided to take a vacation in the middle of a school week with Chewbacca over there," he throws his hand towards Vito, "and Megan's little sister."

"Listen, Erin wouldn't even be here if it wasn't for your weasel of a brother!" I retort coldly.

Vito's stance has changed. He is ready to blow.

"I know about my brother. I think he is being an ass too. But I'm not my brother."

"And you're not Megan's boyfriend either. Glad we cleared the fucking air on that." I say derisively.

Megan's door opens, and she comes out dressed in a t-shirt and jeans. She has pulled her hair back in a ponytail, and all I want to do is wrap my hands in it.

"Meg, is everything all right?" Troy asks. "Are you okay?"

Megan steps up to Troy and gives him a quick hug. I bristle. Troy shoots me a smug smile. I want to rip his face off and tack it to the front of his dorm.

Megan's defeated expression makes me think she wants to spill her guts to Troy. I slowly shake my head at her. She can't tell Troy about her father being the Cleaner. That puts everyone in danger.

"Our house was broken into the other night," she starts and sits on the couch. I watch her. "It was really frightening."

"Who broke into your house?!" Troy asks, shocked.

"Oh, just some crazy guy," she says, leaving out the fact that the 'crazy guy' was 'guys' and they wanted to kill her family.

Troy looks at me and says, "This is because of you, isn't it!"

"Me? Why are you blaming me?" I spew at him. Vito moves to go after Troy, and I put my hand out to stop him.

"Troy, it isn't because of Antonio. It happened, it's over. My dad wanted us to come here for a while to get away."

"Well, you didn't need to bring an entourage with you." Then, says softly to Megan, "I thought it was just going to be us."

That did it. If he speaks intimately one more time to her; I am going to slowly break each finger on his hands then all of his toes.

"How's Erin?" Troy asks.

"Between the break-in and Connor cheating on her, not good." Megan sighs. "We'll just have to see."

"If there is anything I can do, let me know." Troy says placing his hand on her knee.

I roughly grip Troy's shoulders from behind and yank him back against the couch, looking down at him. "Don't. Fuckin'. Touch. Her." I release his shoulders and shove him forward.

Megan doesn't say anything, but she gives me a dirty look. I'll be hearing it later about roughing up her friend.

"Thanks for the warning," Troy keeps his sarcastic tone. "There is a party tonight on campus. Why don't you guys come and relax?" he offers.

No one says anything right away. Erin is now standing in the doorway of her room.

Megan sees Erin and answers Troy. "That sounds great."

Megan:

Antonio is ready to rip Troy apart. I hadn't given much thought to what it would be like for all of us to come to see Troy. I guess all that has happened and all the secrets I've learned will do that to you.

Going to a party on campus is probably just what we all need. It will take our minds off kidnappings, beatings, and the horrors we left behind in New Jersey.

"It's at Dillon Hall, eight o'clock," Troy says, getting up.

Erin's doorway is now empty. She must have gone back in her room. Antonio is standing by the door to the suite, graciously waiting for Troy—NOT! Vito is poised like a bodyguard by the kitchen table. The tension in the room is palpable.

I stand too and walk with Troy to the door. Antonio opens it and scans the hallway before standing out of the way for Troy to leave.

"Thanks Troy," I say. "See you tonight."

Troy's face is sad when he says goodbye. He looks at Antonio and walks away.

Antonio shuts the door and bolts it. Our eyes lock, and Antonio's are possessive and needy. My breath hitches and expectation radiates through me. His hands find my hair and, in a flash, I am crushed against him. My back hits a wall and Antonio is smothering me...kissing me. My pulse races and my stomach clenches in a delicious way I'm not used to. Holy Shit!

I barely register Vito clearing his throat. Antonio picks me up so that I am straddling him and carries me through the adjoining door to our suites. He kicks it shut with his foot. We cross their living room to his bedroom, and he flops me down on the bed. He strips his t-shirt off and lies on top of me, kissing me roughly and passionately. This has never happened to me before. If it did, I wouldn't have wanted it from anyone else.

I wrap my arms around his beautifully sculpted ones. His skin is hot. He is so focused on me...intent. His hands run down my sides, then back up, never breaking our ardent kiss. He cups my breast in his hand and moans into my mouth. A zing of pleasure travels through my body dazing me.

His intensity is pleasurable and frightening all at once. No one has ever made me feel this way, and I don't want it to stop. I trail my hands down his back and over his flannel pants. The muscles underneath are tight. His hips start moving against me. Even through my thick jeans, I can feel the hardness of him. Oh God! So sensual and gratifying!

Knock, knock...

Vito calls out, "It's your Pop." The doorway is empty.

"Fuck!" Antonio curses, and crawls off me. His pants are tented and his chest is bare. I blush. Still sprawled out on the bed, I turn away.

I can hear Vito and Antonio out in the hallway whispering.

"You can't go out there like that. Erin is on the couch," Vito says.

"Get me a pen and a piece of paper," Antonio says, his voice husky.

"Hey Pop." (pause) "Everything's okay, so far." (pause) "Yeah, I can do that. Where was he last seen?" (pause) "Got it."(pause) "I will. Love you too, Pop. Bye."

"I gotta go after a runner today," Antonio says to Vito. "You'll have to stay with the girls."

"What do you mean? All the way out here in bum-fuck nowhere? Fanabola!"

"Pop did some checking on someone that has been evading Donny for a while. They think he's here. I gotta check it out. He owes Pop a lot of scarol."

"Marrone, Tonio! Your work is never done," Vito says.

Listening to their conversation, I lie on my side. Vito is right. Antonio's life is never going to change.

Chapter 6

Scarol (ska-roll): money!

Megan:

Around six, Antonio comes back. His eyes glint with that chilling look that fascinates and scares me. He says nothing as he walks in. He just scoops me into his arms and kisses me. His body slowly releases tension as he melts more into my arms.

"You are so calming," he whispers in my ear.

Vito had taken Erin and me to the library on campus today. It was an amazing building, lined floor to ceiling with every book imaginable. I signed up for a library card, and we checked out a couple of books. Vito just stood by watching and listening. He scanned our surroundings like his was guarding rock stars.

The only time he wasn't on total hyper-vigilance was when he was watching Erin. A few times, I caught him reading over her shoulder. I immediately thought that he just felt really bad for my sallow-faced, duped sister. Then I saw something in his gaze as he studied her that I didn't like.

My strength and wits returned today. The queasiness and shock of the past couple of days are finally waning. Wrapped up in Antonio's arms last night was comforting and powerful. I am actually excited to meet some students on campus tonight.

Antonio goes to shower, and Vito is cooking in our kitchen. He is opening drawers and chopping vegetables. The smell of homemade pizza wafts through the suite.

Erin comes out of her room holding a novel she is reading and sits down at the table. Vito has his back to her getting plates out. He turns and yelps, "Shit! You scared me!"

I truly don't think that happens too often with Vito. And I highly doubt my fourteen-year-old sister, very soon to be fifteen, would be the one to scare him. She lets out a small giggle. Holy Crap! That's a good sign.

We all converge at the table and Vito cuts the pizza. It smells heavenly. He has made it with all fresh ingredients — basil, hand cut tomatoes, mozzarella and ricotta cheeses. He slides a piece onto a plate for me. It is perfect. I hold the pizza to my mouth and bite. Boy, can Vito cook!

"This is absolutely delicious," I tell him.

"I don't know about that, but it's better than the crap we had last night," Vito says, humbly. Wow, is he embarrassed at a compliment?

"Yeah, it's good, man," Antonio says, agreeing with me.

We all clean up together. Antonio steals kisses as we work.

We dress and get ready to go to Dillon Hall. I pick a tight fitting pink cashmere sweater and jeans.

Erin eyes are vacant. Her face makes her look like she's been dead for three days and no one told her to lie down. I put some gloss on her lips and blush on her cheeks. It helps a little. She dresses in jeans and a sweater too. I brush her long red hair for her. As I move the brush down her long hair I speak softly to her. My sister has never looked her age. She can pass for seventeen or eighteen easily, even though she is tiny.

I finish getting Erin and myself dressed. I grab our jackets off the bed and head out into the living room. Standing by the door waiting are Vito and Antonio. They both have leather jackets on.

Antonio looks yummy. His wavy dark hair is brushed but it is ruffled like he's rubbed his hands through it about ten times. A pack of cigarettes sticks out the side pocket. He smiles at me.

Vito is twice his normal size in his jacket and his normal size is big. It makes him look broader and unapproachable. I push a reluctant Erin in front of me.

We had to park on the street because of all the hall parking spaces are full. Antonio holds my hand. It is dark out, only the beams of streetlights are visible, and the shadows of buildings and bushes surround us.

The party is much more rowdy than I envisioned. Tons of people are here. There is a riotous essence in the air. Music is blaring and thumping. Every single person inside and out is carrying a plastic cup. Girls are wearing strapless or sleeveless tops and no jackets despite the fall chill.

A steady stream of people crosses over the threshold to the dorm, coming in and out. It dawns on me that finding Troy will be like finding a needle in a haystack.

Antonio and Vito are cautious scanning the crowd. I'm watching the flirty glances and nods of approval these college girls are giving my boyfriend, and that makes me want to scratch their eyes out. I should be empowered and hopeful since I will be coming here next year. But I'm not. I am territorial and leery.

Even Vito gets the stares. My sister is only watching the ground. She's not meeting anyone's eyes. She definitely doesn't want to be here. Maybe this was a mistake.

Antonio and Vito stand out like chocolate chips in vanilla ice cream. Everyone here is paler and with a myriad of different hair colors — blond, red, light brown. Actually, in the looks department, Erin and I fit right in. Antonio and Vito are the ones who don't blend in. But they always look like they could have starring roles in the Godfather movies.

Come to think of it, won't Antonio be the Godfather someday, the Mob Boss of Palmetto? That's unsettling. I tighten my grip on Antonio's hand.

"Hey, Meg!" I hear. It's Troy.

"Hey, Troy," I say. "How did you find us?" Troy's wearing comfortably worn jeans and a long sleeve t-shirt. He's seems in his element, relaxed. The college life agrees with him.

"I spotted your Italian henchmen first," Troy smirks.

A crowd starts chanting and yelling from under one of the spotlights glowing from the building. The group is in a circle and the circle moves with whatever is going on inside it. The yelling gets louder, then part of the circle scatters. Two guys fall over on the grass, grunting and hitting each other. Cheers erupt as the guys bang the crap out of each other.

Antonio pushes me behind him then tugs on Erin's arm. She is frozen watching the fight. The onlookers move and shift with the fighters, and they're getting closer.

Vito gently moves Erin farther away, and Antonio and I follow. Troy shifts with us to a new location...just far enough away to observe.

"What's going on?" I ask Troy.

"The Gauntlet," he says matter-of-factly.

"Huh?" I ask. Not liking the sound of the word Gauntlet.

"It's simple, really. Two guys step up to run the challenge. Five girls line up with five beers. Each challenger drinks them as fast as they can. Then they run over to arm wrestle Bubba and Jake over there." He points to a couple of guys at a folding table. "The first one to win, if they win, runs to the circle and fights the last guy standing from the last round. They fight their way to the Irish flag over there." He points to a tiny flag on a stake in the grass which is barely visible in the dark. First one to grab it is the winner." Troy says triumphantly.

"Cool," Vito says.

"Cool?" I exclaim. "That's barbaric!" Antonio, Vito, and even Troy give me weird expressions. I laugh at myself. Considering the turns my life has taken, it is just boys having fun.

"No one is forced Megan," Troy reassures me. "It's their choice. And if you can't make it through the first trials you can't do the last, the fighting." True.

"Have you done it?" I ask him.

"No, no... I'm too pretty for that." Troy says joking, as he motions towards the ruckus of fighting.

Antonio snorts. He moves behind me and wraps his arms around my waist, a loving and possessive gesture.

"The next one is just about to start. See the girls lined up over there?" Troy asks.

We walk towards two lines of girls holding large plastic cups. Two guys stand at the end, shirtless and barefoot in the cold. They are pumped up, hooting and hollering. The word 'GO!' echoes through the crowd.

The guys run to the girls and start drinking. They are gulping and sloshing the beer all over themselves. After they finish each cup, they ceremoniously throw them down on the ground. They move down the line fairly quickly. Cheers and chanting follow them. One guy even wastes precious seconds kissing one of the girls. "Ooooh..." resonates among the spectators.

Kissy-Guy finishes first and runs to the arm wrestling table. Sweat and beer fly off him as he shakes his head trying to clear it. He sits down and lines himself up for arm wrestling.

The other guy, quite ungracefully, trips into the table. He is fighting the fuzziness of the beer. Kissy-Guy is already immersed in wrestling. He is struggling to gain an advantage. The challenger doesn't have a chance; he can barely keep his hand straight. His opponent is laughing at him.

Vito is watching this whole thing delighted. Finally, Kissy-Guy flips Bubba or Jake's arm to the table. Then he runs with difficulty to the waiting crowd on the other side of the grass. Standing in the middle is the winner of the last round.

Kissy-Guy gets a punch in and tries to run towards the flag, but the challenger grabs his legs and flattens him to the ground. They struggle, punching and kicking. We watch and, occasionally, I hear Antonio snickering in my ear. He thinks this whole gauntlet thing is funny.

"How 'bout a little fun, Tonio?" Vito says mischievously, rubbing his hands together like he's waiting for his Christmas gifts.

Erin is quiet and shakes her head. She still hasn't looked at Troy.

"Nah, man," Antonio says chuckling. He is nuzzling my neck. "I already beat the shit out of someone today." Troy's head swings around to Antonio, shocked. I reach to touch his hands that are laced across my stomach. His knuckles are swollen and rough. It never dawned on me that he might have caught the guy his dad had him chasing. "You go. I'll stay with the girls."

Vito's face lights up. Oh yeah, it's Christmas! Then he grins at Troy, "Where do I sign up?"

Troy and Vito walk away from us, heads together, talking. I think Troy might have made a new friend.

A few people converge on them as Antonio, Erin, and I stand back towards the road. We still have a great view though. Through the throngs of people, we see Vito emerge shirtless and barefoot.

"I guess there wasn't a very long line," Antonio says is my ear.

"I guess not," I say. "I'm nervous." Antonio shifts me so that I can see his face.

"Don't be," he says smiling.

Erin takes my hand, apparently worried too.

Someone yells 'GO!' and Vito and his challenger are off. Vito is much broader and larger than his opponent, definitely more cut. They're on beer two. Vito chucks his cup to the ground smiling. Beer three. The pretty girl who hands him the cup tries to steal a kiss. Vito shuts her down by waving his finger at her in a nuh-uh gesture. The crowd gives a low "Ooooooh..." The dissed girl gets angry. The guy next to Vito is slowing down. Vito keeps going. His body is quickly getting slicked with beer.

Beer four and five are a blur. "How is he not affected?" I ask Antonio. Vito is running to the arm wrestling table. He sits down not even fazed by the alcohol he just chugged.

"We've been drinking a long time," Antonio says with mirth. "It started with the wine Nonna makes in her cellar. It was downhill from there."

Vito slams the arm of the wrestler onto the table with little effort. It happened in seconds. WOW!

He runs to the other side of the grass. Kissy-Guy was out. This guy had won two rounds at least. Without ceremony, Vito punches the guy square in the face. He goes down hard, like a sack of potatoes. Vito runs right by him to the flag and grabs it. He holds it up. Everything happens so fast. The crowd, Erin and I stand with our mouths open, dumbfounded. Antonio cheers for his friend, breaking the semi-silence.

"Woo-hoo, Vito!" he yells.

Vito marches over to us. Antonio and Vito clasp arms and slap each other on the back. I feel cold with the loss of Antonio's arms. The smell of stale beer emanates from Vito. Erin glances up at him. He puts a reassuring hand on her shoulder and smiles down at her.

"How was that?" he asks. "You need a little entertainment." He is grinning wickedly at her. She pushes his arm off her shoulder and walks away.

At that moment, tons and tons of people from the party come over. Smacking Vito, high-fiving him. Girls wiggle their way closer to him, flirting. Gushing about how they've never seen anything like that. We are encircled with people. I am uncomfortable.

Apparently, Vito isn't finished. He has to fight the next guy to make it through the Gauntlet, a sour voice tells him in the din. Troy is ecstatic about Vito's performance.

"Dude! You were awesome!" Troy yells.

I can see the outline of Erin sitting on the grass by herself way away from the crowd. She is shrouded in darkness. I walk over and sit on the grass with her.

"You okay?" I ask her.

"Yeah," she replies, playing with a blade of grass.

I sigh, "Looks like we could be here awhile."

Erin shivers. A body flops down next to her. It's a guy. He startles us both.

"Hi," he says.

"Hi," I return.

He speaks to Erin, "Not happy to be here, huh?"

Who is this guy? He's cute. Light brown hair, lean but not too skinny. It's too dark to see his eyes.

"No... It's okay." Erin says meekly.

"I'm Jake." He holds his hand out to shake with her. Oh, one of the arm wrestler guys.

"Erin," her voice is so soft, almost a whisper.

I feel him before I see him. Antonio is hovering over Jake, staring down at him intimidatingly. I know that look well now. Troy appears too.

"This is Jake." Troy declares. "He lives in my dorm." Antonio seems to accept this and sits down behind me. His warmth is cozy and soothing. "Well, Vito is making an impression."

"Yeah, college life seems to agree with him," I deadpan.

Vito is waiting for his next victim. He is dancing in place, hooting and shouting. Girls try to stand on their tiptoes to kiss him and hang on him. They are giggling and laughing like he's a celebrity. He doesn't even acknowledge them, except the really forceful ones, he pushes them aside gently.

"Too bad the actual studying part doesn't agree with him," Antonio says into my ear making me shiver.

Someone replaced Jake at the arm wrestling table. More and more guys are getting in line to try and beat Vito. The Gauntlet is just firing up. Vito takes down three more challengers. The crowd around him thickens and grows. We can barely see him now.

Antonio whispers, "I hope someone can beat him soon." He nuzzles my neck, moving my hair aside. "I want to take you back to the suite to finish what we started." His words sizzle under my skin. I lean back ever farther into him enjoying his soft caresses.

I am so caught up in Antonio that I don't notice that Troy has gone back to Vito, and Erin and Jake are having a quiet conversation.

"How long are you here for?" Jake asks.

"I don't know," Erin replies.

"What do you think so far? Is college life all you dreamed of?" Jake chuckles softly.

Erin, playing with blades of grass, shrugs her shoulders. Then she drops the grass and rubs her arms like she's cold.

I'm about to say something when Jake takes off his coat. He gets up on his knees and places his jacket on the front of her. It's backwards covering her chest and arms. Antonio immediately hardens at Jake's movements, but doesn't say anything.

"Maybe we should wait in the car," Antonio says. "Or go inside."

"Sure," I say. "I'm getting thirsty." Antonio unwraps himself from around me and helps me up. He reaches for Erin to help her too, but Jake is already doing that. Hmmmm... Jake takes his coat off Erin and places it on her shoulders.

Cheers erupt as Vito wins another round. The four of us head into the dorm. It is crowded. We push through, but everyone is close — too close — invading my personal bubble space. I reach for Erin's hand behind me.

The hand I reach for is already occupied. Jake has her hand and is maneuvering Erin through the mass of partiers. He is with us, tagging along. Unexpected, but whatever. He seems like a nice guy. We are forced into a single file line, Antonio is leading the way. Plastic cups and beer bottles litter the floor as we enter. The couches in the lounge area are filled with bodies. The music is much louder in here.

Words that sound on the cusp of a roar echo behind us over the music, "Who the fuck is this?!"

Antonio swings around shoving me behind him in a defensive move. It's Vito. Dirt and grass cover his chest that glistens with sweat and alcohol. The crowds of people disperse, and we are all alone in the spacious room, like an island all our own. People are staring at us. Troy comes up behind Vito.

"That's Jake. He's my friend. He lives in my dorm." Troy slaps Vito on the back congenially. "Come on, some guys from the football team showed up. They want a shot too."

But Vito doesn't move. His eyes are glued to Jake and Erin. His expression is savage and vicious. Antonio moves first. Erin, Jake, and I are rooted to the spot we froze in.

Jake anxiously glances between Erin and me, his hand fastened around Erin's. The music continues to thump and pump so loudly that I can feel it through the floor. Vito still faces us, but his eyes have shifted to Antonio. Antonio is saying something to him I can't hear.

Vito turns to leave. Antonio comes back sighing. "Don't touch her dude," he says to Jake authoritatively.

Jake reluctantly drops Erin's hand. Erin runs out of the dorm, Jake's coat dropping to the floor.

"Whoa, Erin!" I yell, and chase after her.

She takes off fast. Antonio passes me, and then yanks me along with him running in the direction she went. Prickles of panic build because I can't see her.

Antonio curses under his breath, "What the fuck? How fast can a fourteen-year-old girl run?"

Erin runs and we chase. Even Jake is with us. The darkness envelops her. I hear sniffling, and we find Erin crouched behind a car on the street.

I lean down and squat next to her.

I've had enough, Meg," Erin sobs. "I hate this."

"I don't know what to say Erin," I say, frustrated, and wanting to wave a magic wand to change it all.

"I do," Antonio says with stern confidence, "Don't ever fuckin' run from me again! You're my responsibility."

Erin flinches and Antonio softens, "Fanabola... I know you've been through a lot but you're gonna have to toughen up that skin of yours."

Troy comes over, "What's going on?" he asks.

"Go away Troy! I don't want to see you!" Erin screams.

"Hey, don't take this out on Troy." I tell her.

Jake moves forward and stands, listening and observing this exchange. Then he says, "I'll hang out with her for a while 'til everybody cools off." His voice is sympathetic. Erin and I are still crouched on the ground; she's sobbing.

"I don't fuckin' know you," Antonio spits. "Vito's right, you shouldn't have been touching her!"

"What?!" Jake ricochets back. "I was just being nice, keeping everyone together! I wasn't making a move!"

I know from the short time we've been together that Antonio is about ready to go after Jake. He's getting angry. I move to hug

221

Antonio from behind. I feel the hard, rough outline of a gun in the waist of his jeans.

"Hey, Jake's a nice guy!" Troy pipes in.

This is turning a mole hill into Mount Everest.

"Why don't we go wait in the car for Vito?" I suggest.

Tension leaves Antonio a little, a very little. I am learning quickly his triggers and responses. I reach down and help up my humiliated sister.

"Come on, Jake," Troy says quietly. "Let's go see how Vito is doing."

Antonio pulls out his cigarettes and lights up as Troy and Jake walk away.

"I can't believe you did that to me!" Erin yells when Troy and Jake are out of earshot. "You and Vito can go to hell!" Erin storms away towards the car, the darkness swallowing her up again.

I look to Antonio who's taking a drag off his cigarette. He shrugs his shoulders and blows out smoke. "Well, at least it's better than being curled up in a fuckin' ball," he comments. I shake my head, and we follow Erin.

Antonio and I get in the front and Erin sits in the back. We settle in, and Antonio turns around.

"I know you're naïve but a guy doesn't take a girl's hand like that who barely fuckin' knows her unless he's interested... He's not just nice."

"Well, maybe I was interested. Did you ever think of that?" Erin is seething.

"Nope. Not gonna happen," Antonio says matter-of-factly, laying down the law. "That chooch is too fuckin' old for you."

"What?!" Erin screeches. "Who died and made you boss?"

"Nobody yet," Antonio says playfully. "But I'm still in charge."

We sit in silence for a minute or two when the side door opens. Vito is standing there holding his coat, shirt, and shoes. Most people would probably look exhausted after taking on some many people, but Vito is glowing. I bet he could do this all night.

"Troy said you guys went to the car," he says. "Hey, what's up with you?" he says to Erin, and taps her on the knee.

"Are you kidding?" she yells, then directs her anger back to Antonio. "How come Vito can touch me?" her voice escalates. "And...sleep in my bed?!"

Antonio responds calmly as he backs the Porsche out of the spot, "Because he's like a big brother, not a pedophile."

"Pedophile! What am I three?!" she yells again.

It is clear that Erin is going through some phases. They must be related to what has happened. First she was unresponsive, now she's getting overtly angry. She definitely has a lot to overcome.

Chapter 7

Sfatcheem (s-fa-cheam): a pain in the ass!

Megan:

We made it back to the suite with less yelling. Vito was quiet. We all disperse when we got back. Erin went to her room and slammed the door. Vito mumbled he was showering and going to bed. It's Antonio's turn to sleep on our couch.

Antonio and I are alone in the living room. He takes my face in his hands and kisses me slowly. My body immediately responds to his touch. He lays me on the couch. I run my fingers through his hair and down his back. We lay kissing and touching for a while. Then without warning, Antonio picks me up. My legs wrap around his waist like this morning. He walks me to my room and lays me on my bed.

Heat pools in my belly. Antonio skims his hand up my thigh, my waist, my stomach, and rests it on my breast.

"Are you ready?" he asks huskily, staring into my eyes.

I flush and cover my face with my hands, embarrassed. I know what he means; I'm just discomfited at the question.

"I don't want to do anything to scare you or fuck this up...so I'm asking. Are you ready?"

I pause and don't answer.

"...or do you want to wait?" he adds.

Through my fingers I reply, "Yes, I'm ready." I really am. I'm just nervous.

Antonio closes the door to the room and kneels back on the bed. The only light is soft from outside. He gently lifts my sweater over my head, I shift to help him. His eyes are dark and lustful. He cups my breasts again, and I moan in- voluntarily. He reaches behind me and unclasps my bra. He slides it down my arms and tosses it aside.

"I want nothing between us," he whispers. He strips his own shirt off and kisses me again. He unbuttons my jeans and slips them down my legs. My heart hammers.

"I want you so much Megan," he says as he slips off his own jeans and covers me with his body.

We wake up naked and wrapped around each other in my bed. I shift, and I feel a faint soreness between my legs. Images of last night flood back to me, and I reel from happiness. Antonio shifts beside me, and I snuggle against him tighter.

"I love you, Megan," he says.

"I love you, too." I reply, and we fall back to sleep.

*****

Antonio:

No nightmares last night, I think to myself... I didn't hear Erin screaming. Last night, despite the drama, was the best night of my life. Megan is mine, and I'm never going to let her go. Ever.

My phone rings. It's on the coffee table in the living room. I get up and throw my jeans on. I scoop up the condom from the floor. I need to hide it in the trash before anyone else gets up.

I get to the phone. It's Pop.

"Eh, Tonio, how's it goin' there?"

"Good, Pop."

"Any trouble?"

"No. Nothing."

"Good. That's good."

"You get anything from the asshole yesterday?"

"Not yet. That guy is so strung out. He is on some hard core shit. I bet he didn't even feel his fingers breakin'. I think he's a lost cause, Pop."

"Tail him, see what he's doin', who he's getting his stuff from. The money has to come from somewhere. He's got one week, Tonio."

"Okay," I say.

I walk to the bathroom while talking to Pop.

"Alright, Tonio. Love you, bye."

"Love you too, Pop. Bye."

I hang up and take care of business in the bathroom. I walk out and see Vito coming out of Erin's room yawning. He is shuffling straight to our suite.

I call out to stop him. "Why are you comin' from Erin's room?" I ask.

Vito turns to look at me. "She was having a shitty night." He points to her room. "Well, you would have known that if you weren't 'busy'." He uses his fingers to air quote.

"I was right next door. How did you know she was having a bad night?"

"I checked on her a couple of hours ago. I figured you were in Megan's room when you weren't on the couch. I guess I was right," his voice is sarcastic.

"I heard her in the next suite last time," I say, annoyed.

"She wasn't screaming, but she was fidgety and restless—talking in her sleep."

"What was she talking about?"

"Ugh...a lot of shit. Mannegia! I gotta piss." Vito walks away.

I make coffee. Vito joins me back in the kitchen. He grabs a mug and fills it.

My phone beeps with a text. It's Patrick.

How are the girls?

Fine. Mostly. You want to talk to them? I type back.

Not yet.

Erin comes out of her room. She is clearly still angry.

"How'd you sleep?"

"I think I'd sleep better if you get the ox out of my bed," she throws out defensively, heading to the bathroom.

"Get changed. I'm taking you to breakfast," I order.

"What? Just us?" she asks.

"Yeah, just us."

All I wanted to do was crawl back into bed with Megan, but this was something I had to do. I let Vito and Megan know that I am taking Erin to breakfast alone. There's just some shit that needs to be sorted out. This kid has to face the music.

We pull up to a little diner off campus. It's small with a neon sign that says Breakfast and Lunch — straight and to-the-point advertising. Erin is quiet for the ride. We sit in the last booth in the back. I face the entrance. I always face the doorway in restaurants. Theaters and public places too. You always need to know exits and points of entry.

This shit about her Dad has been bothering me since yesterday. "I want to talk about your Dad."

Erin looks up from her computer-printed menu surprised.

"I want to explain things to you in a way that will hopefully help you," I continue. "A fireman doesn't hesitate. He just runs into that burning building. He just does it. It's who he is."

"What are you talking about?" she asks, annoyed.

"I'm trying to explain things to you."

"What things?" Her voice is condescending and sassy.

"Don't pull that shit with me." My voice is low and commanding.

"What shit?"

"That shit. Stop giving me attitude. I'm not the one who has been lying to you for fourteen years. I'm given' it to you straight."

Erin stops and looks ashamed.

"Listen, sometimes we're born to do things. Take my pop for example. When his Pop died, he acquired the business. He doesn't force anyone to borrow money — they come to him — whether it's for gambling debts, drugs, or whatever they need it for. Pop doesn't force them, and the people who borrow know the consequences. There are rules, unwritten guidelines. These people are not innocents. They're into big shit."

Erin's eyes fill with tears. "But why does my Dad kill people?"

I glance around the room as the question leaves her lips and tap my fingers on the table.

"It's in his blood. It's what he knows... He's obviously good at it. He's been doing it a long time. Your father dishes out the ultimate consequence for not paying or running...or even trying to push my pop out."

"Why would anyone want to push Mr. Delisi out or take over?"

"That's simple—power," I answer.

"Power? Why?"

"Power can be a more dominant drug than meth or heroine. It makes them feel important. They need it."

Erin stops to consider this. I can tell the wheels are turning in her mind.

"But this is the most important part," I say. "No one knows your Dad is the Cleaner. It's important that they never do."

"Why?"

"People would come after you. Just like the other night. The anonymity of the Cleaner keeps people loyal and fearful."

Erin wipes her tearing eyes with her fingers. The waitress comes over and takes our order. I monotonously order bacon, eggs, and coffee. Erin orders a muffin.

My phone rings. It's Uncle Tutti.

"Eh, Tonio. How are you?"

"Good, Uncle. How are you?" Erin just sits in the booth, watching me talk on the phone.

"Where are you, kid? Haven't seen you around?"

"Oh, you know... I'm all over, doing stuff for Pop." Obviously, Pop didn't tell Uncle Tutti where I am or what I'm doing, so I'm not about to.

"You chasing a runner?" he asks.

"Yeah, something like that." Well, it's not totally a lie.

The waitress plops dishes on the table in front of Erin and me.

"I'm out having breakfast and it just arrived."

"Oh, okay. Talk to ya soon, Tonio. Bye."

"Bye." I hang up.

"Who was that?" Erin asks.

"My Uncle Tutti. He is my grandmother's younger brother."

"Why didn't you tell him where you were?"

"This is a good lesson. Information is very important. You never share it if you don't have to. My pop didn't tell him where I am... I, sure as hell, am not telling him."

"But he's your uncle. You can't tell him?"

"No. Never give anyone extra information they don't need to know. He doesn't need to know where I am."

She considers this. "Does he know about my father?"

"Not that I know of."

"Then who does?"

"Up until a few days ago, my pop and my mom, your father and mother, obviously...and the fuckers who broke into your house."

"You didn't know?" she asks incredulously.

"Nope. I had no reason to know." I push my eggs around on my plate.

"How did you find out?"

"Umm...I ran into him."

"Ran into him?"

"Look, you don't need to know how I know. I just know." I ramble out.

Erin grins and starts laughing, "Its information I don't need to know?"

"Now you're catching on." I say and I wink at her.

We eat in silence for a while. The waitress refills my coffee.

"Does Vito know?" Erin asks quietly, picking at her muffin.

"He hasn't come out and said he knows, but, yes, he does."

"Why hasn't he said anything?"

"He's smart and knows the rules."

"Who makes up these rules, anyway?" she asks, disgusted.

"Life in the Mafia makes the rules," I tell her. "And sometimes they're hard finite lessons."

We come through the door of the suite and the T.V. is on. Megan is on the couch watching the news. She smiles up at us.

"How was breakfast?" she asks.

"Insightful," Erin deadpans.

Erin goes into her bedroom, and I immediately drop beside Megan on the couch. I reach for her and pull her close. I kiss her like I haven't seen her in a week, not just a couple of hours.

"You okay," I whisper.

"Better than okay," she whispers back, and I kiss her again.

"I have to go out again today."

"I figured," she says, disappointed. I rub her cheek with my finger.

"I would much rather stay here with you," I tell her.

"Antonio, what if we're here a long time? Erin is missing a lot of school."

"Don't worry about it. We'll have her read some books. The teachers will let her write some reports about them or something. Pop will take care of it."

"I was thinking maybe we could sit in and observe some classes while we're here. That would be a great experience for her."

"For you too," I say, and kiss her freckled nose. "Talk to Troy, find out when his classes are. Vito will go with you. I can't do anything until I finish up this business for Pop."

For the first time that his name has come out of my mouth, I don't feel jealous. I'm okay with Troy. Last night was incredible, and I know Megan is mine. I kiss her, hard.

I murmur, "You are so beautiful. I want you again."

Megan's eyes flash with lust at my declaration and she says, "Me too."

Chapter 8

Moola (moo-laa): money

Antonio:

Back on the highway, I drive towards Chicago. I didn't even tell Vito that I was leaving the state to chase this fucker. It's only about seventy miles from South Bend. Vito was right — this guy Allen isn't in a bum-fuck town. He's in the big city of Chicago. I could get messed up just for being here if anyone caught on to who I am. I am out of my territory.

You can chase runners into others territories, but the head boss is supposed to know about it. It avoids conflict and confusion...and loss of life.

Pop's informant is a good one because it only took me two hours to track him down to a sleazy bar off the main drag. When I open the heavy wooden door, the smell of stale beer and body odor assaults me. Marrone! This place stinks.

The bar is dark with only a few scattered lights here and there. No windows and an entrance to a kitchen on the left. Two people sit at the bar. The bartender stands behind the counter. All eyes turn on me.

I tap out a cigarette from the pack I take from my jacket pocket and light up. I know it is Allen sitting on a bar stool. He is slouched over. He is facing me, but his glassy look makes me think he is seeing passed me.

I puff out some smoke and my adrenaline starts humming. My body is prepping itself to kick some ass. I crush out my cigarette on the dirty floor and approach him. His broken fingers are taped together haphazardly; his face is swollen from where I punched him yesterday.

"You got anything for me, Allen?" I say sinisterly.

"He ain't got nothin' for you," the bartender answers.

"I'd like Allen to answer me," I return.

"He's so fucked up, he can barely talk," the bartender says.

"That's not good, Allen," I say, approaching.

Allen's glassy unfocused eyes struggle to find me through his long stringy brown hair. I reach out and yank him off the stool with one hand. He doesn't even struggle.

"Hey, you Delisi's kid?" the bartender asks.

I am taken aback by his question. I am still holding Allen up, my fists clenched in his filthy clothes. Nonna would have a fit if she saw this guy.

"No, I work for him," I lie. What's this guy's angle? No one should know my name except the Boss. I hope Pop has done his due diligence. This could get ugly. The Chicago underground is three times the size of Palmetto's.

I drag a limp Allen through the bar area to the kitchen. I kick the swinging door open and spot an outside door. I tug him through it out into an alley. The alley stinks worse than the bar. Holy Shit!

I toss him to the ground. I rifle through his pockets. I don't find a thing, not even lint. Nothing.

"Okay, Allen. Where do you get the cash to get high?" I ask.

He doesn't answer. I kick him in the ribs. He moans.

"Hey! Allen! I asked you a question. Where do you get the money to get high?"

I circle him when he doesn't answer. I tap his shoulder with my foot. He mumbles unintelligently.

"Allen. I'm asking one last time," I say. "Where do you get the fuckin' money?!" I yell it this time.

"No...money..." he slurs.

"What?" I ask.

"No...money..." he slurs again.

"Sorry, Allen, wrong answer," I say, and I swoop down and grab his leg and twist it with a hard jerk. SNAP! "I'll be back in forty-eight hours. You better have something for me."

I leave him lying in the grubby alley. I light another cigarette as I make my way to the car. My phone vibrates. A text from Vito:

Why am I in a fucking college English class?!

I guess Megan convinced them to hang out with Troy in his classes. I smile at the thought.

*****

Megan:

The sights and sounds of the English seminar flow over me. This is so awesome. The room is a lecture hall with stadium seating. We are in the back by the door. Vito wouldn't let us sit any further down. He said we had to be where he could see the door. Whatever! I am just happy to be there.

Erin is hanging on every word the professor says. The class is studying The Odyssey. I have read it before, but the points and inferences the class is discussing shocks me. I learned amazing things in just the short time we had been there.

Vito is playing a game on his phone, not caring at all about the discussion. The girl sitting in the row in front of us keeps turning around. She is trying to be nonchalant about watching Vito. He doesn't even notice. Troy nudges me.

"More muscle than brain," he says, gesturing to Vito.

"I heard that, chooch," Vito whispers, never moving his eyes from his game. "Tonio is on his way back," he adds.

My heart does a little fluttery thing at Vito's words. Awesome! I can't wait to tell him about our day.

The professor dismisses the class, and Vito jumps up ready to bolt. But he has to wait for us, obviously, so he's getting antsy.

"Come on. I'm starving," he says.

"There's a great little sandwich shop on the main Green," a sweet voice says. It's the girl that was sitting in front of us.

"Yeah," Troy says. "Let's go there. You can get Falafel."

"Falafel? What the fuck is that?" Vito asks.

"It's fried chick peas," the girl answers.

"Hmmm, that sounds friggin' appetizing," Vito says sarcastically.

"Cool. It would be great to try something different," I say.

Vito adds, "English class and Falafel...what a terrific day! Yipp-fuckin'-ee!"

"I'm Darla, by the way." Darla sticks her hand out to shake with Vito.

"Hi," he says disinterested, shaking her hand. Erin does a dramatic eye-roll, and we file out of the lecture hall towards the Green.

Troy, Erin, and I debate about the lecture on The Odyssey while Darla tries to keep a conversation going with Vito. He just isn't interested. He throws out one word answers, and continues to play with his phone as he's walking. Vito has a reputation as a player. This girl is attractive. What's his problem? She's a college girl, no less. I think that would be a pretty big score for him.

We sit at a table in the corner big enough to fit all of us. Darla joins us. The waitress comes over, and we all order a falafel wrap with fries except Vito. He orders a chicken sandwich.

I observe my sister, and she is slowly turning back into her old self. Thank God! Antonio is amazing. That talk with her this morning must have really helped.

Troy tells us about some of the crazy things that have happened to him in college. We laugh at his animated stories. Troy could always make me laugh, even Vito chuckles every once in a while.

"Should we bring a sandwich back for Antonio?" I suggest.

"Who's Antonio?" Darla asks.

"He's my boyfriend," I answer, I sense Troy stiffening a little at my reply.

"Not that shit," Vito says. "Get him something normal."

"How about ham and cheese?" I ask.

"Yeah, that's good," he says.

The waitress comes over, and I order a to-go sandwich for Antonio. Darla is talking to Vito but now he is flat out ignoring her. He reaches in his wallet, pulls out a hundred dollar bill, and hands it to the waitress.

Darla's eyes go wide.

"Take it all out of that," he says.

"Dude," Troy says. "I can pay for my own lunch."

Vito puts up a hand. "I know you can. I jus' wanna get out of here and take a nap." He scrubs his hands down his face.

"What's the matter?" Erin asks, cockily. "Didn't sleep well last night?"

"As a matter-of-fact, no, I didn't," he replies. "This little redhead I was sleeping next to kept hogging the covers."

I didn't miss a beat. Vito was saying he slept in Erin's room again. WHY?!

I give him a knowing stare, and the waitress puts a brown paper bag and Vito's change on the table.

"Thank you. Come again."

"Well. Sleep in your own bed then," Erin retorts. "I'm going to the ladies room."

"What was that about?" Troy asks.

"It's nothing I can't handle," Vito says.

"Megan?" Troy asks me.

"She's been having some bad dreams," I say.

"So? Why does Vito the bodyguard need to sleep in her bed?" Troy asks vehemently.

"Troy... She sleeps better when someone is with her."

"Why don't you sleep with her?" he asks.

"I am not having this conversation with you," I say. "It's truly none of your business." His brother cheated on my sister. I don't want anything getting back to Connor about Erin's nightmares. Connor can wonder and wallow in self-pity for all I care.

Darla was listening to this conversation like she was watching a tennis match, back and forth.

"Oh... I get it. So you can screw Antonio!"

Troy's words slap me in the face. But I don't get a chance to even come back with a response because Vito's face is mere inches from Troy's face.

"Don't. You. Ever. Make. It. Sound. Like. She's. A. Whore. Again." Anger and intensity radiate off Vito. His fists are clamped by his sides. In a very low voice, that would frighten Superman, he finishes, "Erin thrashes and kicks when she sleeps. Antonio doesn't want Megan to get hurt. Got it asshole?" He pokes Troy in the chest.

Darla steps way back from us, way back. Erin is coming from the bathroom trying to figure out the scene. Vito's hand goes behind Erin, and he gently guides us towards the exit leaving Troy and Darla standing with gaping expressions.

It was going so well with Troy. I thought we were overcoming this rivalry/jealousy thing. I step outside; the sun feels warm for October. I need to feel it. The warmth helps to cleanse the ickiness away. Troy's hurtful words replay in my mind. I hope Vito doesn't repeat them to Antonio.

"Come on," Vito orders, and we walk back in silence to the suite.

Chapter 9

Gabroni (ga-bro-nee): dumbass

Megan:

Antonio comes through the door an hour or so later. The pang of truly missing him hits me. The day was so busy and filled with more drama. Vito had gone to lie down in his own room, and Erin and I were watching T.V.

"Hey, how's the college girls?" he asks joking.

"Good," I say getting up to greet him with a kiss.

"Where's Vito?" he asks.

"Vito decided to lie down. Today took a lot out of him."

Knock, knock...

Antonio swings around his hand immediately goes to the gun at his waist. He motions for me to move over. I do. Erin stays frozen on the couch.

He looks through the peephole. "It's Troy. And that kid from last night," he says. I bristle with anxiety. What are they doing here? Antonio puts the gun back and opens the door, checks the hallway, and allows them inside.

"What's going on?" Antonio asks. He has no clue about what went on little while ago. If I could read Troy's mind, he is worried whether or not Vito had talked to Antonio.

Troy looks around the room. "Where's your sidekick?"

"Sleeping in the other room," Antonio answers.

"I was wondering if I could speak to Megan...alone?" Troy asks.

"Sure," Antonio says, right when I'm about ready to protest his vehement 'No!'

Jake stands near the doorway. Antonio turns to him.

Jake puts his hands behind his back, grinning. "I'm just here to see how Erin's doing after last night. See? I'll keep my hands behind my back," he says, joking.

Erin is blushing. Jake smiles at her. He walks towards the couch with his hands clasped behind his back. Erin giggles.

"Megan?" Troy's voice is soft. "Can I talk to you?"

"Umm, sure. Let's go in here," I point and walk Troy into the unused living room in Antonio and Vito's suite.

I stand there. I'm not going to be the one to say anything. He hurt me.

"Meg, I'm sorry," Troy says sincerely. "That was way out of line. I don't want anything to mess up our friendship. I keep screwing up and I'm sorry."

"What's goin' on out there?" Vito calls out groggily.

"Nothing!" I yell back. I reach for his door and close it.

Troy continues, "...and I'm really sorry about Erin. My brother's a dick. Erin is a great kid, and she didn't deserve that."

"Thanks Troy. I appreciate it. I don't want to ruin our friendship either."

"Jake's sorry too, about last night. It was just messed up. Meg, he really is interested in Erin. Call off the hounds!" he says is a fake British accent. "He's a nice guy."

"He seems really nice." I pause. "It would be great for her to make some new friends. Take her mind off things. Antonio voiced his opinion on Jake last night... He's uncomfortable with Jake's age, being in college, etcetera." No need to repeat what Antonio said and how he said it. "She's been through a lot. Being friends is fine, but I have to agree with him."

"He's not looking for marriage. He just wants to get to know her. Besides, Jake is a 'young-un', he's seventeen." Troy adds dismissing my apprehension. "He graduated a year early and is getting groomed for the football team. He's good. I bet he makes second string quarterback in a couple of years."

"Really? That's awesome."

"Are we good?" Troy asks. "I'll work on not being an ass." Troy gives me sad, puppy dog eyes.

I smile. "Yeah, we're good."

"Great, let me make it up to you. Jake and I want to take you all out to dinner and a movie. Ladies pick."

"That's nice, but let me check with everyone," I say.

"Come on, Chewbacca paid for lunch. Let me do this."

Vito's door flies open, he's got tired-but-hasn't-slept written all over him. "Aw! Boohoo, you're sorry. Wah wah... You're lucky you apologized. Now let me fuckin' sleep!"

"Don't you have little furry people to save on a planet far, far, away?" Troy asks mockingly. Vito slams his door shut.

Troy yells to the closed door, "And you really need to work on your fake crying! I didn't believe you for a second!"

Back in my suite, Jake and Erin are watching T.V. and talking. Antonio is on his phone in the corner. He hangs up when he sees us.

"Troy and Jake want to take us out tonight," I announce.

"Oh yeah, where?" Antonio asks. Erin and Jake look over at me.

"Dinner and a movie."

"It's ladies pick because I'm an asshole," Troy says with mirth.

"Well then, it will always be ladies pick, because you'll always be an asshole," Antonio quips back. He walks over to me and gives me a peck on the lips. "Whatever the girls want is fine with me."

We meet Troy and Jake at a restaurant just outside South Bend. Italian food is out because I didn't want Vito keeling over in horror over its less-than-authentic taste and presentation.

We go to a burger place. It's one of those that offer at least twenty different toppings and types of burgers. The menu is huge. We are all crowded around a round table by the bar.

I am sitting next to Antonio. His hand is stroking my leg while his other one is holding his menu. Little tingles shoot up and down my thigh. I silently hope that we can be alone again tonight. I glance at him. His dark eyes immediately find mine. We are both hyper-aware of each other.

Troy's on the other side of me talking, but it takes a minute for it to register.

"Huh, what?" I ask turning his way. Antonio silently laughs.

"I asked if you are coming to class again tomorrow?"

Vito breaks in, "Tonio, please tell me you don't have to go anywhere tomorrow."

"No, I'm good."

Jake is sitting next to Erin and says, "You could come to Western Civ. with me tomorrow if you want?"

"No, she can't." Vito says quickly.

"Yes, I can," Erin says.

"Uh...no. You. Can't." Vito says back harshly.

"Yes. I. Can!" Erin flips back.

"Whoa, enough," Antonio says. "Sorry Jake. One of us has to be with them at all times. Vito went today to class. I'll go tomorrow."

Erin sits back and pouts at Antonio's words.

Jake leans in and whispers in her ear. A big smile crosses her face and she laughs. My sister is clearly enjoying the attention.

Without warning, Vito reaches out and jerks Jake away from her. A stunned Jake asks, "Dude, what is your problem?"

"Whatever you need to say to her can be said in front of all of us." Vito lets him go.

"I was just jokin' with her. I was asking if she was a princess that escaped from her castle with her guards. Geez! Get a grip."

Vito looks back at his menu stone-faced. What is with him? He is so intense. I thought Antonio was, but Vito might even surpass him.

Everyone is quiet. Antonio breaks the silence by announcing that he's having the Texas burger.

"Yeah, that sounds good, but I think I'm having the Bleu Cheese one," I say. "What are you going to have, Erin?"

"I don't know. Why don't you ask Vito what I can have?" Erin says childishly, trying to make a point. And I kind of can't blame her. She seems to be trying to pull herself out of her funk, but Vito is really making it a struggle for her.

Vito doesn't miss a beat, "You're having the All-American minus the onions. If you're a really good girl, I'll let you pick the kind of cheese you want."

Everyone at the table just stares at Vito.

"Vito? Erin? Outside!" Antonio commands. The two of them reluctantly get up and follow Antonio to the exit. I'm left with Jake and Troy at the table.

"Sorry," I say to Jake. "Vito's a little..." I can't find the right word.

"Psycho?" Jake finishes for me.

"Well..."

"Is he a brother, a step-brother, cousin?" he asks.

"No..."

"He's from Megan's neighborhood," Troy says.

"He takes what he's asked to do very seriously," I say.

"And what was he asked to do?" Jake asks intently.

"Ummm, look after her," I respond. "By my dad."

"I wasn't going to bring this up, but these guys act like gang members."

Troy laughs.

"No, they're not in a gang," I clarify.

*****

Antonio:

"What is up with you?" I ask Vito.

"Nothing. I'm not sitting in class with Jake the Jackass."

"Hey! Don't call him that. He's nice," Erin says.

I rub my temple. "This is fuckin' ridiculous. Vito, back the fuck down. You." I point to Erin. "Order your own damn food, and don't give Jake any ideas 'cause they're not happening."

"My father just wants you to watch out for us, not run our lives!"

"Oh!" I say, clipping the word. "Remember what I said this morning, watch the attitude. I don't know this guy. I need to feel him out more."

"At least my father let me date Connor!"

"Yeah, and look what that got you! If I ever get my hands on the fuckin' weasel, you won't even recognize him!" That shuts her down. She knows I'm right. "Everybody take it down a notch. Let's enjoy our dinner and try to relax."

We made it to the movie theater early. The line is long. We waited a few minutes. Jake is trying to lighten the mood. He kept waving his fingers at Erin.

"Oh no, Erin. I might touch you, look out." He makes her laugh, that was cool. After a few more minutes, I was getting antsy. I nod to Vito. He knows what I want to do.

My arms are wrapped around Megan's waist, so I shuffle us forward. We walk to the ticket collector by the entrance to the theaters.

"What are we doing?" Megan asks.

"Going to the movies."

Jake, Troy, and Erin follow. They are immersed in their own conversation.

Vito slips the ticket collector a hundred. The guy pockets it and unhooks the burgundy rope to let us through.

Jake asks, "What are we doing?"

I give him my patented, Shut the fuck up look.

The theater is empty. Megan let Jake pick the movie. I think she felt bad about the scene at the restaurant. It's an action movie. At least, I don't have to see a chick flick, although I would if it would please Megan.

"Can I say something without getting my ass kicked?" Jake asks.

"That depends," I say.

"You guys are crazy. We have illegally gained entrance to the movie theater and it cost twice the amount than if we waited in the line."

"And?" I say.

"I'm just pointing out the obvious for my own benefit," Jake responds. Smart guy.

I sit next to Megan and lift the arm rest between us so I can snuggle her closer. I think I'm addicted to her. When she's around, I can't stop touching her. I need it like a drug.

"Hey," Troy says. "We're supposed to be treating you. Not the other way around."

"You paid for dinner, we're good."

I can't keep my attention on the movie. My hands roam over Megan. I am thankful that it is so dark in here.

"I think you need to go to the bathroom," I whisper in her ear.

"I do?" she asks.

"Yup, right now."

I stand and pull her up with me, her hand in mine. I lean over to Vito. "I'm taking Megan to the bathroom."

He waves me away.

We head out the door. I scan the hallway theaters looking for an empty one.

"This way."

I open the door to a dark theater. No one is in here. I immediately grab her by the waist. I take her by surprise and crush my lips against hers. She tastes so fuckin' good! She holds onto me and gives just as good as she's getting.

"I hope that movie is over soon. I want to take you back to the suite and do everything we did last night all over again," I tell her and she melts in my arms.

Chapter 10

Culo (cool-yo): ass

Antonio:

The next couple of days continue like this. We go to some classes and watch movies on T.V. Vito cooks some nights, some nights we go out. Occasionally, Troy and Jake come over.

The drama seems to have subsided, though. This trip is like a vacation for me. Every chance I can steal to be alone with Megan I do. Every morning we wake up entwined. Erin has to know that we're sleeping together, but she doesn't say anything.

I go find Allen again, and he still has nothing. I leave him writhing on the ground in pain in the same alley. Simple. Done. This druggie only has two more days, and I'll have to call Pop.

Unexpectedly, I wake up the following morning with a cold. I feel like shit. I haven't been sick in ages, and it sucks. My throat is sore, my eyes hurt, and my nose is completely stuffed. My immediate thought is I hope Megan doesn't catch it.

I come out of the bathroom hacking and coughing. Erin sees me and puts her fingers together as a cross.

"Stay away," she says.

"Yeah, yeah...I know," I say.

Vito hands me a cup of coffee.

"Dude you want me to go out and get some cold medicine?" he asks. "You fuckin' sound like shit."

"Nah, I'll be fine."

Megan comes out of the bedroom and comes up behind me and wraps her arms around.

"Oh my God, Antonio! You're burning up! Heat is pouring through your shirt."

I sit on the couch, and Megan puts her hand on my forehead. "You're really hot."

"Thanks," I say smugly.

"I'm serious. We have to get your fever down."

Vito grabs the keys to the Cayenne off the counter.

"I'll be back soon. Anyone else need anything?"

"Get some good tissues; you know the ones with the lotion," Megan says.

"Ay, I hate those. They feel like someone already blew their nose on them," I complain.

"They're the best for you, so your nose doesn't get raw," she says to me. And get some juice," she orders Vito.

"Is that your solution for everything, juice?" I tease her.

"Yes. Now back to bed."

"Only if you come with me," I whisper to her.

Megan puts me to bed. I can't fight her. She is just too cute.

"I'm going to see if I can find any tea," she says.

"Tea? Are you serious? How about I just have some of that cure-all orange juice? There's some in the fridge."

"Okay."

I'm definitely getting worse. My head is pounding and fuzzy, and my arms feel like lead. My muscles are slowly starting to ache. Megan comes back, and I drink the juice. It burns going down my throat.

I must have fallen asleep because the next thing I know, Megan is trying to wake me up. My shirt is off, and I feel a soggy washcloth on my head.

"Here take this," she says.

It's an electric blue liquid in a miniature cup.

"What is this shit?" I croak out.

"Just drink it. You'll feel better. It will help you to sleep."

"I was sleeping," I say, and gulp it down. "Ugh, that's gross. Are you trying to kill me?"

"Lie back," she says. "Your fever should go down soon."

I open my eyes and it has to be late afternoon. I check the time on my phone. It's after three. Wow, I slept a long time. I still feel horrible, but at least I slept. I try to get up, but the room spins. I quickly sit back on the bed.

"Megan!" I call out.

"I'm right here," she says, coming into the room. "How are you feeling?"

"Like shit."

"The medicine probably wore off. It's hours past the time to take it." She rests her hand on my forehead again. "But you're much cooler now, so it is helping. Let me get you another dose."

Vito comes in the room. "Shit, dude. You look like hell."

"Thanks."

"There is no way you can go after that runner tomorrow."

"I'll be fine," I say. "By tomorrow, I'll be a lot better."

Talking was exhausting me. It is wishful thinking believing I could take care of business tomorrow.

"Let me go," Vito says. "I can handle it. If he's got nothin', I'll rough him up and call your Pop."

My head is hurting again. "Okay. The address of the bar is in my phone. He's been there the last two times. His name is Allen. He has gross brown hair, brown eyes, and will be as high as a kite. If you don't find him there, just come back."

"Got it," Vito says. "Rest, man, I'll handle it."

Megan comes back in with the weird blue crap. I drink it. Erin comes in with soup. I take a couple of spoonfuls, but I'm just not hungry.

I recline on the bed again and close my eyes. I am out of it. Megan sits on the bed next to me, holding my hand.

Chapter 11

Malocchio (malo-kya): evil eye or curse

Antonio:

Blackness.

I try to open my eyes, but I can't fully wake myself up. I can tell that it's night by the darkness in the room, but my eyes won't cooperate and stay open. I hate not being in control. It's a weakness.

"Megan," I call out hoarsely.

No answer.

"Megan!" I call louder. Or I think it's louder. It could be a whisper for all I know. I'm so friggin' tired. I reach for my phone to check the time, but it's not there. "Megan!" I stagger to my feet to look for her. I need to know she's okay.

I reach the door and stumble trying to pull it open. In the faint light, I see Megan curled up on the couch. Thank God! I move towards Erin's room to check on her too.

Erin's alone sleeping peacefully. No Vito. Megan stirs on the couch.

"Antonio," she says in the darkness. "You feeling better?"

"No," I grunt. "No more of that blue shit. I can't think."

Megan gets up and helps me to the couch. "It got your fever down. I thought we were going to have to take you to the emergency room. Are you hungry?"

"No." I rest my head on the back of the couch. Megan touches my forehead and runs her fingers through my hair.

"Do you want some orange juice?" she asks. Even with my foggy brain, I have to laugh. For Christmas, I'm buying her a case of it.

"Okay, I'll have some orange juice," I say. "Where's my phone?"

"I'll get it. You got a text from your father. Vito handled it."

"Hmmm...?" I didn't process what she said. "Huh?"

Megan hands me my phone. I go to messages. A message from Pop:

Runner is at bar in Chicago tonight with supplier, go now!

"What the fuck is this?!" I yell.

"What do you mean?" Megan answers. "Vito saw the text and said he had to leave. He didn't say anything to me."

I jump up, slightly sobered.

"Vito's not here?" I ask. She shakes her head no.

An ugly dark panic settles in my stomach. Vito's not here! I dial Vito's cell. No answer. I spew orders to Megan.

"Call Troy right now and tell him to get over here. Don't tell him why. Then get Erin up. Both of you need to get dressed, now!"

I rush in to the bedroom and dress in sluggish, sloppy movements. Megan follows me.

"Antonio, what's wrong?"

"Vito could be in a lot of trouble. Don't think, Megan, just do it. Do what I tell you."

I check my gun, and get my shoes on. A minute later Megan comes back in the room.

"Troy's on his way over. Erin's dressing."

She runs to her clothes and changes into her jeans.

"Do we have regular aspirin, no funky shit?"

"Yeah, Vito got it yesterday, I'll grab it."

I stand and double check everything. In the living room, Megan hands me two aspirin and more orange juice, and I suck the pills down. I try Vito's cell again, nothing. A dizzy spell hits me, and I sit down on the couch to settle my spinning head.

I curse, "Where the fuck is Troy?"

"Antonio, what is wrong? I can't help if I don't know what's wrong."

I look up and see two Megan's. My vision is blurry.

"I've been set up," I say. "Pop doesn't text. I always speak to my pop directly for instructions."

"So who sent that text?" she asks, horrified.

"I don't know. Someone either hacked Pop's phone or used it."

Knock, knock...

I get up and the room spins again. Megan notices.

"Sit down, it has to be Troy," she orders.

"Check the peephole first," I tell her.

"It's Troy."

Troy comes in, and I attempt to stand again. I do a little better.

"I need your keys," I command.

"What?"

"Don't ask. Just give me the keys." I hold my hand out. He puts them in my palm. "I am dropping you all off at your dorm. Don't answer the door unless it's me. Got it?"

"Delisi? What's going on? You look like death warmed over," Troy says.

"Antonio, you can't possible drive," Megan states.

"I have to find Vito, and I need to do it now."

Erin is in the doorway to her room. "We should all go," she says quietly. "You're sick, Antonio."

"I'll drive to the dorm, and we can figure it out in the car," Troy suggests.

We pile in his car. The night air feels good, I'm burning up again. He drives us to O'Neill hall.

"Antonio, let me drive to where ever you need to be," Megan says.

"No, it's too dangerous."

"Troy can stay with Erin. You are in no condition to drive," Megan says.

"No!"

"Everyone out! I gotta go," I command again.

"Antonio, be reasonable. I'm not getting out of this car. I'm driving you."

"She's right Antonio, you look like shit."

The energy I exerted to even get dressed and in the car was debilitating. I don't even think I could hold my gun up.

"Erin? Troy? Out!" I order. "Megan drives." Erin starts crying.

"Meg, be careful," she sniffs. "Find Vito."

Troy leads Erin towards the dorm. Megan gets in the driver's seat.

I pull up the GPS on my phone with the address.

"Get on the highway," I tell her.

*****

Megan:

My hands are shaking on the wheel. I am pushing Troy's car over the speed limit. The GPS is giving me directions from a muffled voice on Antonio's phone.

Antonio is resting, eyes closed.

"Where are we going?" I ask. "The sign back there said Chicago fifteen miles."

"Yeah. We're headed to Chicago to a seedy bar with a drug addict. It's a great place to take your girl to," he says sarcastically. "Give me your phone. I want to try Vito again."

I hand Antonio my phone. Vito doesn't pick up. Disgusted, he punches the dashboard. He dials his father. No answer. He tries his house phone. His mother answers.

"Ma, tell Pop someone either hacked his cell or used it." (pause) "No, I got a cold." (pause) "Yeah, I'll be fine. Listen, tell Pop what I said, and I'm forwarding him a text. Vito left hours ago. I'm going to find him." (pause) "I will. Tell Pop I'll call him when I find Vito." (pause) "Love you, bye."

Antonio ends the call, and reaches into the back of his jeans to pulls his gun out and lays it on the center console.

I flinch at the sight of the gun. I am reminded of only last week when I had to handle one — a gun that belonged to someone who wanted to kill my family.

"Megan, you need to listen to me. Where we're going is dangerous. Do not leave this car no matter what. Keep it running and drive away if you have to. Stay low and doors locked. Understand?"

"Yes," I answer.

We approach the city. Tall high rise buildings surround us. We travel under overpass after overpass. The lights from the city illuminate the inside of the car. There are more cars on the road here. Despite the time, the city is awake.

The GPS directs me down a side street. Antonio sits up now. The street is littered with papers and trash. There are lampposts every so many feet, but only half of them are working. The towering buildings on either side of the street make it even darker. I strain to see with just the headlights of the car.

"Over there," Antonio points.

I roll to a stop by the curb under one of the only working street lights. The car is still running.

"I'm going in that door," he points. "Get down."

I slouch down in my seat.

"Lower," he orders.

I move lower. It's uncomfortable. He reaches for his gun and takes it.

"Lock the doors as soon as I'm out. Anything happens, just drive the fuck away. In your phone is that address I gave you. You remember? Where to meet if we get separated?"

"Yes," I answer.

"I love you, Megan." He cocks the gun checking it one last time, and flings open his door to go into the bar.

Moments tick by, and my heart is hammering at an extreme rate. My phone rings, and I jump. I silently pray it's Vito.

It's Troy.

"Hello."

"Megan! It's good to hear your voice. I was trying not to call, but I couldn't take it anymore. The wait is killing me. Your sister's been crying non-stop since you left. Are you okay?"

"Yeah."

"Where are you?"

"Umm...I can't tell you, but I'm okay. I'm waiting for Antonio, he's in some bar."

"Wait a second. Erin wants to talk to you."

"Meg? Did you find Vito?" she asks through tears.

"No, honey, not yet," I say.

BANG! The car shakes. What was that?

Dread crawls up my throat and strangles my voice. I can't see anything from my position. Something hits the car again. BANG! I am paralyzed.

"Meg? Are you there?"

I am just about to give myself a mental pat on the back for not screaming, in this fear-inducing situation, when a face pops up in the windshield right above me.

"AHHHHHH!" I screech so loud, I hurt my own ears. I don't think, I just do, like Antonio said. I drop the phone, sit up, and throw the car into drive. I slam my foot down on the gas. A tha-thump sound comes from the side of the car. Holy Shit! I hit someone with Troy's car!

At the cross street at the end of the road, I swing the car around in a perfect three-sixty. Danica Patrick would be proud.

I am now facing the other way. The headlights illuminate a person staggering in the street. I inch the car forward to get a better look. Oh my God! It's Dino! What is he doing here in Chicago?

He limps forward towards the car and flips me off. Uh, excuse me? You're the one who scared me within an inch of my life, asshole! I want to yell at him, but something doesn't sit right with me. What's he doing? Why is he here? Where is Antonio?

I faintly hear my name being called. I look all around me. My hands are clutching the steering wheel, and my foot is itching to know my next move. My phone is still on. I reach down for it, using a split second, not wanting to take my eyes off a stumbling Dino.

"Hello."

"Holy shit, Meg! What is going on?!" Troy is shouting.

"Ummm...right now? Nothing I can't handle. But that could change at any second."

"Meg! Get out of there!"

"No! I'm not leaving Antonio," I yell, my heart thumping and sweat starts to form above my lip.

"Meg, Antonio would want you to leave!" Troy pleads.

"No. Never leave a man behind."

"What?! Are you in a fuckin' Army recruiting commercial? Get the hell out of there!"

I put the phone down without turning it off. Dino stops advancing. We are staring each other down. The lights from the car give his appearance an eerie glow. Then a horrific thought occurs to me, not only horrific, but sick and immoral.

I could mow Dino down with this car, and call my father to take care of the mess. I have that kind of power. My dad could make Dino go away, and no one would know. My thoughts curdle my stomach.

The door to the bar flies open, and a body rolls out onto the sidewalk. I am momentarily stunned. The body pops up in a fluid motion and fires a shot at Dino. Oh, it's Vito!

Excitement at seeing him surges through me. He scans the road. Dino is on the ground clutching his leg. He's been hit with a car and shot. Wow, that's gotta suck!

Vito sees me, and I wave like crazy. I pull the car forward to the door. Antonio is right behind Vito exiting the bar. I scramble to unlock the doors.

They jump in the backseat. Vito yells at me, "GO! GO!"

I slam my foot on the gas again. The tires screech, and I miss Dino lying in the road by mere inches.

"Fuck! Fuck! Fuck!" Antonio coughs out. "Are you okay?" He is hanging over the console from the backseat. "Megan?" He shakes me as I drive. "Are you okay?"

"Yeah, I think so. What happened?"

"It's Prazzo! It's the fuckin' Prazzos!" Antonio yells through coughs and pants.

In the rearview mirror, I see Vito breathing heavy too, shaking his head. The elation at the fact that they're okay overwhelms me. Tears start rolling down my cheeks, but I'm not upset, I'm happy. Antonio crawls over into the front seat.

"You did good, honey. You did good," he repeats. He leans over and kisses my cheek. "Don't cry."

"I'm just so happy you're okay," I say between tears. I don't know what I would do without you."

"Don't cry, we're okay," he reassures me.

"Antonio?"

"Yeah."

Sniffling, I say, "I feel like we're Bonnie and Clyde."

"Nope, just Antonio and Megan."

I hear a faint voice calling again, 'Antonio!'

It's Troy. I gesture to the phone with a trembling hand. Antonio picks it up.

"Yeah."

"What the hell was that all about?!" I can hear Troy yelling through the phone.

"Everything is fine. Vito's here."

"What happened?"

"There is an address programmed into Erin's phone. Take her to that address."

"You've got my fuckin' car!"

"Then borrow one," Antonio says.

"It's 3:15 am! Where would you like me to get one?"

"You're on a college campus. There must be a party going on or some geeks studying at this time of night." Antonio shuts the phone off. "Shit, I need more aspirin."

"What about our car?" Megan asks.

"If there is anything left to it, Vito and I will try to get it tomorrow. We'll have to get a new rental anyway."

"We're going to have to check out this car in the morning. I hit something with it. I want to get it fixed for Troy if there's a dent or a broken light," I tell him.

"What did you hit?" Vito asks.

"Dino."

"What?"

Antonio looks at me dumbfounded. "You hit Dino with the car?"

"Yes."

"On purpose?" Vito asks, chuckling.

"Well, sort of."

"Honey, what do you mean?" Antonio asks, as he plugs in a new address to the GPS on his phone.

"He scared me. He hit the car a few times and jumped on the windshield. I threw the car in drive and took off. I'm pretty sure I hit him, because he was limping. Then Vito shot him, so I definitely think he's down for the count."

Together, the two of them start laughing, hard. Vito could barely catch his breath.

"You better watch out for this one, Tonio! She's got the devil in her," Vito says, still laughing. "Mannegia! That's some funny shit."

I freeze. Vito's words trigger my mother's haughty expression anytime Antonio is mentioned. He's got the devil in him! I shake it off. Dino was coming after me. I defended myself. I wasn't doing anything, but waiting for Antonio.

We zig and zag through the streets to the highway. Antonio is definitely suffering with his fever.

"So are you going to tell me what happened in there?" I ask softly.

"Let's just say, when Pop hears about this, Palmetto's inhabitants list is going to be short by a whole family."

Chapter 12

Stugatz (stu-got-s): got nothing

Antonio:

The last thing I wanted to tell Megan was that we barely made it out of there. Luigi Prazzo wants leverage over Pop. He hired some dumbasses here in Chicago to kidnap me. Well, they took the wrong guy.

I should have known that Allen was a set up. There is no way he had any money. Luigi's goons must have kept the guy drugged up enough to be out of it and compliant. They used him. They knew the guy owed Pop a lot of money.

Luigi and Dino want to 'dethrone' my Dad. And they planned to go through me.

The whole frittata with Sommersville last week was a set up too. They broke the truce. It all makes sense now. We were walking into a trap. A trap that backfired. Either Sommersville got yellow and ran, or the plan just failed, I'll never know. That bullshit scene with Dino in a knife fight must have been part of the set up too.

The Prazzo's must have promised Sommersville something my pop wouldn't give them. Kidnapping me in Chicago was their new plan. I get it now. The Chicago underground is so large; it was probably easy to set this whole thing up.

They're exposed now though. The mole is out. Now it's kill or be killed.

"How much further?" Megan asks me.

"Another couple of miles to the hotel. Vito will check us in under a fake name, and then you and I will go in a back entrance. I don't even want the concierge to see you," I say.

We arrive and Vito goes in. A few minutes later he comes out with two room keys. The hotel is just a mid-class in which you get a coffee and muffin in the morning and they call it breakfast.

Megan drives around to the back, and Vito uses a key card to open the door. I call Troy.

"When you get here, drive to the back and call me, we'll let you in," I say and hang up.

The rooms are small and clean, with two double beds each. They are adjoined by a door in the middle like our suites. Vito and I check both rooms and the hallway.

My phone rings. It's Troy. I go back to the entrance and let them in. My headache is getting worse.

"Thanks for bringing her," I say, but my words are garbled because Erin throws herself at me. I hold her tight. I reassure her by telling her, "It's okay."

I take her hand and lead her to our rooms. Troy follows behind us.

Megan opens the door, and Erin extends to hug her. They embrace. Megan's eyes are tearful, while Erin's are streaming. I gently force us into the room, wanting to close the door.

Erin releases her sister, and sees Vito sitting on the bed. She runs to him and flings her arms around his neck.

"I was so scared!" she says. "I'm sorry!" she wails.

Vito gently shifts her on to his lap, and lets her hold him around the neck.

"Shhh, everyone is fine,"

"I'm sorry," she says again.

"For what, babe? You didn't do anything," he asks perplexed, rubbing her back.

"Yes, I did. I was a brat to you. I'm sorry."

Vito laughs, "No, I've been hard on you, I'm sorry."

Erin snuggles into Vito's arms and closes her eyes.

"Well, all I can say is that this evening aged me about five years," Troy says. He wraps his arm around Megan. "I was so worried. I could hear stuff going on, but couldn't do anything. It was so damn frustrating."

The tiny hotel room is crowded with all of us in it. I sit on the desk in the corner.

"Troy, if you want to stay here for the rest of the night, you can. We're all tired."

Every time I blink my eyes, they burn. I definitely still have a fever. The adrenaline has faded. I am struggling again, I need to sleep.

Vito lifts Erin, and lays her down on one of the beds. He goes over and locks the outside door to the room.

"Come on, Troy," Vito says. "I want the bed on the left," he yawns.

Megan is quiet and pulls the covers down on the opposite bed from Erin. I lay next to her. My eyes close, they sting for a minute, and then I'm asleep.

*****

The next morning, I wake up first. Everyone else is sleeping. My mouth tastes bitter. Dwelling on the Prazzos betrayal is useless. They made their bed, and now they have to lie in it.

It's time to plan our next move. We could go back to the campus and check things out. Maybe move to new suites. I question whether or not they know we're at Notre Dame. Sommersville and the Prazzos kept leading me to Chicago. Or maybe we should check into a hotel near the campus.

I drift in and out of consciousness. Megan shifts on the bed, and I wake again. She rolls over and snuggles up to me. I wrap my arms around her.

"How are you feeling?" she asks drowsily.

"Okay. My head is still a little cloudy."

"You feel cooler today. I think your fever broke."

"Good. I don't have time to be sick right now," I say. "I gotta call Pop soon."

"I'm sorry about this whole thing," Megan says.

"Not as sorry as they're gonna be."

I reach for my phone and dial Pop. He answers on the first ring.

"Tonio! What the fuck!" my father yells.

"Hey, Pop," I say calmly.

"What the hell is going on? Is everyone alright?"

"Yeah. I was set up. We got out of there."

"The Prazzo's are going to wish they never stepped foot in Palmetto. They touch one hair on your head and I'm gonna serve their asses for Thanksgiving dinner." Pop sighs. "You gotta keep your head straight, Tonio."

"Yeah, Pop."

"Patrick is right here with me. He's gonna take care of some things. I need you to stay low."

"We will, Pop."

"Patrick wants to talk to Megan."

I hand Megan the phone. "It's your dad," I say.

Megan takes the phone. Her eyes are conflicted.

"Hello." (pause) "No, we're okay." (pause) Her eyes fill with tears. "It was scary." (pause) "Some hotel Vito found." (pause) "Erin has been very upset." Megan goes to the bathroom and shuts the door to talk to her dad.

I stand by the bathroom door waiting. A few minutes go by. I hear the door click and see the knob turn. I can't wait anymore, so I push the door a little.

I make my way into the bathroom. I shut the door, and pick Megan up and sit her on the counter. My phone is in her hand, when I grab her face and kiss her, hard. I push her legs apart and stand between them, getting closer. I reach over and lock the bathroom door, never breaking away from her. She tosses the phone on the counter and squeezes me to her. Her legs wrap around my waist, and we are molded to each other. The kisses are fierce and wanting.

I strip off her shirt and stand back an inch to look at her. She must have shed her bra in the middle of the night. Her skin is hot cinnamon candy. Her beautiful face is flushed, and her eyes dance with desire.

Megan's fingers slid up my sides, taking my shirt with them. She lifts my shirt over my head and pulls me close. I take her mouth again. I run my fingers through her hair, over her shoulders and down her chest. Holy shit! This girl is going to kill me.

I reach over and turn on the shower. We strip each other out of our clothes. When the water is steaming, I put her under the spray. I use the complimentary soap and lather my hands. I rub my soapy hands all over her body, slowly. Megan moans, and her head falls back.

The water drenches her red hair making it a dark crimson. I spin her around, so her back is to me, and continue my leisurely sudsy adventure.

If I had to pick perfect moments in my life, they would all be from the time when I took this incredible girl to the riverside and kissed her. Rubbing my hands all over her body, makes me want to profess my undying love, and slap a ring on her finger.

So I do what I can do. "I love you so much, Megan," I whisper in her ear. She turns around, looks me in the eye, and says, "I love you too, Antonio." And I kiss her again.

*****

I dress, and leave Megan in the bathroom to finish putting her clothes on. On the floor by her side of the bed, I find her bra. I grab it and take it to the bathroom for her.

Vito pokes his head in through the adjoining door. Looks immediately at Erin, and then finds me with his eyes by the bathroom.

"What's next?" he asks. I shake my head at him in a give-me-a-few gesture.

Facing the hard reality of the Prazzo's disloyalty to the family prickles at my skin, no matter how much I tell myself that this is their choice, it doesn't make it sting any less. But I have to live by my father's motto —Don't think, just do. What I have to do, right now, is figure out a plan, keep everybody out of the line of fire, and wait it out.

I decide to slip out of the room to go have a cigarette outside. I need to clear my head. The murkiness of being sick and the cold truth need to puff out of me in smoky circles.

It's chilly. The fall air is awesome though, crisp and clean. I'm not alone long. Troy comes out too.

We're quiet, not looking at each other.

"You got something to say to me?" I ask him, a stream of smoke caressing my words.

"What have you gotten her into?" he asks.

"Dude, I am going to say this once. This isn't all me. You don't know everything," I challenge.

"Then tell me." Troy says irritated.

"You know everything you need to know." I crush my cigarette with my fingers and toss it into the dewy grass. "Thanks for taking Erin last night. I've gotta move the girls. I'll keep you informed."

I move to go back into the hotel. Troy stops me with a hand on my arm. I look down at it. Why the fuck is he touching me? I could easily break his hand in about two seconds. But I don't.

"Do you love her?" he asks.

I lower my head, and I give Troy the honor of my confession. "Yes... I think I always have."

"Keep her safe," he says, and drops his hand. We walk back to the rooms in silence.

"Everyone, get your stuff together, we're leaving," I command when I enter the room. Erin is sitting up on the bed. Vito is sprawled on the other bed watching T.V. Megan is on her phone.

"We need to get the SUV and return it to the rental place. I want to find a new location to hold up. Vito, go downstairs and get another map."

Vito leaves. "Troy we need to borrow your car for a little while longer. Better yet, let me have the car you borrowed. We will take it back to the campus later."

Troy nods, and we switch keys. I notice that Megan is still on the phone. I walk over to her.

"Yeah," she says into the phone. "Okay, bye." She hangs up.

I don't have to ask because she tells me.

"That was my dad. I called him back..." Her expression is sad. "I just... I just...wanted to know why he and my mother haven't bothered to call."

"I'm sure she wants to, honey, but your dad probably told her not to," I say comfortingly.

"Dad said that, but I don't think it's true," she says.

"Come on, let's go. We have a lot to do today."

I take her hand and lead her towards the door.

Chapter 13

Feekanaz (Fee-ca-na-zz): sneaky or nosy person

Megan:

Antonio appears to be better this morning. Thank God! I don't like seeing him sick.

We go to pick up the Porsche from where Vito parked it a couple of blocks away from the bar. It appears fine. Antonio pulls up on the opposite side of the street from it. No one touched it. I find that very lucky considering the neighborhood.

Antonio is driving Troy's borrowed car. Vito gets out with the rental keys in hand.

"We'll meet you back at the campus," Antonio says to Vito. "Then we'll clean out the suites. I want to be at a new location before dinner."

"Got it," Vito says and gets out. He walks by the front of the car, and heads to the SUV. He gets the door open.

"I'm gonna go with him," Erin says, quietly from the backseat, as she opens her door.

Antonio takes a breath to speak, when we hear a small squeak. Erin falls out of the car onto the pavement.

"Ouch!" she says.

"Erin you okay?!" I call out to her.

"Yeah. I missed the curb and twisted my leg," she says, slumped on the sidewalk. Antonio opens his door to help her.

BOOM!

An explosion rocks the car. Pieces of fire-leaden debris land on the hood of the car and the surrounding area. A couple of spidery cracks form in the windshield. I am stupefied. I quickly look through the backseat to Erin's open door. Horrified at what I might see. I'm confused when I see the back of a leather jacket. Vito's leather jacket. He is crushing my sister to the pavement.

Antonio yells, "Move!"

Vito scoops up my sister in his arms and jumps in the backseat holding her to his chest. I am turned around, frantic, checking her for injuries, running my hands up and down her legs. My breath is shaky and my lip quivers, my body wants to cry, but I force it back.

"You okay?!" I ask panicked. Vito slams the door, Antonio revs the engine, and we screech away. I stare at the devastation that was once the car we were riding around in. Bile fills my throat. Vito was almost in there! He would have died! I clamp my eyes shut, wishing the unpleasant thoughts away.

"What the fuck?!" Vito yells.

"Had to be a timed detonator," Antonio says, weaving down the street. "Set to explode seconds after the door opens. He smashes his hand against the steering wheel. "They were waiting for us! That was way too fuckin' close. You okay?" he asks Vito.

"Yeah! I saw Erin fall and was going over to help. Then it blew the fuck up!"

Erin is whimpering in Vito's arms. I check her legs again, lifting her pants at the hem this time. Her ankle is swollen, and the skin on her leg is rubbed raw and bleeding.

"Buckle up, there's nothing you can do until we stop," Antonio says softly to me. I sit back in my seat, heart racing.

We are all quiet for a few minutes digesting the blast. I wipe a few stray tears from my cheeks. The hood of the car has black, charred marks all over it. Every once in a while a stray piece of wreckage flies up and over the top of the car. Antonio continues to speed away from Chicago.

"Ummm...guys?" Vito gets our attention. "Does anybody know the signs for shock?" His voice is odd. "I think Erin might have it." I turn around again. My sister is convulsing. Her body is tipping and rocking, rough and jagged. Her eyes are half-closed and empty. Vito is desperately trying to hold her steady.

Vito's words come out frightened, which I never have heard before.

"What do I do?!" he asks.

I am losing it too. I start to freak out.

I shout at her, "Erin! Look at me! Erin!" I get no response.

Antonio speaks calmly, "Vito cover her up. Megan, use my phone to find the nearest hospital."

Vito works to shrug out of his coat and hold Erin at the same time. I didn't smell it before, but I do now. Burnt leather. There are holes, burn holes, all over the back of Vito's coat. He lays it across a shaking Erin.

I set the navigation on Antonio's phone. "Two miles away," I say, taking off my coat too. I lay it over Erin's legs.

We spin into the parking lot by the emergency room. Antonio pulls right up to the door. He races around to help Vito with Erin.

"Run in, Megan," he says. "Tell them were coming."

I sprint through the automatic doors to the desk.

Through heaving breaths, I say, "My sister...she's convulsing... Help!

Chapter 14

Moosh a moosh (moo-sh-a-moo-sh): feeling yucky

Megan:

The nurse quickly rounds the desk to the doorway. Vito is carrying a shaking Erin. A stretcher immediately appears and Vito lays her down on it. She is shaking so much I'm afraid she'll fall off it. I'm about to say something, when a guy dressed all in white, pulls the sides up on the bed. He forces the bed to move and quickly rolls it through double doors into the main hospital.

The nurse turns to me. "Her name please," she asks.

"Erin. Erin..."

Antonio cuts me off. "Smith. Her name is Erin Smith," he finishes for me.

The nurse looks at him oddly, and hands me a clipboard. "Please fill out these forms."

We walk to the waiting area. From behind us, the nurse calls out, "Excuse me?" and rushes over to us. She touches Vito, and he flinches. I move behind him too. His back has severe burn marks scattered all across it. His shirt has more holes in it than a slice of Swiss cheese.

"Holy shit!" Antonio says.

"You need to come with me," the nurse tells Vito, matter-of-factly. He complies and follows her.

I hear her say "Name please." Vito responds with "Jimmy Smith." The nurse shakes her head, and leads Vito away.

A few minutes later, the nurse comes over with another set of forms. "Here you go. These are for Jimmy," she says.

Antonio takes them.

"How are they?" I ask.

"Are you family?" the nurse asks. Now what difference does that make, we're the ones that brought her in here.

"Yes, I'm Erin's sister," I say.

"And, are you Jimmy's sister too?" she asks skeptically.

"Yes." I don't even hesitate.

"Yeah, I can see the resemblance," her voice is light with sarcasm.

"Ma'am," Antonio breaks in. "How are they? Can we see them?"

"Erin is stabilized. We are giving her some fluids, and we gave her something to help her sleep. The doctor is dressing Jimmy's burn wounds."

"Can we see them?" Antonio asks again.

"In a little while," the nurse says and walks back to her desk.

"I gotta call Pop," Antonio tells me.

Antonio paces in front of me as he relays the events of the past hour to his dad. I am itching to call mine too. I want to tell him everything that has happened, but I don't call. I let Antonio handle it. His father will certainly tell mine.

"Pop, she's not right. This shit is messing with her mind. She is not handling things well at all." Antonio's conversation halts my own thoughts. "I think we're going to have to send her somewhere."

"What do you mean?" I ask, interrupting him.

"Hold on Pop," Antonio says. "Megan...when this is over, I think you are going to have to send her away."

"What?!" I can't believe what I'm hearing. "Are you saying you think we should have her committed?"

The nurse calls out, "You can go in now."

"Pop, I gotta go. I will call you after. We can discuss things then."

We follow the nurse, and she takes us to Vito. I push Antonio's words to the back of my mind. Vito is lying on his stomach on a hospital bed. He butt is covered with a thin sheet. His back is totally exposed. The burn marks glisten with medication. A few of them are covered in gauze and tape. The doctor is leaning over him examining his work.

"So," the doctor speaks continuing to tape up Vito's back. "Is anyone going to tell me what happened? I'm not getting anything from this guy."

"Fireworks," Antonio says.

"Fireworks?" the doctor repeats, digesting it.

I spot Vito's clothes on a chair in the corner, and think about the gun he is carrying. Will they call the police if they find it? I fold the clothes and tuck the gun in tightly, hiding it.

Vito grunts as the doctor puts more salve on his back. Antonio walks over to him to survey the damage him himself. "Is he gonna be okay?" Antonio asks the doctor.

"Yes. Definitely. He is going to be in a lot of pain though. Burns are a nasty thing. They'll be some scarring. If he follows the treatment routine, they shouldn't be too bad. It looks like he's fortunate though.

Facing the other way, he would have been burned all down his face and chest."

What the doctor doesn't know is that, if Vito stayed with the car and didn't come over to help my sister, he would be dead. Or, if Antonio was the one to get the Cayenne, it could be him lying there or worse. The thoughts of what could have been make my stomach heave.

I summon my inner strength, and put the putrid thoughts away in a compartment in my brain. We are all okay. We need to stay smart. Trust no one. Solve one issue at a time. This mantra gets going and sticks.

The doctor hands Antonio a large tube of cream. "Put this on him twice a day for two weeks. Keep the areas clean and bandaged until they start to scab over. Then leave them uncovered. He is going to be uncomfortable for a while. Watch for infection and fever. Bring him back if that happens." He rips off a small piece of paper and hands it to Antonio too. "For the pain."

Antonio and I nod.

"Thanks Doc," Antonio says.

The nurse gives Vito a scrub shirt. His has to be thrown out. We leave the room while Vito gets dressed. The nurse takes us to Erin's room.

Erin is lying on her back, eyes closed. She is sleeping. Her leg is raised up in a sling hanging from the ceiling. Her breathing has evened out. Her skin is pale, and she looks helpless and lost in the big utilitarian room.

I walk to the bed and cover Erin's limp hand with mine. Her leg is in a soft cast. There are some bandages on her arms, probably from falling. Vito landed on her to block the firebombs of debris. If Vito didn't shield my sister, she would be a blistering mess of serious burns.

"How long will she sleep?" Antonio asks the nurse.

"She'll need to stay here for observation."

Yikes. How are we going to leave her here? Vito comes in the room. He bypasses us and the nurse and stands over Erin's bed.

"Thank you," I choke out around a lump in my throat. Emotion overwhelms me. He is my sister's savior. I will forever be grateful for everything he has done for her over the past week.

Antonio puts his arm around me and squeezes. Deep images of roaring flames invade my mind. The explosion resonates and twists in dancing pictures.

I lean down and kiss my sister on her forehead. Vito takes Erin's hand. Antonio follows behind me and kisses her too.

Antonio whispers to me, "She's gonna be okay."

We gather in the hallway by Erin's door.

"How you doing, man?" Antonio asks Vito.

"It didn't hurt until Nurse Cratchit pointed it out," he says.

"I'm going to call Pop. She needs a private room somewhere in the hospital away from everyone. I'm gonna see if Pop has any guys around here he can call in a favor to."

Antonio calls his father and briefly tells him what he needs. Vito goes to the cafeteria for coffees. A few orderlies and other hospital staff shuffle in and out of Erin's room while we wait. After about twenty minutes, Erin's bed is rolled out of the emergency room she was in to the fourth floor. We ride in the elevator with her.

At the very end of the hall, they put her in a huge room. There is a couch and two chairs with a small refrigerator. It is decorated totally different than the rest of the hospital rooms we saw. It is like they mixed a lounge area and a hospital room.

Vito finds us on the fourth floor. He's carrying coffees in a tray in one hand and a vase of purple flowers in the other. He places them on the coffee table in front of me.

"They're beautiful," I say. "Maybe we should put them on the table by her bed."

Fussing is the only thing I know to do. I have flattened the blankets out on the bed. I organized her rolling tray with a water pitcher, tissues, and the remote for the T.V. Erin is sleeping soundly. Her leg is now perched on a stack of pillows to keep it elevated instead of from the ceiling.

I haven't paid much attention to what Antonio has been talking on the phone about. I thought he might have been talking to a car dealer. He discussed price and delivery.

I move the flowers and sip my coffee. Vito lies down on his stomach on the couch and scrunches a pillow under his head. He takes his gun and stuffs it under the pillow.

"You in pain?" I ask him, softly.

"Yeah, my back is starting to sting."

"Maybe I should go and get that prescription filled," I suggest. Antonio waves a finger at me and mouths the word no. He is still on the phone.

From my view near the doorway to Erin's room, I see patients and nurses in the hallway all turning to look at the huge dark complexioned men coming towards us. They stride in the same confident and intimidating way that Antonio and Vito do. Oh yeah, they're mob.

They stop inches from the door and peek in. Antonio's face fills with recognition and he smiles.

"I gotta go. Make sure they are here by Tuesday," he says and ends the call.

I step back towards my sister's bed, unsure about these guys.

"Hey, Carlo," Antonio says, and slaps henchman one, Carlo, in a hug. Glad that Antonio knows these guys, I relax a little. But I get the feeling that we can't trust anyone. Vito gets up and hugs Carlo, too.

"Whoa, easy paesan," Vito says. "I got a mess of burns on my back." Carlo backs away.

"I can't believe how long it's been since I've seen you guys," Carlo says. "Remember the time you came up behind Sister Mary and tugged her habit down," he says to Vito. You scared the shit out of her." Carlo laughs. "Father Gio made you clean the church for a month."

I look at Vito. "Are you serious?" I say disbelieving. Antonio, Vito, and Carlo are laughing it up.

"Hey Carlo, this is my girlfriend, Megan," Antonio says pulling me to him.

"Eh, I see you found a nice Italian girl," Carlo jokes. "Pleasure to meet you, Megan. These guys treating you right?" he asks. "Because if they're not..." he trails off.

Antonio gives Carlo a playful jab. "This is Adolfo," Carlo says introducing the other guy. Adolfo is standing hands crossed watching the scene of old friends catching up. He's tall and expressionless. He is wearing his sunglasses inside, playing scary henchman number two perfectly.

A deep hello rumbles out of him. He turns and stands by the door facing the filled hallway of intrigued onlookers. He spreads his legs slightly and crosses his hands in front of him again. Oh, yeah, bodyguard.

Carlo sits down in one of the chairs, and Vito lies back down on the couch. Antonio gestures for me to sit in the other chair. He leans against it.

"Adolfo!" Carlo calls out, and Adolfo shuts the door. "So, Antonio, what can we do for you?" Carlo says switching to all business.

"Megan's sister has to stay here a couple of days, and Vito's been hurt. I need some extra eyes and ears on these girls."

"So that's the princess in the bed?" Carlo asks.

"My sister," I say, interjecting. Carlo gets up and walks to the side of the bed. I bristle with protectiveness. I go over there too. Antonio follows.

"What happened?" Carlo asks.

Antonio puts his hand on my back before I can say a word.

"She fell," he says.

Vito is watching every move Carlo makes. I think he might not trust these guys either.

"If you could stay here with Vito and Megan that would really help me out."

"Sure, no problem," Carlo says. "I think Adolfo and I can handle that.

Antonio pulls me aside. "Listen. I have to go take care of some things. Stay here with Carlo and Vito. Don't leave to go anywhere in the hospital without someone."

"Vito needs his medicine," I remind him.

"I know. I'm going to send Adolfo downstairs to the pharmacy to get it."

"Be careful. And call me. I want to know your safe," I say, wrapping my arms around his waist, and leaning my head against his chest.

"I will. I'll call you." He puts his hands on my cheeks and kisses me. "I love you."

"I love you, too," I return.

Antonio says good-bye to Vito and shakes hands with Carlo. He opens the door and speaks to Adolfo. Then he is gone.

My cell phone rings. It's Troy.

"Hello."

"Meg? Where are you guys?"

"We ran into some problems," I tell him.

"Problems? What kind of problems? Are you okay?"

"I can't tell you, but we're all alive."

"What the hell does that mean?" Troy gets heated.

"Tell me where you are right now, Meg. I'm coming there." Carlo shakes his head at me. "Troy, I wish I could, but I can't. We're okay." I try to reassure him.

"Meg, this is getting out of control."

"You're right," I tell him. He is right. Things are crazy, and Erin is lying in a hospital. I glance at my listless sister who looks small and helpless.

"Jake and I can come and get you guys," Troy says. "I want to help."

"Troy, I will definitely call if we need you. Thank you so much. You're friendship means more to me than I can tell you.

"Where's Antonio?" he asks.

"He had some things to do. Vito is with us."

"Meg? Tell Antonio I will do anything he needs. Be careful..." Troy says hesitantly.

"I will. Bye," I feel empty when I hang up.

Adolfo comes back with the medicine for Vito. Vito pops a pill in his mouth dry. Yuck! I gag thinking about it.

A nurse comes in and changes a bag on my sister's intravenous. Erin has not stirred or opened her eyes since I saw her shaking in Vito's arms.

"Excuse me, nurse?" I say.

"Yes?" she asks politely.

"Is she going to wake up soon?"

"It is hard to tell. We gave her a strong sleep and pain medicine. I'm her nurse till eleven. I'm Brenda. If you need anything, let me know."

"Thank you." The nurse leaves.

Adolfo assumes his position again outside the door. Not only did he bring Vito's medicine, but some snacks, a novel, and a deck of cards.

"Hey, Vito," Carlo says. "How about a little friendly poker?"

"Nah, man. I'm going to try to get some sleep. My back is killing me."

Vito hasn't moved from the couch. He has been drifting in and out since Erin was moved up here.

"How about you, little lady? How about a nice game of cards?"

"Uh, okay," I respond. I want something to keep my mind busy, or I'm going to fix the blankets on Erin's bed a million more times.

"What'll it be?" Carlo asks, shuffling the cards with his long dark fingers. We sit opposite each other with the coffee table between us.

"Whatever you want?" I say.

"Do you know how to play poker?" he asks, defying gravity by flipping the cards around in the air, so that they look like a waterfall.

"No."

"How about blackjack?"

"Yeah, that's twenty-one right?"

"Sure is," he says giving me a wink. He deals the cards. "I've never seen anyone with Tonio before. You must be really special." I blush at his words.

"Tonio is known as a loner in a lot of ways. He is very loyal," he continues. "Are you gonna stay or do you want a hit?" I bend my cards so I can read the face down one.

My cards total fifteen, so I say, "Hit me."

Carlo throws down a five for me and a three for him. I now have twenty. "Stay," I say.

Carlo flips out another card for himself. An eight. He shakes his head. "Flip um."

Carlo is over twenty-one. He swipes the cards off the table and deals again.

"So, you and Antonio used to be close?" I ask, checking out my cards.

"I used to hang out with these guys when I lived in Palmetto. My pop acquired an interest in a casino in Chicago, so we moved here."

He emphasized the word acquired. I notice that many times Antonio and his friends, and even his father, use formal words that allude to whatever they're talking about as unlawful.

I win another hand, and Carlo scoops up the cards and deals a third time.

"How did you meet him?" Carlo asks.

"We go to high school together. I live in Palmetto."

"Figures Antonio would be taken with the only medigan in Palmetto." He shakes his head and checks his cards. Vito's light snoring gets louder. I look over my shoulder and check on my sister. She is still out, sleeping soundly. I want to protest that I'm not the only one. My friend Raven isn't Italian, but my phone rings. It's Antonio.

289

"Hi," I say relieved.

"How are things going there, honey? How's Erin?"

"Still sleeping," I say.

"Is that normal?" he asks.

"Yeah, I asked the nurse. She said that they don't know when she'll wake."

"And Vito?" Antonio asks.

"Snoring..." I roll my eyes at Carlo and glance over at Vito. "...loudly," I finish. Carlo laughs.

"Let me talk to Carlo," Antonio says.

I can't hear what is being said, but Carlo answers with yes. He listens for a minute, then says bye. He hands the phone back to me.

"Antonio?" I say, making sure he is still on the line.

"Yeah. Try to get some sleep. Don't let Carlo keep you up playing cards. He's addicted to it, and he sucks at it," Antonio says chuckling.

"Okay. Love you."

"Love you too. I'll see you soon. Bye."

"Bye." And I end the call.

Chapter 15

Mamaluke (mama-luk): something foolish

Antonio:

I hated leaving them. Megan's sister and Vito both hurt. But I had to. I hope I can trust Carlo and his guy Adolfo. I haven't seen him in years. Time changes people.

I picked up Troy after I left the suite where I filled up the luggage, packed up the kitchen, and moved it to the car. I would have picked up Troy first to make him help me, but I wasn't sure what I would find. No point in putting him in harm's way if I didn't have to.

"What the hell?" Troy exclaims looking at his friend's car.

"There was a hail storm." Troy walks around the car in disbelief.

"Hail?! Was the hail on fire? Holy Shit!" he shouts.

"Don't worry. I'm buying this guy a new car. It'll be here on Tuesday."

"What did ya do to my car? There is a huge dent in the front," he asks incredulously.

"I'll get it fixed for you."

Troy stands there, shaking his head. "I just talked to Megan. She wouldn't tell me where she is. She sounds scared."

I wish I didn't hear that shit. I don't like her being scared. Not that it's not warranted, I just don't like it.

We transfer all our stuff to Troy's car and return the borrowed car to a very stunned freshman. I tell him his new car will be here on Tuesday, a brand new Ford Taurus. I got the kid's cell phone number to make sure he gets it.

Troy drove me in his recently dented car to Hertz. I rent another SUV, a Suburban.

After Troy leaves me, I get a call from Patrick.

"Hello," I say.

"I'm at the airport. Pick me up," he says and hangs up.

Okay... Surprise visit from the Cleaner, great!

I drive to the airport where we started this journey and grab a smoke outside the automatic doors before making my way to the arrival gates. Airport security is flanking both sides of the area. I'm careful not to walk too close to any metal detectors. My gun is secured in the waistband of my jeans.

Passengers flock to their loved ones and baggage claims. Everyone seems to be in a hurry. Patrick saunters with the crowd, keeping pace but not appearing to be rushing. He is just naturally fast. He is carrying a large duffle bag and a rigid expression.

"Let's go," Patrick says, and I fall into step with him. He doesn't say anything else until we get outside. I'm going to need some supplies."

Supplies are weapons and whatever he needs to chop up people into little pieces to make them disappear.

Inside the parking garage of the airport, I click the doors to unlock and I walk around to the driver's side.

Thoomp, thoomp!

Something stings my leg. I automatically reach down to see what it is. A bee is the first thing to come to mind, but it's a dart. A tranquilizer dart. I yank it out. My body becomes numb and I hit the door of car. I crash to the cement, paralyzed. I hear a thump from the other side of the vehicle and people running. Then, darkness consumes me.

*****

Megan:

We play a couple more hands of blackjack, and I win all of them. Antonio is right. This guy is terrible at cards, which is surprising for someone whose father owns a casino.

"I'm going to check on my sister, then try to sleep a little," I inform Carlo.

"Yeah, it's getting late. I'm gonna go stretch my legs and get a coffee. You want anything?"

"No thanks."

Nurse Brenda comes in and takes my sister's blood pressure. I hover over her, watching. She takes a needle from Erin's arm and sticks it in a red box on the wall marked, used needles. She replaces the needle gently, and then shakes a bag of saline. Nurse Brenda hooks up the new bag and tosses the old one away. The door is open, and I can see Adolfo's frame by the door in the hallway.

"She was pretty dehydrated when she came in," the nurse comments, checking Erin's pulse.

"Well, she was sick a few days ago and not eating and drinking too much. It was hard to get her to have anything."

"Her vitals are good. She just needs rest." The nurse fiddles with some buttons on a monitor and leaves, closing the door.

I go to the closet and find an extra blanket and another pillow. I snap the lights off so that there is only a glow from the bathroom. I hunker down in my chair and close my eyes. Ending a night with a kidnapping and rescue, then starting the next day with a car-bomb, makes you bone-achingly tired.

My body is tired but my mind is racing. Replays and images thrust themselves in my thoughts unwanted. I wonder about Antonio, what he's doing, if he's okay. I think about my mom and dad. I want to sort out the hows and the whys, but I can't. Anxiety won't let me.

I flip around in the chair trying to find a comfortable spot. My eyelids are heavy but restless. The door opens quietly, and I see a shadow of Carlo. I can smell his coffee.

It's definitely late because the hallway is much quieter. Earlier, the hallway was bustling with nurses, patients, and visitors. We've been here all day, and I just want to sleep. Find that relaxing comfortable state and succumb to it.

Chapter 16

Mooshadda (moo-sha-da): someone who is stupid

Megan:

I am startled awake and unease creeps its way through my bones. It's dark in the room. I feel someone behind me, lingering over my chair. I tilt my head up and even in the shadows and dim light, I recognize the guy. It's Antonio's Uncle. I am momentarily appeased and ready to say hello, but something is not right.

A large rope comes around my neck choking me. My heart rate spikes knowing my body is in trouble. I dig my nails into the fiber of the rope desperately. I pull hard and it doesn't move. My throat crushes in on itself, and I gasp. I frantically search the room for Carlo and Vito. Vito is still on the couch and Carlo is on the floor in a heap, his body twisted. I strain to see the bed. My sister looks exactly the same as before.

"You've caused me a lot of trouble, you little bitch," Antonio's uncle hisses quietly to me, putting his lips right up to my ear. The rope is burning my skin. Vito is not far from me. I kick out, trying to get his attention.

"You won't wake him, Irish whore," he says, and yanks harder on the rope. I choke and spit runs down my chin. I try again to pull the rope away, but Uncle Tutti regathers his hold on it.

I kick Vito hard in the shoulder, and he moans.

"I want you to know that I've been dreaming about killing you for a long time," he taunts. "Patrick's number one daughter — helpless. I wish he was here to see it. But daddy won't be coming. He's run into a little bit of trouble, just like you."He laughs quietly and maniacally. I strike out at Vito again with my foot. I manage to land another solid kick on his shoulder and he rouses.

"What the fuck?" he grumbles, his eyes still closed. Another figure comes out of the shadows and grabs Vito and hauls him up. "Shit! What's going on?" he slurs, the pain medication making him slow.

"Keep him quiet. I have plans for him, too."

Stars form in front of my eyes, my strength is weakening. The darkness is getting thicker from the lack of oxygen. Very soon, I'll be out cold, then dead.

Quick snapshots of my father subduing our attackers at our house, and Antonio snapping the leg of some guy he was told to beat up, surface. Then an image, one I can only remember from my dreams, hits me. It's me. I'm on the floor, a wooden floor. I have a gun in my hand, and I fire at shadows.

Don't think, just do. I stamp my feet and push my chair over with my jellied legs towards the couch. The thump the chair is loud. Uncle Tutti loses his hold on the rope, and I tear away from him. I scrabble on my knees to reach under the pillow for Vito's gun, all the while coughing and gasping. I am grabbed by the waist and hauled up before I can reach it.

"Oh, no you don't, bitch." I am lifted in the air. I kick and let out a raw scream. Uncle Tutti clocks me in the head. It stuns me for a moment, but I recover and shift in his hold. I kick him with all my might. "Son of a bitch!" he yells.

I catch a glimpse of Vito. He is fighting the other guy. It's a struggle because he's not himself. His punches are slow and he's slurring his curses. It registers who the other guy is that Vito is fighting and it's Adolfo. Shit! Anger burns and replaces my flight response with fight. That disloyal asshole!

There is a light knock on the door, and we all stop for a split second. I take that opportunity to backhand Uncle Tutti in the face with my fist. He reels back, but doesn't let go of me.

"Is everything okay in here?" The door opens. It's a new nurse, not Brenda. Adolfo slams the door on her. She yelps from behind it, probably hurt.

Vito finally manages to tackle Adolfo. He is stunned on the floor and Vito reaches for me. Uncle Tutti is older and can't fend off Vito and hold me, so I wrench free of his grasp. He and Vito struggle. There are grunts and fuck-yous bouncing off the walls. Vito calls out, "Fuckin' traitor!" and lands a solid punch to Uncle Tutti's face.

I crawl away to the other side of the bed. Erin is motionless. Nothing wakes her. I reach into the red used needle bin and pull out three. I rest them in my fist and crawl back towards Vito. But a foot steps on my hand crushing it to the hard linoleum. I screech and look up. Adolfo is standing over me. I swipe my free arm back, and jam the needles into his leg. My trapped hand is immediately freed and I yank the needles out. He picks me up and shakes me. The weight of my body is insignificant to him as he wields me in the air, cursing me. He is fucking angry. Well, so am I.

I thrust the needles into the side of his neck. I stab them so hard, they ram right up to the plastic. He hollers and drops me, I don't let go of the needles. They rip and tear at his flesh. I can feel wetness on my hand — blood. I am back on the floor.

Adolfo staggers, tripping over a chair, and yanks the door open. Harsh fluorescent light pours in the room. I am momentarily blinded. I spin around and jab Uncle Tutti in the leg with the needles. He yells and kicks me, while defending himself against a medicated Vito. On a good day, Vito could have taken this guy with one hand while the other held an ice cream cone.

I am sprawled against the wall, spent. I try to shake off the spinning room unsuccessfully. I see Uncle Tutti rush out. I hear people yelling in the hallway, but I can't get up.

Chapter 17

Guinea (gin-nee): a derogatory term for an Italian

Antonio:

I wake up to the smell of rotting meat and a massive headache. My arms are heavy. I open my eyes and see a large slab of frozen beef inches from my face. I scan around to find a doorway, and when I do, it's upside down. It's upside down, because I am hanging upside down by my feet. They are bare and bound; the rope is secured on a meat hook. It's cold, and I am stripped down to only my jeans. A few yards away is Patrick, suspended from the ceiling too and unconscious.

I immediately assess our situation. Clearly, the Chicago underground uses this place like we use the restaurant, and Sommersville uses a Laundromat. We are in one of the hundreds of meat processing plants in Chicago. They wouldn't deliberately take us here unless they plan on killing us. And since they haven't yet, I can only assume they plan on making it slow and painful.

"Aww, look, Pop, he's awake," sarcasm and scorn drip from Dino's words. He limps in through the door, Luigi behind him. They saunter over to me.

Dino lifts his head up to look at me threateningly and grabs my nipple twisting hard. "Is it cold in here, Delisi?"

I shove his hand away, and the movement causes me to swing.

"What?! Seriously?! Is that all you got? You are such a fuckin' pansy! Always have been, always will be," I grind out.

Dino does exactly what I expect him to do. He raises his fist to hit me. I reach for it and grab him before he can land one on me. I use his own force and push. He falls back, crying out in pain, "Fan-gul!" My body swings, and I collide with a side of beef.

"So, Dino, what hurts more? Vito shooting you in the leg, or my girl hitting you with a car?" I goad as I rock back and forth in the air. His face inflames. He's mad.

"The great Antonio Delisi has found a little bit of trouble for himself," Luigi says spitefully. "I love seeing you up there like a dumb animal caught in a trap."

Dino laughs, "I'm so sick of hearin' his name, Pop. Antonio this and Antonio that." Dino spits at me. I duck and throw my fist out. It connects with the side of his head. I was going for a full jaw punch, but I'll take what I can get.

Dino doesn't come at me again because Patrick starts to come to. He is waking up. He shakes his head trying to clear it, a confused expression on his face as he looks around.

A guy comes in and says, "He's back." Luigi and Dino don't say anything, but leave in a hurry.

Patrick flails and struggles, his burly hands and arms sway.

"Patrick," I whisper. "Patrick," I say a little louder.

He's dazed, but sees me.

"Shit," he says, and closes his eyes.

"Patrick," I call again.

"What?" he says, annoyed.

Is he aggravated with me? Are you fuckin' kidding me?

"You got any ideas?!" I ask.

"I'm thinking," he says.

"Well, think fuckin' faster. I'm freezing!"

Our conversation ends because we hear people coming back. They're talking and coming our way. Dino hobbles in first, then two guys I don't know, must be Chicago mob, then Luigi. Following behind them all...is Uncle Tutti? Holy Shit! My uncle!

"Patrick and Antonio, how nice to see you here in Chicago," my uncle's voice is callous and severe. I examine my uncle. His face is blotchy, and there are bruises along his cheek.

My legs are getting very numb. I question whether I'll be able to stand on them, if I could get down. My hands feel thick and hot because of all the blood that has settled in them from being upside down. My uncle's betrayal settles in my stomach like rancid hamburger on a hot summer night, maggots and all.

Uncle Tutti walks over and stands right next to Patrick. "It's too bad your daughter couldn't be here." My head shoots up, and Patrick stills. "She's a feisty one, I'll give her that." He is taunting us. "But she got what was coming to her after all these years." Patrick's face darkens. I can tell he's trying not to take the bait. He wants to ask what he's talking about and if she's all right.

So I take the bait. "What are you talking about?"

"What a sweet girl she is. Plays the harp. Smart. My brother was smart too."

"What the fuck are you talking about? You don't have a brother."

"Oh, no, Tonio, I did," he says to me, walking my way.

"He was young when he went to live in Ireland. He was sent there to train with the Irish mob." He pauses then explains. "It's sort of like an exchange student thing." He adds pensiveness and mockery to his voice. "It builds alliances and opens up territory. He loved it there and decided to stay."

"You never met him because you were only a little boy when Miss Megan fired a shot right through his heart. He bled out on the floor in lone cottage on a hillside in Ireland."

"Nonna never mentioned him," I hiss.

"She couldn't," he says. "The Boss wouldn't allow anyone to talk about what went down in Ireland." Vengeance seeps into his words." It was humiliating to have two enforcers murdered by a five-year-old," he yells. "It was dropped, forgotten, a mistake! They pushed it under the rug, and stomped on the memory of my brother."

"You're blaming a child who shot someone that was breaking into her house, probably to kill! Are you crazy?!"

"No, I'm not blaming just Megan. I blame him," he points to Patrick.

"What the hell does that have to do with me?" I seeth.

"I'm killing two birds with one stone," he says. "Your father has been boss long enough, Tonio. He's been ordering me around for years. I'm entitled. I'm crushing his empire one person at a time." He smashes his fist in his palm for emphasis.

"So you hooked up with the Prazzo's?! You are oobatz!"

"No, I'm not crazy, Tonio. I'm smart." Uncle Tutti walks towards Patrick. "The hospital was quiet. What a nice room too, at the end of the hallway."Adrenaline singes through my deadened legs. She has to be okay. She's with Vito, and Carlo. "Megan was pretty, and so was her sister."

I freeze and red forms over my eyes. Now I know for sure that he's gone after her. My throat tightens with a lump at the vile and appalling thought of Megan hurt. Patrick is stone-faced, dangling.

Rage, feral and raw, bubbles under my skin. My fists clench. He is totally baiting us. I've been around this life too long not to know this. But the fury and anger build all the same. The need to crush everyone in this room manifests itself, so that, when the time comes, I will have no control.

Chapter 18

Bellissima (bel-e-see-ma): beautiful

Megan:

I wake and find myself in a palace. Creams and golds line the walls with huge moldings and chandeliers. Ornate furniture decorates the room, bigger than my living room in Palmetto.

I turn my head and see Erin. She is lying is a hospital bed in the middle of this strange room. On a cot no higher than coffee table, is Vito, lying on his stomach.

I look down at myself, and I'm wearing a satin nightgown. The movement of my head causes me to cry out. My throat burns and scratches. I feel the skin at my neck, it is sore and inflamed. I move to get up, and my back screams in protest, halting me.

"You shouldn't get up yet," a youthful voice says. In the seating area in the middle of the room is a young girl curled up with a book. "Doc Howie says you all need lots of rest."

She is pixie-like, small with dark hair, bluntly cut, and huge brown eyes. "I'm Clarissa," she says, coming towards me. "My brother brought you here." Her brother? "Are you hungry?"

I shake my head no. I speak but my voice comes out scratchy. "Where are we?"

"La Bella Regale. My pop owns this casino." She sits on my bed.

"Carlo's your brother?" I whisper.

"Yeah," she says smiling. Clearly, she loves her brother a lot.

"How's my sister?"

"Doc Howie says it's gonna take time." I don't like the sound of that. At the hospital, they said she would be fine, her vitals are good, that's he just needs rest.

"He'll be here soon. He is coming back to check on you."

"What times is it?"

"Five a.m."

"The doctor is going to come here that early in the morning?"

"He lives here."

"He lives here?" I question.

"He's on staff here," she says, like that's the most normal thing in the world. Great, resident doctor...just like Michael Jackson!

"Do you live here?"

"Yup. My dad and brother too."

Just then, Vito stirs and sits up. "Shit," he sighs. He manages a glance around and sees Erin's hospital bed. He gets up and stands over it, holding on to the bedrail. He checks her out then turns to me.

"Are you okay?" he asks from across the room.

"Yeah."

We are quiet just staring at each other. Without Vito's help, I think Uncle Tutti would have accomplished his goal of killing me. I suck in a breath. Adolfo!

"So did Adolfo work for Uncle Tutti?"

"I guess so," Vito says.

"He worked for us for the past year," Clarissa interjects.

Vito sees the young girl perched on the end of my bed. Clarissa blushes and looks down at the blankets,

"Hi," she says shyly.

"Hi," Vito says. "You Carlo's little sister?"

"Yeah." Clarissa is bright pink through her olive skin. I didn't think that was possible.

My eyes fill with tears when I think about Antonio. Where is he?

"Vito? Where's Antonio? Can we call him?"

"Yeah, Red."

"Carlo tried to call a bunch of times...no answer," Clarissa states.

"Will he find us here?"

"Don't worry, Red. I'll go looking for him."

Vito walks to the phone on the nightstand and dials. I wait, the anticipation killing me. He shakes his head. "It just goes to voicemail. Mannegia!" He slams the receiver down.

A door on the other side of the room, probably the length of a baseball field, opens.

A tall man with glasses comes in. He's carrying a clipboard.

"Oh, you're awake. How is everyone feeling?" he asks congenially. Without waiting for a response, he says, "I'm Doctor Marco. But, please, call me Howie."

Vito steps forward and shakes hands with Doctor Howie. "You've got some serious burns young man. I'd like to take another look at them in a little while, if you don't mind. It's important to keep an eye on them."

Vito nods as the doctor comes over to me. He gently lifts my chin, examining my neck. "Nasty," he says, wrinkling his nose. "Open for me please. Let me take a look at your throat." He pulls a tiny flashlight out of his pocket. I open my mouth, and he shines the light in.

"You are a very lucky young lady. If that rope dug in anymore, you could have some serious complications." He shines the light in my eyes, examining me closely. I can smell his breath.

"So far, so good," he holds my wrist and takes my pulse, counting on his watch. "Good," he says again.

He pulls a stethoscope out and helps me to sit forward. He puts it on my back and listens for a minute. "Good." Vito stands over me watching all of this.

"Clarissa? Could you go get me that bottle on the counter over there and a glass of water?"

"Sure," she says brightly, popping off the bed. She reminds me of my sister.

"What about my sister?" I ask Doctor Howie.

"Well...she's a different story." Ugh, not good.

Chapter 19

Sticazzi (sti-ca-zee): I don't give a fuck!

Antonio:

Gunfire erupts in another room, the sound unmistakable. Dino grabs a gun out of his jeans and hobbles behind the crowd of thugs that captured us, rushing to the commotion. We are alone again.

Without hesitation, I bend myself in half, reaching for the hook in the ceiling. I grab it. I shimmy my tied feet off and let them drop. I'm about five or six feet off the ground. I let go, and fall to the filthy cement, landing on my thigh. I sit up and untie my legs, all the while, glad that I stay in shape.

I run over to Patrick. The floor is sticky with butcher-sludge and grime. How the fuck do I get him down?

"Get the table," Patrick says, pointing.

A large metal table, the height of a counter, is against the wall. Bits of bone, sinew, and all sizes of knives are on it. As I drag it, it scraps and squeals across the cement making a racket, but it still isn't as loud as the shoot-out in the other room.

I position it under Patrick and jump up on to it. I grab one of the butcher knives and reach up to cut the rope.

"Ready?" I ask.

"Just do it," Patrick breathes out, steadying himself to hit the table. Patrick falls onto the table, quite gracefully for a middle-aged guy. He grabs a knife too. Then takes another one and puts it in his pocket. We climb down.

So, two guys, barefoot and shirtless, three knives, against guns and a shit-load more than two people... Not good odds.

Using his knife to point, Patrick motions me to the side of the doorway. I go, and he stands on the other side. He nods, and I poke my head around the corner. Just an industrial style hallway, no windows. I nod, and Patrick moves. We stay low and quickly move towards the mayhem, our knives held high. I check behind us every so often, making sure no one else is coming.

A bullet wizzes by my ear. Both Patrick and I dive to the floor, clutching our knives, and flip over to see where it came from. Running fast is a guy I have to assume works for the Chicago mob or Uncle Tutti. He fires again, and the bullet pings into the wall above our heads.

In seconds, he is on top of us. I don't give him a chance to aim again. I jump up and kick him square in the chest. He flies back. Patrick moves quickly and is up too. He wastes no time and hammers the guy, sprawled on the floor, in the face with his elbow, crunching bones. Then Patrick jams a knife in his chest. I swipe the fallen gun off the floor. Patrick takes it from me, and shoots the guy in the temple. This whole thing goes down like we have rehearsed it a million times. Our motions are fluid and precise.

We make it to the fray. It's the storefront of the butcher shop. Large white display cases with the glass blown out are all around the room. Shredded fragments of meat litter the floor and stick to the walls. The front windowpanes are just jagged pieces of hanging glass. Patrick and I crouch down in the doorway, weighing the enemy.

Three people are lying on the tiled floor. I search the faces. None of them are Uncle Tutti. He's not here. That spineless son of a bitch! I need answers! Megan's beautiful face flashes through my mind.

The gun-fire slows, and I hear a voice yelling from outside. There is no one left standing in the room. They're either gone or dead. The sun is just peaking over the horizon, and soft natural light pours in through the gaping hole in the front windows.

Patrick moves forward to the side of a metal case. He puts his back to it. This place is just a mess of carnage — blood, glass, and soured meat. I put the back of my hand to my nose in a feeble attempt to block the smell. Fuck! It's a nod or I won't soon forget. My stomach lurches.

I hear my name. Someone outside is talking about me. The voice sounds like Carlo. I slither to the case across from Patrick. A lifeless body is lying next to it, gore coats its shirt. I strain to hear what is going on outside. Patrick is listening too. Muffled voices, only a few words audible, travel through to where we are.

"Carlo!" I call out.

I strain to listen for a response, and a hand grabs my leg. I just react. I jam my knife into the person's chest. I look at the face. It's Dino. He has two slugs in his chest and now a knife hole. He is rasping. His breathing is quick like a rabbit. His eyes are wide open, struggling for life. I wrench my knife out, slick with Dino's blood. His hand wraps around my leg.

Betrayal. It's ugly. It is a cavernous wound, seen and unseen. I run my eyes over the bodies again, this time looking for Luigi, he's not here. He left his son to die.

"Tonio! You in there?" Carlo yells to me.

"Yeah!" I shout back.

"We're coming in!"

Patrick stretches for a gun lying in a puddle of aftermath, and throws it to me. I tuck myself tighter behind the case, not sure if I can trust Carlo. Dino is lying next to me, sucking in strangled breaths.

Sirens sound in the distance, Patrick and I brace for what's to come.

"Tonio?" Carlo calls from in the room.

"Drop your weapons!" Patrick says, evenly and demanding. He lifts the gun and locks it on Carlo. He is standing with three other guys I don't know. They immediately raise their weapons and train them on Patrick.

It's a stand-off. Who's the bad guy, who's the good guy?

"What happened to Megan?"I am peering around to watch him while he talks.

"Fuck, Tonio! Your uncle must have paid off Adolfo." He kicks a body on the floor. Adolfo! "He came into the hospital room...drugged me and, I think, Vito. I tried to hit him, but the stuff knocked me out too fast. I don't remember anything but the nurses and some security guards trying to wake me up."

"Where are they?" I ask coldly, but truly apprehensive to know. Everyone is still wary, guns ready. The air is cold with friction.

"They're at the casino. My pop moved them all there, even your girl's sister so Doc Howie could look after her."

I ponder this. I know Uncle Tutti has tranquilizers — he used them on us. I decide to take my chances with Carlo. He was with Megan when this shit went down.

Dino is rasping, and bleeding out from his wounds. If this situation were different, I would call for an ambulance. I'm not sure of the outcome, and my ass is on the line. I know he would kill me if given the chance.

"I'm coming out." I say. I raise my hands so they can see them. I stand slowly and walk towards Carlo. Patrick is watching every action.

"I'm sorry, dude. He came out of nowhere," Carlo says remorsefully.

I look him right in the eye to gauge his sincerity...and I see it.

"How are they?" I ask, my guard falling slightly.

"They're okay."

Sirens and tires screech to a stop outside. Four police officers flank the storefront, guns drawn. There is a glow of flashing lights in the early morning mist. Carlo turns.

"Stand down," he demands. The police immediately lower their weapons, and one steps through the broken window.

"Carlo! What is all this?" The officer gapes around the room at the massacre that it's been transformed into.

"A problem we have to take care of," Carlo says unemotionally.

I nod. Patrick gets up, unfolding his large frame.

"Come back in an hour," Patrick says. The officer shakes his head, and the police leave. They don't arrest or question us. They aren't even fazed by the bodies lying in their own fluids on the floor. "I need some things," he says to me. I know what he is referring to. He needs stuff to take care of this mess. It's what he does; it's what he is good at. "I'm going to see if they have what I need in the back." Patrick lowers his gun and departs to hunt for supplies.

Getting to Megan right now is my only concern. I don't want to wait, but we need to clear this away before the cops come back. The entire business district is going to be waking up soon, arriving at work, opening stores. I don't want any trouble for Carlo's dad. He appears to be our only ally. The casino is an excellent hideout — if I can trust them. That place is floor to ceiling high-tech security. It puts the Pentagon to shame.

Carlo takes out his cell. He dials and hands me the phone. "This is the direct line to their room." Someone picks up on the second ring.

"Yeah." a deep gravelly voice answers.

"Vito?!" I proclaim.

"Tonio, holy shit!" he yells into the phone. "Your Uncle fuckin' attacked us!"

"I know, man. How are the girls?" I am rigid as I wait for his reply.

"They're good considering how bombaleed this is."

"I'll be there soon. I've got some new stuff to take care of."

Patrick finds alcohol, tarps, and meat wrapping paper. One of Carlo's guys follows behind him with a bucket and mop. This fuckin' frittata conveniently happened at a butcher shop where they clean up animal blood on a regular basis.

"Vito, I gotta go," I tell him when Patrick gives me a get-off-the-phone-look.

"Alright, dude. Megan really wants to see you," he says.

"I'll be there as soon as I can," I repeat. I am thankful that they're okay.

Carlo tells his guy to move an SUV to the loading dock in the back of the butcher shop. Another one of Carlo's guys starts mopping. The slosh of water and the overpowering smell of alcohol fill the room. I can hear the loading dock door rise. Out of the corner of my eye is Dino, and he is still breathing.

"Carlo?" I call out. "Do you have another vehicle here?"

"Sure, Tonio. What for?"

"Have one of your guys take Dino to the hospital."

Hearing my request, Patrick's head shoots up from his work. He is wrapping up Adolfo's corpse. I can read his mind in his expression— Don't think, just do.

Thinking has forced me to have a spark of pity for Dino lying there. Dino would have killed me if he had the chance. He betrayed not only my family, but all of Palmetto. God knows what he would have done to Megan if he got to her the other night. Then he and his goons trussed me up like a chicken just waiting for the go ahead to 'off' Patrick and me. If he was already dead, I wouldn't give it much thought. But he's not. He is fighting for his life, here and now.

Patrick gets up and walks over to Dino, gun in hand. He lowers it, and aims at Dino's temple. Shots ring out in the quiet. Patrick finishes him off in the traditional mob-way, two shots to the head. Dino is gone.

Chapter 20

Uffa (ooh-fah): "I'm fed up!"

Megan:

Clarissa helps me to the bathroom, it's enormous. Marble everything. A gilded mirror stands against the wall from floor to ceiling, very chic. I am shocked at what I see, though. My neck looks like someone tried to hack my head off with a butter knife. My chin is purplish, and I have brownish bruises on my forehead running into my hairline. I have fingertip-sized welts all along my arms. I look like the Bride of Frankenstein in a satin nightgown.

Walking is a chore. I am stiff and awkward. I hurt in places I didn't even realize could hurt. I need Antonio. I need to know he's okay.

Voices come through the bathroom door, muffled and unintelligible. The last person I expect is my mother. It is the holier-than-thou cadence that alerts me that she is here.

Vito taps on the door. "Red? Your mom is here." Clarissa opens the door a crack, and I shuffle over to it.

"Your mom is here," he says again, lower. I notice light starting to pour in through the enormous windows behind Vito. His face is a hard to read mask. "And I talked to Tonio. He'll be here soon."

"Thanks," I tell him, and relief washes over me. Thank God! I try to give Vito a warm smile, but my mother's unannounced visit irks me.

Where the hell has she been? Why hasn't she called to check on her children? Erin is lying in a hospital bed in a coma-like state. My contempt for my mother is palpable.

Small snippets of my past edge their way in to my thoughts. Over the years, my mother has been condescending and blatantly cold. When I was eight, I came home from school angry and upset. Two boys at school were making fun of me. They called me carrot-top and fire-crotch. The little assholes even said my father was a drunk.

Tears streamed down my face, even though my blood boiled with anger. I remember those tears vividly because they weren't from a scraped knee or a fall, but from injured feelings. Those boys were cruel and callous. They stopped harassing me years later when Antonio caught them.

And my mother accused me of making it up to get attention. She didn't believe me. She made me feel like there was something wrong with me. I can still see the look of disdain on her face. My whole life, my mother has treated me like less of a person than Erin. She has been manipulative and severe even to the point of being bitterly hostile.

Clarissa senses my uneasiness. "Everything will be all right. Antonio will be here soon."

"I know," I meet her eyes. "He has been a savior."

Vito knocks on the door again a few minutes later. "You okay in there?" he asks.

I suck in a painful breath. A brutal reminder of just hours ago. I prepare myself to face my mother.

"Yeah, we'll be out in a minute," I answer through the door.

Clarissa puts her arm around my shoulder and she squeezes gently. I open the door.

Doc Howie is attempting to calm my mother down. Her tone is accusatory and grating. I see her across the wide expanse of space, the grandeur of the room hollowed with her antagonistic presence.

"What do you mean you don't know when she'll come out of this? I want her to see a specialist. This is no place for her," she yells. "My daughter is sick and needs the best in the field! Not some hack scrounging off the Mancuso's!"

My mother's words are venomous, not grateful for Carlo's family's help or Doc Howie's. She is crowing over Erin's bedside, her arms waving in protest at Doc Howie's assessment of Erin's condition.

Doc Howie tries to console my mother. "Erin's condition is the result of psychological shock. Her body is repressing traumatic events and images. The brain shuts down because it cannot process it all. The physical reaction is reduced blood flow, and the vasovagal nerve has become overstimulated."

"You can spout all the medical mumbo-jumbo you want! I want her in a top notch facility!"

"Mother!" I chastise. "That is no way to talk to the Doctor."

"And you!" She hisses as she spins to me. "This is all because of that devil boy, Antonio." She waves her finger at me. "He has brought this all on us." Her accusation and assessment is so totally off base, it is scary to think that she is my mother. I register that Vito is near me, restraining his irritation at my mother's rudeness.

My resolve snaps in the one quiet second between her rantings. How dare she? How could she possibly blame Antonio, or Vito, or me for that matter. This is all a result of my father's chosen profession and the circles it has put us in. Antonio and Vito have done nothing short of take care of Erin and I the best that they can in the situation we're in. Is she blind? Or just stupid?

"Mother, you owe Doc Howie an apology."

Her eyes open to their capacity, exposing all of the white around her irises. I have always known my place. I always kept my mouth shut, even when she acts this way. Not anymore!

"Mother, did you hear me?" I ask coldly.

"I don't respond to disobedient children," she admonishes.

"From now on, I'm not responding to ignorant parents," I say sarcastically, giving her attitude right back. "Why are you here, Mother?"

She ignores me and turns back to Erin. I walk right up to the other side of Erin's bed wanting to force my mother to look me in the eye. But she doesn't. I sense a change in her demeanor. Her gaze is on my neck. I involuntarily rub at it. Then she strokes my sister's forehead with her hand—a display of motherly nurturing.

Clarissa has been quiet through this exchange, hanging in the background. Doc Howie clears his throat and says to Vito.

"How about I take a look at those burns?" Vito agrees to let Doc Howie look at his wounds. They walk over to a couch way on the other side of the room. Clarissa follows them.

"I'm here because of you and Erin is sick," Mom says. I want to yell at her that it is partly because of her and dad, but I don't. We stand there for a minute watching Erin.

Erin lurches forward and releases a high pitched scream shocking us. Her lifeless countenance is now distorted in horror and her eyes are closed. I reach out to settle her and clasp her shoulders. Erin's shrieking escalates.

My mother is dumbfounded at Erin's behavior. Erin swings her arms and just misses hitting me by an inch. I can't hold her, and my mother just stands there stunned.

Vito sails over furniture and leaps to Erin's bedside. He pushes me out of the way to reach Erin. She hits Vito in the shoulder. He grasps Erin's arms and pins them. He speaks softly to her, in contrast to her yelling. He finds a way to sit on the bed, and places her in his arms. Very slowly, her screams and movements become less and less.

Doc Howie has a syringe in his hand. Vito steadies her as he injects it into Erin's arm. My mother watches Vito in bewilderment as he strokes her hair and continues to sooth her.

Doc Howie checks Erin's pulse and listens to her heart.

"Clarissa, please get me the blood pressure cuff," he says calmly.

Clarissa rushes to grab it over near my bed while I hold my sister's hand. Vito rocks my sister back and forth like a child, and I catch a glimpse of his burns again. Raw, blistery, red skin shows through the gauze. Vito had taken his shirt off for the doctor. He must be in so much pain.

Careful not to touch his back, I wrap my arm around Vito and lay my head on the top of his. The three of us are cocooned together. Thank God for Vito!

A door opens at the end of the room, Antonio and my father walk in, followed by people I don't know. A tunnel of light filters through me. The vision of Antonio soaked in blood and dirty, is heavenly because the look in his eye shows me how much he loves me.

The tears come as Antonio peels me off Vito and Erin, and lifts me up to kiss me. He cradles me in his arms, sits down in a chair, and buries his face in my hair.

"I was so worried, Megan," he whispers. I wrap myself tightly around him. The tightest I have ever hugged anybody. The tears continue to flow, but I don't care. Antonio is safe and right here with me.

We stay like this awhile until I feel my father kiss the top of my head. I had blocked out the entire room and all the people in it.

My father's deep voice shakes. "Are you okay, Meg?" I feel his fingers on my back in a consoling gesture.

I unhitch myself from Antonio and turn to face my Dad. He is blood soaked and half-naked like Antonio. "Are you hurt, Dad?"

"No," he says with a small smile, very uncharacteristic of my dad. "I'm fine." I have to see for myself, so I stand. I take in his body from head to toe, trying to identify any type of injury. He reaches out and hugs me. "I'm sorry," he tells me in my ear.

*****

Antonio:

Desire to get to Megan was practically unbearable while we cleaned the butcher shop. As sick and grotesque as it sounds, I learned a lot from Patrick. Cleaning up crimes scenes and disposing of bodies is a gruesome art form. We got out of there before the cops came back. Ennio, Carlo's dad, sent a couple of more guys to help.

Ennio offered for Patrick and me to get cleaned up and some new clothes, but neither of us wanted to waste time. We needed to see the girls.

One of Ennio's enforcers punched a code in for a private elevator. We rode in it to the reserved floor of the casino. The entire elevator car's walls are mirrors. Our images are reflected at every angle. Even though I'm Italian and Patrick is Irish, we look the same, shirtless and haggard, coated in layers of blood and dirt.

Megan, Vito, and Erin are enveloped in a bizarre hug when I walk in. My eyes lock on Megan. Beauty and compassion are written all over her face. She glows with strength.

I can't control myself. I walk over, scoop her up, and hold her to me. Nothing else matters other than knowing she is safe.

My heart almost screeches to halt when I see her neck. Indentations of rope shadow the delicate skin under her chin. Upon closer inspection, I find bruises and marks on her face and arms. The monster in me rears its head, aching to wrap its hands around Uncle Tutti's neck and squeeze until his eyes pop and his last breath fizzles to nonexistent.

After Vito lays Erin back down, everyone convenes in the sitting area in the suite Carlo's father, Ennio, is letting us use. Patrick and I take turns showering. Carlo gives me a change of clothes. I come out of the bathroom. Ennio and Patrick are talking in a corner.

"Tonio?" Ennio calls me over. I head over to them.

Ennio has always been good to me and my family, especially when he lived in Palmetto. My pop kept up the relationship all these years. We see the Mancuso's at least once a year. They come to Palmetto and visit. Let's hope the bond is strong enough to withstand betrayal and track the traitors.

When the casino became Ennio's, my family came to check it out. I remember being floored at the sights and sounds of the games. Tons of people pumped money into the machines. Every table had people squeezing together to play. I was with my father and Ennio when they discussed the type of security and surveillance that was to be upgraded. The cost alone could feed a small country.

Ennio envelopes me in a traditional Italian man-hug—back slapping with the gentle neck grab. Breakfast is brought in on a rolling cart.

"Tonio. Eh," he says pulling away to look at me. "No one is talking. I've got my enforcers scanning the streets. Nothing. It's gonna take some time."

I shake my head in understanding. Sorting this shit out, taking down the right people, and testing the waters is going to take time and manpower.

I scan the room and find Megan on the couch. Clarissa fills a plate with food and hands it to Megan.

"Thank you," she says.

Clarissa then continues to fill plates, handing them out to the somber crowd. Even Megan's mother is quiet for a change.

"Can my daughters stay here?" Patrick asks Ennio. "I don't want to intrude, but I need them somewhere safe."

Clarissa holds out a plate to Patrick beaming. The idea sounds good to her.

"Oh, please, Daddy," she pleads with Ennio.

"Of course they can stay here. Doc Howie can look after Erin. Clarissa's governess would love to have more students."

Clarissa rolls her eyes playfully at her father's statement.

Megan's mother finds her voice again. "Oh, you have a governess?" she asks sounding very pleased with the statement.

"Pop likes to call Lucia my governess because it makes us sound prestigious. She's just my tutor, and she lives on the floor below us."

"Regardless, we have plenty of staff here."

"What about what happened with Adolfo?" I question.

"Adolfo worked on the Casino floor as a bouncer. He never had access to this level. Very few people have ever seen the living quarters."Governess, living quarters... It is funny to listen to Ennio. His choice of language mixed with his cavone accent is comical.

A phone rings. It's Ennio's. Patrick's and mine are long gone.

"Hello."

"Yup, right here." Ennio hands me the phone. It's Pop.

"Tonio!"

"Hi, Pop."

"I can't fuckin' believe it! That God Damn traitor! After all I've done for him!"

"I know."

"You get an opportunity, you pump no less than five holes in his fuckin' chest, you hear me!? Not one fuckin' less!"

Pop is so loud; everyone is looking over at me. They can probably hear him. I go into the bathroom and shut the door.

I pace as my father continues to yell more obscenities into the phone. After about a minute or two, he calms down.

"Tonio, this is big. Bigger than what we have dealt with before."

"Yeah," I say, knowing full well that he is right.

"Your uncle is making alliances, big ones. You get me?"

"Yeah, I get you."

"What about Luigi?" I ask. "What the hell has he got himself into?"

"That fuckin' slime ball! He couldn't shoot the head of an elephant. He's with Tutti. Take 'em all out, Tonio."

I pause. My father is asking me to kill everyone. I actually have never killed before. Beat the shit out of them, even shot them, yes. But I have never been the end reason for someone dying.

This thinking is short lived because the monster, angry and untamed peaks over the top of my consciousness ready to kill. I have been primed my whole life for this. Megan's life is in danger. Uncle Tutti started this...and I'm going to finish it.

"I got it, Pop. You comin' out here?"

"I can't. I am trying to fuckin' control Sommersville. With you and Patrick gone, I am running low on people I can trust to get the job done. You can handle it, Tonio. Keep those girls safe. With Vito and Patrick, you have a good team to sweep and clean. I trust Ennio."

My instructions are clear, take down Uncle Tutti's crew. I hang up with Pop and walk out of the bathroom. Vito is by Erin's bed with Megan's mother. Ennio and Patrick have left. I sit next to Megan on the couch. She leans her head on my shoulder. Her soft hair touches my cheek. I put my arm around her and squeeze. She lifts her head and kisses me gently. It is just as sweet as the first time.

She tilts back to look at me, and I see the rope burns and the bruises. Adrenaline, hot and fierce, pumps through me at the sight.

"Antonio... Is everything all right now?" she asks.

"No." I say, staring into her eyes. "It is just the beginning."

I have to kill them all!

End of Part two

BOOK 3

Mobster's Vendetta

There are three sides to every story. Mine, yours, and the truth.

Joe Massino, Mob Boss

Chapter 1

Capo: Captain of boss's enforcers

Megan:

If anyone asked me I'd tell them I've known Antonio my whole life–intimately. This isn't because we have spent every waking moment with each other since birth. In fact, we never spent any time together until recently.

But, my soul was drawn to him even when my mind didn't want to be. It isn't about the danger or his dark beauty. It's the connection I feel. He makes me feel at home even though I am miles away from it.

We have been apart now for three weeks. I have been caged in this gilded prison for three weeks. Fancy meals, workout room, pool, repeat.

This separation is painful. If you get something, something powerful, then lose it, desolation takes over. It's both unhealthy and right all at the same time.

"Meg!" my sister, Erin, calls weakly.

"Coming!"

I just finished working out. I use the gym here every day. I have never worked out before, but boredom took over. Well, boredom and my run-in with Uncle Tutti, Antonio's uncle. Near strangulation is a great motivator. It inspires me to become stronger.

The only time that I leave the family floor of the casino is during the slow times. A bodyguard takes Clarissa and me downstairs to get ice cream from the small Ben and Jerry's stand in the midst of the high-priced shops that line up and down the main lobby hallway. I always look forward to this escape. Sure, it's a diversion from the top floor of *Mancuso Mafia Penitentiary*, otherwise known as La Bella Regale Casino, but it is something I have to get me through.

The bodyguards are relatively nice. Joey is typically the one on duty when we get our treat. It still surprises me that Clarissa has been living like this her whole life. I don't know how she does it. I, on the other hand, feel like an animal in a cage, even if it's a comfortable one.

I typically bring Erin a huge sundae. Chunky Monkey is her favorite. I think she is well enough to come downstairs with us, but she chooses to stay upstairs.

"Meg! Joey's here."

"I'm coming!"

I walk towards the front of the suite. It's not a short walk. Think studio-style with palace-like, heavy gold furniture...an old-world palace in a modern-day skyscraper.

"Hey, Joey," I greet him.

He grins at me. Joey is a good looking guy...well no, he's gorgeous. He fits right in here with his black, floppy hair scattered around his forehead, but his eyes seem to set him apart from everyone...they are a pale green. I can see why Clarissa and my sister, Erin, giggle every time he's around. He is quite charming. When he smiles, two dimples appear on each side of his mouth. It's sweet and endearing. But, all the same, I probably wouldn't want to meet him in a dark alley.

Clarissa is sitting on the couch next to my sister. Her short-cut bob of rich brown hair swings when she turns to me flashing a warm smile. Our stay has been a treat for her.

Erin and Clarissa have their heads together, snickering. I roll my eyes at their immaturity, but it also fills me with happiness to see my sister entertained. They have become very close during our seclusion. Clarissa truly has been a lifesaver by pulling Erin back from the darkness of recent traumas.

The traumas run deep. Connor, her ex-boyfriend...what an ass! He cheated on her. There isn't a minute that goes by when I think of his betrayal that my blood doesn't boil. And the truth about Dad's work, being bound to a chair in our kitchen with a gun pointed at her head...these events revealed my sister's insecurities and vulnerabilities.

Clarissa is good for Erin. She is a tough cookie. She gives my sister coping skills that she desperately needs. Being immersed in the Mafia lifestyle, even though she's trapped at the casino, makes Clarissa a force to be reckoned with. She has learned, like Antonio, to handle and deal with tough situations.

Joey is the son of Ennio's right hand man, Julio. Julio is head of security and an enforcer...I've heard him also referred to as Capo. Joey is in the beginning of his training, at the very early stages. Being a bodyguard for us is one of the things he has to do. He is pretty close-lipped about it, but I still ask a ton of questions and he typically caves. As much as what goes on scares me, it also fascinates me. I'm not sure if that's because I'm in love with a mobster or if it's because I've been born into this life, albeit ignorant of it.

"You ready?" Joey asks.

"Yeah. You coming, Clarissa?" I ask, grabbing a sweatshirt.

"I think I'll stay with Erin."

"You don't have to," Erin interjects.

"It's okay. Make that two Chunky Monkeys today, Meg."

"Got it. We'll be back."

Joey and I leave the suite and head for the family elevator. The red and gold carpeted hallway gleams all the time. I have mused to myself that little elves come in the middle of the night to scrub it.

Joey pushes in a security code and we wait.

"How are things going today?" he asks.

"Ugh. Same ol'," I shrug.

A door opens at the end of the hall. We both turn to look. Alex, another enforcer, sticks his head out. My face automatically moves to offer a greeting, but, when he sees Joey and I, he quickly pulls his head back in and shuts the door. No hello. Alex is another one of the people I've met here that I really like. He seems genuine and has been extremely helpful with anything that Erin and I have needed, so this behavior is a little odd.

"What was that about?" I ask quizzically.

"Who knows," Joey responds.

The elevator dings, and we step in. Mirrors line all of the walls. I know behind those mirrors are cameras. There are cameras everywhere.

"I think I'm going to take my ice cream upstairs too. I'll eat with Erin," I tell Joey.

"Nah, eat downstairs. It's your big adventure to the casino floor," he coaxes.

"I'd rather eat in the suite with Erin and Clarissa. Erin's birthday is tomorrow, and it's not too early to start celebrating. Besides, I always feel guilty when I leave with you."

Joey raises his eyebrows at me.

"Why? Do you have a thing for me, Miss O'Neill? You're a beauty, but I don't need my face knocked in by Tonio," he jokes, his dimples deepen when he laughs.

"Ha ha," I deadpan.

Everyone knows that Antonio and I are in love. I miss him so much. But I am struck by what Joey said. Joey is in his twenties, much older than us...and he's afraid of Antonio.

Joey's phone buzzes in his pocket, and he shifts his coat to the side, his gun and holster poking out, as he takes his phone out and answers it.

"Yeah...(pause)...No...(pause)...I can do that...(pause)...Okay."

Joey hangs up and presses a new floor button - B.

"Are we are going to the basement?" I ask skeptically.

"Yup. We're going on a field trip." He scrubs his hands together maniacally. He is joking, but an eerie feeling overcomes me. Mice and gross things are usually in basements. Is there a special mob morgue down there? My mind is running away from me. I have been cooped up too long.

Joey grins at me. "What's wrong with you?"

"Nothing." I shiver. "I'm just not a big fan of basements."

Joey shakes his head and laughs at me. "It'll be fine. Don't worry."

Says the mobster - *Sure, no problem!*

The elevator dings. The doors slide open.

Chapter 2

Enforcer: Mafia henchman, who *enforce* the rules

Megan:

A half-dozen enforcers are lounging around on leather couches. All faces turn to us. All conversation stops.

"Hey!" Joey calls out to no one in particular.

This place never ceases to amaze me. The basement is like a whole other world. The conversations resume. The doors slide shut behind us as I scan the room.

The first thing I see, because you can't miss it when you step out of the elevator, is a huge screen television. It swallows the whole back wall of the basement. A football game is on. The players are enormous like in a movie theater. In the corner is a kitchenette. Mini stainless steel appliances, complete with a Keurig coffee pot. The granite counters are covered with open chip bags and salsa, metal food trays, and plastic dishes.

"Hey, Meg," Ty yells over when he sees Joey and me.

He is another enforcer/bodyguard that I see a lot. I wave as I continue to examine the fortress. A poker table for eight sits against another wall. Over to the left is a massive steel door with a huge glass window next to it.

"So, Meg, this is where we hang out." Joey gestures around the room.

I have never met most of these guys before, and feel their eyes follow us as we make our way through the room. Ennio, Clarissa's father, owner and boss, is very strict about who is allowed on the family level.

Joey walks me over to the steel door and opens it. Lined floor to ceiling are television screens. Levers and switches cover a desk. Every inch of the building appears to have a camera trained on it. I knew this, but seeing it freaks me out. Not that I have never thought of it before, but seeing the actual place where they come together is unsettling.

"Here is the command center where we can keep our eye on everything." Joey winks at me.

Tables, entrances, and slot machines are all on the screens surrounding the room. Joey shuffles me in front of him. "This is Gilly. He sits a lot."

Gilly punches Joey in the arm. The man appears to like his doughnuts and coffee. Two empty boxes sit next to him, piled on top of each other, and a bunch of coffee cups overflow the trash can. Gilly has a sweet face with a stomach the size of a basketball.

"Don't listen to him, Megan. I hit the floor too."

I have never met Gilly, but he knows my name. He has probably seen me through the cameras. I hope there isn't one in the suite. I scan the frames trying to find my room, but don't have time to finish searching because Joey takes me through another door.

"Come on. I have to grab a couple of things," he says, waving for me to follow him.

Inside the door is a huge bowling alley style room, but it's not for bowling. Large targets are at one end - huge black pinned up outlines of people with circles on their chests hang from the ceiling.

A firing range.

Makes sense. They must need to practice shooting. I have seen first-hand that Mafia is a tough business.

"What do you think?" Joey asks pulling me from my thoughts. He is rifling through some boxes and putting some equipment together.

"Umm. It's nice. Very high-tech." I wonder to myself if the police have anything so spectacular.

Guns and ammunition hang on the walls. Steel boxes are piled in a corner. There are five firing lanes with goggles and headsets positioned at every station.

I walk over to the first lane. A small handgun rests on the counter, seemingly innocent and arbitrary. I pick it up. It's cold and heavy in my hand. But it's not as weighty as the one the guy had trained on my sister only weeks ago.

I take aim, wistfully. The gun is a natural fit to my hand. My eye's predisposition draws to the center of the target. I've done this before. The feeling conflicts my memories, ghostly recollections of the past.

Joey startles me. He is behind me while I observe the target.

"You wanna give it a try?"

"What? Me?" I ask, shocked. *He wants me to fire a gun in here?*

"Let's see what you got, O'Neill!" he eggs me on.

Joey grabs the hand gun from my hand and slips the clip out, replacing it with another he grabs from the metal boxes. It clicks in place. He turns the butt of the gun to me, expecting me to take it.

"Uh...I don't know about this. Why don't you take some shots, and I'll watch?"

I'm very uncomfortable about this. The last time I held a gun was over the guy that broke into my house. I do my best to not touch any of Antonio's weapons, even though they are around all the time. I'm not sure why I picked this up.

"We'll fire together," he suggests. He gestures for me to take the gun by waving it at me slightly.

An image flashes in my mind.

Shadows.

Danger.

There are tall shadows, and I'm so low and small.

I shudder.

"Come on. It'll be fun," he encourages. The gun still hangs in the air between us.

I take it.

"Move right over here." Joey gently places his hand on my back and lines me up at the firing range. "Stand here and put these on."

He hands me goggles and a headset and grabs a set of his own from the next station. His voice is muffled when he speaks again.

"The safety is off on this gun, so there is nothing to do. Just hold it in front of you, point, and pull the trigger."

Joey stands behind me, all business. My fingers and hands seem to slip into the right position. It feels familiar, and I have held a gun before.

I readjust myself and get comfortable. It feels intuitive, like I know what I am supposed to do. My mind flashes again with images of tall men in shadow. I shake it off.

"Now, look right here. It's the site. Aim right for the heart on the target," Joey says bringing me back to the here and now.

My heart beats faster as I hold the metallic object in my hand. My hand fits perfectly. My index finger is lying comfortably on the trigger.

"Take your time," Joey says to me in my ear. "Focus. Look only at the target."

A hysterical giggle wants to erupt from inside me, but I don't let it.

I suck in a breath, focus myself, and squeeze the trigger. The gun bucks slightly as the bullet releases. I can feel the shot all the way down my arms and into my chest.

Joey freezes.

I freeze.

He pushes a button on the panel. The target, suspended on a wire, rushes towards us. It has one hole in it. And the hole is through the heart...perfectly.

After a second of silence, Joey jumps and fist pumps the air.

"I knew it!" he yells. "The minute you picked up that gun, I knew it!"

I'm confused.

"You knew what?!" I yell, partly because it's hard to hear with the headset and because I am scared. *What did he know?*

"You're a sharpshooter! It's gotta be in your blood. Holy Shit! I knew it!"

Joey grabs the door to the security room.

"Dude! Get the guys. They gotta see this! *Mannegia!"*

Joey is beaming as he comes back to me.

"Do it again!"

I'm flustered. *I'm a what? Sharpshooter?* Don't you need to go to like some kind of gun school for that...or years of training?

"Come on, do it again! I bet you can do it every fuckin' time!" Joey pleads. "Go through the same hole! Come on!"

He pushes the panel button and the target swishes back to its position. The room fills with enforcers and bouncers. The huge expanse of the firing range becomes very small.

The hulking guys are pushing each other and fooling around, being guys. Joey stands behind me again.

Ty starts chanting my name like he is waiting for me to score the winning touchdown. Some of the others join in.

Joey gives me some last minute instructions. I push out the noise and commotion behind me. Joey must raise his hand or something because the room becomes very quiet.

I suck in a breath, focus myself, and squeeze the trigger just like last time. I fire and the gun bucks.

The room is still while Joey pushes the panel button. The silhouette target dances towards us again. I concentrate on it before it makes it to us. Another hole. This one overlaps the other in a figure eight form with the middle missing. I was off by a millimeter.

"HOLY SHIT! She did it!" Joey exclaims, and cheers erupt in the room. "I have to save this for Delisi!"

I feel hands on my back. Multiple hands clap my back and congratulate me. Joey pulls me in for a half-hug.

"You are the awesomest *medigan* I have ever met!" Joey yells and unclips the paper guy from the wire. He holds it over his head. "Fuckin' awesome!"

Everyone hovers around us as Joey examines my bullet holes. The flock of guys are all gasping and chatty like little girls.

"Only Delisi would find a girl who can shoot like that," Ty says to his friend.

Joey pulls his phone out. It must have been ringing, but I didn't hear it over the noise.

"Yeah we're coming," he shouts into the phone. "Nope, right now." He ends the call and looks at me.

"Ready to head back upstairs?" he asks grinning.

"What about the ice cream for Erin?" I ask. I don't really care about me, but I want to at least bring it for Erin and Clarissa.

"Don't worry. I'll have someone bring it up."

The hallway is silent as usual. In the elevator, Joey stares at the target the entire ride. He certainly is proud. I am surprised by my own ability. Maybe it was just luck. Maybe, maybe not. It felt right. I just knew what to do. It was easy. *Why is it so wonderful? Can't other people do that?*

341

At the suite, Joey puts a code in, and the door opens. I walk in to darkness. The suite is completely black. Where is Erin? I immediately snap to alert.

I hear Joey click the lights on.

"Surprise!"

It takes me a second. The entire room is filled with people.

Clarissa and Carlo.

What's he doing here? He supposed to be with Antonio. I quickly scan the room for Antonio's face, but sadly don't see him.

Doc Howie and our governess, Lucia. Okay, she is really a tutor, but I go with the flow. It's what Ennio calls her.

Alex, one of our bodyguards and enforcer stands off to the side with a deep grin on his face. He is a tall drink of cool water like the rest of them. Natural dark skin, intense brown wavy hair, and built in all the right places.

My mother is not here. She went to stay with the O'Connell's back in Palmetto. Once Erin started getting better, she left. She didn't even ask us to go with her, probably knowing I wasn't going to listen to anything she said. I want to at least be in the same state as Antonio, and Erin's proximity to Doc Howie is vital for her recovery and safer than any hospital in Palmetto right now.

Troy!

Troy is here. He sweeps me into a hug and spins me around just like he used to.

"Oh my God! I'm so happy to see you." My eyes adjust as the room spins. I can't believe it. Troy is here. Ennio was so adamant that no one could come to visit. "How? They let you visit?" I fumble my words.

Troy still holding me, whispers in my ear.

"They blindfolded me. They fuckin' blindfolded me," he says as he puts me down. "It was the only way they would let me see you."

"Oh." His words make me falter, but I recover because I am just so happy to see him. I missed my friend so much and hug him again.

Shock consumes me and Erin comes up to me.

"What is this all about?" I ask.

"This is for you," she says.

"But it's your birthday tomorrow, not mine," I say puzzled by all this.

"I wanted to do something to thank you."

"For what?" Now I was really baffled.

Tears spring into Erin's eyes. "For taking care of me." She pauses. "And putting up with me."

I reach out and hug her.

"Oh, Erin, I am just so glad you're better." Tears leak out onto my cheeks, too.

There is nothing I won't do for my sister. As fragile as she is, I would do everything I could to help her. Over the past few weeks, the dark circles under her eyes have lessened. Her rosy complexion has come back, and her strength is returning.

We break our embrace, and Clarissa comes up to hug me, as do Lucia and Doc Howie. I am so busy talking that I don't notice Alex trying to get my attention until he taps my shoulder.

"Come on over here," he says. I follow him across the room. Troy and Erin are right behind me. Staff from the casino mill in and out of the room offering stuffed mushrooms and little egg rolls.

Near the windows facing the windy city of Chicago is a sheet draped over something huge. I stand in front of it as everyone else makes a semi-circle around me. Alex rips the sheet off...

A harp!

The most gorgeous harp I have ever seen. Intricate scrolls and designs cascade down the sides. A cherub with hands extended, graces the top arch. It is absolutely magnificent!

"It's the most beautiful thing I have ever seen," I breathe aloud in awe.

I step closer and gently strum my fingers across it. *Perfect!*

"What is this for?" I ask no one in particular.

"It's from Tonio," Alex answers. "He knows you miss the one at your house."

My chest tightens and my cheeks burn. I ache for him so much.

"Play something," Alex says. Everyone in the room mumbles and nods encouragement.

"Yeah, come on, Meg," Troy urges.

Erin sits down on the sofa, and Clarissa follows. Slowly, each person in the room finds a seat as I settle behind the enormous instrument. I caress it easily, loving the feeling of the strings. I play a few chords, learning the composition of it.

Beginning slowly, Ave Maria glides out of my fingers into the strings and out into the air. I am home.

Chapter 3

Take Out: Kill

Antonio:

"This fucking sucks!" I toss my phone hard onto the dresser. I won't be surprised if it doesn't work later.

"Tonio? I thought we were going to the casino tonight?" Vito asks, coming out of the bathroom with a towel wrapped around his waist. His black hair is wet and longer than usual.

Vito and I are staying in a scummy hole-in-the-wall hotel in the heart of Chicago's hit area. It sucks, but we have no choice. Pop wanted me home for a week to take care of some business for him, then come back here. I said *No fucking way!* I am not leaving without Megan.

I am miserable. Vito is more ornery than usual, too. Crossing our path is bad luck for anyone and everyone – even the poor guy that sold us coffee at Starbucks.

Vito walks to the bed to put on his jeans. I get a good view of his back. His scars are pink and angry from the burns. It's been three weeks since the car bombing. We are no closer to getting Uncle Tutti than we were then.

"Dude, Pop called," I huff out, disgusted that I even have to tell him this. "We have a meeting down on Charleton Street at six. We'll never fuckin' make it to the party," I tell him.

Three weeks of chasing.

"*Mannegia!*" Vito growls.

Chasing after Uncle Tutti and Luigi Prazzo is playing on my fucking nerves. *This is bullshit!* I have to kill them. Sadly, that's not what's eating me alive...the biggest fuckin' stab is being away from Megan.

I really want to see her face when she receives that harp. It's the most expensive thing I have ever bought in my life. Pop had to take money out of an overseas account he has for me to pay for it.

"What the fuck is goin' on now?" Vito spits, aggravated.

We both wanted to see Megan and Erin tonight. We've both been on edge. I'm starting to question my own sanity. Days are running together. My mind feels edgy and frustrated.

For weeks, Pop, Patrick, Vito, and I have been scouring Chicago and Palmetto for Uncle Tutti's men. And now, we are forging another alliance...tonight. Ennio's family, the Mancuso's, arranged a meeting with another Mafia family in Chicago, the Furlotti's. Pop is coming to Chicago tonight especially for this meeting.

I pull my shirt over my head as I walk to the bathroom, ready to shower. Vito is pulling his jeans on.

Knock, knock.

We both become motionless, and then spring into action. Vito grabs the two handguns off the bedside table and tosses one to me. We flank each side of the hotel room door. I nod to Vito, and he opens it.

"What do you want?" Vito barks out.

I infer by Vito's response that the person at the door is an undesirable. I stiffen, bracing myself to react.

A very female voice answers.

"*Marrone!* Is that anyway to talk to me?! I've known you since you wore diapers."

"Get in here," Vito scolds. "This is no place for you!"

"Nice to see you too, asshole."

Alessandra steps over the threshold.

"Tonio!" she beams at me and throws her arms around my neck. I embrace her back. I bury my head in her thick brown hair.

I have missed her. Besides Vito, she has been my closest friend. When everyone else was fake or stayed away from me, she never did. She has been tried and true...like a sister. She calls me on my shit and never lets me get away with anything.

I pull away. "What are you doing here?" I ask much gentler than Vito and throw a glare his way.

Vito reads my glance, hugs her, and then stands back, arms folded across his chest waiting for an answer.

"School's out for holiday break. I was bored. My parents flew me out here. I rented a car, and here I am."

"Who told you where we are?"

"Carlo," she says. "Hey, where is he? I thought he said he would be with you?"

"He is back at the casino. I wish we were, but some stuff has come up," I say aggravated.

"Oh...he said something about a party there for Megan?"

"Yeah, but now we won't get there 'til later."

"So, let me get this straight," I question, "Carlo told you to come here and not go straight to the casino?" Something is not right.

"Well...no. He told me where you were staying, and I decided I meet you here and go with you guys over to the casino. You know, to surprise Megan. How is she doing?"

"So, Carlo expects you at the casino?" Alessandra is obviously trying to change the conversation, but I don't drop it.

"Um, yeah..." She looks ashamed.

"When you drove into this neighborhood, did you not start to get a clue it might not be the best place?!" Vito spits at her.

I sigh. "We'll have to drop her off before the meeting."

"I can drive myself," San huffs.

"There is a lot of shit going down, Alessandra. I would feel better if we took you."

I pick up my phone and call Carlo.

"Hey, man," he answers.

"Alessandra's here."

"What?!"

"She is at the hotel."

"I sent a guy to the airport to pick her up!" he says annoyed.

"They must have missed each other because she is standing right in front of me."

"Do you want me to come and get her?"

"No. We'll drop her off."

I click the phone off and walk to the bathroom to shower. I make it a quick one and dry off, dressing quickly. Vito and Alessandra are having a heated conversation in the next room. The door is so paper-thin that I can hear every word.

"Don't play me, Vito! I know you like her."

"Just shut up, San! You don't know what the hell you're talking about?"

"The hell I don't! I see the way you look at her. You follow her with your eyes at school!"

"She was at school for what, two weeks, before all this shit went down," grumbles Vito.

"Don't play me, Vito. I'm not stupid!"

"Yes you are! You came here by yourself. You are fuckin' stupid."

San huffs and curses under her breath.

"Carlo has been filling me in. He said you bend over backwards for that girl."

"Why the fuck are you starting shit with me?! Stay out of my business!" Vito sounds at his limit.

Who the frig are they talking about? My brain kicks in. Shit!

"What the hell does Carlo know? We've hardly seen him in years. Besides, I'm supposed to be watching out for her. She is my responsibility," he adds.

"...and he said you haven't been doing your usual screwing anything on two legs! To me, that sounds like a man who is whipped!" Alessandra is pushing.

"What the fuck did you call me?" Vito's voice is alarmingly sharp.

"Wh-ip-ped! Would you like me to spell it, dumbass?"

I yell through the door, "*Sta-zitto*! Now!"

Their voices lower.

"San, I'm gonna say this once. She. Is. A. Kid."

"And I'm gonna say this once. Does. Not. Matter."

Oh, shit! Erin!

We pile in the SUV that we are using, courtesy of Ennio, and leave San's car at the hotel. I'll send someone for it later.

The two of them are uncharacteristically quiet.

How did I not see it before? Am I dense? Am I losing it? Have I been so caught up in my own shit? Getting her to drink and eat...freaking out over that *chooch*, Jake...sleeping in her bed to get her through her nightmares...sitting at her bedside... Fuck! He's got a hard-on for her!

Deep down, Vito is a nice guy, but that stuff did seem over the top even for him. Come to think of it, I did catch him watching her a lot. Not that he has had much opportunity, but San is right, he hasn't gone after girls...hasn't even mentioned any.

"So, San, how's school?" I ask.

"Boring without you guys," she mutters.

Vito snorts.

The ride gets quiet again but then Alessandra speaks up.

"How are Erin and Megan?"

Vito stiffens noticeably beside me.

"They're safe. I haven't seen Megan in a few weeks, but I get regular reports and call her. She hates being there."

"I'm sure she does. She probably feels like a caged animal. Poor Clarissa, I don't know how she has done it all of these years. Ennio keeps a short leash on her."

We pull up in front of Regale Casino. A doorman opens Vito's door, but Vito waves him away and points to the back where Alessandra is.

"Aren't you coming in at least for a minute?" she asks.

"If I go in there, San, I'll never come out," I say, meaning it. It has been so long since I've seen Megan that I'm not going to want to leave.

Alessandra gets out, and Carlo shows up at the curb. His face is stern. He is pissed at Alessandra. Carlo knows better than to tell anyone where we are staying. San made him look bad, and I will have to talk to Carlo later. It's not that we can't trust Alessandra, but you never give out information someone doesn't need to know...she didn't need to know. It is important to maintain discipline between enforcers and associates within the families.

Vito plugs the address into his phone, and we arrive a few minutes early for the meeting. I get out of the car and light a cigarette, taking a deep puff. I watch the smoke mixed with my breath in cold in the night air.

Business is always the same, no matter where we go. Dark alleys, warehouses, seedy bars. We are constantly reliving the same smells and the same sounds. The air reeks of cat piss and rotting trash.

The mob underworld never changes. It hides itself deep in the cities. The rules, people, and danger are a given. Sometimes I wish things were different, but they're not.

I take one last drag of my cigarette and toss it on to the pavement. Vito is standing beside me, partially in shadow from the street light. His figure is intimidating. Menacing is what we need right now. Forming alliances brings out territorial bad asses wanting to strut their shit. They want to let you know how tough and dangerous they are. They'll try to challenge us tonight...one sit down is not going to cut it. This is not a simple thing, but a process, just like everything else in the Mafia.

The door is a huge metal one with a chain that lifts it. I rap on the metal, and I can hear the rattle of the chain as the door rises. A shiny, gray cement floor is revealed. Round tables and folding chairs create a makeshift meeting place, just like we do in Palmetto. My father is leaning against a wall talking to Donny, who looks really good. A bullet doesn't keep him down for long. Others are milling around, talking. Pop spots Vito and I.

"Tonio!" he beams at me.

I walk to Pop and Donny, Vito behind me. I approach my dad and in a flash I can see myself for the first time...really see myself...what I am meant to be...who I am meant to be.

"Hi, Pop." I smile.

My father's stance is confident and sure. It is very good to see him. I miss him and Ma. I reach out for the typical, half-hug with pats on the back. But Pop grabs me and holds me tight.

"I missed you, son," he says.

"I missed you, too," I say into his shoulder.

Donny clasps me on the back, and I turn to hug him. It's weird. Donny and Pop have been friends since they were kids, the same as Vito and I.

Vito greets Donny and Pop, too.

"Eh, Vito, you look good! How's the back?" Donny asks.

"It's healing up."

"If everyone will take a seat, please," Mr. Furlotti says.

I pull out a chair and think that I can't wait for this meeting to be over. I just want to see Megan.

We all take our seats accordingly. Pop and Donny have a couple of their enforcers with them from Palmetto. Ennio also sent a couple of his own...Julio, his head enforcer, and a couple muscle thugs, people who take care of the little shit.

Don Furlotti is a short, balding guy and the boss. Next to him sits his underboss, Mikey Fingers. Mikey scans the room like everyone is a threat. He started out in this business as a cleaner, his specialty being dismemberment. He starts with the fingers. The thought crosses my mind that he has a lot in common with Patrick.

"Loyalty!" Mr. Furlotti calls out, and slams his fist on the table as he launches into a long speech about alliances and what it means for all of us. It is all the common blah, blah, blah, that has been ingrained in me since I was a child.

Then he brings up Uncle Tutti, and my fists clench.

"Tutti has taken the wrong road. He's going away from his boss, going away from us all. We cannot let him come into his own power.

Palmetto's boss and son are here to form an alliance. It is a tradition that our first order of business is a challenge."

The room buzzes with everyone talking quietly amongst themselves. I drink in the vision of the mobsters around me...all similar to me. We all know the rules. We all know the game. We all know the lifestyle. Once you're in, you're always in, and it is very difficult to get out.

"Tonight there is going to be a fight. Don Delisi, please select someone from your family."

I stand. I don't even want to give Pop a chance to pick anyone. I know my place. It is my responsibility. Don't think, just do.

"I volunteer," I say.

Pop nods at me with pride.

"Okay, Antonio," Mr. Furlotti replies.

I glance over at Vito, and he regards me with annoyance. A glacial stare at me that says he wanted to offer himself for the challenge. But it's my obligation.

A door opens up across the warehouse towards the back and slams with an echo. A tall man approaches. I recognize him, and he is someone I wouldn't choose to spend time with. Demetrius! He emerges from the darkness and to the harsh light of the warehouse. His demeanor runs at a constant zero-degrees coldness to the trained eye. To the unsuspecting or ignorant, he may appear charming and friendly, but it is all a front. I'm sure the ladies love him and he has a new one on his arm all the time...until they learn what a sick fuck he is. Stories fly about him. The truly saddest part of all the rumor shit running rampant is that it's true.

Demetrius walks towards the table never taking his eyes off me. He sits down next to his boss, Furlotti.

"Now, from the Furlotti family, who chooses to fight?" The words aren't even finished when Demetrius stands.

This is a set up. I should've known that they would do something like this. Demetrius wasn't even at the meeting. They kept him in the back on purpose.

Demetrius is a lethal thug feared by the entire underground, disturbed on a level that rivals the worst mobster. He is mentally unbalanced, and, in this business, that's scary. He defies the rules and breaks them as a habit. People avoid Demetrius and his attention at all costs.

"Oh, hell, no!" Vito yells. My father silences him with a steely glance.

He's impulsive, volatile, and a plain fucking psycho. He's *oobatz* in the head. I can't believe I need to fight him for this damn alliance. Pop needs this though. Good relations are an important step to putting Uncle Tutti down.

As I walk towards the ring, I strip off my shirt and start jumping up and down to warm up my muscles. I clench together my fists a few times and roll my head side-to-side, stretching out my neck.

If I had to picture what the devil looks like, I would pick Demetrius. His eyes radiate death and hate. He watches me with sharp eyes - staring at me like he wants to eat me alive with a fork and a knife...like a cannibal.

Pop leans over to me, and I stop jumping.

"Tonio, you can take this guy. Focus. Use everything you've learned...everything you've been taught." He puts his hand on my shoulder, reassuring me that he has faith in me. Donny leans over as well.

"Tonio, this kid is crazy. Give 'im everything you got. Don't hold back. Give this kid everything you got!" he repeats. The room gets louder, everyone gearing up for a fight.

Vito scrubs his hands down his face, worried. Dammit! He shouldn't be showing it. He knows to keep his face stoic and his eyes straight. Never show an emotion. It's the only way to win these things. This alliance is important. This fight is our first set up, our first test. I start jumping again.

Money starts exchanging hands. Everyone in the room begins betting. This underworld makes everything about a pot of money, power and gain. Hands switch and swap cash. Cigarettes and cigars hang from foul mouths. For probably the first time in my life, I want to throw up at the smell of the smoke.

Demetrius is cool, cold, calculating, and blood-thirsty, these traits oozing from his pores. He's as big as Vito. But I'm not afraid of getting hurt, I'm more afraid of losing. Pop is counting on me. Tonight is one step closer to a valuable alliance happening.

I need to put Uncle Tutti in the ground, and here I am in a boxing ring with a psychopath waiting to beat the shit out of me. I love a beautiful girl who is waiting for me in a suite at the casino. Megan's face flashes before me, a welcome vision.

Ennio can't be here tonight because it is one of his biggest casino nights – and they all know it. I think to myself that his absence is another reason why they are doing this. They know Ennio won't be here. These fuckers wanted to see what were made of...without friends or supporters.

I guess I'd play the game the same way if the tables were turned. I'd want to know their weaknesses and true grit.

I step into the dirt of the ring. It kicks up around my shoes. Demetrius walks in, his confidence and instability evident in his eyes. The announcer calls out last bets, and we face off, waiting.

The announcer talks about the rules. Basically, there aren't any. Stay in the ring. Only fists, no weapons, and it all ends when someone is down for the count of ten. You can kick, punch, hit, slam...do whatever you want. Really, there are no rules.

I put out my hand to shake Demetrius'. He grabs mine hard. There is no bell or formality, only the announcer yelling go. Demetrius slams me with a punch that has me reeling. My legs falter, and I stagger back a solid three feet. I shake it off, and he is right there in front of me again.

"How does this feel, golden boy?" he asks, pounding and knocking me in the jaw again and again. Blood spills out of my mouth, and I watch it hit the dirt, darkening both to a redish brown.

Vito is yelling. The whole room is shouting, cheering, booing, and calling out. The only person I can't hear is Pop. Donny is barking out instructions and things to do... like tear Demetrius's throat out.

"I hear you've got a piece of ass that everyone is hard over," he grates at me. "Can I fuck her, too?" His crazy eyes center on me and bile rises in my throat. The idea of him with in a hundred feet of

357

Megan makes me want to kill him. My focus returns, and red forms over my eyes, a flash at first and then it becomes a solid haze as my adrenaline peaks. I use a simple leg swipe and watch Demetrius' massive form crash onto the dark dirt. Obviously, he has not had mixed martial arts training like I have. I need to use it to defeat him.

I swing around, lift up my fist, and jam it square into his stomach. With all the force that I use, I can hear the air flow out of his chest. Demetrius clutches his stomach and rocks back. I take the opportunity of his weakness to grab his arm and twist. He lets out a yell that is muted because I knocked the wind out of him. I begin to snap his arm back, but Demetrius recovers way too quickly.

He twists and seizes me by the waist, hoisting me up. I hover above his head for seconds before he smashes me into the dirt. Dust clouds in my mouth as I sputter and choke on it. I think all of my bones feel the connection to the ground and hard cement underneath.

Demetrius reaches for me again, and I roll away. He misses me by a mere inch as I kick up onto my feet. I am upright again and my body screams in agony from the hit to the floor. But I push on and dance around him until I get my bearings. He towers over me...David and Goliath.

Demetrius seizes my hand and swings me around, and I land against the ropes knocking them down. The mobsters watching pick me up and toss me back into the filthy ring. Demetrius is coming at me again. Relentlessly, he kicks and wails on me. He uses my jaw and face as a punching bag. Vito yells for me to get out of the way, but I can't move.

He has me in a snare, and it is a vicious cycle I can't get out of. I feel myself losing consciousness, tipping and sliding. I am going to fall over soon. I can't let him get in another punch...I have to stop the sequence. I have to stop the beating. I have to get him down.

I step over to the side just two inches, he misses me this time. His confidence in his ability to hit me makes him stagger when his punch doesn't meet me. Before he can recover, I roundhouse kick and thrust my foot into his kidneys, knocking him to the ground. Not wasting one second, I jump on him. I throttle him with my fists everywhere I can reach. I beat him, hard. The red stays over my eyes, and I just keep hitting him. I don't think I could stop myself if I want to. Blood and spit slip under my fists after every blow.

The announcer comes forward and pulls me off Demetrius. He is telling me it is over, and I don't even know it. I struggle to get a breath, so tired from hitting him. Blood runs down into my eyes, and my fists feel four times their normal size. *I did it!* I put Demetrius down, exactly what I needed to seal the deal. I am swollen and hurting when I leave the ring.

Vito appears beside me. He clutches my shoulder whispering, "You almost killed me, dude."

Pop walks over with Donny, right over to me, and Pop wipes the blood off my face. My breathing is labored.

"Good job, Tonio. Good job! I knew you could do it. That's my boy."

Everyone reassembles at the tables...phase one is complete. So far we're going to follow through with the alliance.

We will meet back at this warehouse in a couple of days. Pop may have a solid start to a new alliance, but I made a new enemy, Demetrius. Demetrius is not going to let this go. His pride is hurt, and I'm going to pay for it.

*****

Megan:

I need some space. The party, the harp, seeing Troy, all of it is overwhelming and I escape to the hallway. I walk towards the elevators and lean against the wall. A deep breath I didn't realize I was holding escapes.

The same thought repeats over and over. *How did I end up here?*

It's not bad. I'm safe, well fed, I have company...but it's not enough without Antonio. I have a constant worry in my heart until I hear his voice over the phone. As soon as we hang up, the worry starts all over again. I walk up and down the hallway with restless energy.

A ding sounds and the elevator doors slide open. Carlo steps out with someone. A girl. *Holy crap! It's Alessandra.*

I launch myself at her. We have never been really close, but we have a connection that is Antonio. She helped me when I was lost.

Alessandra actually lets out an *'ooph'* and steps back on her spiked heels, then hugs me back. She never stops looking like the Italian diva that she is.

"Hey, have you been working out?" she asks, taking a minute to look at me.

"Yes, I'm going stir crazy!" Tears sting my eyes as I laugh at my own response.

"Come on," Carlo says. "Let's go into the party."

Alessandra puts her arm around my shoulder like we are besties, and we walk into the suite together.

It is so nice to see Alessandra. I can't believe that she has shown up here all the way from Palmetto. I can't believe it's already school break. I've lost track of time and days since I've been here.

She looks incredible as always. We head into the party, Alessandra and I arm-in-arm. All heads turn our way. Erin comes up to us.

"Hello Alessandra, how are you?"

Alessandra embraces her. "I'm fine. How are you?" She truly sounds sincere. "You look amazing. I'm so glad to see you."

"Thank you," Erin says. "It's been a little rough, but I'm getting better."

"That is great to hear," Alessandra says sincerely.

Clarissa comes up and hugs Alessandra as well. The girls know each other, being in the same "family." Ennio doesn't allow anybody up here without connections... that's why I was so surprised to see Troy here.

Alex, across the room, is craning his neck and watching us. He's tall, so I can see him over everyone. I'm sure he must know Alessandra, everybody is connected around here. But Alex's expression is a little taken aback, as though he is surprised to see her...or he doesn't even know her.

Troy comes over, munching on some sausage rolls.

"Hey, you look familiar," he says to Alessandra, his brows are furrowed as if he is trying to place her.

"Yes, we met this summer," she beams.

I butt in, "Troy, we went to get ice cream and sat with Alessandra and her friends."

"Oh yeah," Troy recollects. I find it hard to believe that Troy doesn't remember a beautiful girl like Alessandra.

Mingling ensues, and later I notice Alessandra hanging around Troy. He is pleasant and nice, and Alessandra actually seems interested in Troy. He doesn't seem to be returning the interest though.

Alex comes up to me when I was just filling up another plate of food. Seconds...working out makes me very hungry.

"Who is that?" he asks me, all secretive.

"That's Alessandra. You don't know her?" I ask, shoveling bread and butter into my mouth. "I thought you all knew each other."

"Well, I've certainly never seen her before."

"She lives in Palmetto," I tell him. "She's friends with Antonio which is why I kind of assumed you would know her."

"No, but...she's beautiful. You need to hook me up with her."

"Hook you up? You need my help?" I ask incredulously. His dark brown eyes turn to me, annoyed, and I laugh. "Really? What's the matter? With all that Italian testosterone, and you can't go meet her yourself?"

"Funny," he says deadpan.

"Alessandra!" I call out. She is talking with Troy and looks over at me. "Come on over here."

"Shit! What are you doing?" Alex is flustered.

"What you asked. What is your problem? Sheesh." Alex is acting pretty juvenile for someone who routinely kicks ass and takes names.

Alessandra comes over to Alex and me. She could be a runway model, she is that perfect. Smooth brown hair, big eyes, high cheek bones, olive skin. She smiles at us as she approaches.

"Alessandra, this is Alex." I gesture to him for effect.

"Hi," she extends her hand. "Nice to meet you."

"Hi," he returns and follows that up with...nothing...silence. *This is a badass enforcer?!* He's acting about ten not twenty-two.

I try to fill the void. "Alex is an enforcer here."

"Oh, this, um, must be a great place to, uh, work," she says. I can tell she senses the awkwardness.

Continued crickets from Alex, and I roll my eyes.

"Are you hungry?" I ask. "There is a ton of food." I point to the buffet tables.

Troy walks up behind me. "Hey, Meg, how are you liking your party? This food is wicked good," he says shoveling pasta and meatballs in his mouth.

Alessandra bats her eyelashes at Troy. I seriously didn't think women still did this. He ignores her.

"It's great!" I say. "I can't believe it. I just wish Antonio were here."

Troy snorts, "I am sure Delisi would be here if he could."

"Are you leaving tonight?" I ask, my melancholy drifting to the surface.

"I don't know. I'm assuming they'll take me out, the same way they brought me in," he says quietly.

"I wouldn't say 'take me out' too loudly in here," I chuckle.

Alessandra agrees jokingly.

Troy laughs too and says in an Irish brogue, "It's a fine mess you've gotten yourself into Miss Megan."

I smile, "And I wouldn't have it any other way."

Alessandra tries to engage Troy in a conversation again. "So how's college?"

"Actually, it's been quite eventful since I've gotten here." Troy says, giving me a knowing look as he walks away. *What is up with him?*

Around midnight, the party breaks up. Troy gives me a big hug as he leaves. I truly hope he gets home okay. I tell him to call me when he gets there. He never mentioned Jake. He was fun to hang around with while we were at Notre Dame, and he is a great new friend to Troy. I meant to ask him how he's doing. Next time I talk to him, I'll have to ask how things are going with Jake.

I am still feeling dispirited because I haven't seen Antonio yet. My gaze shifts to my gorgeous harp. Moonbeams filter in through the windows lighting up its golden color. It is just so beautiful. I can't even venture to guess how much something this magnificent costs. But I love it. It's just what I need in this prison...something to take me away, to give me some peace, even if it's only for a few minutes or the length of a song.

Clarissa is picking up crumpled napkins and throwing used plastic glasses away. Alessandra is putting chairs back around the kitchen table. Everyone's movements are leaden. I help to gather up some trash.

"Okay guys, I'm going to head back to my suite," Clarissa says once things are mostly cleaned up. "Are you staying with me, Alessandra?"

"Yep, I'm coming. Wonderful party, Erin," Alessandra says. "I'm so glad I got to come."

"See you tomorrow," I call out very pleased she is here..

Erin and I continue to clean up party debris. I know in the morning they'll be staff here to help, but I figured we might as be as useful as we can.

"Thank you so much, Erin. I had no clue."

Erin lifts her shoulders like they are heavy and says, "I'm so lucky to have you as a sister, Megan. I don't know how I would've gotten through this without you...and...I'm sorry."

"What are you sorry for?" I ask her, surprised.

"I'm sorry that you can't see Antonio. That he's been gone for so many weeks. I know that it's very hard on you and that you miss him."

I flash a bittersweet smile at her.

"I miss him too. I think he's great, Megan. Don't let him get away," she adds earnestly.

"Thanks. I'm glad someone in our family approves of him. If I have to listen to Mom one more time, berate and trashing him, I am going to lose it."

"Meg, I wouldn't listen to Mom. This whole thing has made me see a lot of things I'd never seen before. It has really opened my eyes."

Erin throws a bunch of disposable plates in the trash and continues thoughtfully. "Actually...I think Mom is jealous of you."

"What?! That's nuts," I say disbelieving.

I can't imagine that. *My mother's jealous of me? How is that possible?*

"She's jealous of your strength. She's jealous of who you are. You're confidence and intelligence...your ability to get through tough situations." I'm a bit surprised by the conversation...that is quite a mouthful for my sister lately.

"Good night," Erin says and comes over to hug me. I hug her back.

"Good night," I say quietly as she slips out of the room.

Erin goes to her bedroom and closes the door. I am left standing in the large suite alone, reflecting on her statements. Is my mother jealous of me? How can she be jealous of her daughter? Parents are supposed to love unconditionally...not have those petty feelings.

Chapter 4

Don: Head boss, family leader

Megan:

I sense a hand on my thigh. Sleep has settled so deeply that I barely register being touched. Whisper light kisses feather across my ear and temple. I feel a heaviness in the bed in addition to my own. Familiar hands brush against my neck. I open my eyes, but I can't see. The room is in pure darkness.

"Antonio?" I sigh.

"Yes," he says softly. "Who else would it be?"

"Oh, you know, any number of boyfriends I've accumulated over the past few weeks," I giggle, sleepily.

"Really?" he asks with a smile in his voice as he tickles me.

I laugh, happy to have his hands on me. I relish in his closeness.

"Well, I'm going to make you forget all about them...right now." His voice is so seductive and needy that my breath catches.

He pulls the covers off me slowly. I am in a tank and boy shorts. Antonio runs his hands over me, and I involuntarily buck off the bed.

"I missed you so much," he whispers against my lips.

"I missed you too."

His hand slides in between my thighs and parts my legs. He shifts his body and drapes it over mine. I wrap my legs around his hips. He feels so good I could cry. I want to stay like this forever. His weight is welcome. It is comforting and protective. He caresses and holds me as I kiss him. He pulls away. I feel his breath against my face.

"I love you," he says, and draws lazy circles on my shoulders with his fingers.

"I love you, too."

I take his face in my hands and kiss him hard. He parts my mouth with his tongue. My belly tightens deliciously, anticipating what is to come. I run my hands down his back and feel his muscles tense and contract with urgency. He lifts my shirt and I am gone - lost in a haze of passion.

*****

Megan:

The next morning I wake up tangled up in sheets and Antonio. It is a marvelous feeling. It's been so long. I love this man so much, and he feels absolutely wonderful.

The sun is streaming in through the windows. I feel it's warmth on my face, even though I know it's bitterly cold outside. I snuggle closer into Antonio's chest. I see his body, his chest is scattered with bruises. I probe farther up, and I look at his face...cuts and scratches, a huge one across his forehead near his hairline. His eyes are shadowed black and blue.

"Oh my gosh!" I cry out.

Antonio's eyes open lazily. He looks down at me and grins. It's the most attractive thing I've ever seen. Even with bruises, cuts, and scrapes, he's the most amazing man I've ever seen.

His voice is rough when he says, "I missed you so much." He leans over and kisses me.

"What happened to you?!"

"Nothing too bad. Do we have to talk about this now?" he sighs.

I sit up and stare at him incredulously, the sheet barely covering me. I need to hear what happened. I give him the tell-me-or-else look.

"Okay. I had to fight this dude last night."

"What do you mean you had to? Oh my gosh! I have never seen you like this."

"It's for the alliance. Don't worry about it. It's done."

I exhale and rest my head on his chest again relishing in his closeness. I feel that pain again in my heart, it's from knowing that he's been hurt. Last night's party comes back to me...I'm partying, he is being beaten to a pulp.

"Did you win?" I ask softly.

"Yes," he says. I can hear his answer vibrate in his chest.

"Thank you so much for the harp," I whisper after a few moments, wanting to change the subject to forget his bruises. "It's gorgeous. I have never seen anything like it in my life. It looks like it belongs in a museum."

"I'm glad you like it," his voice is raspy. "Anything to make you happy, Megan. Will you play it for me today?"

"You're staying!" I ask excitedly. "I'm so happy to get you for the whole day."

"You get me for the whole weekend."

"Why is that? What happened?"

"We're forming a new alliance with the Furlotti family. So we are taking a few days off, regrouping."

Antonio rolls us so that I'm beneath him. His breathing becomes uneven and his hands more urgently skim over my body. My stomach involuntarily squeezes delectably as he moves. He presses soft kisses on my neck as his hand works its way up. He uses his knee to push my legs apart and he settles in deeper between them.

The daylight reveals the mars on his skin which make me starved for him. My hunger flares with how much love him. I want to make his hurt go away.

*****

I wake up alone. Antonio isn't here. I throw on a robe and push my feet into pink fuzzy slippers. I walk out into the suite kitchen area.

Antonio is sitting at the table with a bowl of cereal. Sprawled out on the table is a target. My target. The target that I shot at the night before with Joey.

"Good morning, beautiful," he says with heated eyes.

I walk straight to him and give him a kiss. He pushes back his chair as he pulls me into his lap and kisses me deeper. Erin's door opens across the room.

"Give it a rest already," she mutters.

Antonio and I break from our kiss.

"Happy birthday!" I say.

"Happy birthday," Antonio calls out too.

Without warning, Vito gets up from the couch. He must've slept there last night. I didn't know. He startled me.

Vito's sweatpants lay low on his hips, and he is bare-chested as he stretches with a mild roar and drags his feet to the bathroom. His hair is tousled from sleeping.

"So, my girl's a hell of a shot," Antonio says squeezing me.

I turn to him; our faces are close my body thrilled to be in his lap.

"I guess so. Joey seems to think so," I respond modestly.

The bathroom door reopens, and Vito comes out. Erin is by the counter listening to us. Vito walks straight towards Erin and grabs her by the waist. He picks her up and plops her by the table so she is no longer blocking the coffee area.

"Hey! Do you mind? Standing here!" Erin huffs, then, as though she thinks better of further comment, she ignores him. It is so good to see my sister slowly coming back to her old self. "What do you mean she's a good shot?"

Antonio holds the target up for Erin.

"Wow, Meg, you are a good shot."

Vito scratches himself, sips his coffee, and walks over to see what we're all looking at. He hovers over Antonio's shoulder before glancing at me. "Hey, you did that?"

I nod. "Yeah, I did it last night," I say.

"Cool. We could really use you," Vito says. Antonio shoots him an ugly stare. "Dude, I'm just sayin'. She's good."

I got a really good look at Antonio's face during this exchange, the swollen skin and bruising. He doesn't seem to mind though. He drinks his coffee and eats his cereal like nothing happened last night.

There is a knock on the suite door and it opens. Doc Howie walks in.

"Good morning," he says with a smile. "And happy birthday, Erin." Doc Howie plops down his medical bag then rifles through it, pulling out a stethoscope.

"Thank you," she says.

"And how is the injured party this morning," he asks.

Antonio says, "I'm fine."

Doc begins taking out a stethoscope, some ointment, and gauze from his bag. I get up from Antonio's lap and shift to a chair.

The doc listens to Antonio's heart and dresses some of his face wounds. He tips Antonio's head back and forth examining him and tells him to take his shirt off.

Antonio swiftly removes his t-shirt and his bruises are defined against his olive skin.

"You got some doozies," Doc says.

"Yeah, Demetrius got in a few good ones."

Vito snorts.

"A few good ones," Vito comments sarcastically. "He got a lot of good ones in."

"Who's Demetrius?" I ask.

Antonio and Vito look at each other, it is clear that they don't want to answer me.

"He's just another guy in the Furlotti family," says Antonio.

"He's a Furlotti?" I ask.

"Well, no, he's not a Furlotti, but he's in that family."

I shake my head disgusted. I'll never understand all the connections and mob talk.

Doc Howie interjects, "You're staying in today right, Antonio? You need to rest."

"Yeah, I want to hang with my girl today. And we're going to celebrate Erin's birthday," he says.

I didn't even know Antonio had planned anything. I thought Erin and I would have a quiet day. I was going to give her a gift from the casino gift shop, and that would be it. Erin hasn't been up for much lately because of her condition. But she has gotten a lot better.

Antonio shoots me a wicked smile. "It's the kid's fifteenth birthday, we need to do something special," he says. Erin's face lights up.

"Okay," I say. "So what did you have in mind?"

"Don't worry. I've got it all taken care of. Everybody get dressed." Antonio says he's got it all taken care of…I doubt this will be a boring day.

Vito stands at the sink drinking his coffee. Erin and I rush to our rooms to change our clothes. I can't help but wonder what Antonio has in mind for today.

I slip on my jeans and a beige sweater. I fluff my hair with my fingers, then I decide to run a brush through it. Antonio comes in the room while I'm standing at the mirror. He slips his arm around my waist and his other hand reaches for my hair. With a gentle touch, he strokes my hair with his free hand. He picks up a handful and holds it to his nose, breathes deeply and sighs.

"I can't get enough of you," Antonio whispers.

My heart rate spikes, and I feel a rush of lust again. It doesn't take much when he's around. I lean back into his chest as he caresses me, his chin on my shoulder.

"What are we doing today?" I ask, relishing in Antonio's touches.

"I thought we would eat at the restaurant downstairs. I know you guys haven't got out of the suite much. Then I thought we would take your sister shopping at some of the stores here, have her pick out something for her birthday."

"That's very thoughtful of you, but the boutiques here are so expensive. Shouldn't we go out somewhere?"

"Megan," Antonio spins me around to face him. "You don't have to worry about money."

Blood money! The thought flashes through my mind. Everything that Antonio has ever bought me has been with blood money. Money he has worked hard for, that's for sure, but blood money all the same. It is hard for me to get used to this lifestyle, this way of life.

But now that I see the whole picture, I shouldn't let myself think that way though. Everything my parents have ever bought for me has been with blood money, too...I just didn't know it. My ignorance makes me feel guilty. Just because I didn't know doesn't make it right. But I have to accept that this is the way things are and have always been, whether I knew it or not.

My thoughts shift to my parents. I wonder if they'll call Erin today.

"Have you seen my dad?" I ask Antonio.

"I've talked to him a few times on the phone. I'm not sure when he's coming back to Chicago. But I saw my dad last night. He looks really good. So does Donny."

"They were there last night? At the fight?"

"Yeah, my dad is here. He has some business with the Furlottis."

"What kind of business?"

"I really don't want to talk about business today. This is the first time I've seen you in three weeks. One of two things is going to happen right now...I'm either going to take you and your sister shopping downstairs, or I'm going to throw you on the bed and have my way with you. Business is not a part of either of those two things." Antonio reaches for my hips and pulls me towards him. His hands trail down my thighs and up to the back pockets of my jeans. I shiver in his arms. "I really hope you pick being thrown on the bed. I can send Vito with Erin shopping." Antonio's face is mischievous as he leans down and kisses me.

Knock, knock.

"You guys ready?" Vito is at my bedroom door.

375

"We're coming!" Antonio calls out.

Erin is leaning against the door frame that leads out into the hall. She is dressed very casually like me in jeans and a sweater. This is the first time that Erin has left the family floor since our arrival. She is eager and her foot is tapping.

I turn to Vito and his attention is completely on Erin. He has a certain gaze in his eye that worries me, one I have felt uncomfortable with since day one. One that resembles a wolf stalking its prey.

But I can't complain, because Vito has been nothing but protective and helpful to my sister. If it wasn't for him, my sister's face would be covered in burns...or worse.

I grab my pocketbook off the back of the kitchen chair, and we all head out towards the elevators. Antonio punches in the code and the doors open up. Inside stand Joey and Clarissa.

"Hey guys!" Joey says.

Clarissa hugs Erin. "Happy birthday!"

Erin beams at her friend and hugs her back.

Joey claps Erin gently on the back. "Hey Erin...I guess it's fifteen birthday spankings today," Joey jokes. Erin smiles at him.

Clarissa laughs along with Joey, but I don't think Vito found it too funny. He steps in between Joey and Erin and hovers, ominously challenging Joey.

"Hey dude, I was just kidding. Take it easy!" Joey reassures Vito. Antonio taps Vito's arm in a give-it-a-rest motion.

Erin moves to the back of the elevator saying nothing. The ride to the casino level is a quiet one. Antonio is holding my hand, and that small gesture feels wonderful.

The elevator slows at C-level. The doors open revealing Carlo. Standing directly behind him, to my surprise, is Troy.

I release Antonio's hand and give Troy a hug. I whisper in his ear, "I guess you made it out of here alive."

"Yes, I did. The bag over the head wasn't so bad the second time," Troy jokes drily, trying to be funny.

I am so fixated on Troy that at first I don't see Jake standing barely two feet away.

"Jake?! How are you?" I exclaim. It's nice to see Jake. He was fun to hang around with while we were at Notre Dame, and he's been a great friend to Troy since Troy started college.

"Good. How have you been?" Jake asks.

Erin, Clarissa, Antonio, and Vito, along with Joey, gather around Troy, Jake, and I. It's the morning, so the casino floor isn't too loud. Normally, you have to speak in a yell to be heard over the bells, whistles, and shouts of the gamblers. Erin gives a shy wave to Jake, and he immediately takes that as a sign to approach her without waiting for a response from me. He speaks softly to her, and I can hear a happy birthday in their conversation, which is cut short by Carlo.

"Let's head over to the shops, they're waiting for us."

"What does he mean by 'they're waiting for us?'" I ask Antonio.

"You'll see." He smiles.

If Antonio means that all these guys are coming shopping with us, that's weird. In my entire life, I don't think I've ever been shopping with this many people, let alone men.

Slot machines cover the walls and are lined up like soldiers in the middle of the floor. The brightly lit machines with their colorful electronic designs mesmerize the passerby. Against the far wall are tables with every gambling game you can imagine in the casino - roulette, blackjack, some peculiar games I've never heard of before, and, of course, craps. One whole section of the casino is dedicated to restaurants and shops. A gigantic waterfall separates the gambling floor from the shopping. It is noisy as it cascades down the enormous man-made rocks. Small drops of water splash on the granite tile floor.

The first shop is a high priced active wear store where you can get a pair of sweatpants for a hundred dollars. The guys steer us right by that store. Antonio slows down at a boutique called Calypso, which sells everything from jewelry to high-end dress shoes. Standing next to the salesperson near the register is Alessandra. She dashes towards us on her sky-high heels and pulls Erin into a 'happy birthday' hug.

"I couldn't stand waiting anymore! I almost went to get you guys." Alessandra stammers out. She jumps up and down like a kid in a candy store. "Erin, wait 'til you see the gorgeous stuff they have here!"

Troy and Alex watch Alessandra bounce around with excitement.

Alessandra takes Erin's hand and pulls her into the store. Flustered, Erin follows and allows herself to be towed in as Alessandra sits her down in a chair and waves to the clerk. Antonio motions for Clarissa and me to sit in the chairs next to Erin. Our chairs are lined up facing the back of the store. We sit down as our gang of guys stands behind us. This feels weird.

Alessandra is too excited to sit still. It takes me a moment to figure out what was going on.

A woman struts out of the back room dressed to the nines in a sharp black dress with thick silver heels. She parades across the store modeling the dress for us, and Alessandra's excitement bubbles over as she explains the plan to Erin that she can pick out whatever she wants.

"I selected the best outfits here, and these ladies are going to model for you. Seriously, pick out whatever you want. Isn't that cool?!"

Clarissa clapped, "Goody!" She and Alessandra are giddy, but Erin looks as stunned as I feel.

"Uh..."

"Awesome! A fashion show!" Jake announces, then quietly says to Troy. "Hot ladies in fancy clothes."

"Mmmm... yeah..." Troy nodded in agreement, smiling devilishly.

The next woman marches out dressed in a red silk gown with a slit up the right leg. Her shoes must have a four-inch heel and red satin straps lace up and down her feet, very chic. Clarissa screeches in delight and claps her hands as we watch the model spin and turn. Vito stands stoically, shooting glances at Erin, gauging her reaction.

Joey strolls up beside Jake and gently punches his shoulder. "This is my kind of shopping," Joey says as he leers at the model. Jake nods his head in approval.

I peer behind me at Antonio who is speaking quietly with Carlo by the entrance, probably about business.

Shifting my attention back to the models, I try not to appear ungrateful, but these outfits seem way too sophisticated for my sister, unless she is going to a prom or something.

"I love the next one," Alessandra says as a model parades back down the runway, sounding like a host on the Home Shopping Network. "You can wear it for dinner at a nice restaurant or to a club."

It is a little more youthful, but still probably cost more than my entire wardrobe. A black pantsuit with a form fitted jacket. The material looks expensive. Underneath the jacket, the model is wearing a fancy shell that reveals her well-endowed cleavage.

"If we're voting, I totally vote for this one," Jake blurts out.

"Me too," Joey chimes in.

Vito glare at the guys, his expression is murderous. He has been out of sorts.

Erin looks to me for guidance. If I can read her face correctly, she's not only astonished, but a little embarrassed. Before this whole shit-storm of trauma, Erin would have been acting like Alessandra; totally into it and high on the fun of shopping. But the recent events have changed her. She has become more reserved. It is good and bad. While I hate to see her changed, I must admit that I am pleased to see her a bit more cautious.

Antonio breaks from his conversation with Carlo. "Do you see anything you like, Erin?"

She looks at him blankly. I turn in my seat to regard him and speak for Erin. "I think she's maybe a bit overwhelmed."

The clerk frowns, probably hoping for a major sale today. I give my sister a reassuring pat on her knee. The clerk says hopefully, "The models are changing. The next one should be out in the minute."

Alessandra leans towards Erin. "We can try another store," she says quietly.

Clarissa leans in to be part of the conversation.

"Everything is beautiful," Erin says to Alessandra, pausing to say more.

One of the models steps out from the back with a new outfit on. She stops mid-step when the very quiet Vito speaks up, piercingly. "Just give her one of each outfit in her size," he says severely to the clerk. Vito looks at me. "We're moving on. Let's go." He looks back at the salesperson saying, "We will be back to pick the stuff up later." The lady is beaming; she probably made a week's worth of sales in an hour.

He reaches down and takes Erin's hand gently. He helps her to a standing position and pulls her towards the exit. Hmm...Okay... He hands a credit card to the clerk.

Troy looks over at me looking as dumbfounded as I feel. My sister's birthday celebration is turning extravagant. A small evil thought gleefully creeps its way into my mind...Troy will probably share with Connor the treatment Erin is getting and the expensive gifts. Good! I want Connor to know that my sister is fine without him.

"You ready?" Antonio asks me. I nod my head, and he takes my hand.

Troy, Jake, Joey, and Carlo follow us out while Alessandra and Clarissa stay behind to speak to the salesperson.

Leaving the store feels abrupt and awkward, but that's Vito for you, straight and to the point. I keep wondering who is going to pay for all of those clothes. All that will cost a small fortune. Is Vito buying her that stuff?

Vito releases Erin's hand as we walk towards a new store. As Alessandra and Clarissa catch up with us, Alessandra discreetly whispers in Vito's ear, antagonizing him. He practically growls. Alessandra, triumphant, moves closer to Erin smiling.

"Those clothes are to die for! You are so lucky," she purrs.

"You have to let me borrow that red dress!" Clarissa begs. "What do you think, Meg?"

"Now, you just need someone to take you out," Joey says.

Vito stops short and glares at Joey, his face icy. If actual steam could come out of Vito's ears, it would be doing just that right now.

"Are you fucking askin'?" he practically yells at Joey.

Antonio steps forward, intervening. Jake motions with his hands on his neck in a cut-it-out motion to Joey. I remember that Jake has been on the receiving end of Vito's anger before.

"Dude, calm down," Antonio says directly.

"What is your problem?" Joey asks, highly annoyed.

Vito shifts away, but doesn't appear to calm down. Alessandra smiles smugly as she pulls Erin to her and links their arms. They lead us into a cute little store with more expensive clothing. The mannequins in the window even look posh, all posed distinctly with their sharp edges and lines like robots. Alessandra steers us all towards the sales desk in the shop, a small Asian woman approaches her and shakes her hand.

"Good morning," she says. "What can I help you with today?"

Antonio steps forward. "We're looking for some nice things for this girl right here?" Antonio points at Erin.

The nice Asian lady looks Erin up and down and smiles. "Let's see what I have."

All of us, including the guys, walk around the store. Jake picks up a pair of tacky platform shoes and holds them up. "Didn't one of the band members of Kiss wear these shoes?" Erin walks over to him and laughs as she holds the shoe in her hand.

"Wow! These are heavy," Erin says. "I think I want these, Antonio."

Antonio examines them and laughs. "I don't think these are shoes, I think they're weapons. Pick again." Antonio tosses it with a thunk back on the rack.

Erin seems to be warming up, laughing at something Jake mumbles. I watch her with him, seeing how brings out the best in her. Erin and Jake go to a display of hats. They each try a few on, and Jake uses his phone to snaps some pictures of the two of them making silly faces. Erin dissolves into stitches as he makes comments about each and every one.

Vito leaves with a huff and goes to hang outside the store with Carlo. Troy and Joey decide they're bored and go to hang out outside the store too. But, I catch Troy surveying Alessandra's every move as she and Clarissa stand admiring the jewelry with the salesperson.

Antonio talks with the clerk. He pulls out a wad of cash from his back pocket as I join them. "Here you go," he says, handing the cashier a ton of money. "Bag it up those outfits in her size. We'll be back for it later."

I call out for my sister and the others. "Come on." I have no clue what all Antonio has purchased, but I am sure it is more than Erin would ever need. He is so good to her.

We all stroll out into the main area. By the looks of Vito, I would say he is seething.

Carlo speaks to Antonio softly, "We're going back to that first place to settle up, and then Vito, and I will meet you at the restaurant."

I guess that answers my earlier question. It appears Vito is buying Erin a closet full of new clothes.

"Okay," Antonio says as he waves them off. Then he glances at me. "Let's head over to Bella Bistro. I'm starving."

"I could eat to," Troy says.

"So could I," Alessandra adds, smiling broadly at Troy. He looks away seemingly uninterested. Hmm...

I think she is still seeming interested, although Troy... not so much?

Standing at the entrance to Bella Bistro is Alex. I wave as we approach. He waves back as he eyes Joey and the rest of the group, but zeroes in on Alessandra. I realize that Alex is not alone, though. Next to him is a tall man with a black eye and bruises down his dark face, very similar to Antonio. He is an enormous. Not fat...broad and muscular in a way that rivals Vito. This guy radiates a domineering viciousness.

I develop a very bad feeling in the pit of my stomach. Something seems so very wrong or off about this guy. He smiles at us, but it doesn't reach his cold eyes. There's no sincerity. Actually, he looks quite malevolent.

Antonio squeezes the hand that he's holding in a warning. It dawns on me that this is the man Antonio fought last night. The bad feeling in the pit of my stomach turns acidic.

"Hello, Demetrius," Antonio says deadpan.

Chapter 5

Favor: Illegal business that you need help with

Megan:

"How are you feeling this morning?" Demetrius asks a little too kindly.

"Fine." I notice that Antonio doesn't reciprocate the question.

Antonio takes my hand and uses it to tuck me behind him marginally. His eyes never waver from Demetrius'. But this doesn't stop Demetrius's eyes from locking on me. This brute of a guy trails his them up and down my body rudely.

"So... this is the famous Megan." He offers his hand. Antonio stiffens. I hesitantly hold my hand out, but instead of shaking it, he brings it to his lips and kisses it. Antonio swiftly pulls my hand away. Demetrius chuckles at Antonio's reaction. "So the rumors are true...she is stunning."

Demetrius' cold but pleasant demeanor transfers to behind me, where Erin stands with our friends.

"Ah, this has to be her lovely sister, Erin," Demetrius fawns bogusly. *How does he know our names?*

Clarissa shoves forward. "My father doesn't like you here." She gets close to him, almost in his face. Joey reaches his hands out, takes Clarissa by her shoulders, and pulls her back.

"Ah, the sweet Clarissa. How are you? It is so nice to see you amongst other people." His comment is boiled in sarcasm.

He moves himself closer to Erin and stands above her small frame. Antonio immediately reacts along with Joey. I've learned to read his signals, and this isn't a good one...he is ready to lunge.

"Happy birthday, little Erin," Demetrius says lightly.

Sensing Antonio's indicators and catching on, Troy reaches around from behind Erin and wraps his arms around her shoulders, hugging her to his chest. "Yup, this is our little birthday girl!" Troy quips, his voice jovial and upbeat against the tense situation.

"And who might you be?" Demetrius asks nastily.

"I'm Troy, a close friend of the family," he holds up one hand in a sharply exaggerated manner to shake Demetrius', without letting go of Erin. Demetrius does not shake Troy's hand, rather scowls down at it with disgust. Joey and Jake converge on Troy.

"Troy, why don't you and Jake take the girls inside and get us a seat?" Antonio asks, but it comes out as a command.

"But I'm not done saying hello to old friends," Demetrius pointedly shifts his attention to Alessandra. She turns away from him and grabs Clarissa's hand, click-clacking in her heels on the marble floor as she nods for me to follow. Antonio releases my hand as Troy, Erin, and Jake follow Alessandra and Clarissa into the restaurant. Following them, I twist to gaze behind me. Joey, Alex, and Antonio face-off to Demetrius, then the walls of the restaurant swallow me up.

*****

387

Antonio:

"What the fuck are you doing here, Demetrius?"

"Now, now, Antonio, that's no way to talk to someone you are forming an alliance with."

He is fucking with me! And so it begins.

"What do you want?" I ask.

"Come on, Antonio, we're practically family. I just wanted to say hi." Demetrius laughs and drops of his act. "But now that you mention it..." he starts, then pauses and looks around. "So, where is Vito?"

I already have enough on my plate. I don't need this asshole dicking me around. I wrestle with the urge to punch him square in the face. I don't know what his game is yet, and it makes me furious inside.

"He's around. Why are you here?" I mutter.

"I need a favor."

Shit! A favor in this world doesn't mean he's going to ask me to babysit his pet snake while he goes on vacation. Favors are one of two things either a test for the installation of new members into a family, or some business that needs to be handled delicately or on the sly. With the mention of a favor, Joey and Alex slowly back away, knowing their place. What Demetrius is going to ask or say isn't for their ears. Demetrius and I move farther away to a more private area.

I have been gritting my teeth since seeing him standing with Alex, and my jaw is starting to ache. Being in Demetrius's presence irks me on an instinctive level and produces a foul taste in my mouth.

"I have a very important shipment for the Furlottis coming in. I need an experienced associate." Demetrius shrugs.

"When?"

"Forty-eight hours."

I can't say no. Forming alliances with other families is all about one hand washing the other.

"Where?" I ask, knowing he won't answer that question. After all, I don't need to know until it's time.

"I'll contact you." Demetrius begins to walk away. As he's walking he can't seem to help but comment, "By the way, your girlfriend is one sweet piece." He recognizes how to rile me. I stand still not trusting my own body to react to his words. She is my Achilles' heel, and he knows it. "I wouldn't mind a little of that...or maybe you could set me up with her sister?" He laughs arrogantly and finally strolls through the tables.

Alex and Joey immediately approach me. Joey has a worried look. "What was that all about? You okay? You looked like you were gonna pounce on him!"

I evade the questions. "Let's go have lunch."

At a large round table in the back of the restaurant sits Alessandra, Clarissa, Erin, Troy, and Jake. I don't see Megan, and my body immediately shoots a warning to my brain. *Where is she?*

Troy reads the question on my face because he said, "She went to the ladies room."

I move quickly, rushing to the restrooms, pushing wait staff out of my way. My fears aren't for nothing. Up against a wall stands Megan, pinned, wisps of her red hair dance on the wall...Demetrius has her trapped.

"Let me pass, please," Megan says to him, looking annoyed. She has a sassy hand on her hip.

Demetrius tightens his stance by leaning his hand against the wall by her face. I automatically react, thrusting my body between them and forcing Demetrius back. The edges of his mouth twist up into a grotesque smile. I feel Megan's shaking hands rest against my back. She's afraid.

"Relax, Tonio. We were just talking," Demetrius hisses the words like the snake that he is.

It is taking everything I have to maintain my self-control. My whole body hums with agitation. My fists scream at my brain to let them fly. But it's a bad idea. Starting anything with Demetrius right now will cause more problems in the future.

Before I can respond and diffuse the situation, Vito and Carlo come rushing around the corner. Vito doesn't hesitate or even know what is going on. He strides forward, seizes Demetrius by the arm, and flings him into a nearby empty table, crushing it as Demetrius goes down hard.

Megan gasps behind me knowing a fight is coming. My only concern is her.

Carlo reaches down and pulls up Demetrius roughly, anticipating retaliation. Demetrius doesn't counter. Instead, he laughs and brushes himself off as the commotion rings through the restaurant. Security officers come running, along with our lunch party.

"What happened?!" Alessandra calls out.

"Holy shit!" Troy says.

I keep Megan trapped behind me, still uncertain about what Demetrius might do. He is a loose cannon. Vito's breathing is harsh, and he is clearly ready to go at it with Demetrius. Carlo holds up a hand to stop the security officers and let them know he's got it covered.

Surprisingly Demetrius speaks up. "It is just a misunderstanding," he says, his hands raised in surrender.

The gesture means nothing to me, because I can see him calculating something ruthless in his eyes. He's not the type to do something for nothing. I steal a look at Erin, her hand covering her mouth with shock. Jake puts his arm around her shoulder, comforting her.

"Go back to the table," I order. I gently take Megan's hand and lead her over by the rest of the group, giving them another warning order to go back to the table.

They reluctantly leave. Security flanks Carlo waiting for instructions on what to do. I step forward with Vito, Joey, and Alex standing behind me.

Vito's decision to send Demetrius flying into the table was rash, but what's done is done. I can understand Vito's reaction. Almost everything Demetrius does is hostile, so you can never be too careful.

"Sorry about that," I say to Demetrius.

Uncharacteristically, Demetrius shrugs his shoulders in a nonchalant way. But then Demetrius approaches Vito. It's a standoff. Neither one of them moves or backs down. That would be a sign of weakness.

"Why don't I show you out," Alex offers, moving towards Demetrius.

"Tonio," he says but is staring down Vito. "I'll be in touch." His voice is ominous as Alex walks him to the entrance. Security follows.

"What the fuck was that about?!" Carlo asks, annoyed.

I scrub my hands down my face aggravated at the whole situation. I don't like this kind of shit happening with Megan around...and Erin witnessing that...not good.

Vito's regretful gaze lands on me, resting for a moment on my blackened eye. "That fucker is lucky I didn't do worse than throw him into a table."

Any other day, I wouldn't care. Vito could beat Demetrius to with an inch of his life, and it wouldn't bother me in the least. But with the girls around, with us being under the hospitality of Ennio, it's not cool.

I ask Joey and Carlo to go back to the table. Words don't even have to leave my mouth as Vito follows me over to the slot machine smoking section. A couple of people are sitting at the terminals we're near. Vito looms and shoots them a lethal glare, and they suddenly have the urge to try a new machine elsewhere.

I tap my cigarettes until one comes out. Vito folds his arms over his chest watching me. I grab my lighter, clicking it with the cigarette to my lips; I stoke it until it catches and inhale deeply, each curl of smoke entering my body, one by one, relaxing me.

Vito is waiting patiently. We've been friends long enough for him to know I need a few puffs before I enter into this conversation.

"Demetrius wants me to do a favor," I start.

Vito tightens up at the word favor, and his face gets hard. I know what he is going to say before he even says it.

"You are not going alone!"

"Don't start this shit, you know I have to."

"What the hell? I don't like it! Who knows what that psycho has going on his head!" Vito yells. I motion for him to calm down. "When?" he asks.

"In a couple of days."

I take another drag off my cigarette, feeling Vito's irritation and rage bouncing off my skin. His opposition is warranted because I feel the same way, knowing it's all probably a set up for something bigger. But I have to follow through - for the family.

I stamp out my cigarette in an ashtray near me. Alessandra is walking towards us, and we meet her half way.

"Erin wants to go back upstairs. I think it's for the best. Let's have lunch brought up."

"That's fine," I agree.

Chapter 6

Racket: Illegal business

Antonio:

The silence is deafening on the ride to the top floor of the casino. For most people, it's not every day you ride in an elevator with two people who have cloth bags over their heads. It's the only way that Troy and Jake can come upstairs.

Erin had buried her face in my chest and cried when Carlo pulled out the bags. "Please Antonio, don't let Carlo do this," she begged. But I explained the reasons, and she calmed down some. Security is non-negotiable.

Joey has some work he had to do, so he doesn't come with us. He probably has to go write up a report about today's events.

"I guess this is one of those things I shouldn't ask questions about huh, Antonio?" Jake asks.

"Yup," I clip off. "No questions."

Erin stands in the middle of Megan and me, each of us holding one of her shaking hands. Clarissa and Alessandra appear unaffected, and Troy already seems to know the routine. Jake just makes light of it all. Alex squishes himself in the back of the elevator. I watch him in the mirror as he stares at Alessandra for the whole ride.

The elevator stops at the family floor, and I step out with Megan and Erin. Alex and Carlo maneuver Troy and Jake, leading them since they can't see. The door slides shut, and Carlo removes the bags.

Jake is already smiling when his face is exposed. "You know I felt like that crazy scarecrow in that old 80's horror movie." He snaps his fingers a couple times, trying to recall it. "I can't remember the name of it..."

"Dark Night of the Scarecrow?" Alex suggests.

"Hey, yeah! Hollywood didn't have to pay too much for that costume, huh? A burlap bag with a few holes in it."

Everyone laughs. Jake definitely has a way of breaking up the tension in the air.

We step inside the suite. Garment bags are lying all over the furniture and hanging on the backs the doors. Clarissa squeals. "It's like Christmas in here!" she yells. "Erin, please tell me you are going to share?" she jokes.

"It looks like someone brought the whole store up here," Troy says.

Megan's mouth hangs open in either horror or amazement as Alessandra and Clarissa begin unzipping bags.

"Are you going to buy her a bigger closet, too?" Alessandra asks me.

"I didn't buy all of this," I say, and leave it at that.

Alex helps collect the bags with Alessandra. They carry them into Erin's room. Erin trails behind them with Clarissa.

Troy and Jake have made themselves at home, sitting at the kitchen table and snacking on chips they must have found in the cupboard. Carlo is on the phone ordering our food. Vito quietly disappears into the bathroom. It's not my place to say that he bought all this shit. When Carlo and Vito took off earlier, they must have carried all the stuff up here for Erin.

Megan examines me keenly. The look she gives me makes me feel like I'm in trouble, like she thinks I'm lying. I kiss the tip of her nose, loving the way she's observing me speculatively.

"It's not all me," I whisper to her.

I have a seat at the table with Troy and Jake, pulling Megan down to sit in my lap as I hug her to me. I want more than anything to scoop her up, take her to her room, and lock the door. With all these people here, I'm thinking it's not going to happen. A guy can wish though... I run my hands up and down her smooth skin as she talks to Troy and Jake. I have no clue what they're talking about...I'm in my own world with Megan in my arms. I come back to reality when I hear Connor's name.

"Your brother's turning fifteen this week too?" Jake asks around a mouthful of chips.

"Yeah, Connor is the same age as Erin," Troy adds.

Megan shifts in my lap, noticeably uncomfortable with the conversation.

I want to rip Troy a new one for even bringing his asshole brother's name up. I keep my cool, though, not wanting to start trouble. Thankfully, Erin is still in her bedroom sorting her new clothes.

Alessandra comes out of Erin's room and heads to the refrigerator for a drink. I'm still a little pissed off at Troy, and then he stares at

Alessandra's ass with no shame. I want to snatch his fucking tongue out of his throat and hang him with it. I wish I could shoot metal daggers out of my eyes. I reach across the table and whap him on the back of the head.

"Owww! What did you do that for?" Troy yells.

"Don't be a *chooch*," I rumble. Jake tries to cover up his mirth. Carlo, also noticing Troy's behavior, bursts out laughing. Megan looks at us all quizzically as Alessandra sits at the table with her iced tea. Her big brown eyes dance as she beams at Megan and me.

"There are some truly spectacular clothes in that room over there," she says.

"I'm sure there are. What we saw at our own personal fashion show was fabulous," Megan agrees.

Alessandra doesn't even look at Troy. I'm glad she's not interested in that *chooch*. She wouldn't stop talking about him before, so she must have come to her senses. In the back of my mind, I was questioning why she really came here, thinking the reason might have been Troy. But she's giving him the cold shoulder...that is a relief!

Alex comes out of Erin's room and walks over to me. He leans down, whispering, "I'm going to get the cake.

"See how they're doing with the food, too," Carlo adds.

I see Vito lounging in an armchair with his feet up on the coffee table flipping through the channels. Erin comes out of her bedroom, clearly happy. Clarissa talks up a storm to Erin about how to match up different outfits.

"Antonio, thank you so much!" Erin exclaims. "This is the best birthday ever." She leans down and kisses me on the cheek near my bruised eye, then she gives Megan a hug. I say in a low tone, "Vito bought most of it." They turn their heads to him as he monotonously clicks the remote, his head resting on his fist. Erin pats my shoulder, letting me know that she isn't going to say anything to him right now.

The group gets up and makes their way over to watch TV. Jake sprawls out on the couch next to Erin and Clarissa. Troy finds a leather armchair to crash in. Alessandra sits in the matching one. Vito sets the remote aside after finding an old eighties movie. His melancholy mood has not lessened with the passage of the afternoon. Carlo senses it too, and he pulls a deck of cards out of his pocket, offering to play with Vito. Vito nods in agreement.

I snuggle up on a small loveseat with Megan. Her body is pressed against my chest. The clean scent of her hair tickles my nose. The movie holds no interest for me. It is hard to think when she's this close.

Alex opens the door ahead of the wait staff who carry an enormous light purple cake and large silver trays which they place on the counter. Carlo and Alex organize and fix a lunch buffet.

"Come and get it! Birthday girl first," Alex calls out. Erin dishes up a plate as the others gather around the food. I grab a plate and pile it with gnocchi and meatballs. Megan follows behind me.

"This looks delicious," she says.

"This is my favorite," I tell her.

"This is awesome!" Jake says. "I wish my mother could cook like this."

Everyone is shoveling food in their mouth, and the room quiet until, one by one, each person finishes and gets up and throw their plate in the trash.

"Meg, why don't you play something for us?" Alessandra asks.

"Great idea," Erin says and her eyes light up.

I gently kiss Megan's temple and squeeze her shoulder in acknowledgment. This is something that means a lot to me. I have never heard her play the harp. The one and only time I had the opportunity was in church, but I ended up knocking out Dino Prazzo for making a lewd comment about Megan and I had to leave quickly, missing her performance.

"Sure," Megan replies shyly.

She slowly gets up and walks to her new instrument. Her expression is dazzling when she sits down behind it. The exquisite harp was made for her. Everyone gathers back at their seats waiting with anticipation.

Megan leans forward and positions her fingers gracefully above the strings. She begins plucking them like a professional at Carnegie Hall, and the music sails and flows across the room, just as mesmerizing as a track on an iPod. The whole room is captivated and unflinching as they watch and listen to the magic that pours out of the harp.

Too soon the song ends, and Megan steps from around the harp. Erin immediately stands and claps, giving her sister a standing ovation. Troy hoots and follows suit. The rest of the room stands. Megan blushes faintly.

"I didn't realize how much I missed hearing you play the harp, Meg," Erin says.

"That really was incredible," Jake says in awe.

"I could listen to you all day," Alessandra comments.

I am speechless. Megan is more captivating with every new thing I learn about her.

"Cake time!" Clarissa calls out.

Alex lights fifteen tiny purple candles that are spaced evenly across the top of the cake. Clarissa starts us off to sing happy birthday. At the end, Erin blows out her candles and everyone claps.

*****

Antonio:

After cake, it is time to escort Jake and Troy back out. There are some things Vito and I have to do. As the rest of us head to the elevators, Erin, Clarissa, and Alessandra say their goodbyes in the suite. It is obvious that Erin doesn't want to see them with bags over their heads again. That's fine. I think she did really well today, considering it was her first trip off the family floor. Too bad that whole shit storm with Demetrius caused a slight setback, but it seems to be forgotten now. I force the unwanted thoughts of the favor to the back of my mind.

Megan hugs Troy tightly when we get to the floor of the main entrance.

"Thank you so much for coming," she says. "I know visiting Erin and I is a little unconventional."

"No," Troy says sarcastically. "Never."

Jake shakes my hand. "Thanks for the very, um, interesting day."

"No problem," I tell him. As Alex escorts them out, I turn to Megan.

"Come on. I need to get a few things."

Vito and I need additional fire power. Pop called Carlo while we were taking the girls shopping to talk about a tip Carlo got from one of his enforcers. Apparently, a guy named Zee over on Pine Street is working for Tutti. Pop wants us to leave early on Sunday to chase this guy down before we have our next sit down with the Furlottis.

Megan, Vito, and I get back into the elevator and ride it to the basement. We walk into the range, which is just how I remembered it, except now there are neatly stacked boxes against the wall filled with ammo. Vito immediately begins packing up what we need into a bag.

I glance at the targets at one end of the range. "Megan, I'd really like to see what you've got. Why don't you come over here with me and fire a couple rounds."

I put my arm around her back and gently guide her over to one lane. I pick up a pistol and check the stock. It is loaded. I pick up some ear protection and gently place them over Megan's ears as her eyes find mine. Her gaze makes my heart melt - so warm. She looks so cute with the headphones on, and I can't help but kiss her. I gently twirl her around and hand her the pistol. Megan drapes her hand over mine, the pistol beneath our intertwined hands. She takes it from me and raises her arm and focuses. I gently reposition her, just slightly, and step back.

She fires, the blast echoes throughout the room. A perfect shot, straight to the heart.

Joey comes running in. "Aww, I missed it!"

"Glad she's on our side," Vito says.

"I wonder how she would do with moving targets?" Joey asks thoughtfully.

I snake my arm around her and kiss her neck. "You did great!" I say congratulating her.

She pulls off her headphones. "Honestly, I'm not really sure how I'm doing it."

"It doesn't matter, just keep doing it," Vito tells her. He's right.

Chapter 7

Faction: Mob family

Antonio:

The day ends too fast. I really want to spend another night with Megan, but I need to take care of some business. Being with Megan doesn't help with my focus, so Vito and I go back to our shitty hotel room.

Chasing Uncle Tutti is the most aggravating thing I've had to do in a long time. There are too many places to hide in Chicago, too many people to shield him. Allies are easy to come by here for him. Add on top of that the shit with Demetrius and life just keeps getting more complicated.

Vito and I stop by Starbucks, the same one we've been going to for the past three weeks for morning coffee. It's early Sunday morning, and I am in a foul mood. The shit-hole we're staying in doesn't even have a coffee pot. Vito sits at a table in the back while I go to the counter.

"Hello!" a perky girl says.

"Hi, I'll take two Grandé coffees, black, and a couple of those weird pastry things."

"Would you like lemon poppy seed or ginger spice? We also have chocolate chip," she chirps brightly.

"Whatever is fine."

The waitress dips her hand in the case of baked goods.

"Do you live around here?"

What a line? I roll my eyes.

"No," I deadpan.

"So, where are you from?"

"I'm not from around here. Jus' visitin'." I clip my words off hoping she gets the idea that I am not interested.

"Oh, visiting friends? Or family?" She tallies up the order.

"A little of both." I throw a twenty on the counter trying to end this conversation. "Here, keep the change," I say as I grab the bag and coffees.

"Thank you!" she calls out, but my back is already to her, walking away.

I sit down next to Vito. He is playing on his phone. I place the coffees on the table and shove the pastry bag towards him. He sticks his hand in.

"What the hell are these?" Vito breaks one in half and shoves it in his mouth. "Ugh, it's dry."

"Whatever, dude, just eat it."

I take a piece. Vito was right, it is crap.

"Where are we going today?" Vito asks.

"Tonight we've got another meeting, so I really wanted to follow up again on Carlo's lead. He thinks Zee is getting sloppy."

Vito chews the foreign pastry slowly as he stares at the wall of Starbucks.

"I'm going with you," he says matter-of-factly.

I sigh. "Not this again. I have to deal with Demetrius on my own."

"I don't trust that fucker!" Vito says, eyes flashing with severity.

"Neither do I." I finish my strong as hell coffee and stand to leave.

We toss our cups in the trash and step out onto the street. We get in our borrowed SUV, and I drive us towards Pine Street. Vito is silent. He is stewing. Vito doesn't like to be told no. He'll follow orders, but it doesn't mean that he likes it. I understand his frustration. I would feel the same way. I wouldn't want Vito dealing with a sick fuck like Demetrius on his own. Vito's loyalty runs deep.

The street is pretty much deserted. I slow the car down to a crawl, and the two of us scan in between buildings and down alleys. The new intel reported that this scumbag, Zee, has an apartment over here. Carlo says that this guy is an underling for another family he screwed when he took up with Uncle Tutti. What my uncle has to offer him has to be worth a lot to justify the bullshit of taking off from the other family. This idiot is taking a big chance because, if the family he left wants to, they can mark him...then he'll be as good as dead.

My cell phone buzzes in my pocket. I pull it out while I maneuver the car to the sidewalk. It's Patrick.

"Hello," I say.

"How's Erin?" Patrick grumbles out.

"She's doing better. Did you even know it was her birthday yesterday?" I had to ask. It pisses me off that neither of her parents called her on her birthday. I know it bothered Megan. She was just closed lip about it.

A long pause hangs on the other end. "Of course I did." He sounds pissed, but that doesn't mean much with Patrick since he constantly sounds bad-tempered and cross.

"You could've called." I wasn't holding anything back about how I felt. These are his daughters. He and his wife should be more involved.

"Don't lecture me," Patrick says sternly.

I decide to play nice. "Megan and Erin are doing great. I took them out yesterday in the casino, and we bought Erin some new clothes."

"Who's we?"

"Vito and I." I hear Patrick suck his teeth. "You have a problem with that?"

More silence fills the line. Patrick clips off a short, "No."

I got the impression from the conversation, or lack thereof, that Patrick feels beholden to me for taking care of his girls. It doesn't sit well with him.

"I am not doing this as an obligation. I'm doing this because I love Megan and, in turn, her sister. I would do anything for your daughter, never forget that."

"I know." His voice is deep.

"I'm chasing somebody down, so I have to go." I say and take the opportunity while on the phone to check the street again.

Wait! What's that?

In a flash, Vito's door flies open and he takes off running. I click my phone off, grab the keys, and shove my phone in my back pocket. My legs take over, and the chase is on.

For a big guy, Vito is fast. The slime-ball slips in between two brick buildings and zips towards the back. He reaches a chain-link fence, jumps up, grabs on, and starts scaling it. Vito is only seconds behind him. Using his height to his advantage, Vito leaps and grabs the guy's leg, yanking him to the ground. Zee yells as his back collides with the cement. He clutches him by the shirt and wrenches him to his feet. The loser is sweaty and pale. He must've taken something.

"I don't know nothing!" he yells.

Vito pulls back his arm, clenches his fist, and punches the guy directly in the face to shut him up.

"Don't knock him out," I say, but I'm too late. The guy goes slack, his legs giving out, and Vito is holding him up by only the front of his white t-shirt.

"*Mannegia!* What did you do that for?" I huff.

"I didn't hit him that hard. The fucking guy is a *chooch!*" Vito says remorsefully.

"Come on," I say, a little disgusted, and move back down the alley towards the SUV. Vito drags this Zee guy along by his shirt behind me.

I pop open the back, and Vito shoves the guy in. He binds his hands and feet with duct tape and shoves a rag in his mouth. I call Carlo.

"We got him. Be there in fifteen. Have the room ready," I instruct.

I drive us right past the casino main entrance to a small underground garage entryway at the back of the building. Carlo is waiting there. He moves a sawhorse out of the way, and I steer past him into the basement of the casino.

The bluish-tinted lights are bright in the hollow expanse of underground. Noises and voices echo in the cavernous space. I was going to interrogate this guy in the alley, but Vito knocked him out, changing my plans.

I push the button for the back door to the SUV. Vito hoists Zee out and throws him over his shoulder, still unconscious. Across the private garage is a room specifically made for this kind of thing, similar to a police interrogation room...except this room includes many forms of, um, illegal components to *physically extract* information. A two-way mirror, metal table, and chairs are probably the only things in the room that are not made for hurting someone.

Alex meets us there. The four of us have some work to do. No one likes doing this kind of shit, but it is necessary and part of the code to keep people in line. Finding Uncle Tutti is my primary concern right now, and this fucker is supposed to have answers for me.

My adrenaline starts to pump and flow. Vito carries the guy into the room. Against the wall are shackles, and Alex helps Vito by binding the traitor to the wall. The guy's head hangs to his chest, and his arms and legs are spread eagle.

I walk behind the two-way mirror. Carlo is arranging the equipment we need. He slips a clip out of a pistol, checks it, and clicks it back in. On a shelf in the room is a bottle of smelling-salts.

"You ready?" he asks me.

"Ready when you are," I tell him.

I try to suppress my monster. It is seething, gearing up for what it knows is coming. My thoughts antagonize my body, getting it set.

This guy defected from his family, is helping my uncle...an uncle that attempted to strangle the life out of my girlfriend, a man who wants to see my father taken down. My loathing and hatred grows with every thought.

In the other room, Vito and Alex wait. Carlo and I come in, and I stand in the back while Carlo waves the smelling-salts underneath the nose of the defector. He rouses slowly, his unconsciousness battling the harsh aroma. Whatever this guy shot up or took before we found him is probably wearing off. Carlo waves the small bottle again. The second time is more effective and a small moan escapes his mouth. His pasty, greasy skin is more evident as he slowly awakens.

"Wake up, Zee!" Carlo says loudly.

Unintelligible rumbles sound from the guy's chest. Carlo raises his hand and slaps him. Zee groans with the harsh contact. His limbs shake and sweat pours down his face. He's obviously going through withdrawal. A hint of recognition forms in his eyes. Carlo slaps him again on the other cheek, a whimper escapes his lips.

"Where is Tutti?!" Carlo yells at him.

"I don't know anythin'!" Zee cries out.

"Don't bullshit me, you fuck!" Carlo is pissed. He rears back his fist and punches the guy square in the stomach. Agony is clearly written on the traitor's face. It is going to be a long day if this asshole keeps it up.

"Let him hang there for a while," Vito says. "When his hands and feet go numb, he'll talk."

I nod my head. I agree. If we just let this guy hang here, he'll talk eventually. We all leave the room and go to stand behind the mirror. My phone buzzes, I pull it out. It's Patrick.

"Hello."

"When you get what you need from Zee, call me," Patrick says.

He hangs up. *Hasn't Patrick ever heard of small talk?* I think sarcastically.

Carlo calls upstairs to the casino kitchen to order lunch for us.

He hangs up grinning wickedly. "How about a little blackjack while we wait?"

"Dude, you are so fucking lame at blackjack! Why do you torture yourself? I don't mind taking your money, but I'm also your friend. You suck!" Alex exclaims.

Personally, sitting down and playing blackjack while my girlfriend is upstairs does not interest me anyway. I have the urge to head to the top floor to see Megan.

"I'm going upstairs. If anything happens or you think this ass smartens up, call me, and I'll come back down," I tell them.

"No problem, Tonio," Alex says, grabbing a deck of cards. "We'll take care of it for you."

I pass through the door out to the garage towards the elevators. I feel a presence behind me. It's Vito following me upstairs. I press the elevator button and tap in the code. My heart rate accelerates wanting to be close to Megan.

"Aren't you going stay with the guys?" I ask while we wait.

"Nah, I'll come upstairs."

Erin's upstairs. The thought clicks like a light switch. I'm not sure what I think of his interest. Alessandra is thoroughly convinced that Vito is in love with Erin, but, seriously, he's too old for her...too rough. Erin needs a nice quiet guy. Someone who is not involved in all this *shit*.

The elevator doors open and Joey steps out.

"I heard you have someone down here. How is it going?" he asks.

"He needs to hang around a bit before he spills what he's got." I tell him. Vito laughs at my stupid pun.

"We'll catch you later," I say as Vito and I enter the elevator.

*****

Megan:

I am shocked when Antonio and Vito stepped through the suite door. I hadn't expected to see him again for a long time. My body had a mind of its own when I raced across the room and threw myself at him. He picks me up, and I wrap my legs around his body. He squeezes me tight and laughs into my hair.

"Well, hello to you too," he says chuckling.

"What are you doing here?" I ask breathlessly.

"I have some business here, but it can wait until later." He puts me down, but doesn't remove his arms from around my waist. "*Where is Erin?*"

"She's sleeping," I answer.

As he sweeps me up in his arms and carries me towards my bedroom, he glances at Vito who is getting himself a cup of coffee. "Let me know if anything happens."

"Yup," Vito clips without turning to see us.

Antonio kicks the door closed with his foot and plops me on the bed. He follows me down, kissing me with a drugging passion...like we didn't just see each other yesterday.

*****

Megan:

An hour or so later, Vito knocks on the door. "He's awake."

"Who's awake?" I ask. Antonio's heated eyes find mine as he begins to rise.

"Nobody." He kisses me again. "But I have to go," he says reluctantly. He pushes himself off my bed, and I feel the loss of his warmth.

As we come out of my room, Erin is in a chair with her legs curled up reading a book. Vito has the TV remote in his hand as he sits on the couch looking bored. Vito and Erin apparently aren't speaking.

I've noticed that they tend to avoid each other lately. It confuses me, even more when I think of Vito buying all those expensive clothes for my sister. I haven't asked her yet if she's thanked him. We've all been through so much together; their sudden aloofness towards each other is odd.

Vito pops off the couch, tosses the remote on the coffee table, and stretches, his muscles rippling under his shirt. Antonio reaches for my face and kisses me gently.

"I have to go," he says. I don't want him to. "I love you."

"I love you, too." And they leave just as quickly as they showed up.

*****

I have barely sat down when the suite door opens.

"How about some target practice? Not that you need much." Joey quips as he comes in. He observes Erin and me.

I look over at my sister, not really wanting to leave her. I'd love to get out of here, though. I am so sick of staying cooped up. Especially since Alessandra left this morning for Palmetto and Clarissa is at dinner with her family in their suite.

"Can I come too?" Erin asks. Joey is as dumbfounded as I am.

"Umm, I guess so," Joey says, unsure. Erin dashes into her bedroom for her shoes. "That's new."

"I know. But, it's a good sign right?" I ask Joey, perplexed.

"Yeah. It's better than locking yourself in the suite all the time."

We arrive at the basement floor. This time when the doors open, no one is there.

"Where is everybody?" I ask.

"It's Sunday. Everyone is on the floor. Those seniors can be pretty rough." Joey chuckles. "It is usually arguments over machines...someone hogging too many."

"Oh."

Erin's eyes are like saucers when she takes in the sophisticated room. "I didn't know this was all down here," she says in amazement.

"Only security, bodyguards, and enforcers are allowed down here," Joey tells her.

Joey takes us through to Gilly's room, and he's is sitting at the multitude of screens chomping on a powdered doughnut.

"Hey, what a great surprise!" Gilly exclaims.

"Hi, Gilly. Nice to see you again," I say. "This is my sister, Erin."

Gilly's face is beaming. He obviously doesn't have many visitors down here, probably just sees the same guys every day.

"We'll be in the range," Joey states.

Joey walks Erin and I into the range. Erin takes my hand, which is understandable as the room is very cavernous and intimidating.

"I think we're going to try a rifle today," Joey says.

He picks up a long, heavy-looking gun with a round black thing on the top. Erin steps back as Joey moves me towards the lane. I pick up the headphones and place them on my ears, and Joey hands me the rifle. He picks up another headset, handing it to Erin who covers her ears. After he has put on his own ear protection, he moves me into position.

"Put the butt of the gun against your shoulder. Like this." He moves my hands and arms into the correct spot. This doesn't feel as comfortable as the pistol. The rifle is heavy and awkward. "Look through the site," he instructs. "Aim it so that the cross is in the middle of your target."

He moves my hands a little bit more, adjusting them. I turn my head to look at Erin, just to check on her. She is watching in awe as I prepare to fire.

"How's this?" I ask him. He stands back to admire his handiwork.

"Looks good. Whenever you're ready, fire."

I lean down focusing myself. I force my eye to look through the site. I line it up...and pull the trigger.

The gun bucks wildly, jamming into my shoulder painfully. I let out an *OUCH!* I was not ready for that.

"Are you okay?" Joey asks in a panic. He rubs my shoulder. "I forgot to tell you about that! Sorry!" My shoulder feels as if someone rode a motorcycle over it.

Erin comes over to examine me. "You okay, Meg!"

"I'm fine. It just startled me, that's all," I say letting out a breath.

Joey hits the button on the panel. The target swings towards us. There is a hole just off the center of the heart. Good. But not as good as my shooting with the pistol.

"Wow, you still had a great shot though!" Erin says excited. "Can I try to?" she asks Joey.

Joey's face becomes indecisive. "Well..." He pauses a long time.

Erin speaks up again. "I'd like to learn how to defend myself. I'm tired of feeling helpless and weak."

Joey and I share a look. I can tell in his eyes, and he can probably tell in mine, that this is a big step for her, and we shouldn't dismiss it.

"Okay. Meg, why don't you keep practicing. I'll set Erin up over here."

Joey and Erin walk all the way down to the far end. He selects a small pistol. I watch for a minute as he points out the different parts of the gun and stuff. He is showing her how to hold it, how to load it. I can't really hear them with my headphones on, but I note how my sister looks so tiny next to Joey.

I position myself again with the rifle, attempting to remember everything that Joey has shown me. This time though, I rest my elbows on the counter and bend down.

I fire off a couple of shots until the ache in my shoulder becomes too much. I relax for a few seconds and stand up straight, working the cramp out of my shoulder.

I feel rather than see the door open, and suddenly I recognize a new presence in the room. I turn my head to see a man I don't know standing about ten feet from me.

Joey yells, "Get down!"

Don't think, just do. I drop to my knees and throw my body under the counter between the lanes. Clutching the rifle, I sneak a peek at the stranger. His clothes are torn and he is talking to himself wildly as he bounces around the room like a monkey in an unwanted cage, trapped.

An instant later I see Antonio and Vito in the doorway, breathing heavily. Without a thought, my body raises the rifle and aims. A familiar kind of protectiveness overcomes me. Antonio sees me at the last second and yells to me, his hand raised, "Just nick him! Don't kill him!"

I fire.

My bullet flies through the room and punctures the guy's leg, blood sprays in slow-motion onto the cement floor. I crippled him. He falls hard, groaning.

I pull off my headphones and I hear Joey yell, "What the fuck?"

My eyes immediately search for Erin. She is pinned underneath Joey against the wall. The room fills with more people...security, I think.

Antonio scoops me up off the floor, takes the rifle, and holds me.

"It's okay," he says soothingly. "You did great."

"What happened? Who was that?" I question, my hands shaking.

"Zee. He's a guy we're interrogating," he sighs. "We left the guy for a couple minutes with a rookie," he informs me, angry at himself. "When we were walking back, we saw Zee taking off down a hallway."

"Why did you tell me not to kill him?" I ask, trying to catch my breath.

"I saw the look in your eye. And you're a great shot," he laughs. "But, I still needed to ask him questions."

The thoughts that had run through my mind were not of killing, rather of protecting. I don't know where I would have shot him if Antonio hadn't yelled to me.

417

"What are you doing down here?" he asks me.

"Joey brought us down here. He was showing me how to use a rifle. And Erin wanted to shoot, too," I spill out in a rush.

I look over Antonio's shoulder to see two security guards dragging this Zee out the door, leaving a trail of blood. Behind them is Vito lifts Erin, and, cradling her is his arms, walks to the doorway cautiously to avoid the blood. Antonio and I follow him out into the main room. Gilly is not at the security cameras. He is sprawled out on the couch with a bag of ice. I hurry over.

"Gilly, are you okay?" I ask.

"Yeah, he hit me on the back of the head...put me out for couple minutes."

"Do you need anything?" I ask. Gilly looks so vulnerable lying alone on the couch.

"I'll be fine," he says good-naturedly.

I look around the room, but can't find my sister among all of the people. Every face I see is male.

"Where is Erin?" I entreat Antonio.

"Vito must've taken her upstairs."

The elevator seems to take forever to arrive with all the different people coming and going because of the chaos this guy, Zee, started. Antonio tries to call Vito, but it goes immediately to voicemail. My patience is fried, and I am about to suggest we walk up the stairs when finally the elevator is free. Antonio punches in the family floor code, and, thankfully, we're off.

Chapter 8

Marked Man: Slated for death

Megan:

As soon as we walk into the suite, I can see that things are not good with Erin. Doc Howie and Ennio are already there, talking quietly when we come in. Clarissa is sitting at the table with her head in her hands. Seeing Ennio surprises me the most...we haven't seen him in over a week.

We quickly say our hellos, and I rush directly to Erin's room. She is on the bed enfolded in Vito's arms; her head is against his chest. She is silently crying. I cautiously sit on the bed next to them and brush the hair out of her eyes. My sister again seems fragile, like a porcelain doll.

I am guarded by what I should say. Her behavior has been so erratic when it comes to these types of things happening. She spent thirteen years not having to deal with it, and now, unfortunately, scares like this are a constant fixture in our lives with only short reprieves.

A soft knock on the door jam. Doc Howie comes in. He checks her pulse, and Vito shifts Erin so that Doc can listen to her heart. His expression is unreadable.

"Ennio would like to speak to you," he says to her tenderly.

Suddenly, a voice I recognize travels through the main room. *My father!* I have mixed feelings when I see him. I'm angry that he hasn't kept in touch with us or even contacted Erin on her birthday. But at the same time, I miss him. That twinge consumes me as I walk directly to him and encircle my arms around his waist, hugging him to me. He leans down and kisses the top of my head. That fatherly gesture releases some of my anger.

After all, the phone goes two ways. I could've called him. But a niggling voice in the back of my head stops me...a whisper that reminds me what he is probably doing. I'm not really sure why I can easily accept the lifestyle from Antonio, but not my father. I'm certain it has something to do with the fact that I've always known Antonio's legacy and decided I wanted him anyway. My father lied blatantly for years and years.

"Why don't we all sit down?" Ennio suggests.

I release my dad and feel a hand on my shoulder. I turn my head...everything in the world that makes life worth living is standing there beside with love shining in his eyes. Antonio takes my hand and leads me to the table, and we all sit down. Clarissa is quiet.

"Clarissa is going to a boarding school for the next semester. It is very safe there. Many influential people and A-list celebrities send their children there," Ennio rushes out. He must think that running his words together quickly will lessen the blow.

Tension starts in my neck and runs all the way down to my toes. *They're sending her away!* That's why my father's here. Antonio brought this up before, but I thought the idea had been forgotten. Antonio squeezes my hand reassuringly. I already know his opinion on the subject.

"Doesn't that cost a lot of money?" I ask.

"Don't worry about that," my father rumbles. I suddenly realize lately that my parents must have been squirreling away the *blood money* he's made over the years. I've never seen any of it, that's for sure. We have lived very frugally for as long as I can remember.

My biggest objection is that I won't be there with her. It is an unbelievable opportunity, and she will be with Clarissa...but I can't help having an issue with losing some control. I glance over at Clarissa, she has an unreadable expression. Maybe she doesn't want my sister to go with her?

"It seems as though this has already been decided," I say quietly. Clarissa stiffens, and I reach out a hand and place it on top of hers. "If you don't want Erin to go with you, maybe there is another school she can go to...one that is just as good...just as safe?"

"Why would you think I wouldn't want her to go with me? I have been so afraid that you wouldn't want her to go. I am so excited that I won't be alone, I can hardly contain myself," Clarissa says earnestly. Her face brightens.

"If everyone thinks it's the best thing...I just want my sister to be happy and safe...to get past all of this," I say.

Ennio and Clarissa are obviously pleased. Clarissa claps her hands in delight. My father is exactly the same as he was when the conversation started...unmoving and stoic.

"I'm going to be sending Joey with them as added security," Ennio continues. "Even though the school is a fortress, most attendees bring their own security."

It is obvious by the way everyone is speaking that they were expecting a fight from me. But I could never take anything away from my sister. I agree with all of them that it could be just what she needs. It gives me a great deal of relief to know she will be with Clarissa...even more to know that Joey will be there, as well. My father gets up and goes to Erin's room.

Antonio kisses my cheek and whispers in my ear, "You're doing the right thing."

Thirty seconds later, Vito storms out of Erin's room. His face is chiseled into a frown. With fists clenched at his side, he walks straight out the door into the hallway, leaving. Antonio follows him.

"Now that that is settled, I need to get back down to the casino." Ennio says his goodbyes, and it's just Clarissa and I left in the room.

"I can't wait! It is going to be so much fun!" Clarissa squeals.

A few short moments later my father comes back out.

"She's sleeping," he says quietly as he approaches me and hovers over my chair. "Come with me," he orders. As we walk by the kitchen counter, I notice two new cell phones that weren't there before. "Those are for the two of you," my father scratches out.

I stand frozen in place, unsure of what this is about. The awkwardness between us is palpable. We have had no parental supervision in weeks. Basically, we've been living on our own with the generosity and company of Clarissa's family. My father motions me out into the hallway.

As we exit the suite, Antonio and Vito are in a heated close-knit conversation. They abruptly stop talking when they see us. Antonio sends me a half smile, but Vito won't even look our way. His head is hanging. Hair drops down around his cheeks, his appearance is crestfallen. Antonio doesn't ask any questions as my father and I get on the elevator...he just watches us leave. I don't even have the courage to ask my father where we are going, but I don't need to wonder for long as he presses the button for the basement.

The enforcer area has cleaned out since the mayhem earlier. My father takes me over to the door that houses Gilly, who is there looking healthier than he did an hour ago.

"Hey, Gilly...how are you feeling?" I ask.

"Much better, thank you," he says in a chipper tone. "How are you doing, Patrick?"

That is an interesting tidbit. He knows my father. Well, I guess, in a way, Gilly knows everybody. I suppose my father does, too.

"Fine," my father clips off.

The firing range has been cleaned thoroughly. The remnants of ammonia invade my nose. Not one drop of blood remains. I am numb to the whole thing right now, which must be a defense mechanism. When these types of things happen, there's a disconnect between my body and my brain. My soul takes over...like it knows exactly what to do. It sends signals to my body to protect itself. Self-preservation and defense rule me. Fight, flight, or freeze...I fight.

I take a deep breath and ask "How's Mom?" I want to know the answer to this more than I care about what we're doing down here.

"A little lonely without you girls," he says unemotionally.

"Why doesn't she call us?" I hated the sound of the pleading in my voice. It gives the impression that I'm needy or weak, and I don't want anyone to feel that way about me...especially my father.

He loads a gun I've never seen before. It's small and black. He doesn't look at me when he talks. "I told her not to."

"Why?!"

"It's better for everybody. The less your mother knows, the safer it is for her...and you. Hasn't that boyfriend of yours taught you anything?"

"She could've called us, Dad!" I yell at him, my temper rising. "The phones are secure. You and Antonio use phones," I admonish. "I had a phone in South Bend."

"You can talk to your mother when Tutti is put down. I just gave you new phones, use them wisely."

"What about Luigi Prazzo?" I ask. Antonio speaks about them as though they are a package deal. My father does not even look at me during this entire conversation as he loads and checks the gun.

"He's already dead," my father says with absolutely no emotion.

I want to suck in a breath and think, *How horrific!* But I can't. Only thought that runs through my mind...One down, one to go.

Chapter 9

On Ice: *Dead!*

Antonio:

Zee managed to give us important information before he got fucking loose. While he spilled his shit about Prazzo, I already knew that he was dead. Patrick had already got him and surprisingly gave me the details. No one will ever find Luigi Prazzo unless they decide to take down the new high-rise over on Lexington.

The important intel he gave us was about Uncle Tutti...the only one left. Zee put up a fight but we convinced him to talk. Tutti's men have been hijacking tractor-trailer trucks all over Illinois, selling the stolen goods on the black market. Following the routes and tracing them back is the best way for us to trap him. Figures Tutti would be doing shit like this...hijacking and fencing stolen property is a low form of organized crime.

Afterwards, we dropped Zee on the doorstep of the family he defected from. Literally...we threw him on the sidewalk. Let them deal with him.

It will be a relief when this is all over. Maybe we can go back to school and finish out our senior year, although Megan probably doesn't even need to do that. Lucia has been tutoring her, and, with all the credits she already had, her diploma is as good as being in her hand. I would love to take Megan on a vacation. A real one this time. Anywhere she wants to go.

*****

Antonio:

Vito is a live wire. He says he's just pissed because Patrick was an asshole to him. He's lying. He could give two shits if Patrick acted like a jackass to him. I didn't mention the discussions of sending Erin with Clarissa to boarding school. I wasn't sure it was going to happen, and I never let my suspicions sink in regarding his feelings toward Erin. It's hard for me to see her in that way because of her age...and the fact that I only have eyes for one person. But Vito has done an excellent job of taking care of Erin. She has been a difficult responsibility. The combination of her volatile emotions and reactionary behavior has been a cross we've all had to bear. I wish I knew a way to help him deal.

I'm hesitant to take him with me to the meeting tonight. His explosive mood could really be a problem. If Demetrius is there, that will only add fuel to the deadly fire already burning.

Back at the hotel, we change and head to the car. The meeting is at the same place, so we don't rush. We know how to get there.

I smoke my cigarette as we had out towards Charleton Street.

"Dude, you okay?" I ask.

"Yeah. Fine."

"Keep your cool tonight. Don't go fucking *oobatz* on me. I need your head on straight," I order. I toss my cigarette out the window as we park and walk over to the building. I rap on the metal door, and the chain rattles lifting it, just like the last time we were here. The meeting place looks exactly the same except the makeshift boxing ring is gone.

Pop and Donny are here. They have been staying at a high-end hotel in downtown. One of Pop's colleagues owns it. Pop had been promising to visit forever...these unfortunate events gave him just the opportunity.

Demetrius is standing behind Don Furlotti's chair. He nods at me to follow him. Vito visibly tenses when he sees Demetrius.

"I'll be back in a minute," I say. Vito must be watching me because I can feel his eyes on my back. With certain things Vito can hide his emotions extremely well...with others they run right at the surface ready to implode.

Demetrius and I stand in the shadows of the corner away from everyone else. "Three a.m., dockside on Elm," he tells me in a brute command.

I nod and walk back to Vito.

Everyone seems to have assembled that needs to be here. There have been no problems with the alliance over the past few days. Negotiations are going forward. Don Furlotti calls everyone to order, and we all take a seat. Chairs scrape along the cement and the talking dies down. First order of business is to mention the death of Luigi Prazzo.

"The first defector, Luigi Prazzo, no longer remains among the living," Mr. Furlotti announces. "As for Tutti, attempts are still being made by Don Delisi's son to find him."

It is my duty and obligation, as assigned by my father, to take care of Uncle Tutti. I relish the opportunity after what he attempted to do to Megan and Pop.

"If there is no new business, we will proceed with the alliance," Don Furlotti finishes.

Pop stands with Don Furlotti, each at the head of the table. Donny stands as well, as he is the capo. He takes a switchblade out of his pocket and it clicks open. Don Furlotti's capo does the same. An incision is made on Pop's and Mr. Furlotti's fingers. Per the ritual, each Don meets in the middle and solidifies the alliance in a blood bond. An enforcer I don't know steps forward with rosary beads and a picture of St. Francis of Assisi. He drapes the rosary beads over their adjoined hands and places the picture underneath them. A bond is formed through blood and family. Bottles of Chianti are opened, and wine glasses are passed around. Pop makes a toast.

"To our new family members, thank you. It is an honor to become one with you. Salute!" Pop raises his glass and everyone follows. A chorus of salute bounces off the walls.

The meeting breaks up, and the group seems pretty content with what went down. This alliance benefits everyone. Demetrius stares at me coldly, and I shrug it off.

"How are things going, Tonio?" Pop asks me as we step into a private corner.

"I am making some headway. Hopefully, I will have everything taken care of in a week or so."

Pop affectionately taps my shoulder. "Your mom misses you. We look forward to having you back at home." He pats my face with his palm. "You're a good boy."

"Are you leaving tonight?" I ask.

"Yes. I have a meeting with Sommersville very soon."

"How's that been going?"

"Now that Tutti took off, they don't have the backbone. Everything's falling back into place...like it used to be."

I see Donny waiting for Pop. Pop pulls me in for a tight hug. "Love you," he says. "We have to go." I hug him back.

"Love you too, Pop. See you soon," I tell him.

Vito's disposition is marginally better as we get back in the car.

"That went well," I comment.

He shrugs his shoulders noncommittally.

"What did Demetrius say?" he asks in a low tone. I am surprised at Vito. He knows I'm not supposed to discuss it. I don't respond right away. "I don't trust him," he adds. "I'm not trying to break any code; I'm just looking out for you."

"I know," I sigh.

We sit in silence. The hum of the motor and the softened radio are the only sounds.

"Have to go tonight at three a.m." If I can't answer these types of questions with Vito, then there is absolutely no one. Someday, he'll be my head enforcer. He was born and bred for it.

*****

Antonio:

I catch a couple of hours sleep before I have to meet Demetrius. Vito is snoring loudly, sucking the air out of the room. I take a quick shower attempting to wake myself up and throw on some old jeans, a T-shirt, and a jacket. I grab my keys off the nightstand.

I arrive at the docks and let the car roll along slowly in the darkness. I don't see Demetrius, but I'm a little bit early. I am well-prepared, with a semi-automatic rifle stuffed under the driver's seat and a glock in the back of my jeans.

Being part of a crime family, you would think that crimes wouldn't bother me, but they do. I find it easy to shrug off what my father does...those people know what they're getting themselves into. People who take part in gambling and money-laundering are typically their own victims. If they can't pay or get in to deep, it's their own problem, their own fault. But shit like drugs and racketeering, those things create more faceless victims than I ever care to think about...Pop would tell me not to think. *Don't think, just do.*

A black Camaro pulls up next to me, its windows tinted. Leaning forward in my seat, I reach into the back of my jeans and pull out my glock, holding it below the steering wheel...ready for anything. The window rolls down on the car next to me, and Demetrius leans over the seat.

"Follow me," he says brusquely.

I hold my gun in one hand and steer with the other as I follow him down the thin road and out behind a crumbling brick building. Parking next to him, I wait for him to get out first. He slams his car door, and I notice his hands are empty, so I put my gun back in my pants and get out.

Each time I am in Demetrius's company, I am reminded of his sordid and violent past. His impulsiveness and disregard for the rules makes him two things - feared by the underworld...and a target.

"Come on," Demetrius says and waves for me to follow him.

I do.

Side-by-side we walk into the rundown building through a dilapidated steel door. The misshapen door has been kicked numerous times and now it bows ungracefully. It is dark inside with only a few streetlamps casting shadows and illuminating certain areas. It is hard to see in the dimness, but I can smell decaying fish and mold. It is overpowering, and I cover my nose with the sleeve of my jacket, trying to get relief from the foulness.

A figure steps out of the shadows. I brace myself preparing to attack if necessary.

"Do you got the stuff?" a scared voice asks.

"Yeah. Do you?" Demetrius says bitingly.

Paper rustles and the unknown person steps forward, handing a package to Demetrius.

He opens it gradually saying in a low tone, "You better not try to fuck me."

The guy in front of us is visibly shaking. That's not good. That's just as bad as someone like Demetrius. This guy could start going crazy...do something stupid. I train my eyes on the guy, watching carefully his every move.

Demetrius licks his pinky finger and dips into the package. He brings his finger to his mouth tasting it. He growls.

"What is the shit?" Demetrius barks. "I told you I wanted the pure stuff only!"

All hell breaks loose, and I am ready for it. Demetrius tosses the shitty cocaine to the ground and pulls out his gun. I do the same, jacking my body forward to grab the guy. He's skinny and quick, and he dodges my grasp and runs for the door. I chase after him while Demetrius ducks through another doorway, attempting to cut him off in the next room. I grab the guy's shirt and yank him back. He lands on the ground crunching the broken plaster that litters the floor. I shove my foot on his chest holding him down and train my gun on him in the thick darkness.

He pleads with me as Demetrius walks up and hovers over him, too. The red has already formed over my eyes in fight mode. It takes a few minutes to register what he is saying.

"Don't leave me with him!" he repeats over and over.

He is talking to me, asking me, the man with the gun on him, not to leave him alone with Demetrius. There is definitely something wrong with this scenario. I look to Demetrius to see what he wants to do. This is his show, not mine. He is eerily quiet as the man on the ground grovels.

If this was my business to take care of, I'd beat him up, and tell him to get better stuff or else. In my mind, it seems simple enough; you can't get clean cocaine from a dead man. But I have never dealt in drugs, so I am not really sure what's going on here.

And if this kid was marked, it wouldn't be my business to take care of it. It would be the cleaner's.

Then the entire bullshit situation dawns on me.

Demetrius is a Cleaner. Fuck!

A gunshot rings out startling me, but it's not mine. Blood splatters my jeans and I feel the wetness soaking through to my skin. I realize Demetrius shot the groveling kid in the face. I take a moment to recover and relax my hand. I drop the gun to my side.

Mistake number one.

Demetrius mumbles under his breath, "No body, no crime."

His eyes, even in the blackness of the grimy room, are vacantly hateful. He shifts his eyes to me, and in that look I know...*I'm marked!*

I play it cool, paying close attention to where his arm is pointing. I'm not sure what he has planned for me, so I don't want to alert him that I am onto him. Knowing this sick fuck, he'll make me help him clean this mess up and then off me. I give him the intro he needs to see where this is going.

"What's next?" I ask. My hands are steady as always, and I keep my breathing even.

A new shot whizzes by us and embeds itself in the wall behind Demetrius. It startles both of us. I immediately hit the ground and roll close to the wall. A garbled screech roars through the ancient building. I keep moving and stay low to the ground as I scan around me looking for an exit. I don't know where Demetrius has gone. I'm like a rat in a maze. But my prize for figuring it out isn't a crumb of cheese...it's getting out of here alive. I say a silent thank you for my father being a bastard when it came to training.

I keep my gun poised and set. More shots are fired and pump into the walls, shattering and collapsing them. The yelling continues between the shots, and I can finally make out what this person is shouting.

"You killed my brother!"

Sobbing wails bounce off the crumbling enclosure as whoever is out there kneels over the dead body. "You son of a bitch! Demetrius! Where are you?!"

I strain to listen. I definitely know where the shooter is. This person is clumsy and inexperienced. I don't know where Demetrius is...and that is a problem.

I can't stay here. I'm too exposed. I stay low and shuffle across the floor, but only get about ten feet when I recognize the shooter is coming my way. I crouch on the floor near a doorjamb. The tip of a sneaker comes into view and slips forward cautiously. I slide my gun in the back of my jeans, needing two hands.

Don't think, just do!

With another step forward, I lunge and grab the person around the middle trapping their arms. A startled yelp bellows out. I clasp my hand over their mouth.

Holy shit! It's a girl!

Her cheeks are slick with tears. I tighten my grip, squeezing her as she tries to free herself. She is attempting to raise her gun, struggling. I jerk her over to the wall and press her face against it. She whimpers. I whisper in her ear as her long black hair flies wildly in my face.

"I'm not Demetrius. Stay calm, and I'll get us out here," I say, attempting to sound comforting.

She nods her head, but I can't trust her. She's too unstable and upset. I keep my hand in front of her mouth and my other arm securely around her, pinning her to me. I hear the familiar crunch of plaster.

He's coming!

I pick her up, inches off the floor, and make a run for it. I dash over the threshold, and we're out into the night air. I see two people crouched by the side of the building. I immediately throw the two of us down onto the ground, and grab for her gun. She screams into my hand. Within a second, I'm aiming.

"Tonio! It's me," a voice says that I identify instantly.

Vito!

I relax my hand, lowering my gun, as Vito rushes over to me. Behind him is Patrick.

"What the fuck are the two of you doing here?" I spit, angry at Vito for totally disregarding my instruction to stay away.

The girl who tried to blow my head off earlier, although I truly think she was aiming at Demetrius, begins sobbing uncontrollably. The crying racks her body and makes it convulse in defeat.

I'm not sure if the danger was over. I have no clue where Demetrius is now.

"Help me get her up," I say. Vito reaches down and scoops her up into his arms. I hang onto her gun.

"We need to find cover," Patrick orders. I agree.

Patrick and I flank Vito as he carries the crying girl in his arms.

"Who is she?" Vito whispers.

"No clue. She was shooting at us earlier."

Patrick silences us with a look. He stalks cautiously around the side of the building towards my car. Demetrius's Camaro is gone. It's a good guess that he probably screwed. But Demetrius is very sly; we still need to make sure that he's gone.

"Vito, put the girl in Antonio's car. Antonio and I will check the perimeter and the inside of the building." Patrick directs. *Who the hell put him in charge?*

We cover Vito and make it to the Camaro. He slides her in the back seat. Her hysteria seems to have died down, and she just makes the occasional sniff. Vito closes the car door then stays low behind the car. Patrick and I do a sweep and move over the entire area outside, but we find nothing.

We head inside the building. Patrick pulls out a flashlight. *Mannegia*, he comes prepared! The only thing we find is the corpse of the drug dealer that Demetrius killed. Patrick leans down and examines the body. Then he casts the light of the flashlight around the room.

"What are you looking for?" I ask.

"Something to wrap the body in."

436

"Why would you clean up Demetrius' mess?" I ask incredulously. "Let's just get the fuck out of here."

Patrick sighs. "I don't want there to be any trace of you ever being here." he says unemotionally. "I need to get a few things out of the SUV."

We stop by my vehicle and pile in to have Vito drive us over to the other car, which is parked a block away. The girl is curled up, not moving, not speaking, mentally checked out.

"You get any information out of her?" I ask Vito.

"Nah, she is out of it," he replies as he puts the car in motion.

He drops us off and waits while we get in the SUV and start it up. We head back to get rid of the body, Vito behind us.

"So what is the plan?" I ask Patrick as we get out and stand over the body. "I think that he is that girl's brother. Do you think she's gonna want to bury him?"

"We're just moving him. Getting rid of any evidence here." He unravels a large plastic sheet and lays it next to the body. "Help me move him."

I lean down and grab the legs as Patrick takes the gory area where the guy was shot. On the count of three we lift and place him in the center of the sheet. Patrick carefully wraps the sheet around the guy, then picks him up and tosses him over his shoulder. I open the back of the SUV, and Patrick puts him in the back, motioning for me to get in the passenger seat. We drive for about a mile, Vito still behind us.

Patrick pulls over at another deserted place. He turns the off headlights and the overhead lights in the car so the car remains in darkness when he opens the door. He opens the back and drags the body out, tossing it over his shoulder.

"Stay here," he orders me. He walks away as if he has done this a hundred times.

A few minutes pass, and Patrick comes back, and I stay silent as pulls up beside Vito.

"Hop in with Vito, and you two drop that girl off somewhere. When she comes to, she'll find a way home."

"Where do we drop her?" Vito asks as I get out of Patrick's SUV and jump in with him.

"Behind a club or something," Patrick says matter-of-factly.

Cold! That is the only word to describe Patrick. He has daughters. Would he want someone dropping them off comatose behind a club?

"Okay," I say. Vito looks at me stunned. "We'll head back to the hotel after we take care of her."

"You should get a new room," Patrick clips and drives away. *Bye to you too!*

Vito looks at me like I've grown a second head. "We are not seriously dropping her somewhere...random?"

"Of course not!" I reply gruffly. "Head to the casino. I want to question her. We'll give her to one of Carlo's thugs to drive home when she's awake."

The events of the last hour hit me. The game is in full swing. I wrestle with the idea of whether or not I should tell Vito about Demetrius. I wonder if Demetrius has marked me on his own or if someone else has put out a contract on me. My adrenaline is slowing down, and the plague of this new information haunts me.

Vito calls Carlo. "We need a secluded room," he tells Carlo quickly. "And a guard for the door." He hangs up.

The girl is sprawled across the back seat, very quiet. Her chest rises and falls slowly and her eyes are closed, as though she's in a deep sleep. So the skinny kid with the bad drugs was her brother. This is the ugly part, the destruction of family through drugs. She could've gotten herself killed too. How did she know it was Demetrius though? I have a lot of questions for this girl when she is coherent.

Chapter 10

Hit: To kill

Antonio:

It's 5 a.m., and there are still people coming in and out of the front door of the casino. *Don't gamblers ever give it a rest?*

Alex and Carlo meet us in the underground garage as Vito tries to get the girl to come around. Even the jostling of moving her doesn't get her to respond, so he carries her into the casino to the elevators. We ride to the fourth floor and make our way a single room down the end of the hallway. Alex opens the door and Vito places her on the bed.

"What do we do with her now?" Carlo asks.

"I need one of you to stay with her, see if you can get her talking. I want to talk to her when she wakes up," I order, and no one questions my instructions. "Vito and I are going back to the hotel to switch rooms, and then we are going to catch a couple of hours sleep. We'll be back later to question her."

"No problem," Carlo says.

"Make sure the Doc checks her out."

*****

Megan:

The early morning sun wakes me. I stretch and yawn under the covers, my body tired and limp. I shuffle to the bathroom and come out to find Erin sitting and waiting for me.

"What's up?" I ask warily. Erin is never up this early.

"What do you think about me going with Clarissa to boarding school?"

I sit beside her. "I think it's great. You should go back to school, and you and Clarissa will have a great time."

"I'm afraid," Erin says, ominously.

"Sometimes we have to face our fears."

"I spoke with Doc Howie. He thinks it's the best thing for me, and he tells me he believes I'm strong enough to go," she says, as though she doesn't quite believe it herself.

"Once you get involved in classes again and meet new people, it is going to help you to move forward."

"I'm going to miss you," Erin adds. Tears fill her eyes.

"I'll miss you too," I smile sadly.

Clarissa burst into the suite. "Carlo has a girl in a room downstairs on the fourth floor!" she says excitedly.

I can't imagine why Clarissa would be so excited that her brother has a girl staying here at the casino. She sees my confused expression explains. "Not a girl for him! There was some big commotion last night. One of the enforcers told me they saw Vito and Antonio drop her off."

My jaw drops as I go from melancholy to jealous in point three seconds. *What the hell is Antonio doing with this girl?!* Not only am I green with envy, but hurt that he was here and didn't come to see me. Anger flows through my bloodstream like a disease taking over my body, even though the rational part of me knows that there has to be some kind of explanation.

"Come on, let's go see her!" Clarissa encourages.

Even though we're not supposed to leave the family floor without an escort, I feel rebellious right now. And all of a sudden I'm very intrigued to find out what this mysterious girl's story is.

Erin and I head to our rooms to change out of our pajamas. I stop short at my bedside table, glancing at the small black handgun on my father gave me. I remember shooting it for him last night in the range. I remember him telling me that he felt better knowing I had protection of my own defend myself. He made me fire the weapon repeatedly, and every time I hit the target he requested. I could tell that he was impressed and proud.

I now hesitate by the gun. My father told me he wanted me to keep it on me wherever I went, so I pick it up. I'm not taking a purse, so I check the safety and slip it into the back of my jeans like Antonio does. It is bulky and uncomfortable, cold against my skin. I pull my sweater down over it. I check myself in the mirror and meet Clarissa and Erin in the hallway.

Since Clarissa lives here, she knows all the elevator codes and taps the right one into the keyboard. Erin is noticeably uncomfortable, but I'm invigorated. This feels like a secret mission, and I'm locked and loaded.

Clarissa gives Erin a playful shove. "Come on. Lighten up! It'll be fine," she reassures. "We're just going to say hi."

Erin gives us both a forced smile. "I know," she says.

The ride is quick to the fourth floor. The hallway is just as grand as the one leading to our suite. I see Alex standing at the end of the hallway. It is totally deserted except for him. Clarissa waves, but I can tell by Alex's stance that he's annoyed. We shouldn't be here.

"What are you guys doing down here?" he asks, irritated. Alex is tough and is trusted with many important tasks around here, but when it comes to Clarissa he is a softy.

"We came to see the girl!" Clarissa says pointedly.

"You shouldn't be here," he shakes his head. "No, you can't see her. Go back upstairs." Alex ticks off his sentences like a list...or maybe they sound rehearsed because he's had to say them to Clarissa before.

"Come on, Alex!" Clarissa pleads. "We'll say hello, that's all."

"You are a pain in the ass," he says.

"I know, but you love me," she smiles with a singsong voice.

Alex hangs his head in defeat. "I was giving her a little time to rest, so, if she's sleeping, you are NOT going in there. Hold on a minute, let me check."

He slips a key card into the door mechanism and slowly opens it. Clarissa tries desperately to see around him.

He speaks softly, "There are a couple people here to see you." There's a quiet moment, and Alex steps aside and lets the three of us in.

Resting on top of the covers of the bed is a girl probably about my age with long thick black hair that could seriously use a good brushing. Her eyes are red and puffy with a vacant glaze over them.

"Hello," Clarissa calls out. The girl continues with her empty stare. "I'm Clarissa. This is Megan and this is Erin." She gives her a minute, and then tries again when she gets no response. Erin and I stand back waiting feeling uncomfortable. "Can we get you anything? Or do anything for you?" Clarissa asks.

The girl turns her head with effort and says in a ghostly voice, "If you can bring people back from the dead, I'd like my brother please."

The shocking and unexpected words tear through the tension in the air, filling it with friction. Her words even stop Clarissa in her tracks.

Alex sticks his head back in, he must have heard. "Okay. You're done. You said hello," Alex says severely.

I silently pray that Antonio wasn't the person who killed her brother. The notion creeps its way to the forefront of my mind. But I can't hold my tongue. "Sorry about your brother. Do you know who killed him?" It is a totally inappropriate question.

"Demetrius..." The words spill from her mouth and past her lips in slow-motion. Tears gather in her eyes. I've upset her.

"I'm sorry," I say again, shameful.

Erin surprises me. She doesn't even know this girl, but she sits by her on the bed and takes her hand. Erin gazes at her with sympathy and understanding.

"How about we just sit with you for a while?" Erin suggests.

The girl does look like she needs a friend. I can't imagine what she's going through losing her brother. Alex backs off when we don't ask her any more questions. Clarissa goes over to the television and flips it on, then sits on the edge using the remote to find something halfway decent to watch. I sit in a chair by the window, and Erin stays put on the bed. We're all quiet for a long time. My good mood from this morning is all but vanished. Meeting this poor girl has blackened it. Her tragedy reminds me of the danger around us.

Alex comes in a little while later carrying his phone. He holds it out to me and leaves.

"Hello?" I say the greeting as a question.

"Megan, it's me," says Antonio. My mood immediately brightens of its own volition as I unfold myself out of the chair and head out to the hallway to have a private conversation.

"Where are you?" I ask.

"I'll be there soon. Did you find anything out from that girl?" he asks. I am surprised...I thought we were in trouble for visiting her.

"Find out anything? I don't even know what's going on." I say bewildered. "She said Demetrius killed her brother."

"All right...Vito and I will be there soon. We had a late night last night."

I stiffen at his words. *Does he mean he had a late night with this girl?*

"Who is she?" I demand.

"I don't know. She was there last night while I was taking care of some business. That is all I can tell you over the phone. Hang tight, and I'll see you in a little while," he says. "Love you..."

I melt a little inside. "Love you too," I return.

Alex is by the door, and I hand him his phone. "Thank you," I tell him. "Antonio is on his way."

I walk back into the room, and Clarissa immediately asks me, "Are you in trouble?"

"No," I say emphatically.

"Whew! I didn't want to get you guys in trouble," Clarissa says relieved.

The girl gets up to use the bathroom. She shuts the door.

"Has she said her name...anything?" I ask.

Erin shakes her head no.

The bathroom door clicks open, and the zombie-like girl comes back to the bed to lie down. I'd find out information for Antonio if I knew what I was supposed to ask. I guess her name is a good start.

"I hope this isn't a rude question, but what is your name?" I say, thinking that came out horrible.

"Lisa," she says with effort.

"Where are you from?" I ask. I am trying to encourage easy conversation.

"I live here in Chicago." Her monotonous voice and expressionless face is an indicator to me that she's in a mild state of shock; Erin was exactly the same way. Lisa isn't as bad off as Erin was, actually. "Demetrius killed my brother," she repeats.

I nod, although she has already told us this. I guess she needed to say it again.

Doc Howie walks in carrying his medical bag. He absorbs the scene in the room, smiles warmly, and approaches Lisa, giving us all a general hello.

"I'd like to check your heart rate," he says to Lisa. She nods, allowing him to do it. "How are you feeling?" he asks.

Lisa doesn't respond, she just stares forward. He presses his hand against her forehead.

"I used to date him," Lisa says out of the blue. "He gave my brother a job." *Demetrius?!*

"Does anything hurt?" Doc Howie asks, methodically.

She shakes her head no and continues. "Drugs...he got my brother into drugs," she says with no emotion. "I found out too late. My brother came to me. He said Demetrius threatened him." Lisa stops, emotion overtaking her as a single tear courses down her cheek.

I hear voices out in the hallway...deep ones. *It's Antonio and Vito!* My heart does a quick slam in my chest. It takes everything I have not to run into the hall, but I exit as quickly as possible. Antonio is entrenched in conversation with Alex and Vito. As soon as he sees me he breaks away. I step into his arms, and he kisses me, wrapping his arms around me...and pauses. The gun. He glances at me quizzically, and steps back from our embrace.

"My father wants me to carry it," I explain.

Antonio doesn't say anything. I see in his eyes that he wants me to carry it, too. He quickly kisses me again.

Someone's phone is ringing. It's Alex's. He answers, and suddenly his face twists with fury. "Where!? Are you fucking kidding me?!"

Alex yells into the phone. Anyone on this floor can surely hear him. Alex pulls the phone away from his ear and pointedly looks at Antonio.

"Someone downstairs says that Tutti is out on the street," he rushes out urgently.

Antonio and Vito move quickly. They run to the stairwell at the end of the hall. Vito flings the door open and they're gone. As though my legs have a mind of their own, I'm off running to catch up with them. Alex reaches out to grip my hand to stop me as I rush by, but I shrug it off and bolt through the door. I am cascading down the stairs neatly, allowing the railing to glide under my hand. I make it to the bottom floor in record time and burst into the casino.

The casino is busy, as it very often is. I rush past gamblers and wait staff carrying drinks. I make it to the front doors and see no one guarding them. Through the glass, I scan the street, but I can see nothing. I throw open the swinging door, looking to the left and then to the right. *Where is Antonio?* I take a step forward, looking all around me. This sky is cloudy. It is a dark winter day. I immediately feel the chill with the absence of a jacket. I step forward once again, putting myself on the sidewalk. That's when I hear it.

Gunfire echoes in the air like thunder, in between two large city buildings. Knowing Antonio would want me to stay put, I dive back in to the casino, my face plastered to the glass as I struggle to see something...anything. Sirens sound in the distance, getting closer by the second. Nobody in the casino seems to register the gun shots. Everyone is in their own world, deafened by the sounds of the machines.

My heart pounds with worry. I stand on my tiptoes to see around the parked vehicles on the street and watch three cop cars skid to a stop. Their doors fly open and uniformed officers swarm into the alley across the street.

A hand grabs my arm and roughly pulls me to the side against the wall.

"It's not safe to stand by the door."

It's Demetrius!

Horror grips me. My arm throbs where he clenches it, his fingers pushing into the flesh, bruising me. I wince. He touches my hair with his other hand in a creepy, affectionate gesture. The paradox of his hands, one brutal - one gentle, isn't what startles me; it's the psychotic cast in his eyes. He is capable of anything. I'm paralyzed as he stares me down.

Shouting makes us both turn to look. Casino security is racing towards the doors. Demetrius smiles down at me with a cold look, once again runs his fingers through my hair, and releases me. He disappears.

A deep crowd has formed around the commotion outside. People rubberneck over each other to see the scene. I slump against the wall, the paralysis leaving me. I try to calm myself, fear coming through in knowing that I did something very stupid.

Chapter 11

Underboss: Second in command

Antonio:

Something is off with the intel about Uncle Tutti. He is alone and wandering around aimlessly, seems out of it. The whole thing stinks of a set up.

Vito and I rush outside and sprint across the street, flanking the walls of the buildings attached to a mini-mart and a shoe store. I draw my weapon and hold it at the ready position. Vito does the same. Ahead of us, I see a man who could definitely be Uncle Tutti, but his back is to us. We inch closer, one step at a time.

The guy is talking under his breath, mumbling. He is moving around pointlessly always with his back to us. I don't want to fire without being totally sure. Killing an innocent person is not on my list of things to do today. We creep slowly not to alert him. My focus is zeroed in to see if this is Uncle Tutti. I don't see the sniper on the building to our left.

Shots are fired! Brick pieces fly and crumble bouncing off the asphalt as I duck and dive. I rip my jeans and scrape the shit out of my arm when I land. Vito crouches next to me and points his gun up, checking the roofs of the other buildings. My frustration is heightened when this fucker who could be Uncle Tutti doesn't even turn around. He isn't even fazed by the bullets flying by him.

Sirens whirl and whistle. Tires screech on the pavement. That's our cue to get the hell out of there. We quickly snap open the back door of the mini-mart and shove our guns back in our pants, pretending to look around.

The police are going to be a long time investigating. I motion to Vito that we need to get out of here. I walk to the front of the store and watch as the police rush in to the alley. The clerk and shoppers are pressed against the doors trying to see what happened. Looks like the coast is clear, and we step out the front of the store and head directly for the side garage of the casino. We make it underground. We rest against a giant cement pillar, panting.

"What the fuck was that?" Vito spits.

"A setup," I release in a frustrated sigh. Nothing adds up. My head is filled with questions and the answers right there in front of me, but I'm so blinded by my vendetta that I almost got taken out. The anger and rage is making me sloppy. I need to talk to that girl. Maybe she'll have some answers for me about what is really going on.

Vito thinks for a minute, possibly replaying in his mind the details of the past few minutes.

"Not just a setup...a *contract!* That fucker was aiming at YOU!" His eyes flash with horror and something I rarely see from Vito...fear.

"I think Demetrius has a hit out on me," I tell Vito. Anger pulses inside me. "I also think that he is the cleaner for the Furlotti family."

Vito scrubs his hands down his face, taking it all in. "Okay, so what do we do now?" He asks me earnestly like I would already have a plan. I don't.

Mob assassins like Demetrius and his associates don't have a problem with public executions. It sends a warning to others and it gives them a sick empowerment on the same level with a serial killer. It's a deranged form of exhibitionism.

I find it odd that Ennio has set us up with the Furlotti's. Most mob families typically don't like to draw attention. Public exterminations and drug dealing are huge flashing signs for organized crime. Bosses normally like to keep things quiet, like my Pop. Although, some families get delusions of grandeur and greedy, and think they're untouchable. Flying low on the radar is what keeps many families afloat.

I didn't realize the Furlotti family was like this. They have never been known to be such a high-profile family. Things just don't make sense.

*****

Antonio:

Back upstairs, Alex is standing with Megan. His face is strained as he speaks with her. I quickly thaw when I see her.

"She's gone," Alex informs me as he sees Vito and is storming down the hall.

Dammit!

"What happened?"

"When you left, your girlfriend chased after you. I tried to grab her, but she took off." Alex gives a steely gaze to Megan. "I sent Clarissa and Erin back upstairs because I didn't know what was going down, and I went after Megan. When I came back upstairs, she was gone."

I'm angry, and I flash my eyes at Megan. She knows better than to follow us like that. I don't want to get into it with everyone standing around here. I'll have to discuss it with her later.

"Do you think she just took off?" I ask attempting to stay calm.

"I'm not sure." He flicks his eyes to Megan. "But Megan has something else she needs to tell you," Alex says with a scolding tone.

She stares at the floor, then raises her gaze and looks at me sheepishly. This is getting better and better. I wait for her to respond.

"When I got downstairs, I went to the glass doors to try to see what was going on...and Demetrius grabbed me," she says softly.

A monster so ugly and vicious erupts from deep within my soul. I want to crush the life out of Demetrius for putting his hands on Megan. I can't handle this. What I want to do right now scares even me. I don't trust myself so I walk away - seething in my own rage.

This is a game. A fucking screwed up game. Demetrius is in rare form, and it is all centered on me. I'd bet my bank account that Demetrius took her.

I take a deep breath with my back to Megan and Alex. We need to regroup. I hate this. I take out my phone and call my father.

"Hi, Pop,"

"Eh, Antonio. What's going on?" he asks. Unfortunately, he doesn't know how loaded the answer is to that question. I can't tell him everything over the phone, that's protocol. So I speak in innuendo.

"There may be some problems with our new friends. I'm looking into it. Stay alert."

"Got it. You be careful," he says.

"You too." We hang up.

Letting my father know is important, they could be targeting him, too. This way he will take on some additional bodyguards. The simple solution would be to just call Don Furlotti, but things don't work that way. To accuse him and his family of putting a contract out, or even not holding up their part of the alliance, is a major insult. Having all the facts is key, or you might as well start funeral arrangements.

I call Vito over. "We need to get our stuff out of the hotel. It's too out in the open. We'll stay here where it is guarded and we have what we need. I don't know what Demetrius' next move is. I think we should lay low and wait."

"What about Tutti?"

"I have a feeling that, whichever way this is going, Tutti is gonna be at the end of it." I'm going with my gut on this one. I don't want to be blindsided again. I can be patient, when I need to be. "The celebration dinner is only a couple of days away. We need to be ready for anything."

"And that girl?" he asks.

"We don't know if she left on her own or was taken. I'll have Carlo find two volunteers to go look for her. That's the best I can do."

"I'll take Joey with me and clean out our stuff. I'll be back later," Vito says and leaves.

Alex and Megan are standing silently waiting.

"Take Megan upstairs. I'm going to find Ennio," I order to Alex, not looking at Megan. They get in the elevator, and I take the stairs to the casino.

*****

Antonio:

I find Ennio at the bar opposite the casino from the restaurants and shops. He's taking inventory of the liquor, holding a clipboard, and he doesn't look up as I approach.

"You know I don't like cops at my casino," Ennio's voice is unhappy.

"I understand. It won't happen again," I tell him. It doesn't matter how many cops you have in your back pocket...whenever they show up, it is bad for business.

He puts the clipboard down on the granite bar. "What happened?" he speaks in a low tone.

"Alex got a call from one of your guys saying that they thought Tutti was in the alley across the street. We left to check it out, and there was a sniper on the top of the shoe store building. We took off when we heard the sirens. Somebody must have tipped off the cops."

"Was it Tutti?"

"I don't know. We never got a chance to find out."

"What's that look on your face for?" Ennio asks, sounding like the mob boss that he is.

"I just don't know what to think. The whole thing is just wrong."

"If it doesn't feel right, keep your head down. You know that. I'll do some checking around."

I leave Ennio to finish his task and head straight to the family floor. I need to talk to Megan about taking off on Alex.

Chapter 12

Omerta: Code of silence

Megan:

When Antonio walks through the door, I don't know whether to run to hug him or run to my room and lock the door. I know he's mad...and for good reason. I know how foolish I was to follow them.

Antonio walks over to me, standing over me where I was lounging on the couch. Erin is in Clarissa's suite. *Lucky girl!*

He takes my hand gently, hauling me up to a standing position, and leads me to my room.

My heart pumps wildly in trepidation, and my hand tingles where he's touching me. Even though we're alone, he closes the door. His eyes glass over with need.

"Lie down," he orders me.

Unsure, I climb on the bed and lay down with my head against the soft pillows. I wonder what he's going to do. He stands at the end of the bed grabs my ankles and tugs me towards him. He takes off my sneakers and they thump to the floor. He kicks off his own shoes and kneels on the bed. He throws his leg over my hips and straddles me, pinning me to the bed lusciously.

My belly jumps at the contact, wanting more. I wait - each second killing me. I want to reach up and pull him down to me. I take my hand and slide it under his shirt across his meaty abs. He gathers my hand and holds it. He takes my other free hand then traps them both to my sides.

"Don't. Ever. Follow. Us. Like. That. Again." Antonio's tone is intimidating. I nod my head because I can't move my hands...and I'm afraid to open my mouth. Suddenly, he takes my hands and thrusts them over my head. He leans down and gives me a searing kiss. He kisses me feverishly like it's life-or-death. "I wouldn't be able to take it if anything happened to you," he whispers, intensely staring into my eyes.

I can only continue to nod my head in agreement. Antonio has immobilized me, physically and mentally. After a brief and passionate staring contest, he lets me go. I feel bereft immediately.

"Sorry, you are right," I say quietly, a little afraid to move even now. "It was stupid."

I knew it was dangerous when I did it and ran after him. I felt so empowered, but my run-in with Demetrius was sobering. He could have dragged me out of the casino and down the street. No one would have known. *What was he doing here anyway?* Clarissa said he is not welcome.

Antonio strips off his shirt and lies down next to me on the bed. He draws me to him, spooning my body with his. I snuggle in deeper, breathing in his scent...suddenly feeling his comfort. As he holds me in silence, Antonio's breathing becomes even and wispy. I close my eyes and sleep finds me.

*****

Megan:

I wake up and see Antonio still sound asleep. He hasn't even switched his position. He must be really tired. I sneak out of bed so I don't disturb him.

I halt, hearing voices in the suite as I approach the door. "When are you leaving?" asks Vito's deep voice.

"Next week," Erin replies.

I hear pots and pans clang. Someone is cooking in the kitchen.

"I never thanked you for the clothes...sorry. I really love them." Erin's voice is small and hesitant.

"Yup," he replies, and I hear a cupboard open and close. "Don't you have sea salt around here?" he asks, avoiding Erin's thank you.

"We don't really cook here. Everything comes from the kitchen, except snacks and microwavable stuff."

Without seeing them, Erin's voice sounds so young and slight compared to Vito's masculine low-toned one. They are polar opposites.

Whatever he is making smells incredible. My stomach awakens and growls, but I don't want to intrude on them. I wait and listen by the door, eavesdropping some more.

"What's that called again?" Erin asks.

"A frittata."

"It looks like you pumped air into an omelet."

"It's thicker and fluffier than an omelet. It's a whole different texture," he lectures.

I cover my mouth to keep from giggling. I know Vito can cook, but it sounds funny listening to him. It is such a contrast to his usual unapproachable, beat-em-up persona.

I am ready to give in to my stomach when Antonio stirs. I turn to him. He is so gorgeous lying there on my bed, mussed and groggy from sleep. He stretches, his muscles rippling from the movement, and flashes me his perfect smile.

"What are you doing?" he says sleepily.

"Shh...I'm listening to Erin and Vito," I say, without an ounce of remorse for snooping and turn back to the door.

I yelp when Antonio scoops me up and throws me on the bed. "Hey!"

"You know what we do to spies?" he asks me mischievously.

"No."

He tickles me relentlessly. I laugh, struggling to get a breath in. I try to fight him off, but he is too strong. I snort unbecomingly, and Antonio thinks it is hysterical and he tickles me even more. I twist trying to get away to no avail.

"What's the matter, Megan? Can't you talk?" He torments even more, and I roar with laughter.

"Stop...please..." I try to get out, but my words are cut off as I attempt to suck in air.

A knock on the door halts us.

"Meg? Are you okay?" It's Erin.

"Yeah," I call out. My response is fuzzy from wrestling.

"Are you guys hungry? Vito made dinner."

"We'll be out in a sec," Antonio yells to her and lifts off me. He gets his shirt from the floor and slips it on. I lay on the bed panting. "It smells good," he comments.

Antonio reaches down and helps me up off the bed. He caresses my hips and draws me in, kissing me sweetly. I can't resist, and I wrap my arms around his neck, drinking him in before we head out to the kitchen.

At the table, there are four dishes filled with frittata. A huge loaf of Italian bread sits in the middle of the table. Everything looks delicious. The whole scene reminds me of South Bend. When we stayed at the suite at Notre Dame, there were many nights that Vito cooked. We all sat together to have a *family* dinner, and I miss it. Doing something as simple as sharing a meal together has been lost these three weeks while Antonio has been chasing his uncle.

I notice that is it dark now and wonder how long Antonio can stay before he has *business* to take care of. I push the unwanted thought away, determined to savor the time I have.

We sit down, and Antonio slices up some crusty bread and gives me a piece. Vito digs right into his plate.

"So, have you started packing?" Antonio asks Erin in light conversation.

"No," she says.

We eat quietly for a while.

"This is wonderful," I say to Vito. I am always floored by his skills in the kitchen. If this mob thing doesn't work out, he could always be a chef, I think comically.

He shrugs as though embarrassed by my accolades.

Dinner ends just as quietly as it began. Antonio and I clean up the dishes, putting them in the apartment-sized dishwasher and letting it run. There seems to be an elephant in the room, but I'm not sure what it is...I'm sure, though, that something is bothering Antonio. It's not at the surface; it is buried deep down. His outward appearance shows the same breathtaking, handsome, mobster.

After the kitchen is cleaned up, Antonio sits on the couch, and I lie down, resting my head in his lap. Vito and Erin each sit in a chair. Vito mindlessly presses the channel button on the remote. Like a typical man, he never slows down enough to watch to see if a show is something he might like. He just goes around and around, like a Ferris wheel until he arbitrarily stops on a station that is running the Three Stooges. Erin and I both groan. I've never found them funny. Vito and Antonio howl with laughter. I just don't see the humor, even finding it repulsive at times. I close my eyes instead of watching, and revel in the contentment as Antonio strokes my hair. It feels so good that I could fall asleep again.

I hear, rather than see, Erin pick up her book off the coffee table, settling in for a relaxing evening. Antonio's occasional laughter echoes in his chest.

Erin falls asleep between episodes, and I am in a profoundly relaxed state. Vito reaches over and takes the book out of her hand, careful to hold its page. Leaning down, he lifts her in his arms and carries her to her room. Her head is pressed against his shoulder as she sleeps peacefully. I very subtly notice him incline his head down to hers affectionately, pressing his lips to the top of her head. I look away hurriedly. It is an intimacy that catches me off guard.

Antonio flicks off the TV and we go to my room. There is a weight on him, despite his appearance and behavior this evening watching that ridiculous show.

I reach into my drawers and find a pair of fleece pajama pants and a cozy white t-shirt for bed.

"You won't need those," a husky voice says from behind me.

My belly flip-flops, and I straighten. Strong arms roam down my back and then encircle my waist. I lean into the embrace, passion fueling my shallow breaths. His hands glide freely across my stomach and up to my breasts. I mewl in the back of my throat, already filled with need for Antonio. I let him explore while I stand still enjoying every caress. He spins me around, and I can't hold back anymore. I open to him and kiss him hard. He squeezes my butt and pushes me into his erection, making me squirm delightfully.

He picks me up, and I wrap my legs around his waist. He walks to the bed, and sets me down, moving slowly. He kneads my breasts and nuzzles my neck at a painful pace. I need more.

A plea poises to spill from my lips when I hear his jeans unzip. My pulse quickens, and I am adrift in a hungry passion that is only satisfied by Antonio.

Chapter 13

Underground: Mafia world

Megan:

The next morning I wake up warm and comfy. Antonio's muscled arms are wrapped around me tightly, and I close my eyes to relish in the moment. I could stay like this all day, but the bathroom beckons me. I reluctantly roll out of bed, untangling myself from his arms. I am completely naked. I go to my dresser and pick up the pajamas that I had planned to wear. I slip them on and open the door.

Curiosity leads me over to the couch to see if Vito slept there. I look down and the couch is empty. *Hmmmph!*

As I drag myself towards the bathroom, Erin's door opens and I behold a very disheveled Vito. *Uh oh!* I freeze. This is highly uncomfortable.

In the past when he has slept in her room, it's been to keep the nightmares away and make sure she doesn't hurt herself. Erin's thrashing can be very violent. Lately, though, she has been great and even insisted on sleeping on her own. She said something about wanting to face her own demons. Doc Howie said we should give her space...said that when she needed help, she would ask for it.

"Hey," he says sleepily.

"Is Erin okay?" I ask.

"She's fine," he says through a yawn.

"Oh." I wrestle with asking more.

Vito doesn't seem as uncomfortable as I do. The awkwardness of his lavish purchases makes this whole situation all the more unseemly. *Is he trying to buy her?*

Antonio strides out of my room. The way he looks should make flannel pajama pants illegal. His body is so fit and formed; I find it hard to look away from him.

Vito immediately starts the coffee pot dripping and beats me to the bathroom. I realize I've been standing there a long time, completely dumbfounded. I am trying to put the pieces of the puzzle together, when Antonio grasps me by the back of the neck and pulls me in for a long, luscious kiss before he makes his way to the counter for coffee. The coffee smells heavenly and just what I need to wake me up from my daze. Erin must smell it too, because she comes out of her room.

I can't help but feel a bit uneasy, but I tamp it down and try to enjoy the day. Antonio has a big dinner to go to tonight, so I just want to live in the now.

*****

Antonio:

I dress for the dinner in Megan's room. She is sitting on the bed watching me. She looks good enough to eat. Her red hair dangles down her back and around her face, making her look like a celestial angel...one that is mine.

I button up my dress shirt and start on my tie. It is a tradition carried down from the 1930s to dress up in your best suit for these types of occasions. It is the candy coating over what's really on the inside - mobsters. It makes us appear civilized and refined in the underworld of criminals.

The celebration dinner is a time for the families to get together who have formed an alliance. It is not a business meeting, but a time to be social. It is always a four-course meal with lots of wine. Vito and I need to be extremely cautious. Not knowing where the Furlottis stand is a difficulty. We can't trust anyone right now. Signs of weakness are not an option. *Not showing up? Impossible!* Even when suspecting you are walking into a trap, you go prepared and with your head held high. Fear and cowardice are invitations for mutiny and death.

I am ready, and I kiss Megan goodbye. I don't want to leave her, but I have to. It gets harder and harder each time.

I think about what Ennio told me earlier today. He didn't find out anything out of the ordinary, but we both surmised that it's because of the Omerta, the code of silence. No one wants to talk to him because they know how close our families are. You don't rat on your friends or your enemies. It's part of the code and stays in the family.

The restaurant is located in the heart of Chicago's Little Italy, and is owned by the Furlotti family. The place is shut down to the public for the evening. Vito and I drive to a designated spot a couple of blocks away to meet Pop and Donny. We roll to a stop at their car and park. Vito and I get out slamming our car doors, and Pop and Donny do the same. I light a cigarette and take a puff as we all move to stand in the darkness of the building beside us.

"Antonio!" Pop reaches out to me and hugs me. His demeanor is sour and perturbed. I feel his familiar pat on my back. It's as comforting as ever.

"Hi Pop," I say taking the burning cigarette out of my mouth.

"I got some not so good news, son." He takes out a piece of paper and hands it to me. *A letter?*

I did what your son couldn't. I have Tutti. Send Antonio to the docks tonight where we met before. Same time.

~D

"That filthy Demetrius!" Pop curses on his name. "Do what you got do, Antonio! It's kill or be killed."

"How did you get this?" I ask Pop as Vito stands over my shoulder reading.

"It was delivered to Donny by some flunky."

The sick son of a bitch is playing his hand. My eyesight is as red as the tip of my cigarette, burning as hot as the fires of hell. I want him. The whole package so that he can never do this again. He is going down. He is done shattering lives and not playing by the rules.

"Tonio," Pop growls, "Take as much firepower as you can. He's clever; he's probably figured all this out a while ago. That fucker's got nothing better to do than start a *bloody crime war!*"

If Demetrius succeeds in taking down me and Uncle Tutti, he would be sending a deadly message to rivals. This would put him on an even higher pedestal in the mob underworld...would make him a living legend. But egos like that just shorten your life span. If it wasn't me he was fuckin' with, it would be someone else.

What is it about me that has drawn his attention? He called me *'Golden Boy'* in the fight ring. I was born into this life...I grew up in it. But Demetrius had to work his way in and up. He had to prove himself worthy and get himself noticed.

That note indicates that he wants to shame me. Little does he know that he has done the exact opposite. He has fueled my fury and wrath to a level that I have never felt before. The monster inside me is uncontainable, ready to rip and tear.

"I'm going with you!" Vito spits acidly. "There is nothing you can say or do to stop me! We handle this together!" Vito's tone is livid and unmoving.

I doubt I could stop him. Just like the last time, he will not listen. When it comes to my welfare, Vito's loyalty overshadows and squashes his mafia discipline.

"We'll figure it out," I say quietly, trying to contain my rage. Demetrius has moved into the wrong territory, trying to steal my thunder. Uncle Tutti is mine to deal with.

"It's time to go," my father says, looking at his watch. "We'll meet you over there."

The car ride to the restaurant will take no time because we are only a few blocks away. At first, Vito and I are quiet, both working out a strategy in our minds.

"We need to take Carlo, Alex, and Joey with us," he says out of the blue.

"We'll call Patrick too. I want to let him in on all this," I tell him.

"I agree."

Patrick has been an unusual ally. It is weird to work with my girlfriend's father on such a personal and macabre level. It just solidifies the fucked up way things are.

"Set up a meeting tonight for after the dinner."

Vito makes some calls on his cell phone, while I navigate to find a parking space. I scan the area the best I can in the dark, checking for threats. This could turn out fine tonight...this is the pre-show. Demetrius has planned the main event for 3 a.m.

The restaurant is filled with bosses, underbosses, thugs, and enforcers. Everyone is dressed in sharp-looking suits, even the little guys.

The restaurant is fairly large, and tables in the back are set up with white linen tablecloths, napkins, and big goblets for wine. Candle centerpieces line the middle of each table, the candles lit and casting a golden glow. The maître d' shows us to a table

Mr. Furlotti greets us. "Antonio! Vito! Welcome! *Mangia!*" He gestures with his hand to sit and I tense up. He is being so nice to me, but I'm thinking this guy is a rat. I put on my best façade.

"Thank you," I say, watching his every move.

Vito doesn't even try for nice, he doesn't say anything. *Good choice!*

Pop and Donny come in with a few of the guys from home. They are welcomed the same way and come to join us. Vito and I stand while my father sits. It is the proper way to greet the Boss if you are already seated before him.

The guys from home ask me how I'm doing. I exchange pleasantries with them all while watching and waiting for some shit to go down.

And then he arrives...

Fucking Asshole! Vito is doing everything in his power to not shoot out of the chair at Demetrius. The tension when their eyes meet is thick and solid, not a trace of friendship in them.

Don Furlotti claps his hands. "Everyone please be seated!" he calls out to those who are still standing around talking.

Pop and Donny are completely emotionless. They are masters at hiding their feelings and their temperaments appear genial and friendly.

Pop taps my hand. "Don't worry, Tonio. You'll get your chance."

Pop has complete faith in me. He always has. He trusts me, he confides in me, and gives me the freedom to become what I need to be.

A thin waitress with long brown hair fills each glass at our table with red wine. I think twice before drinking it. She didn't open the bottle at our table. Pop notices too and halts her.

"Please bring new glasses. Open the bottles at our table please," he orders nicely.

"Yes, sir," she says, and scurries away with the open bottle.

Donny gets up and heads to the kitchen to talk to the staff. It is common protocol that wine is opened at the table and is checked by the head enforcer. It is tasted by the senior person at the table to check its drinkability and vintage.

The last thing I am is hungry. Rage fills my stomach and adrenaline quenches my thirst.

Everyone is talking at their own table. A waiter is bringing out the salad. A very flustered waitress comes out with a tray of fresh glasses and an unopened bottle of Chianti. Donny is behind her. He waves away the waiter with the salads and says sternly, "No, thank you. She is the only one who serves us."

The waiter disappears to a new table. Donny is going to watch everything that is prepared and served. The young girl is such a mess that I feel sorry for her.

"Thank you," I say, as I stand and take the bottle. "I can do this. Why don't you get our salads?" She smiles at me with relief and leaves with Donny for the kitchen.

I expertly insert the corkscrew into the bottle and pop it open, letting it breathe for a minute. I then put only a swallow in Pop's glass. He swirls it around and sips.

He nods his head at me. "It's good, Tonio." He holds out his glass for me to fill. Standing gives me an opportunity to scan the room, but it also makes me an easy target for a bullet. Vito holds his glass for me, and I fill his too. I put the bottle on the table for the others to take what they want. It is inappropriate for me to serve them.

Donny comes back and sits as the waitress places the salads at each place setting. Her hands are shaking. A grape tomato rolls off Vito's plate and hits the floor. She sucks in a scared breath.

"It's okay," he says to her.

The guys across the table engage us with news from Palmetto, giving us info on Sommersville and some punks they have had to put in their place. I am only half listening because of the severity of the situation we are in.

After the salads, Don Furlotti makes a toast. He stands and raises his glass. "To our new family. May we have many happy years working together."

My first reaction is to snort at his declaration.

"This is a new era. Welcome! *Salute!*" he says, and everyone clinks glasses and says, S*alute!*

Demetrius looks in my direction and sneers with his glass pointed at me and Pop. I give it right back, not allowing him to rattle me.

Dinner is long and drawn out. I push the food around on my plate. I am running out of patience. Many *goombahs* and *cavones* come over to our table to speak to Pop. My father is admired and respected. They shake his hand, make jokes, and are generally happy to see him.

"When the fuck can we get out of here?" Vito whispers to me.

I totally agree. We need to get out of here and plan for meeting Demetrius tonight. "Soon," I tell him.

We can't leave before dessert; it would be considered an insult, and I am not leaving my father and Donny here with the wolves.

Finally, the waitress comes over to our table with tiramisu. Pop gives her a hundred dollar bill and thanks her for helping us this evening. She blushes deeply and slips the money into her pocket. I make mush out of it with my fork, not caring the least bit about eating. Dinner and dessert...and now it is okay to leave.

We cautiously say our goodbyes, and I am on edge waiting for something to happen. I find it hard to believe that this whole thing has gone down without a hitch or a gun shot.

Outside is a cold Chicago winter night. The wind is howling with the threat of snowfall. I press the remote for the car to unlock the doors, doing my best to search the surrounding area for danger. Pop had left a guy outside… Rawlo is his name, I think. His job is to watch the vehicles and keep a look out. The guy must be freezing.

My phone buzzes with a text from Carlo. *What time?*

I text back.

Leaving now.

*****

Antonio:

Carlo, Alex, and Joey are waiting for us in the basement interrogation room of the casino. Carlo plays with a deck of cards, fanning them professionally. Joey is leaning over a map that is laid out on the table. I appreciate their loyalty and efficiency.

My attention is stalled when I see Megan in a small metal folding chair in the corner, her demeanor uncertain. She is chewing on her nail nervously. *Why is she here?* The words are forming on my lips when Patrick walks in distracting us all. He is carrying a high-powered sniper rifle. It's a beauty.

"Before you flip out, this was my idea," Joey starts.

"What was your idea?" I ask, and then the unpleasant realization dawns. "NO! No. Fucking. Way!"

"Hear us out." Joey talks with his hands like a true Italian. "She is an incredible shot! She will be far away for the whole thing. I'll stay with her. We'll even suit her up in bullet proof gear."

"No! Absolutely not!" I shout.

I examine my beautiful Megan. She looks petrified. Every time I see her, my heart softens in a way that is not healthy for this type of business. She is one of the only things in the world I care about.

Joey pleads his case. "She's your ace in the hole, Tonio. Her ability is going to give you the upper hand with Demetrius."

"You want her to fuckin' kill someone?! You want that on her conscience?!" I smash my fist against the table. "This isn't her acting in self-defense. This is placing her in an *assassination nest!*"

"Can I finish?" Joey asks sarcastically. "You only need her if things go bad. She will be far away. She might not even have to do anything."

I turn to Patrick for his input. It's his daughter - flesh and blood that he brought into the world. He is his typical emotionless, stoic self. *Dammit!*

"Can I say something?" Megan says quietly, standing up. "Antonio, I want to do it. I can live with this. I know I can." I can tell her mind is made up. "What I can't live with is something happening to you, or anyone else, if I could have stopped it or helped in some way," she pleads with me forcefully.

"No, you need to stay here on the family floor. I won't be able to concentrate." I am adamant.

"You can't keep me locked in a tower!" she yells. "I have done everything you have asked of me. I've been trapped for weeks, waiting for this nightmare to be over. I want to get on with our lives. Please let me help."

This is exactly what I didn't want to happen. I never wanted Megan anywhere near this shit. No matter how hard I try, my fucked up life follows and leads straight to Megan whether I want it to or not.

I level my gaze at her. "I don't want this for you. This is my burden to bear. I don't care if you think I locked you in a tower, it's the only thing that gives me comfort." I suck in an angry breath. "Patrick, can I speak to you?"

We step out in the hall with everyone staring after us.

"You know why I immersed us in a rundown shabby hotel? So that I could keep the fight away from them!" I spit out angrily.

"I don't want my daughter involved in this anymore than you do, but, Antonio, clearly she has a talent that rivals the best of them. She's clever, and she has instincts. I will protect her."

"This is *scumbati*! We shouldn't even be having this conversation."

"If I thought she would be in any danger, I wouldn't even consider it. She will be far away," Patrick promises.

I am losing this battle, and the clock is ticking. We still haven't planned what we are going to do when faced with Demetrius tonight. I glance at the rifle in Patrick's hands. It has a half-mile range on it, but even twenty miles away is not far enough for me when it comes to Megan. In this short span of time, with all of the crap that has gone on, I feel like she is more my family than any of my own blood; she is a part of my soul. I didn't even know that was possible in this life.

Patrick and I go back into the room and sit down with the guys and Megan. Even with all of Alessandra's knowledge and experience, she has never been a part of any of this type of *business*. But I know it isn't my decision to make. I just have to have faith in my girl...that when the time is right, she'll know what to do. I silently pray that it never comes to that point.

I let out an exhausted sigh when we finish making plans. Carlo and Alex have an excellent strategy. Hopefully, Demetrius doesn't have a better one.

Chapter 14

Wise guy: Has proven loyalty to the family and taken life

Megan:

I am so uncomfortable. I am padded up ridiculously. Besides a bullet proof vest, I have on the pants that I can barely walk in. To top off my outfit, I have on a helmet that is so heavy it weighs my head down. I look like I should be in a foxhole in Afghanistan, not on a rooftop in Chicago.

My father and I never did a ton of father/daughter bonding activities, and the strangeness of this whole situation makes me feel oddly connected to him as we wait together. I am worried that this is going to be a bloodbath, and my anxiety over Antonio's welfare is brimming over inside my chest.

My father's voice sounds far away when he starts talking to me. The wind whips and howls making it difficult to hear. He is repeating instructions he already gave me at the casino when everyone agreed to the plan of attack. Antonio made it very clear that he needs to confront Demetrius. Demetrius's abduction of Uncle Tutti is a personal attack on Antonio's abilities. Not to face it head on would look weak in the eyes of the underworld.

From what I have observed and seen, there will always be a Demetrius or Uncle Tutti scratching to get to the top. It is the nature of the beast. It happens in all walks of life, and the underworld is no different than the rest of society when it comes to lust for power and greed.

"Don't fire unless I tell you to," Dad says forcefully over the wind.

I nod my head in understanding, and he hands me the rifle. It's a heavy one. Planted next to him is another one, but it is not as fancy as mine.

"Lie down. Look through the scope. Learn the area."

I bend myself the best I can, struggling in these clothes, but I am suddenly thankful for the thick padding because the cement on the roof is very cold. I position my eye to look through the site. The helmet gets in my way, and I push it back a little on my head.

The scope is like using a set of binoculars. Everything looks so close. I do what my father says and use it to scan the area. All I can see is bits and pieces and shadows in the dark.

"How am I to know who's who? I can barely see anything," I ask, terrified of shooting one of my friends.

My father flips the switch on the scope. A green light comes on. He beckons me to look through the site again, and I am astonished.

"Night vision scope," he says informing me. "If things get out of hand, I will get a call and instructions on where to fire."

I nod my head remembering that part of the plan. I have an ugly tickle of nerves at the back of my neck showering me with worry. This could turn out very bad.

My father lays his phone out in front of us. I glance at the time...it is 2:53 a.m. I am so awake, which is odd for me at this hour of the night. It must be the adrenaline pumping through my body, pushing the need for sleep away.

I check the site again to see if there is any movement down below...nothing. This experience is so surreal; like it is out of an action movie. I jostle a bit in an attempt to get comfortable. My father is like a statue beside me...waiting.

I look at my dad's phone again...2:55 a.m. Time has never moved so slowly before. Earlier, the hours of planning flew. Now, time's new trick is to stop.

Waiting.

Waiting.

Waiting.

I obsessively look at the clock on my father's phone...2:56 a.m. Suddenly it lights up, ringing and causing me to jump. My father moves quickly and answers it. I try to listen to what he's saying over the noise of the wind.

"Yes...(pause)...How long?...(pause)." He shuts off his phone and puts it back.

"Who was that?" I ask hoarsely.

"Vito."

I turn my head back to hold my position like I've seen on TV. It is my only frame of reference, fake snipers fighting battles with flying motorcycles. Maybe I should watch more reality TV...or the military channel. I put my eye back in the site. A red light blinds me for a second. I pull back to shake it off.

"What the...?" I say under my breath.

Beside me, my father goes down. Stunned, I look over and he is lying flat on his back. I scramble to get up to get to him. He raises his hand and fiercely motions for me to get down. *My father has been shot!*

I don't hear it, but I feel a bullet whiz over my head. *Holy Shit!* There is a sniper firing at us. Another whizzes by, farther off the mark.

My father stays low and crawls to me. Blood oozes out of his left arm. I panic, my heart thundering in my chest. I reach quickly for the phone to call for help, but fumble and drop it.

Dad puts a gentle hand on mine, stopping me. Another bullet flies by as we lie on the roof flat. *Holy Shit! They're gonna get us!*

"Megan!" he shouts, "Stay low and fire back."

Tears fill my eyes seeing my father hurt. He smiles at me. *Huh?.*

"You can do it!" he says over the blast of wind. "Take em out, honey!" He smiles reassuringly again.

I have to kill someone?? Antonio's words press themselves into my mind. *Don't think, just do!*

If I don't do this, that asshole over there could kill my father...me...Antonio. I have to do this. I *can* do this!

I go into a zone in my brain that I have been to before. My father says I have instincts. I go to them...I call on them.

I stay low and raise my rifle. I move the damn helmet out of my way again. I focus through the site. I lock on a green apparition across four buildings. I aim, suck in a breath, and fire. The figure falls like a sack of potatoes out of my site line.

"Did you get 'em?" my father asks.

"I'm not sure if I hit them, or they hit the deck to get down," I say, unsure of myself.

My father smiles again. "I think you got them." He closes his eyes and winces in pain.

I reach into one of the pockets of the pants I'm wearing and pull out the mini first-aid kit that Joey gave me earlier. I find bandages, unwrap them, and begin wrapping my father's wound. He grits his teeth as I apply pressure.

"I'm sorry," my father says. If I wasn't so close to him right now, I would never have heard him.

"About what?" I ask, quickly sopping up blood.

"I should have told you years ago about this. Me," he says remorsefully. "You would have been more prepared. I thought that if I kept it from you and Erin, you would never have to face it."

I continue working on his arm thoughtfully, all the while, waiting for another bullet to zing by.

"This all started with those gangsters breaking into our house," he says sorrowfully. "I think every day about what could have happened. I wasn't there...but you were. You took care of your mother and Erin. You are an amazing girl."

My father just called me amazing. I can't believe it. *My father thinks I'm amazing!*

"That's me," I smile. "I can play the harp and shoot a tin can right through the center from a mile away." I tie a knot of bandages around his arm in a bow.

"Antonio always saw it," he says thoughtfully. "He has been in love with you since you were little. I saw it...knew it. It scared me." He pauses and touches his arm. "He's a smart kid, though. People respect him and not just because they're afraid. He has a lot of integrity for someone in this business."

The phone rings, and our talk is cut short. It's 3:02 a.m. My father answers, then motions for me to get back in position. I do with a new sense of purpose. I have people counting on me. And my father has faith in me.

My father slides over and joins me once again, hovering next to me. With the phone to his ear, he tells me to aim below.

"Over to the left. Look through the sight," his voice trails off in the wind, but I know what he said.

I see my target, aim, focus, suck in a breath...and fire.

Chapter 15

Contract: Someone is paying to have you scheduled for execution

Antonio:

The kiss I gave Megan before we separated wasn't enough for me. It killed me to let her go, like there is a gaping hole in my chest that gets bigger every second without her. Knowing she is in this sickens me.

Carlo and Joey are positioned dockside. Vito is with me, but is headed to take cover in the trees to the left. Alex has a car waiting a block away. Vito calls Patrick to let him know where almost ready.

The metal of the guns strapped to me feels cold against my skin. I walk to the deserted building where Demetrius killed Lisa's brother, and Vito and I separate.

I gingerly open the door, the click when it opens loud in the air. I stalk as quietly as possible inside, hearing movement in one of the inner rooms. I proceed cautiously knowing full well that my nemesis has no qualms about pumping holes into me. As I take more steps forward slowly, I keep my hand ready to grab my gun at the first sign of trouble. Someone shushes someone else, and the noise in the other room silences. My feet move, taking me closer. I am pinned tightly against the wall. I glance around the corner.

There are four people in the room. Demetrius and one of his goons stand gazing at the object of my search...Uncle Tutti is strapped to a chair, looking bloodied and broken.

Rage forms a red haze over my eyes as I see the images of Megan's raw throat...the attack on my friends. The alliance with Sommersville and trussing me up like a turkey hanging from a ceiling, I'm ready to just pull my gun out and fire. I don't.

I am ready to take care of all of them. One clean sweep. My thoughts falter when my eyes catch movement to the right. Strapped to a chair, just like Uncle Tutti, is the girl from the other night, Lisa. Guilt quickly floods through me, pushing out the red for an instant.

Holy shit! This fucker has got to go!

"Come on in, Antonio, and join the party," Demetrius says maniacally. He walks over to Uncle Tutti and grabs him by the back of the hair and rips his head up. His eyes are swollen shut. "Say hi to your Uncle Tutti." He lets go, and Uncle Tutti's head slumps back down. He's either unconscious or drugged.

Lisa looks frantically around the room for me with fear in her eyes. Her black hair is knotted, and her face is red and dirty. As Demetrius walks over to her, I stiffen, wanting to lunge and crack his head against the floor. He strokes his fingers down her filthy cheek. She cringes away from his touch and he steps closer antagonizing her. She turns her head away disgusted.

"Don't look away from me, bitch!" he sneers.

Demetrius grabs her chin roughly and crashes his face into hers, kissing her. She squirms and wails, but they are muffled by his mouth ravaging hers. *So easy...it would be so easy just to take my gun and shoot him in the back, but impatience causes mistakes. I don't know what traps he has set, how many people are in the shadows.* His thug stands there enjoying the show.

I skim the room looking for any signs of booby-traps, bombs, any sort of device that could be set off. Lisa whimpers again, drawing my attention. Demetrius slaps her hard across the face making her head whip to the side.

He is such a bastard! I seethe with effort to ground myself.

"Awww, Antonio feels bad for the girl," he says, with sadistic sarcasm. "I wanted to take Megan and show her a good time, just like I did for little Lisa over here, but there were just too many people around." Demetrius struts back over to Uncle Tutti with an ungodly amount of confidence. "And Uncle Tutti...God, don't you just hate disloyalty, Antonio?"

He waits for an answer that I don't give.

"I mean seriously, did Tutti really think he could overthrow your father? He's *oobatz*, right?" Demetrius laughs, almost sounding normal. "It's the little guys that think they're big and powerful, but all they are really good for is fish food."

Where is he going with all this bullshit?

I feel a presence behind me... and hear the click of a gun. *The trap is sprung and it seems to be a simple one.* The gun taps me in the small of my back, gesturing for me to move forward. I take a small step, wanting to stay close to the doorway. The gun taps me harder, and I take another step.

"Come on, Antonio. Come right in here," Demetrius offers.

I have to make a move because Demetrius still has the upper hand. Things changed the minute I saw Lisa. I need to get her out of here alive. No one knows she's in here, and I have no way of telling them. I have done everything he's asked me to do. And everything he asks will lead me closer to my death.

I decide I have to change my tactics and talk to him.

"How did you get him?" I ask attempting to sound interested. Uncle Tutti dropped down on my to-do list. Demetrius' interference changed everything.

"It was easy," Demetrius laughs. I paid off some of his guys. It is mind-boggling how little allegiance they had to him. After Prazzo went missing, Tutti couldn't handle his crew."

Faint gunshots sound in the distance. Demetrius looks up at the noise and smiles.

"How nice that you put Megan and her daddy on a rooftop," he says, his ego bloated. His happy tone letting me know he was aware of what we were up to.

I feel the adrenaline kick my body into overdrive at the thought of someone shooting at Megan, and I take advantage of it. I whip around tackling the gunner behind me to the ground. As we wrestle for his gun, it goes off into the air. The recoil throws us back and the gun lands on the floor.

The bullet's trajectory makes a gaping hole in Uncle Tutti's lowered head sending his chair flying backwards with the splat. Lisa screams and knocks her chair over, putting her lower to the floor.

Demetrius's second goon comes at me, and I fight with the two of them with every ounce of anger and fear. I knock the gun out of the hands of the second goon, and it skids across the mangy floor. I am able to grab my own gun, but they both tackle me. Instead of firing it, I can only use it to knock them away from me and the smaller guy goes down easily and unconscious. The bigger guy is a bit more of a struggle. Demetrius simply watches, not intervening, even when his second guy crashed to the ground. Stupidly, I lose the grip on my gun, and it skids across the floor as well. *Dammit!*

I want to lunge for it but I swing around, ready to take Demetrius. Bizarrely, he looks mad, but for some reason it doesn't seem to be directed at me. I stand with my feet splayed and my arms ready for attack anyway. Demetrius seizes the gun out of the back of his jeans. I dive for the floor in the doorway and crouch behind the wall. I lift up the cloth of my jeans at the ankle and pull out a small pistol.

I try to catch my breath as I listen carefully to Demetrius. He is murmuring to himself. "That's not what was supposed to happen. You ruined it!" he bellows.

He fires his gun, startling me. I peek around the corner, trying to see what he's doing. My first thought is Lisa. He is poised over the guy that shot Uncle Tutti accidentally. Demetrius shoots him point blank in the back of the head as the goon lies unconscious, splayed on the floor. Demetrius continues to ramble to himself like the fucked up guy that he is.

I have a shot and I mean to take it, but I turn my head at a very minute sound. Crawling towards me quietly is Vito. I gesture to him that there is one left, Demetrius, and the girl. Vito nods in understanding. He points in the other direction, letting me know that he is going to go in through another door. If I can distract Demetrius, Vito can probably get Lisa out of here.

Carlo and Joey pop their heads up, and I can see them through the broken window. They signal me, and let me know they're coming in. I momentarily get distracted by thoughts of Megan and wonder if she's okay as I turn back and scan the room. Two bloody corpses, an unconscious man, and a girl strapped to a chair that lies on the floor. I pop up, my pistol ready, and my eyes dart around searching for Demetrius.

He's gone! Shit!

Vito comes in the other way, and we meet at Lisa. She is quivering. We set her upright, and I attempt to examine her. He face is cut and she is badly bruised. Vito removes her restraints. Both wrists and ankles are bloody and raw with deep indentations from the rope. Silent tears stream down her face. She gingerly touches her sore wrists.

Carlo and Joey meet us in the room. They flank us ready for anything.

"Where did he go?" Carlo asks quietly.

"I don't know," I tell him. Vito pulls his phone out and dials. He calls Patrick.

"Is everything okay?...(pause)...We will be out of the building in less than two minutes. There are five of us." He ends the call.

"Carlo, Joey, you watch the rooftops," I command. "Vito and I will take the streets. Stay together, and keep her in the middle." Lisa's eyes are cast down onto the floor. "Do you think you can walk?"

She sniffles and nods her head yes. She gets up unsteadily, and I grab onto her arm to help her. She takes a few uneasy steps, but then gets her bearings. I reach down and pick up the scattered firearms, double-checking *unconscious guy* for additional weapons. "OK, let's move," I command. The group takes their positions, and we travel as one unit.

I glimpse at Uncle Tutti out of the corner of my eye. His chair completely knocked over backwards, and his blood is splattered around like spilled red finger-paints all over the flooring. I have no remorse over his death. He wanted to hurt the people I love. His demented views cost him, and there is no one to blame but himself.

Lisa does what she is told, hanging in the center of our group with her arms wrapped tightly around herself. Her image borderlines on that of an unstable mental patient. Carlo helps her along.

Each room we enter is clear. At the main door, Carlo and Joey cover each side of it. Vito goes through first. Joey, Lisa, me, and then Carlo follow. The fresh air is cleansing after the rank foulness of the rundown building mixed with the smell of blood ate at my skin.

Up ahead of us, Vito shoots into the trees. I whip my head up, and we all dive to the ground taking Lisa with us. Two shots clip the building, spraying bits of brick. We quickly low crawl across the asphalt and around the corner. One shot, from far away, sails through the air and into the trees. The shooter in the trees falls with a thud, crushing leaves and sticks.

Vito's phone buzzes, and he jerks it out of his coat. I put out my hand to take it. I answer it.

"Vito, I think I got them all," Megan says excitedly. "Are you guys okay?"

"It's me," I say, and Megan lets out an audible sigh of relief.

"Oh, Antonio! Thank God!"

"Everyone is fine. Stay where you are. We're coming to get you."

"My dad's been shot," she says nervously. "He's lost a lot of blood."

"Where was he shot?"

"In the arm. I put bandages on it."

"Is he conscious?" I ask.

"Yes."

"Put him on the phone." I hear some rustling then Patrick's gruff voice.

"Yeah," he says.

"Is your area secure?"

"Yes. She took out one on the rooftop and one in the trees. We haven't seen anybody else."

"Okay. We will be there shortly."

I hang up and dial Alex. He picks up on the first ring.

"Start coming towards the docks. We'll meet you," I tell him and hang up.

"How do we know there's no one else?" Joey asks.

"We don't. But we can't sit here all night. Patrick said they didn't spy anyone else. They took out two."

"What about Demetrius?" Carlo asks.

"I have no fucking idea." I really don't. The mission now is to get everybody back to the casino in one piece. Lisa and Patrick both need to be seen by Doc Howie. "You're going to need to beef up security at the casino. This isn't the end. Demetrius will definitely try something else. All of your employees need to know what he looks like." Carlo nods in agreement, using his eyes to check everywhere for Demetrius.

We all move succinctly, holding our weapons at different angles ready to fire if necessary. Lisa shuffles along amongst our group. We meet Alex, and he drives into a small alleyway.

The SUV only holds six. We pile in, and Carlo gathers Lisa into his lap, freeing a spot for Patrick. Megan rode on my lap on the way here, as I didn't want to draw attention with too many vehicles.

Alex swings the car around and heads for the building where we left Patrick and Megan on the rooftop. Suddenly, an ugly recollection creeps its way into my mind. Demetrius knew Megan and Patrick were sniping.

"Give me a phone," I yell, panic setting in. *He is going to go after them!*

Joey hands me a phone, and I dial Patrick. We *just* talked to them, so I know they have service. The phone rings and rings, then goes to voicemail. Each ring that echoes on the other end of the phone makes dread circle in my stomach.

"They're not picking up!" I shout to no one in particular.

Chapter 16

Whack: To kill

Megan:

The relief I felt in hearing Antonio's voice could not be compared to anything I've ever known. I settle in to wait for them to come, my mind eased since Antonio didn't seem too concerned about my father's injury.

My father lies next to me resting. I fumble with the strap on my helmet trying desperately to get this hideous thing off my head. I tug and pull. The stupid thing is stuck.

My eye catches something in the dark. A shadow moves slowly, inching toward me. A shot of fear threads its way up my body. I reach for the rifle, not looking away from the threat. A man steps out of the darkness in front of me. Two more men converge, slipping closer. I grasp the rifle and drag it slowly toward me.

"That would be a bad idea, Megan."

It's Demetrius.

"You are an unbelievable shot," he says proudly. "Just incredible."

My heart is pounding in my ears. My father is as still as a stone. I desperately try to clear my head of fright.

"Is Daddy hurt?" he asks mockingly, truly not caring.

I'm immobile.   He is still yards away from us, but his vile ruthlessness permeates the air. I'm trying to figure out where he came from. The only access to the roof that I know of is the one we used.

His two henchmen keep pace with him. I eye them warily waiting for them to make the first move. The gun I have is heavy and clumsy. It will take too much time to line up the shot. A distraction is my only hope.

They inch forward, and fear paralyzes me. I don't know what to do. Demetrius stops directly in front of me and looks down at me. His eyes pierce through me, like he wants something. I look up at him from my position on the ground, scared as all hell. Demetrius' associates hover behind like bodyguards.

My father is only a few feet away from me, and I silently pray that he hasn't lost consciousness.

"How is your sister?" Demetrius asks in a carefree tone. "You know, I love small women. She is tiny and pretty. I would love to take her out one night. You think you can arrange that?"

Is he kidding? This guy is a real nut-job!   What does he expect me to say? Is he waiting for something?

Then I get it. He's trying to bait me… maybe even my father. He is testing us.

My father's gun is beside him, and Demetrius kicks it across the roof. It slides, kicking up pebbles of dirt in its wake. He motions to his colleagues, and they rush forward, locking each one of my arms...trapping me. I struggle and let out a little yelp, but their hold is tight.

At that moment, my father sits up and stabs Demetrius in the side with a knife. *I didn't know he had a knife!* Demetrius curses and backhands my father across the face hard, sending him flying. The force of the hit must have been incredible to throw him back that way...my father is a big man.

"You bastard!" I scream, kicking and pulling my arms and legs trying to free myself to get to my dad.

Demetrius's hand covers his side, where my father stabbed him. Blood oozes between his fingers. He gazes at me and smiles psychotically.

"Let's go!" Demetrius says sternly. I flail my body, scared to death, that if they take me away, I will be lost forever.

"No, no!" I yell. It does no good. They just drag me along, not even fazed by my rant.

I'm so busy trying to save myself that I don't notice my father. He grabs the ankle of one of the assholes attached to my arm. The guy goes down face first onto the hard roof's surface.

With my newly freed hand, I dig my nails into the other guy's skin, deep enough to draw blood. "Bitch!" he shouts at me and takes a swing at my face with his fist. I duck, and he misses me. *I'm free!*

I run across the roof in the darkness, hearing footsteps behind me. I turn, ready to inflict as much damage as I can, and realize it's my father. We take cover behind a large sheet metal vent. His bandages are soaked through with blood, and he is breathing shallowly. He pats my knee.

"Good job," he says through panting breaths.

Voices echo through the vent, and I hear running footsteps. A lot of them. The door to the roof swings open and crashes against the side. Someone is bellowing my name.

"Megan!" *It's Antonio!*

"Over here!" I stand and yell.

Relief washes over me and tingles down my back when I see him come around the corner. His facial expression is murderous. He picks me up and crushes me to his body, my feet dangling. I can barely feel him through all the padding. He kisses me fervently and desperately. The helmet tips forward and clips him on the forehead before I step back, getting my balance.

"Did you get him?" I ask.

Vito steps around the corner looking feral. "He got away!" he yells.

My face falls in disappointment. Not good.

Carlo crouches in front of my father checking him out. My father has a gash across his face from where Demetrius hit him. Carlo helps my father to stand.

*****

Megan:

At the car, Alex gets out of the driver's seat and greets us, opening the side door to help my father in. Antonio has not left my side.

Joey and Vito investigate the area while we get ourselves together after the traumatic ordeal. I tip my head to check on my father when I see a girl in the car. As Antonio opens the door, I see that it's Lisa and suck in a horrified gasp when I see her face. She looks like she did ten rounds with Mike Tyson. My stomach churns knowing full well who did this to her.

Carlo loads the back of the vehicle with all the weapons. I see the rifle I used and wonder if either or both of the people I shot tonight died. The term, *survival of the fittest*, never meant much to me until now. It is kill or be killed, or, at the very least, hurt or be hurt. There is no margin for error.

My father sits in the middle of the backseat. Antonio sits down next to him and pulls me into his lap, and Carlo does the same with Lisa on the other side. We are crushed into each other in the small space. I want to say something to Lisa, but everything I can think of seems insignificant compared to what she's been through. I remain quiet like everyone else.

When Vito and Joey get in the front seat, Alex drives away from the curb in a hurry, and we head back towards the casino. I feel gentle fingers at my chin. Antonio unclasps the strap on the helmet and removes it for me. I am relieved when I'm free of it. I rest my head back against Antonio and close my eyes. I feel a light pat on my knee. I raise my head to see my father weakly smiling at me.

Alex gets us to the casino in record time. He drives us down into the underground garage. I keep my eye on Lisa as I get out. I am worried about her.

I whisper to Antonio, "Is she going to be okay?"

Antonio's face is hard, but softens when he looks at me.

"Carlo will take her to Doc Howie. They'll take care of her." His expression changes again, and I can guess what he's thinking about. His gaze travels up and down my body, even in this ridiculous getup.

My father is standing with Joey and Alex. Pulling Antonio along with me, I walk over to him, concerned about the bullet he took in the arm.

"Dad, are you going to be okay? Do you want me to go with you to see Doc Howie?"

"No. You go get some rest," he says. His expression is different, as though he sees me in a new light.

I am suddenly brutally tired, feeling the effects of no sleep and a highly life-threatening situation. I just want to wash off the ugliness of the night, and I am anxious to get out of these clothes.

Antonio and I step into the elevator alone. He is holding my hand. Since he found me on the roof with my father, there hasn't been a second that he hasn't been touching me. I close my eyes for a second just to rest them.

We make it to my room, my legs are barely carrying me. I unsuccessfully fiddle with the zippers and Velcro on my bullet-proof vest. Antonio notices my struggle and strips me effortlessly out of my gear. My fatigue fades as he strips off the layer of thermal underwear I had put underneath all the padding. I'm standing before him in just my panties and bra. He rakes his eyes up and down my body, and he attacks me passionately. Antonio crushes me against the wall, lifting me by my legs and wrapping them around his waist. If he could unzip

497

my body and crawl in, I think he would. It's like he can't get close enough. My heart thunders wildly as my hands dance in his hair. He carries me to the bed and sets me down. I put my fist in his T-shirt and yank it over his head. My hands brush down his sculpted chest. All my sleepiness is replaced with need. His eyes are black and heated...he is ready to take me. I let him as I spiral down into the glorious abyss that is only Antonio.

*****

We lay quietly in the darkness. I am leaning over Antonio's chest listening to the sound of his heartbeat as it slows down. He uses his finger and traces designs on my shoulder. I relax blissfully.

"Antonio?" I whisper.

"Yeah," he responds huskily.

"Is this ever going to be over?"

I lift my head from his chest and gaze into his glowing brown eyes. Our faces are close. He wraps a thick piece of my hair in his hand and holds onto it.

"Listen to me," he commands and he tugs my hair gently. "The first best day of my life was when I met you. The second best day of my life will be when you walk down the aisle to become my wife. The third best day of my life will be when you have our baby. You are the center of my world. You make the bad all better."

Did he just ask me to marry him?

"Everything that we have been through together is nothing compared to being without you. I can't make you any promises about what other people do or how it will affect our lives, but I can tell you I want everything else. The white picket fence and the two point five kids. Megan, *you're mine*, forever. Making you happy is the only important thing to me."

He puts his hand on my back and pulls me close to his face. We are nose to nose. His intensity scares me sometimes, but it's also something I love about him. I don't let my eyes stray from his because I want him to know that I want it too. I lean down and kiss him. We're quiet again, and after a few minutes, I fall asleep dreaming of big cakes and wedding gowns.

Chapter 17

Made Man: Follows through on contract killing

Antonio:

It's early in the morning, barely 6 a.m. It is the only way to sneak out of here. I grab my clothes and throw them on as quietly as possible. I strap on my gun and put on my leather jacket to cover it.

Vito is sleeping soundly on the couch. There will be hell to pay with him later, but he will just have to deal.

I need Megan. I don't think in my entire life I've ever needed anyone as much as I need her. Just having her close to me fills the void that has grown over my eighteen years of life...the mafia void. It's the coldness that seeps in year after year, fight after fight, beating after beating. My girl wants this to be over. The only way is for me to end it today - alone.

I head to the firing range not speaking to anyone. I wave to Gilly and take what I need from the bins. The underground garage is deserted, everyone is still asleep. I grab keys in the interrogation room, find the vehicle, and get in. I spin out of the garage and up the ramp.

I drive automatically, not really seeing anything but red. I screech to a stop at a building that I know is owned by Don Furlotti. I'm not really sure where he lives, but I'm gonna find out right now.

What I plan to do could jeopardize everything and start a major crime war. I'll have to take that chance...for Megan.

Pumped up, I jump out of the car. There are two guards at the entrance. They don't even see it coming. I clobber the first one with the back of my arm, and pounce on him knocking him out. The second guy is shocked and hesitates too long. In the broad light of day, I yank the guy from behind by his neck and put him down to the cement. I grab my gun out of its holster and point it at his head.

"Is Furlotti here?" I say murderously. The guy struggles, but I squeeze harder on the back of his neck.

"I don't have time to fuck around. Is Furlotti here?" He doesn't answer for a second time, so I knee him in the gut. He chokes and sputters. "Last chance," I say in a deadly tone.

His voice cracks when he says he says yes.

"Thank you," I say sarcastically and hit him in the head with the butt of my gun. I search his pockets for a key card which I find quickly.

I enter the building easily, knowing he's on the top floor. That's where they all stay. I push the elevator button, the lobby is deserted. When the doors slide open, the car is empty. I swipe the key card and press the top floor.

The elevator dings, the doors slide open. I cautiously look up and down the hall… it is deserted too. There is a big fancy door way down the end of the hall. *Jackpot!*

My legs move of their own volition quickly and efficiently. I doubt this key card will open the door. I toss it aside and knock. I move away from the peephole. A deep voice echoes from behind the door.

"What is it?"

I don't respond, and knock again. I plant to myself against the wall.

"What the fuck?" the guy curses.

I knock again, pretty confident that this guy will open the door out of sheer aggravation.

"Dammit! What?!" he yells.

I knock a final time hoping this one will do the trick. The door opens slowly, and I stay patient. I let him come all the way out into the hallway, then I jump him, using the butt my gun again, and send this one into lala land too. *Chooches!*

I move slowly across the entryway. This place is just as palatial as Ennio's place. The apartment is completely quiet. I stay pinned to the wall as I move.

A door opening startles me. I brace myself to react. It is Furlotti coming out of a bathroom.

I lunge grabbing him. I restrain his arms and put my gun to his head.

"Where's Demetrius?" I ask in his ear.

"Antonio? What are you doing?" he asks me. He is stunned and completely perplexed by my actions.

"Where's Demetrius?"

"What the fuck is going on?" he asks angrily.

"Your fucker put a contract out on me," I say seething. "Did you order it?"

"Why would I do that?" he asks.

"I don't know, why don't you tell me?"

"There must be some confusion, Antonio. I have nothing against you or your family." He sucks in a deep knowing breath. "Demetrius is acting alone. I didn't sanction anything."

Around the corner, comes his head enforcer, Carmin. He sees me and quickly raises his gun at me. Mr. Furlotti tells him to stand down. He lowers his gun and puts it on the floor.

"Believe me. Demetrius is more problems than he's worth. He has been fucking out of control. What has he done?"

I laugh a pissed off chuckle. "Besides trying to kill me, playing fucking games, and kidnapping?"

"Antonio, I had no idea." He pauses. "That kid has cost me. You can have him."

Part of me believes him. It wouldn't make any sense to put a contract out on someone in a family you just made an alliance with. It would make you look untrustworthy to the rest of the underworld.

"Then tell me where he is."

"He has an apartment right here in this building." He gestures to Carmin. "Nobody hurts Antonio. Let him do what he has to do."

A look passes between them. Carmin looks resigned that this is the way it has to be. I release Don Furlotti, but stay alert, concerned that they are conceding too easily. He steps away from me.

"I'm sorry. Things shouldn't have happened this way. I should have dealt with Demetrius a long time ago."

"A lot of good it does me now," I say. "Demetrius needs to be taken down."

"He is on the fifth floor. Apartment 501." He says remorsefully. "Tell your pop that this was a big misunderstanding. If there's anything I can do to help, please ask."

"Yeah, you can send *your cleaner* to 501!" I say sarcastically, knowing full well that Demetrius was his cleaner.

I don't stand around anymore. I have a job to do. I realize that Don Furlotti is using me. There is always a certain fear in his eyes around Demetrius. He's allowing me to do a *job* he should have done a long time ago. I am his *out*. It is clear they want Demetrius gone as much as I do.

Instead of the elevator, I take the stairs two at a time down to the fifth floor. His apartment is easy to find. It's on the end. I decide surprise is better than anything else I've got up my sleeve. I take a running start, lift my leg, and knock down the door with an earth-shattering crash. It splinters and falls effortlessly.

With my gun drawn, I hurry inside, spinning around looking for Demetrius. A girl is standing in the kitchen, she screams when she sees me. I motion for her to get down, and she drops quickly. *Smart girl!*

"Get out," I say only loud enough for her to hear me. I hear her start to crawl away, out and over the shattered door.

I rush forward to the room up ahead, expecting Demetrius to jump out at me. Kicking the door down and the screaming was enough to wake the dead. Lying on the bed on his back is Demetrius. I don't hesitate. *Don't think, just do.* I immediately fire two shots into his chest. His body bucks with the force of the bullets.

I slowly approach him. I keep my gun ready and look down at him. He is ghostly white, and his eyes are open and lifeless. I reach down and touch his arm checking my suspicions. I'm right. He is ice cold. He was already dead. *Shit!*

I walk out of the apartment, down the stairs and out into the street, feeling a sense of relief that the fucker is out of our lives. Two new guys are by the door. They let me pass. I am so fueled and hyped up, they are fortunate they didn't try anything.

I get behind the wheel with the keys in the ignition, something makes me look up. Sitting against the building curled into a tight ball is the girl from the apartment...she glances at me, and a spark of recognition hits me.

I turn the car off and get out. Furlotti's thugs watch me, but I don't care. I stand over her and hold out my hand. She looks up at me with a tear stained face and takes it cautiously and with a shaky hand. I haul her up. I feel sorry for her and her family.

"You're...Lisa's sister, aren't you?" I ask.

"Yes." She wipes her face. "How do you know?"

"It was a good guess. Come on. I won't hurt you. Let me take you to her."

I call Carlo since he has been taking care of Lisa, and we let the sisters talk on the phone while I drove her to the casino. She had been looking for her brother and sister. She suspected Demetrius had taken them. Her intention was to get information from him through the use of drugs and sex, but her plan backfired when she overdosed him.

She shook and cried the whole ride. Until now tonight, she didn't know her brother was dead. I think I feel more empathy for these two sisters than I have in my entire life. I wasn't the only person Demetrius was harassing. But he can't harass anyone anymore. Sometimes it's the person that you least suspect, the seemingly weakest one, that will get you in the end.

Death is like sex...you can fool around all you want, but once it's done, it can't be undone. It's taken from you, just like murder, there is no going back.

The bastard is gone...he made his own bed, and he died in it.

*****

Megan:

I am at Lisa's room when we get the call. I had been frantic all morning. No one knew where he was. I thought Vito was going to destroy the place searching.

I run as fast as I can to the garage, leaving everyone in the dust. It is great not to be under lock and key anymore. It seems as though I proved myself.

Carlo is bringing Lisa down to the garage to see her sister, and Joey is calling Vito to let them know Antonio is coming back. Erin is in the suite, patiently waiting with Clarissa for any news.

When I woke up alone, I was angry at first, but then I was just plain worried when we couldn't find him. I curse the elevator as it seems to move oh so slowly down the floors. The doors slide open, and I bolt across the garage just as Antonio is pulling in. He gets out, and I throw myself at him. He catches me, gripping me tightly. I kiss him, then pound on his chest with my fists.

"Don't ever do that to me again!" I yell at him. "Nobody knew where you were! I felt so helpless!"

He ignores me and pulls me to him for another kiss.

*****

Antonio had some things to attend to after the morning's events, so I decide to go check on my father, who is surprisingly staying here at the casino. He doesn't even offer to stay in our room, but he takes his own. I truly appreciate the privacy. I feel as though it's been years since I've lived with my parents, even though it's only been a short few months.

I knock on his door. I hear him pad across the floor to open it.

"Hey, Dad. I just came to check on you. How are you feeling?"

He walks back into the room and sits on the bed with his back straight against the headboard. I take a seat in a small chair by the window.

"I'm fine." He pauses like he searching for something to say. "Is your sister packed?"

"Yeah. And Clarissa is too."

My father stares at the wall in front of him, not looking at me. He hesitates, takes in a breath to speak, then thinks better of it. I decide to help him out.

"I can't believe they're leaving tomorrow. I hope they like it. It would be great for them to meet new people." I add, really thinking it is important for Erin and Clarissa to get out into the world. Being stuck here isn't doing them any good. You can't hide from problems, or people, or the general badness of the world. You have to face it head on. Mostly, it is a great world. It is exciting, eye-opening, and the only way to live is to be a part of it. I lived with forced blinders on my whole life, and that is going to change.

"There is something I've never told you," my father says in his deep rough of a voice.

"There's a lot you've never told me," I don't mean to sass my dad, but I can't help it.

"I've made some mistakes. I think I've made more serious ones with Erin than I ever had with you."

"What do you want to tell me, Dad?"

"This week was not the first time you have shot someone."

"Huh?"

"When we left Ireland when you were five, it was because our house was broken into. Their intent was to kill you, your sister, and your mother."

"Why?"

"The why isn't as important as what happened. You and Erin were sleeping with your mother in our bed. You must have known, even as a little child, that I kept the gun underneath the bedside table.

508

I wasn't there but your mother says you got the gun and shot the intruders in the dark."

I sat still listening to my father's story. I try to search my memories of Ireland for any hint of this. It dawns on me that the shadows and the men that I have seen, the images that have flashed before my eyes at different times in my life, were the memories of that fateful night.

"I just took the gun and shot them?" I ask, wanting more details. He nods his head. "Did I kill them?" He nods his head again.

"Straight through the heart."

I do the nodding this time and I process this. *Self-defense. Instincts.* They have always been there, locked away in the deep recesses of my mind and coming to the surface when I need them.

Deep down, I feel everything that needs to be said about my bizarre talent has been said. I don't want to go backwards, I only want to go forward.

I feel it is only fair to warn my father. "I think Antonio wants to marry me," I tell him honestly. I don't brace myself for a fight or reaction. I'm going to do what I want to do, regardless.

My father looks at the ceiling now. "I know. He has already talked to me about it."

I'm not surprised, but I still get an excited twang knowing that Antonio has already broached the subject with my father. I really want to be girly and giddy, hounding my father for every word said between them. Instead, I take the mature road and leave it be.

I leave my father and check on Lisa and her sister. Carlo is treating them like queens, and Doc Howie is seeing to their wounds, mentally and physically. I think they're going to be okay. They are definitely two strong girls who had the unfortunate experience of crossing paths with Demetrius.

*****

Megan:

My mother arrives at 10:00 a.m. I have mixed feelings about seeing her, but in the end I am glad. Erin is packed and ready to go. Clarissa is so excited that it's the only thing she talks about.

The school is deep in California. It is a boarding school that celebrities, actors, and politicians send their kids to. Erin will be away from the underworld drama, but I am sure she will find a different kind there. Spoiled brats and paparazzi are on the menu for her for the next few months before summer.

I can hear my mother in Erin's room. She is repacking one of her bags. She is so loud that, even in this huge cavernous suite, I can hear her tittering away at Erin and the proper way to pack luggage.

"Where did you get this!?" she booms, chastising Erin. "This stuff is ridiculous! How did you get it?"

Oh no! The new wardrobe Antonio and Vito bought her. Well, mostly Vito. I decide it is time for me to get involved.

I stand in the doorway to Erin's room. My mother's eyes are like saucers as she picks up the clothes with disgust and horror, one by one tossing them aside.

"You're too young for these things!" she says in reproof.

"They were a birthday present," I say flatly.

"Really. From who? *Your boyfriend!*" she scolds. "Who buys a young girl these kinds of clothes? It is improper. They are too sophisticated! Take them back."

"They can't be returned," I tell her.

"Then give then away. My daughter is not walking around in this *stuff.*"

"Mother," I use my best you're-being-unreasonable voice. "Who would they fit? Erin is tiny."

Erin looks at me, then opens her mouth to say something.

"I will not give these away. They are beautiful gifts from people who care about me. From you, I have received nothing, not even a phone call. I am sorry that you are upset about me growing up without you, but that is the way it has to be."

She grabs the discarded clothes and shoves them back in the bag, zippers it furiously, and drags it off the bed.

I want to clap my hands and cheer, but I stop myself. I turn when I feel someone behind me. It's Vito. He walks to Erin ignoring my mother and takes the bag from her, and grabs two more. He carries them through the suite and disappears into the hallway. Erin takes her purse off the bureau and her coat from the hook on the wall. She smiles at me when she passes and leaves my mother standing in the room alone.

Down in the lobby is a crowd of people. They are all here to wish Erin and Clarissa a good trip...to say good-bye. My eyes tear up a little. Everyone has been great during a very rough part in our lives. Even Troy and Jake came.

Erin hugs everyone gratefully. Joey and Alex load the bags into a black SUV parked outside the huge glass doors. Between two fifteen year old girls, there are a lot of them. Doc Howie and Lucia gush and tell them over and over to be careful. Lucia cries. I hope it's not because she'll be out of a job.

Troy wistfully hugs Erin and kisses her on the top of her head. Jake follows, moving forward. The two of them huddle away from everyone. Troy comes over and hugs me too. I try to see around him to spy on my sister and Jake. He moves to go speak with Clarissa.

Jake pulls a small box out of his jacket. Erin grins and opens it. It is a tiny heart necklace. She thanks him and kisses his cheek.

Antonio comes up behind me and hugs me from behind, watching with me the exchange between Jake and Erin.

"Hey, do you think she likes that guy?" he asks thoughtfully.

I shrug my shoulders. "I don't know. I never asked her." I glance at Vito, he is by the door glowering at the floor.

My mother watches the exchange between Erin and Jake suspiciously. Ennio and my father come in from outside. They are preparing to take them to the airport.

"Time to go," Ennio announces. Erin and Clarissa quicken their goodbyes. Erin hugs my mother and comes over to Antonio and me.

"I'm going to miss you," she says to me.

"I want to know everything. I even want pictures. Take them with your new phone."

Antonio steps around me, and envelops Erin in a huge hug practically crushing her. "I'm gonna miss you, kid!"

"Thank you...for everything." They break away still holding hands, and Erin looks at me, then back to Antonio. "Take care of my sister."

"You know I will," he smiles.

Erin steps towards the middle of the crowd and stands next to Clarissa. This is a big thing for Clarissa, as well as Erin. Erin gazes around and looks like she's mentally ticking off in her head her goodbyes.

Erin and Clarissa clasp hands and walk towards the door together...a united front to face a new Chapter in their lives. Erin hesitates by the door. She releases Clarissa and swiftly hugs Vito around the middle, then lets go and dashes through the doors. The last thing I see is her fiery red hair.

Antonio rubs my shoulders, consoling me. Everyone begins to disperse. We're going to be heading back to Palmetto soon.

My father left for the airport with Ennio and the girls, as did Joey and Alex. My mother looks at Antonio and me severely.

"You ready to go?" Antonio asks me, taking my hand.

"Yup."

Antonio nods to Vito who goes to get the car. "Where are you going?" my mother asks, disgusted. "I just got here."

I take deep breaths to tamper down on my aggravation. "We're going shopping," I tell her.

"What do you mean you're going shopping? What could you possibly need?"

"A...ring," I say slowly.

She screws up her face haughtily and unattractively. "What do you need a ring for?" she spits at me. Some things never change.

"Didn't you hear, mother?" I pause dramatically. "The mob boss's son of Palmetto is getting married."

I prepare to enjoy the reaction I know is coming. My mother clutches her chest and opens her mouth in horror. Last night, I received a call from a very ecstatic Antonio's mom. I think we are going to get along great.

"What?!" she yells upset. "What about college?! You're supposed to be going to Notre Dame in the fall!"

"Yeah, I changed my mind," I inform her with my feet planted firmly. Heads turn around to look at us. "I decided I'm going into the family business."

Her face twists into ugly shock, and it leaves her speechless.

I laugh inwardly at how out-of-touch my mother has truly been. She doesn't rule my life anymore. I have to make my own decisions. I've never been as sure about anything.

I was born into this life, and becoming Mrs. Antonio Delisi, Jr., has always been my destiny. Things aren't always going to be pretty and wrapped up in neat little packages. It isn't always going to be rainbows and lollipops, but I'm with the man I love, and that is enough for me.

Antonio brings my hand to his lips and kisses it softly. I look into his eyes, and I am home. He places his hand neatly on my lower back and leads me away. With each step towards the waiting car, the more excited I get. I'm ready to face our future together.

End of Part Three

Bonus Epilogue

Megan:

I never thought I'd be sitting in the principal's office of my high school. Or I guess I should say former high school. The entire campus seems changed now; even the air smells different. I guess it's the freedom. The walls are lined with the achievements of alumni: medals, certificates, and even a few flags of the teams who won championships over the years.

I'm here to pick up my diploma. I squirm a bit in my chair. It's a hard uncomfortable, aged, wooden seat meant for students who've been called here for discipline. I've been waiting for a while for the principal to come back. He wanted to make an extra copy for his files.

Sitting back here in an academic environment reminds me of how I gave up my early acceptance at Notre Dame. Going away to school just didn't seem to be in the cards for me anymore, especially now. My experiences and the knowledge of my father's work in the mob underworld have changed my ambitions and perspective. I'm still going to go to college: I just said that I wasn't to aggravate my mother. I plan on taking classes here at the local college. I think I am going to major in business.

One little phone call to the school from Antonio's father and I'm walking away with my diploma early. Not that I didn't earn it. My

GPA was a 4.0, and I had more credits than I knew what to do with. Most of my senior year would've been spent in study hall or picking up some kind of half-day internship.

As I shift in my stiff chair, a sparkle catches my eye. I look down at my hands and smile. On the finger of my left hand is a gorgeous diamond ring that catches the light with miraculous shine. It has a round center stone with smaller diamonds adorning it in a neat circle. The setting is crisp, shiny platinum.

Engaged at eighteen: never saw that coming. Antonio, my fiancée, wanted me to get something bigger than what I selected. What I picked isn't small, but it's not the humongous rock he had in mind. If Antonio got his way, I would need a pedestal to support my finger when I walked, due to the grandiose size of a five-carat diamond.

The principal comes back in shuffling some papers and a fake leather case. He fumbles with the small official rectangular paper that says I am a high school graduate. He attempts to neatly place it in the case, and then enshrouds the corners with the provided ribbon.

"Here you go, Megan," he says nervously as I watch him fumble with the diploma.

The principal finally gets his act together and hands me my certificate. A smile creeps across my face...finally. I'm done. I'm moving on and *putting away childish things*. I stand up and the principal holds his hand out to me. We shake cordially.

"Thank you," I say.

"No problem. If you need anything else, don't hesitate…" He stops when my phone jingles loudly with a text. It's a rude but automatic reaction to look at the screen.

Antonio's mom!

I just ordered the flowers for the party. I think u r going to love them ☺

I turn back to the principal and he starts again.

"If you need anything, don't hesitate to call."

"Thank you," I say very cordially and smile internally at Mrs. Delisi's text. I think it's a good thing when you actually like your future mother-in-law.

*****

Antonio:

"What do you think?" I ask Vito as I walk around scanning the gleaming metal vehicle.

"I don't know. Whatever."

"I think she needs something classy. Not something sporty."

Vito rolls his eyes as the sales clerk pops the hood. We're checking out a Mercedes sedan, cherry red. The more I look at it, the more I think it's perfect.

"You think she'll like it?" I question. I stick my head in the driver's side window. The smell of new leather bombards me.

"Dude, yes! Who wouldn't like a brand new benz? Fuckin' buy it already." I frown at Vito's curt-ass behavior.

"Draw up the papers," I order the salesman, Gino.

"What is up with you?" I ask Vito. The very happy salesman goes into the dealership to print out the endless paperwork that comes with buying a car.

"Nothin', I just hate buying cars. It takes fuckin' forever."

"You wouldn't be acting so shitty if we were shopping for a ride for your girlfriend," I mock.

"Fuck you!" he spits at me.

"Oh, yeah, you don't have a girlfriend… ass!" I taunt.

"Neither do you. You have a fiancée," he hurtles at me a little too viciously for this mild bantering.

He thinks he's cutting me down with that comment, but he's not. I can't help but smile like a fuckin' chooch every time I hear that word: fiancé. I'm getting married. It's too good to be true in my messed up world. I don't know who is happier, Megan or my mother.

I guarantee this is going to be a full blown choquad wedding, with lots of homemade wine and drunk, ignorant relatives. It's all good if the end result is me spending the rest of my fucked up life with Megan. Maybe then it won't be so fucked up.

Vito taps his fingers in irritation on the roof of a silver C class next to us. He hasn't been the same since we got back from Chicago. Something is bothering him, and he just won't talk about it.

The car salesman, Gino, comes back out.

"The paperwork is ready. How are you planning on paying for this, Mr. Delisi?"

"Cash," I tell him. "It'll be here in a few minutes." He nods exuberantly and goes back into the dealership.

The guy my father normally deals with has had a *small accident* and is out of work for a while. I wonder if this guy, Gino, is aware of what the owner of this dealership is into. He'd best tread lightly.

I called our friend Ronnie to stop at Pop's to pick up the cash. Pop didn't even scoff at the money. I knew he wouldn't, even with my mother spending a small fortune on an engagement party.

"You bringing anyone?" I ask Vito as I stamp a cigarette out of a pack of menthols. I bring it to my lips and light it up with a zippo Pop got me for Christmas last year.

I should probably quit, I think as I inhale. Megan has never asked me to, but it seems like the right thing to do.

"Bring who, where?" Vito growls. His snarl takes me back to the now.

"To the engagement party."

"Who the fuck would I bring?"

"A date, you dick!" I pull another drag on my cigarette in annoyance with Vito. I see the salesman Gino peeking out the window, probably wondering when the "*scarol*" is showing up.

"You didn't have any trouble finding one before," I inform him.

"Aren't you supposed to buy a necklace or something for an engagement gift, not a freakin' car?" Vito asks, in a lame attempt to change the subject.

Ronnie pulls up directly in front of us in his Audi. He's got Louie with him. I toss my cigarette to the ground and crush the life out of it with my foot.

Louie rolls down his window and waves a manila envelope at me.

"Here you go, Dude," he says. I take the money.

"Which one?" Ronnie asks.

"Right there." I point to Megan's new car.

"Sweet!" Ronnie says and whistles.

"Nice color," Louie says. "I wonder why you picked it," he adds sarcastically.

*****

Megan:

I pop back into the family mini-van parked for the first and last time in the high school parking lot and head for home. I never had an opportunity to drive the family car to school. Since I have arrived home from Chicago a soon-to-be-bride, my parents have treated me differently.

I navigate the road parallel to the short path I walked to school day in and day out. The van screeches along like the decrepit metal monster it is. Of course, my father uses it to transport his "work," so it's gotten pretty worn down.

I turn into the driveway. My father is there, loading trash bags into our barrels. I jump out and walk to him.

"I got it," I say happily and wave my new diploma at him.

"Good," he mumbles. He adjusts the barrels and fiddles with the covers. "Are you ready for tomorrow?" he asks, his face colorless.

"Yup," I respond. "Ready and excited."

My father turns back towards the house and climbs the cement steps to the back door. I follow.

In the kitchen laid out along the table are the party favors my mother's been working on. It's her contribution to the engagement party. She's made her own goat's milk soaps and wrapped them in pink netting with bows. I'm surprised that she offered to do anything. She lets me know daily how much she disapproves of my "union" with Antonio. I just block her out now. I couldn't care less at this point. After the way she's treated me, after she left Erin and me in the dark about our family's life, she is lucky that I didn't just run off and elope. In many ways, I'm still hurt and angry with my parents.

Mom is busy sorting and tying the soaps into small round packages. She barely acknowledges me as I enter the room.

"Here it is," I tell her, beaming.

"Uh huh," she mutters as she continues her work.

I decide not to even try with my mom and head up to my room. I place my diploma on my bureau and snap a picture with the phone Antonio gave me. I hit send and the picture of my new diploma goes into the atmosphere, cell tower to cell tower, to California where my sister is at school.

Almost immediately I get a message back from my sister.

Erin: Awesome! ☺

Me: It's a great feeling to be done. I wish you could come tomorrow. ☹

Erin: I wish I could too. ☹ Clarissa, Joey, and I must have said a thousand times this week that we wish we didn't have to miss it.

Me: Is school going okay?

Erin: It's great! Gotta go to class. C ya!

Me: Have fun ☺

*****

Antonio:

Morning strikes and I'm pumped to see Megan. I head to the kitchen for a cup of coffee and pour some sugar in my cup, opting for a little sweetness. Standing by the window, I see a box truck labeled party rentals back in to my driveway. A sharp beep echoes through the air as it pulls in. Mom materializes from somewhere in the house and claps her hands, eagerly.

"The tables and chairs are here!" she calls out.

Donny meets the truck driver at his door. Everything has to be checked. Caution is important in the underworld. This party is very high profile and my mother invited everyone and their *cousins*. Everyone is acting like this is my wedding day and not an engagement party. I shake my head; puzzled at the amount of weight everyone is putting on this party.

I watch Donny check the contents of the truck and the truck cabin. He signs the invoice, and then he and the driver begin unloading the tables. I put my cup on the kitchen counter and go outside and help.

"Eh, Tonio. Big day, huh?" Donny says to me, flicking a knowing smile my way. I yank a white plastic table off the truck lift.

Another large truck pulls up, decorated with a huge picture of yellow flowers on the side. Donny leaves me to the unloading and goes to check out the floral delivery.

The delivery guy and I are just starting on the chairs when a black Cadillac parks out front on the street and Vito gets out. His door slams, and he takes long strides to meet up with me.

"Hey, you're early," I say. Vito takes the chairs I'm carrying from me.

"I'm here to help," he mumbles and walks away to the backyard.

O-kay.

I grab more chairs and follow him.

"Tonio!" my mother yells from the house. "Six chairs to a table, not eight! I don't want people shoved together! It's uncomfortable!"

"Got it, Ma!" I call back.

My mother must've gotten dressed early just to come out into the yard and bark orders at us, I think sarcastically. I find Vito placing vases in the middles of tables. My mother goes over to him and I follow.

"Hi, Honey," she says to him and gives him a hug. "How're you doin'?"

Vito shrugs his shoulders. "Fine," he answers.

"Antonio, don't put that there!" Ma shouts at Pop. "The ice sculpture is goin' there!"

"Ice sculpture?" Vito says quietly.

"What the fuck?" I murmur back to him. "Knowing Ma, its probably some cupid with its ass hanging out."

Vito laughs. It sounds good. I haven't heard him laugh in a long time.

"Don't you make fun, Tonio! I'm doing all this for you!"

Wow, I forgot about her keen sense of hearing.

"Me! I'd be happy running off to Vegas," I tease.

Whack!

Ma clips me on the back of my head with her open hand.

"Don't even kid, Tonio. It's not funny."

Yikes! I crossed a line. Ma would never forgive me if Megan and I eloped. She would crucify me.

The sound of car doors slamming and engines being killed lets me know the town enforcers are showing up. Pop talks to them and they begin positioning themselves all around the yard and driveway... security, in case things go wrong.

It's getting closer to party time. I see Megan's family mini-van pull up to the curb in front of my house. My fuckin' heart races knowing my fiancée is in that vehicle. I miss her even when it is a small period of time since I saw her. She looks freakin' stunning! Her legs trail out from a short skirt. She wears high heels that make her legs look killer.

Patrick trails behind Megan and her mother carrying a tray of weird, wrapped white things with bows.

His face is the same stony, stoic look he wears all the time. I understand him more now, that's a good thing considering he is my future father-in-law and will be working for me when Pop is gone.

Megan's mother has twisted her lips so tightly that her expression looks peeved and pained. She hasn't come to terms with this upcoming marriage, but of course there is nothing she can do about it.

Ma is the gracious one that approaches Mrs. O'Neill first to make small talk. Megan immediately breaks off from her family and walks straight into my arms. I hug her to me and all of the tense and tight sensations inside me melt away. She was made for me.

"Diane," Mrs. O'Neill says. "Everything is beautiful." Her words don't match her tone. What I think she's really thinking is that the party is posh and overdone.

"Thank you," Ma says, smiling civilly.

"Here are the favors I promised you."

"They're wonderful, thank you." Ma takes the tray from Patrick and walks them to a small table she has set aside for them.

Megan whispers in my ear, "This is amazing. You mother did a fantastic job."

"She loves it. She eats this stuff up," I whisper back.

"Tonio! Megan! I want to get some photos before the guests start arriving," Ma calls to us.

She snaps a few, and then positions us like she's a professional photographer. She moves my arms like I'm a puppet and shifts Megan and me like she's playing with dolls.

She corrals Pop and Megan's mother and father.

"Get together everyone." It's an awkward moment, but Ma keeps snapping away.

"I wish your sister could be here, Megan," Ma says, sounding truly heartbroken that Erin needed to stay in California for school.

"I wish she was here too," Megan says with melancholy in her voice.

"Vito!" Ma yells. "Come over here for a picture!"

Vito walks with heavy legs to the *"picture area."* Mrs. O'Neill all but snarls at him. Ma ignores the bitterness and shoves Vito between Megan and me. We pose and my mother asks, "Tonio, where are Ronnie and Louie?"

"They're coming later," I tell her.

"Fine. Vito, take one of me and Antonio with Megan and Tonio."

Pop and Ma stand with us. I glance at Ma and her smile is priceless. Pop clasps my shoulder in approval. They're both really happy for me.

We snap another endless amount of pics and Alessandra comes around the corner.

"Alessandra!" Ma yells happily. "Hurry up! I want some pictures!"

*****

Megan:

Antonio moans at the idea of more pictures. I laugh it off. After all, Antonio's mother honestly and truly out did herself. The yard is spectacularly decorated. Not like an engagement party, but more like an outdoor wedding. Diane waves Alessandra over. Her smile is a mile-wide.

"You guys are so cute!" she coos as she hugs both of us. Her beautiful brown hair tickles my face. We owe a lot to Alessandra. She's been a great friend to both of us.

She pulls away.

"Mrs. Delisi, this place is amazing! I can't believe it. You transformed it like a page out of a fairy tale book."

"Thank you, Alessandra," Diane says affectionately and hugs Alessandra to her.

Commotion catches my eye over by the driveway near the side of Antonio's house. It's Troy! I didn't expect him to come! He must have flown home for this.

"Meg!" he shouts by the very large man who is not happy. *Probably security.*

"Tonio! The angry enforcer says. "You know this chooch?"

By now we are all staring and looking intently at the scene.

"Let him in. He's cool," Antonio says.

I run to Troy and he lifts me up.

"I can't believe you came!" I say excitedly to him. My feet dangle from his uplifting, enormous hug.

"How could I miss it? Two big dudes showed up at my dorm and threatened to rearrange my face if I didn't," he says jokingly.

Antonio comes over and shakes hands with Troy.

"Thanks for coming, man."

Troy smiles and sees Vito over Antonio's shoulder.

"Hey!"

Vito grumbles an intelligible hello.

"As pleasant as always," Troy comments, unfazed.

"How was your flight?" I ask.

Alessandra joins us as soon as the question is out of my mouth.

"Hi Troy," she says awkwardly brightly.

"Hi," he says, unaffected. Then he gives me back his attention. Antonio excuses himself to go help his father move some tables closer together. For a second, Alessandra looks as if she might stay, but soon goes to hang with Vito.

"The flight was good and leaving school for a while is just what I needed."

Our conversation is cut short by an influx of people streaming in from the street. The backyard area gets loud as everyone is greeted and congratulates Antonio. Antonio waves me over.

"Sorry, Troy. I think I need to get over there."

How many people did Diane invite?

I hear people "oohhhing and ahhhing" over the amazing backyard transformation.

My strides to Antonio seem to take forever. His magical eyes are on me as I come to him and I feel a flutter of passion flood through me. *I can't believe I'm marrying such a handsome man!*

Thick crowds of party-goers crowd the yard, blocking our gaze. I have to step around people to get to my destination.

"Move!"

"Move! Move!" Someone is shouting!

People shuffle aside and my heart rate speeds up in fear that something very bad is happening.

I scan the yard, looking for a threat. I ready myself to hit the ground, if necessary. I see my Dad standing very calmly by an ice sculpture, my mother beside him holding a plate of hors d'oeuvres. Their lips are moving quickly in conversation.

Vito and Alessandra remain composed. Suddenly, I hear an engine. It sounds close.

Is someone going to ram the party with a car?

I find Antonio again in the crowd, and he smiles broadly.

"Move!"

"Move!" The faceless voice shouts again.

More shouting as the crowd shuffles closer to the tables.

A car horn sounds loudly, making my jump.

"Move! Step back please!"

A shiny red Mercedes drives right up on the grass. I squint, perplexed. Ronnie's behind the wheel and Louie's in the passenger seat.

What the hell are they doing?

Antonio comes up behind me, wrapping his arms around my waist.

"Do you like it?"

"Huh? What are they doing?" I ask.

"They're doing me a favor. Happy engagement." He kisses my hair.

"Huh? I don't get it."

"It's yours," he whispers in my ear, tickling me.

"You got me a new car?!" I'm shocked.

"Yup."

"Holy…"

"Do you like it?"

"It's beautiful!"

Antonio pulls me towards it. Everyone is standing around watching our exchange. Diane's behind the car taking more pictures.

He opens the sleek door and Ronnie hops out. I peek my head in. Sitting in the backseat is my friend Raven.

"Congratulations, girl!" she says.

"Oh my God!"

I'm so shocked by this wonderful gift. Raven gets out and hugs me.

"You deserve it," she says.

My own car!

"How's my wife going to get around? She needs a car," Antonio teases.

"Antonio, I can't believe it. It's too much! I don't need something this fancy."

"It suits you. A beautiful fiery red car for a beautiful fiery red Megan."

"Wow, Meg, it's awesome," Troy says, coming over to examine my gift.

My eyes fill up with tears. Antonio is so thoughtful. My mind blocks out all of the eyes on me and the noise of the party; for the moment, the only thing I can see is Antonio.

How can someone so terrifying and tough be so sweet? The road ahead of us is going to be filled with uncertainties and danger, but I know we can face it all as husband and wife.

Antonio moves closer, places his fingertips on my chin, and forces me to look him in the eye.

"I love you. Never doubt that. Ever," he says with a seriousness that would frighten anyone else.

"I love you, too. Very much!" I tell him.

He gently presses his lips to mine in a promise that encompasses hope, love, and togetherness.

The entire backyard party erupts into a roar of cheering for us: the future Mr. and Mrs. Antonio Delisi, Jr.

From the author:

Thank you to all of the fans, new and old, of Antonio and Megan and for purchasing this anniversary edition. I can't believe it has been a year!

I have truly enjoyed writing their story and have been blessed with amazing characters that continue to shock me.

Thank you very much to friends and family for your support. Thank you to my husband and son for giving me the time I needed to finish.

Thank you to Toni for pushing me and to Summer and Kim for editing.

What an amazing adventure this has been!

Other books by Amy Rachiele:

Frosted Over

Silencing Joy

Coming Soon

Mobster's Angel Book 4 (Coming Soon)

Sybrina
(Historical Paranormal Romance)

Join me on Goodreads and Facebook:

http://www.goodreads.com/author/show/6150565

https://www.facebook.com/messages/626361887#!/amyrachielebooks

https://www.facebook.com/messages/626361887#!/pages/Mobster-Series/245610882223918

Made in the USA
Charleston, SC
29 September 2013